Look w...............................ut
th................

stephanie BOND

"Red hot, deliciously wicked, fantastically entertaining."
—*Joyfully Reviewed* on *Watch and Learn*

"Sex and humor blend perfectly…this fairy tale of
a story has the perfect magic ending."
—*RT Book Reviews* on *No Peeking…*

leslie KELLY

"*One Wild Wedding Night* features sexy and fun stories
with likable characters, only to end with a sexy story that
floors me with how well it resonates with me. Oh, this
one is definitely wild, but even better, it also aims
for the heart."
—*Mrs. Giggles*

"Filled with humor and heart, *Slow Hands*,
by Leslie Kelly, is a complete delight."
—*RT Book Reviews*

kate HOFFMANN

"Sexy and wildly romantic."
—*RT Book Reviews* on *Doing Ireland!*

"Sexy, heartwarming and romantic…a story to
settle down with and enjoy—and then re-read."
—*RT Book Reviews* on *The Mighty Quinns: Teague*

ABOUT THE AUTHORS

Stephanie Bond believes in the power of books to change a person's life. Reading and writing have taken her on wonderful journeys, real and imagined, and brought her the friendships of a lifetime. Stephanie lives in midtown Atlanta and has, in her words, "the best job in the world."

Leslie Kelly has written more than two dozen books and novellas for Harlequin Blaze, Harlequin Temptation and HQN Books. Known for her sparkling dialogue, fun characters and depth of emotion, her books have been honored with numerous awards, including a National Readers' Choice Award and three nominations for the RWA RITA® Award. Leslie resides in Maryland with her own romantic hero, Bruce, and their three daughters. Visit her online at www.lesliekelly.com.

Kate Hoffmann has been writing for Harlequin Books since 1993. She's published sixty titles, most with the Temptation and Blaze imprints. Kate lives in southeastern Wisconsin with her cats, Tally and Chloe, and her trusty computer. When she's not writing, she works with local high school students in music and drama activities. She enjoys talking to her sister on the phone, reading *Vanity Fair* magazine, eating Thai food and traveling to Chicago to see Broadway musicals.

THE
Blaze
COLLECTION

stephanie BOND

leslie KELLY

kate HOFFMANN

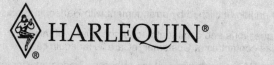

HARLEQUIN®

TORONTO • NEW YORK • LONDON
AMSTERDAM • PARIS • SYDNEY • HAMBURG
STOCKHOLM • ATHENS • TOKYO • MILAN • MADRID
PRAGUE • WARSAW • BUDAPEST • AUCKLAND

Recycling programs
for this product may
not exist in your area.

ISBN-13: 978-0-373-83755-7

THE BLAZE COLLECTION
Copyright © 2010 by Harlequin Books S.A.

The publisher acknowledges the copyright holders of the individual works
as follows:

HER SEXY VALENTINE
Copyright © 2010 by Stephanie Bond, Inc.

PLAY WITH ME
Copyright © 2010 by Leslie Kelly

THE CHARMER
Copyright © 2010 by Peggy A. Hoffmann

All rights reserved. Except for use in any review, the reproduction or
utilization of this work in whole or in part in any form by any electronic,
mechanical or other means, now known or hereafter invented, including
xerography, photocopying and recording, or in any information storage or
retrieval system, is forbidden without the written permission
of the publisher, Harlequin Enterprises Limited, 225 Duncan Mill Road,
Don Mills, Ontario, Canada M3B 3K9.

This is a work of fiction. Names, characters, places and incidents are
either the product of the author's imagination or are used fictitiously,
and any resemblance to actual persons, living or dead, business
establishments, events or locales is entirely coincidental.

This edition published by arrangement with Harlequin Books S.A.

For questions and comments about the quality of this book
please contact us at Customer_eCare@Harlequin.ca.

® and TM are trademarks of the publisher. Trademarks indicated with
® are registered in the United States Patent and Trademark Office,
the Canadian Trade Marks Office and in other countries.

www.eHarlequin.com

Printed in U.S.A.

CONTENTS

Blaze

HER SEXY VALENTINE

stephanie BOND

For Blake, whose creative heart will be missed…

chapter one

This Valentine's Day, Cupid will take no prisoners…

CAROL Snow picked up the cartoonish card sitting on her assistant's desk that featured the celebrated cherub wearing fatigues, with bow and arrow at the ready. She idly opened the card to glance at the message inside.

So your best strategy is to surrender. A white flag waved feebly in the background. The name "Stan" was scrawled across the bottom.

Carol frowned and turned over the valentine, not wholly surprised to discover it was a product of the company she worked for, Mystic Touch Greeting Cards. Stan must also be an employee. She set the card back on the cluttered desk, rankled by the cheerful sentimentality. Thank goodness she didn't have to work on the creative side of the business and be surrounded by that inane fluff all day.

Carol leveled an irritated glance in the direction of her assistant Tracy who had her back turned, whispering low into the phone, where, as far as Carol could tell, was how the young woman had spent most of her day. Carol rolled her eyes—a new boyfriend, no doubt. Probably Stan, the guy who'd sent the valentine. Tamping down her growing frustration, Carol glanced at her watch—at this rate, she'd be late for the monthly meeting of the Red Tote Book Club.

She cleared her throat meaningfully. Tracy cupped her hand over the mouthpiece of the phone and turned in her chair, her face lined with trepidation. "Yes, Ms. Snow?"

"I need to talk to you about this project before I leave."

"Okay."

Carol pursed her mouth at the woman's pause. "And I need to leave now."

Tracy glanced at the clock. "But it's only six…you usually stay until eight or nine."

Carol stiffened at the woman's tone that smacked of an indictment on her personal life. "Not tonight."

"Are you sick?"

Carol frowned. "No. Would you please hang up so we can talk?"

Tracy uncovered the mouthpiece and murmured something low before returning the handset to the receiver. "What's up?"

Carol bit down on the inside of her cheek. "*What's up* is this memo for the quarterly report. It's riddled with typos." She handed over the piece of paper where she'd circled the errors with a red marker.

Tracy bit her lip. "Oh. I'll redo it."

"I want a clean version on my desk when I arrive tomorrow morning," Carol chided.

"Yes, ma'am."

"And Tracy? You've been spending a lot of time on the phone—that puts both of us behind."

The young woman nodded. "Yes, ma'am. I'm sorry."

Carol made a rueful noise, then retreated into her office. Appointed with dark furniture, it was spacious and fitting for the director of Finance. A box window provided a nice view of the Atlanta skyline while leaving enough wall space for the banks of extra wide file cabinets that lined the room.

She straightened her already tidy desk, then retrieved her purse, briefcase and the red tote of books for her book club meeting. When she strode past Tracy's desk, Carol gasped in dismay to see the woman was on the phone again. Shaking her head, Carol walked up to the elevator and stabbed the button. Tracy was going to be sorely disappointed if she continued to put her love life before her job.

Men. Could. Not. Be. Trusted.

Somebody in the creative department ought to put *that* sentiment on a Mystic Touch card.

The elevator dinged and the doors opened, revealing a sole occupant: Luke Chancellor, Director of Sales and resident playboy. A grin spread over his handsome face. "Going home early, Snow? You must have a hot date for a cold Tuesday night."

Carol stuck her tongue in her cheek—she was not in the mood to be teased. "Actually, Chancellor, I've decided to take the stairs."

She turned and stalked to the stairwell, ignoring the man's booming laughter. Luke Chancellor was an outrageous flirt who seemed to have made her his pet project. In an effort to avoid him, Carol jogged down the stairs as fast as her high heels would allow. When she reached the lobby, she was relieved to see the elevator hadn't yet arrived. Juggling the items in her arms, she scooted out the front door of the office building and in the direction of her car. If every traffic light between Buckhead and downtown Atlanta was green, she *might* make it to the book club meeting on time.

"Hey, Carol!"

At the sound of Luke's voice behind her, Carol winced and kept moving. But in her haste, her red stiletto heel caught a raised edge on the sidewalk and she stumbled. Her briefcase, book tote and purse went flying, and she flailed, mentally bracing herself to hit the pavement hard. At the last possible second, though, a pair of strong arms kept her from falling flat on her face.

"I got you," Luke whispered in her ear like a warm breeze in the February chill.

The scent of his earthy cologne curled into her lungs, compromising her breathing. Her body distantly registered the fact that his big hands were touching her, his fingers burning into the skin of her shoulders and brushing her breasts through the layers of her prim suit. Unbidden lust shot through her midsection, reminding Carol how long it had been since she'd been so close to a man. The alien sensation jolted her into action.

"Let go of me," she said through gritted teeth, pulling free of his grasp. She straightened and patted at her clothing.

Luke's legendary mouth quirked into a half-smile. "You're welcome," he said drily, then crouched to gather her things from the ground.

He wore a mocha-colored suit that set off his dark hair and brown eyes. A handful of red silk tie poked out of his pocket, a stab at the formal corporate culture of the company. The man was known for his casual management style and practical jokes. Luke had come to Mystic Touch Greeting Cards two years ago and had leapfrogged through the ranks until he was now a peer of Carol's, a fellow director. The feminist in her had wanted to cry foul on a couple of his promotions, but admittedly, since his arrival, Luke had been instrumental in turning around the flagging sales force.

With only a few days to go until their biggest card-selling day of the year—Valentine's Day—the company was enjoying record-breaking profits. As a numbers woman, she grudgingly respected his accomplishments.

Feeling contrite, Carol stooped to help him with her things. "Sorry," she murmured. "You startled me. Thank you for…catching me."

"No problem," he said easily. "I probably distracted you when I yelled."

"Yes," she agreed, scooping up her purse and briefcase. "What did you want, Luke? I'm late for my book club."

"Whoa." He held up the books that had fallen out of her tote bag and lay scattered on the sidewalk. *"Lady Chatterley's Lover? Venus in Furs? Fanny Hill? The Slave?"* A devilish grin split his face. "What kind of book club do you belong to?"

Heat climbed her face. "None of your business."

He leaned in close. "Do you accept male members?" His tone was innocent, but his eyes danced with mirth at the double entendre.

Instead of responding, Carol tried to snatch the classic erotic volumes, but he held them out of reach. Indignant anger whipped through her. "What are you, ten years old? Give me my books!"

He wagged his eyebrows as he perused the risqué covers. "I knew there was a wild side to you, Snow. You just keep it all bottled up."

Exasperated, Carol realized the best way to diffuse him was to deflect his attention. She crossed her arms. "What did you want, Chancellor?"

As if to answer her question, his dark gaze flitted over her appreciably, stirring up little flutters of awareness in its wake. With great resolve, she managed to maintain a cool expression of disdain.

Luke sighed and his shoulders sagged in defeat. "Okay, back to business. I thought it might be nice to have a company party for Valentine's Day."

She squinted. "Valentine's Day?"

"Why not? We could have it Friday."

"Friday the thirteenth?"

He shrugged. "Close enough. Valentine's is a significant sales day on our calendar. Plus a party would be a good occasion to pass out bonuses—what do you think?"

"I think this company has never issued bonuses," she chirped.

"Not in the past," he agreed. "But Mystic has had such a good year, I thought it'd be fair to spread the love, if you know what I mean. I'm sure the rest of the directors would agree with me."

Ire shot through Carol—doling out bonuses from money that Luke was being given credit for bringing in almost single-handedly would make him a bona fide hero in the eyes of the five hundred or so employees. The man would be Chief Executive Officer before the end of the year…dammit.

Squaring her shoulders, she drew upon her most authoritative voice. "In my opinion, the more prudent move for the long-term health of the company is to take the profits we make on good years and reinvest them in new technology."

His seemingly permanent grin never wavered. "In *my* opinion, you should skip your naughty book club and we should discuss this over drinks."

The pull of his body on hers was unmistakable. His decadent brown eyes were almost hypnotic, summoning her to follow him anywhere. Her breasts pinged in response and her thighs quickened. Her mouth opened and to her horror, she realized she was on the verge of saying yes.

Carol's head snapped back. "That's not going to happen." The words came out more forcefully than she'd planned—for her own benefit? "We can discuss the party and the bonuses at the directors' meeting in the morning—with an audience."

He frowned. "You're no fun."

She extended her hand, palm up, and wiggled her fingers. "My books, please?"

He relinquished his hold as if they were favorite toys. "I've never been second place to a book before."

"That you know of." Carol gave him a tight smile as she slipped the erotic books inside the red tote bag. "Goodbye, Chancellor." She turned and walked toward her car, certain now that she'd be late for the book club meeting because of the bothersome man.

"Instead of reading about life, you should try the real thing sometime!" Luke called behind her.

Carol was tempted to turn and shoot him the bird, but, mindful of their location and the curious stares they'd already garnered from employees loitering in the parking lot, she kept walking. She didn't want to keep the members of the Red Tote Book Club waiting.

And she didn't want to give Luke Chancellor the satisfaction of seeing the sudden tears his parting comment had brought to her eyes.

chapter two

EVERY traffic light between Carol's office and downtown Atlanta was, not surprisingly, red. If it was the city's idea of commemorating Valentine's Day, Carol thought wryly, it was fitting that she was caught in the bottleneck. As expected, she arrived late for the meeting of the Red Tote Book Club.

So late, in fact, that she sat in the parking lot of the branch of the Atlanta Public Library where the group met and contemplated driving away. She glanced over at the box of almond cookies sitting in the passenger seat that she'd brought for the members to share and rationalized the goodies would make her a fair dinner—almonds were chock-full of fiber…weren't they? Considering what was waiting for her inside, she was suddenly gripped with the compulsion to drop out of the group altogether. The other women wouldn't miss her. They might even be glad if she left.

They were probably sitting in there now, talking about her, the rogue member who refused to go along with the experiment their coordinator had suggested: That each member apply the lessons they'd learned from the pages of the erotic novels they'd read to seduce the man of their dreams.

The other women had embraced the challenge whole-heartedly. She, on the other hand…not so much.

Her phone chimed and she looked down to see a text message had arrived.

Are you stuck in traffic? We didn't want to start without you. Gabrielle.

Gabrielle was the coordinator of the Red Tote Book Club. Carol couldn't stop the relieved smile that curved her mouth—they did care. She quickly texted back that she'd be there in a few minutes, then grabbed the box of cookies and the red tote holding the precious books that had filled her lonely evenings over the past few months. After exiting her car, she jogged toward the entrance of the library.

Inside, she stopped to inhale the pungent scent of books and absorb the pleasant hum of computers and lowered voices. She'd been an avid reader most of her young life, but had gotten away from pleasure reading as an adult. When she'd seen the ad for the book club for women looking to add a little spice to their reading life, she'd been intrigued, if a little suspicious. But the group of women who'd gathered on that first night were amazingly like her—in their thirties, educated and single.

Except, *un*like her, they all seemed to be in the market for a boyfriend or a lover, neither of which appealed to her.

Carol wound her way through a maze of hallways to reach the tucked away room where the group met for ultimate privacy. Their book selections and discussions weren't meant for tender eyes and ears. She rapped on the door and a few seconds later, it opened wide enough to reveal the wary, blue-eyed gaze of Cassie Goodwin, fellow member. Cassie's wariness immediately turned into a smile as she opened the door and welcomed Carol inside where the other three club members—Page Sharpe, Wendy Trainer and Jacqueline Mays—sat around a table, with the group's coordinator, Gabrielle Pope, at the head.

"We were just having a toast for Gabrielle," Cassie sang, handing Carol a glass of red wine—contraband smuggled in for the occasion.

Taking a seat at the table, Carol glanced at Gabrielle and noticed the woman had a glow about her. Which could only mean one thing: Even their plain, bun-packing, cardigan-wearing leader had bagged a man. Dread settled in Carol's stomach.

"The toast isn't for me," Gabrielle fussed, although she was clearly pleased by the attention. "To seduction by the book!"

Carol was the last to lift her glass and her smile felt stiff as she looked around the table. Over the past few months, the other four members had chosen erotic books to help guide them in their sensual journey to seduce a man. Now, even their leader Gabrielle had found her match in a lover and, if the light in the woman's eyes was any indication, had found love as well.

And the cheese stands alone, Carol mused wryly as she

drank deeply from the glass of merlot. She remained the lone holdout, refusing to go along with the optional assignment.

The women chorused good wishes and congratulations to Gabrielle and listened as their coordinator relayed happy details about her lover and how their relationship had taken off once they discovered common sexual ground. The woman spoke openly about tantric experiences, mirroring the frank, honest discussions the members had shared about the group's book selections. Gabrielle had declared no topic and no language was off-limits. And while Carol conceded that the candid dialogue had riveted her, she acknowledged that she'd participated less than anyone. And she'd sensed the other women were resentful to varying degrees that she'd observed more than she'd partaken.

As Gabrielle shared the lush aspects of her new relationship, Carol felt excluded. The other women leaned into each other and seemed to share an emotional shorthand she wasn't privy to. It occurred to her that they didn't trust her because she'd refused to be vulnerable, refused to take the same risk they'd taken.

Carol shrank back in her chair, suddenly wishing she had followed her earlier impulse to leave. She knew the women around the table thought she was detached…maybe even thought she was a lesbian. They had no idea she once was like them—dreamy eyed, with an open door to her heart, waiting for the right man to walk through. And he had.

James had romanced her and cajoled her into falling head over heels in love with him. So much so that on Valentine's Day eight years ago, she'd garnered her strength and proposed to *him*. But instead of the wholehearted "yes" she'd expected, the day had gone horribly wrong, shattering her hopes and dreams. Since that day, she'd kept her heart and body carefully under wraps.

When her chest squeezed painfully, Carol gave herself a mental shake, surprised that the mortification of that day still felt so fresh. She dropped her gaze to her feet to gather herself.

That was when she noticed a small white envelope sticking out of one of the books in her red tote.

Being the long-time employee of a greeting card company, she was accustomed to finding cards in her brief-case and scattered around her car and condo—samples and mockups and overruns. But this card was sealed and seemed to have been placed purposely. She glanced up to see if any of the other women had noticed, but they were congratulating Gabrielle and talking amongst themselves. Ignoring her.

Carol removed the envelope, then slid her thumb under the flap, broke the seal and slid out the card.

The front of the greeting card was a photograph of an early spring scene, with the green shoots of bulb flowers poking through the earth. In the foreground, one large, lone icicle glistened spectacularly. She opened the card and read the computer-generated words inside.

Spring came, and still Carol Snow refused to thaw.

There was no signature.

Hurt whipped through her, leaving her skin stinging. She knew she had a reputation at work for being cold, knew that people saw her as unfeeling and rigid. Her mind raced, scanning the faces and names of coworkers, wondering which one had gone to the trouble of putting the note in her book…

And her mind stopped on Luke Chancellor, the cad. The reason he'd detained her today wasn't to talk about bonuses—he'd been looking for an opportunity to plant the card. It made even more sense when she recalled his parting shot.

Instead of reading about life, you should try the real thing sometime!

Tears pressed the back of her eyes and she must have uttered something because suddenly, all heads turned in her direction.

"Carol, did you say something?" Page asked.

They all stared at her expectantly, silently challenging her to step up, to join their sexually active sisterhood. Her reluctance to participate in the seduction experiment was like an elephant in the room. In the beginning, she had justified to herself that she barely knew the other women and therefore, owed them no explanation.

But over the course of the monthly meetings, things had changed. Carol felt closer to these women than to anyone else in her life, and she wanted to fit in, wanted to be accepted. Her pleasure over Gabrielle's simple, thoughtful text message in the parking lot was proof that she needed these women and these meetings.

Judging from her traitorous response to Luke Chancellor today, she conceded she would benefit from the physical release a seduction would provide. But if she seduced a man, it wouldn't be with stars in her eyes…it would be purely for revenge. Revenge for the way men had treated her, especially James, but there had been others who had made her feel powerless…men like Luke…

It would serve the cad right if she seduced him and then cast him aside…play the playboy.

"Are you okay?" Cassie asked her in a gentle tone.

Carol wet her lips and nodded. "I've been thinking…"

Eyes widened in her direction, shoulders leaned. Her bravado fled, leaving a trail of perspiration trickling between her breasts.

"Yes, Carol?" Gabrielle prompted in the ensuing silence. "What's on your mind?"

Her heart galloped in her chest, but she managed a smile. "I've decided to try the seduction experiment."

Congratulations reverberated in the room and happy smiles wreathed the faces of her fellow book club members. They seemed equally pleased and surprised. She wondered how their expressions would change if she told them she planned to use sex to avenge her wounded pride, to humiliate, and hopefully, to inflict pain on her target. Only Gabrielle seemed reserved for some reason, studying Carol over the brim of her wine glass. Carol couldn't meet the woman's gaze.

"So who's the lucky guy?" Wendy asked, practically bouncing up and down in her chair.

"Someone I work with," Carol responded casually. "His name is Luke."

"He sounds sexy," Jacqueline said with a smile.

"He's perfect," Carol agreed through gritted teeth. Beneath the table, she crumpled the icicle card into a tight ball in her fist. Too late, she realized Gabrielle had noticed.

When she met the woman's gaze, Carol saw the flash of something in the coordinator's eye—apprehension?

"A seduction just in time for Valentine's Day," Cassie continued, oblivious to the exchange, as were the other women. "Do you have a plan?"

"Not really," Carol admitted. "Although…there is the possibility of a company party on the horizon."

"Sounds promising," Wendy said with a grin. "Maybe you and Luke can slip away to a supply closet."

The women laughed and passed around the almond cookies that Carol had brought. For the first time, she felt at ease with her fellow book club members. As the evening progressed and they discussed titles for upcoming selections, she contributed to the discussion and felt accepted. But she was aware of Gabrielle's thoughtful gaze on her throughout.

As they left the meeting, Gabrielle walked out into the parking lot with her. Their breath formed frosty puffs in the winter air.

"It's really getting cold," the older woman offered. "I heard rumors of snow flurries."

Carol laughed. "I think the groceries get that rumor started every year so people will go out and buy milk and bread. It never snows in Atlanta."

Gabrielle nodded, then seemed to turn inward. "I confess your about-face on the seduction experiment surprises me. If you don't mind me asking, why did you change your mind?"

Carol attempted a casual shrug. Inside her coat pocket,

she clenched the crumpled card so hard her hand hurt. "Does it really matter?"

"No," the coordinator admitted. "Just be careful with your motivations, else you might be the person who winds up getting hurt."

"That's not going to happen," Carol assured her.

Gabrielle smiled. "Then I feel sorry for Luke."

As the woman walked away, Carol adopted a smug smile. Someone should feel sorry for Luke. Because, just like the cartoon Cupid dressed in fatigues on the sappy valentine, Carol planned to take no prisoners.

chapter three

CAROL sat in her car in the parking lot in front of her office building gripping the cold steering wheel with sweaty hands. She glanced at her watch, fighting the compulsion to go inside. At 7:50 a.m. she was usually well into her workday, but Luke Chancellor always cut it close, so...

As if she had conjured him up, his pewter-colored BMW zipped into view. She followed his car in her rearview mirror, noting where he parked. Then she timed her exit from her own sensible sedan so they would meet on their way into the building. It was a brisk winter morning, with enough of a breeze to send chills up her skirt. Carol tried to ignore the cold, slowing to allow Luke to catch up with her. He was whistling under his breath and tying a yellow tie, his white shirt collar flipped up. When he saw her, he did a double-take and rolled his wrist to check his watch.

"Good morning, Snow," he said with a grin. "Two more minutes and you'd have gotten a tardy slip."

"Good morning, Chancellor," Carol returned as nicely as she could manage given the fact that she wanted to confront him about the icicle card he'd stuck in her book.

"How was your book club?"

"Fine," she said, wondering if the man was, on top of everything else, a mind reader. Her heart pounded in her chest. Could he tell something was different?

"Something's different," he said, looking her up and down.

She stiffened. "What?"

"You're wearing a skirt," he said, appraising her legs. "Nice."

It wasn't that she didn't appreciate the compliment—it was just that she hadn't received a compliment from a man in so long, she didn't know how to respond. "Thank... you?"

He angled his head at her. "Was that a question?"

Flustered, Carol nodded to his undone collar. "Didn't have time to dress at home?"

"Maybe I wasn't at home this morning."

She started to roll her eyes at his insinuation that he'd spent the night elsewhere, then remembered some of the coaching tips the women in the book club had given her—act interested...make eye contact...flirt...touch him...

"So...um...where were you?" she asked, batting her lashes.

"At the gym." Luke squinted. "Do you have something in your eye?"

"Er, yes," she lied, lifting her knuckle for a fake rub.

"Let me see," he said, stopping to turn toward her.

Caught off guard by his sudden proximity, she inhaled sharply, breathing in the scent of shaving cream and soap that emanated from him. Even with her wearing heels, he stood a head taller. The ends of his dark hair were still damp, conjuring up images of him in the gym shower… sudsing sweat from his long, muscular body. He peered into her perfectly healthy eye while she stood stock still in an effort to ward off the sexual vibes rolling off him.

It didn't work. Even standing in the cold wind, her temperature raised a few degrees.

"Hmm," he murmured. "I don't see anything. Wait a minute—there's something."

She cut her gaze to him. "What?"

He pulled back. "A pair of big, gorgeous green eyes."

She wanted to scoff, but the sound came out sounding like…a sigh! Then Carol remembered she was *supposed* to be swooning over him. The sheer push-pull of emotion left her paralyzed.

Luke, meanwhile, seemed to be enjoying himself. He walked ahead, his stride carefree. She shook herself and trotted to keep up as they walked into the lobby of the office building. An elevator car was waiting, open. Luke stepped inside, then looked to her. "Are you coming, or are you taking the stairs?"

He was mocking her now. And she was so nervous, Carol was halfway ready to make a run for the stairwell. Maybe this seduction plan wasn't such a good idea after all. Standing next to him in the open air was unnerving enough…she wasn't sure she was ready to be confined with him on the elevator…alone.

Then another woman stepped past her onto the elevator. The cute brunette with the stylish razor-cut hairstyle worked in marketing, Carol recalled. The woman flashed a toothy smile at Luke and the door started to close. At the last second, Carol put out her hand and the door bounced back. She stepped inside and faced the front. When the doors closed, Carol glanced at her reflection, realizing there was nothing "cute" about the way she wore her coarse, bronze-colored hair clasped at the nape of her neck.

This seduction thing was making her self-conscious.

"Luke, do you have plans for Valentine's?" the young woman asked in a hopeful voice.

"Dinner with a special lady," he quipped.

Carol could practically feel the air whoosh out of the brunette's sails, and she conceded a blip of dismay herself that Luke was dating someone, yet still flirting indiscriminately. Her mouth tightened. All the more reason to bring him down a notch.

At the next floor, the brunette got off, leaving them alone for the ride up another ten floors. Then, to her dismay, Luke reached forward to push the button for every floor in between.

"*What* are you doing?" she demanded.

"Just wanted a couple of minutes to finish tying my tie," he said easily, reaching up to resume the job. "Not sure I'll ever understand why men wear these things."

The elevator doors opened at the next floor and a woman walking past peered inside at the couple, giving them a strange look when neither one of them alighted. When the doors closed, Carol glared at Luke.

"People are going to talk about us."

"It'll do wonders for your reputation…and mine," he said amiably. "It's a win-win situation."

Carol felt a sputter coming on, then reminded herself that she was supposed to be flirting with the man. The elevator climbed, opening and closing on every floor before proceeding. After lying in wait for him in the parking lot, Carol knew she should be taking advantage of this time alone with Luke, but she didn't know what to say.

"How'd I do?" he asked, pulling on the tie.

She glanced over and couldn't help smiling at the crooked knot. "It's lopsided."

"Help me out, Snow?"

When Carol stepped closer, she was struck with a sense of déjà vu she'd always helped James with his ties. That had been so long ago, did she even remember what to do? The size of the knot went in and out of fashion and there was something about putting a dimple in the knot.

The pure silk of Luke's mustard-colored tie felt velvety to her trembling fingers. Beneath the layers of clothing, she could feel the beat of his heart. The electric impulse seemed to transfer to her fingertips and up her arm as she adjusted the knot. She met his dark gaze and for a split second, she thought she saw the same look of surprised confusion she felt fluttering in her stomach. But in a blink, the look was replaced with a teasing light.

"The thought of you reading those naughty books kept me awake last night. It makes me think there's more to you than meets the eye."

His rumbling voice skated over her nerves like sandpaper, stirring responses long-buried in her womb. Carol bit her tongue to keep from asking what the woman he was taking to Valentine's Day dinner would think of that remark, reminding herself that if she was going to seduce this man who had come to represent the Cheating Everyman, she was going to have to pretend that she liked him.

She smoothed her hand down his chest, feeling the wall of muscle beneath his shirt, then conjured up a seductive smile. "You're like a barking dog chasing a car, Chancellor. What would you do if you actually caught it?"

His jaw went slack as the doors to the elevator dinged and opened onto her floor.

"See you at the directors' meeting," she said, then turned on her heel and walked away.

She was pretty sure he was still staring at her when the doors closed.

Carol exhaled slowly. She'd anticipated the nervousness and the awkwardness of being sexually assertive. What she hadn't planned on was the sense of sheer feminine power that filled her chest. It spurred her on to prove to Luke Chancellor that she wasn't the chunk of ice he'd accused her of being.

She would set him on fire, then leave him to burn down.

"Are you okay, Ms. Snow?"

Carol turned at the sound of her assistant Tracy's voice. "Good morning. Yes, I'm fine. Why do you ask?"

"Because you're late," the young redhead said, narrowing her eyes.

"I'm not late."

"It's late for you. And you're flushed. Are you feeling ill?"

Carol straightened. "I'm fine. Did you revise the memo we talked about?"

"It's on your desk." Tracy followed her into her office. "Would you like some coffee?"

Carol set down her briefcase and looked up with surprise—Tracy had never offered to get her coffee before. "That would be nice, actually, since I'm on my way to a meeting."

"The directors' meeting, yes, I know," Tracy said. "There's a rumor that the company might give out bonuses this year!"

Carol frowned. "You shouldn't listen to watercooler gossip. The idea hasn't even been brought before the directors yet. And even if comes up, it would have to be a unanimous decision."

Looking contrite, Tracy retreated to the lobby. Carol glanced out her office door into the large bullpen area that housed the employees that made up her department. Many people were standing and talking over their cubicles, their body language excited. Carol cursed Luke Chancellor under her breath—no doubt, he'd gotten the rumor started, hoping that employees would pressure their bosses to approve the bonuses. It was the height of irresponsibility, a move meant to make him look good. And it put her between a rock and a hard place.

If she were going to seduce the man, she needed to cozy up to him. But could she set aside her business principles and support his self-indulgent campaign simply to get her ultimate revenge?

Carol skimmed the memo that Tracy had revised, shaking her head when she spied two new typos. She circled them with a red marker, grabbed a pad and pen, then exited her office.

"Here's your coffee, Ms. Snow…you take it black, don't you?"

"Yes, thank you." Carol took the cup, then handed over the memo. "Try again, Tracy…I'd like to see a clean copy on my desk by the time I get back from the meeting."

Tracy bit her lip. "Yes, ma'am."

As Carol strode past the offices of her employees, she noticed their animated chatter quieted. They shot furtive glances in her direction and talked behind their hands. She resented the hell out of Luke for raising the hopes of her employees, and was still feeling rankled when she walked into the boardroom where all of the other eight directors had gathered, with one notable exception—Luke. The group had left the chairs at both ends of the table empty. By unspoken consent, one chair was reserved for the person who ran the monthly meeting, and the other was reserved for their hero Luke, who would stroll in late, as always.

Since it was Carol's turn to run the meeting, she took one of the chairs and made small talk with her peers, glancing at the agenda that had been passed out. Luke was scheduled to give a sales briefing, but there was no mention of bonuses. Still, just in the couple of minutes since she'd arrived, she'd heard the word whispered and bandied about in conversation.

The man had his own viral marketing posse.

"Shall we get started?" Carol asked.

"Shouldn't we wait on Luke?" Teresa Maitlin, Director of Marketing asked. There were rumors that she and Luke had dated…or something. Luke did seem to be aware of the dangers and legalities of workplace dating and only consorted with women on his level. As Carol looked around the table, she realized she might be the only single female director he hadn't been linked with romantically. She idly wondered if one of these women was his date for Valentine's Day.

"No," Carol said pointedly, then glanced across the table to another member of the Luke Chancellor loved-him-and-lost-him fan club. "Janet, you're up first to give us an update from the Art Department."

Janet took the floor and passed around samples of cards Mystic Touch would be unrolling later in the year for Halloween, Thanksgiving and Christmas. "We're expanding on designs that have proven customer appeal, including military themes and pop culture themes like music." Janet glanced at the still-empty chair. "I'm sure Luke will fill you in on the top sellers of the season."

Carol made a rueful noise. "I'm sure he will, if he ever gets here."

"Something must have come up," someone offered.

"Right. And the rest of us aren't busy," Carol said drily. They moved down the agenda until it was time for Luke to take the floor and he was still a no-show.

"Guess that's a wrap," Carol said, grateful to dismiss before the idea of bonuses was even raised.

Then the door burst open and a huge bouquet of red heart-shaped helium balloons were shepherded in by a set of long legs that Carol recognized with a sinking feeling. Everyone laughed as Luke went around the room passing out the playful balloons.

Carol accepted one reluctantly, knowing she and everyone else was being manipulated. Luke faced her and gave her a private wink that made her want to strangle him with the ribbon on the balloon she held.

"Doesn't it feel good to get something unexpected?" Luke addressed the room.

While Carol tried not to roll her eyes, everyone chorused agreement.

"And as a greeting card company, isn't that what we're all about? The joy of receiving something unexpected?"

His adoring fans cheered. Carol could only stare at the spectacle. The man was a hypnotist.

"Which is why," he continued with a magnanimous grin, "I propose that we have an impromptu company party this Friday afternoon to celebrate Valentine's Day, our biggest sales day of the year. Since it's not tied to a religious holiday, we don't have to worry about offending anyone, or being politically correct—our employees can just have fun."

From the nods and smiles, Carol knew the party was a done deal. And secretly, she thought it could be fun, although the pragmatist in her would not be quieted.

"As long as we set a reasonable budget," she said.

Luke smiled at her. "I thought I'd leave that to the Director of Finance. And while we're at it, I'd like to suggest that we pay every employee a one thousand dollar bonus."

Carol gasped and any feelings of conflict she'd been having about supporting Luke's idea and seducing him evaporated. "A half million in bonuses? That's outrageous."

"Anything less would be an insult," Luke countered. "We've had a record sales year."

"For one year in a row!" Carol exclaimed. "Next year could be a different story altogether. Wouldn't it be better to take that money and invest in a new high speed color printer, or a state-of-the-art cutter? My department would benefit from new computers on everyone's desk. Or maybe we could kick in more on our employees' health care premiums?"

Luke shook his head. "That's not tangible. Why not give our workers the money so they can spend it however they see fit?"

"Because it's not a prudent investment," Carol said, crossing her arms. Which would've been more menacing if the movement hadn't made the helium heart-shaped balloon bump her in the nose. She slapped at the balloon and lost a grip on the ribbon. It rose to the ceiling where it hit a hot light and burst.

Everyone jumped.

"Now then," Carol continued, "I agree the idea of a company party has merit—if we did something on-site, it could be affordable, and something that everyone could enjoy. But I'm not convinced that employee bonuses are the best way to spend a half million dollars."

Janet bit her lip and shrugged at Luke. "Carol has a

point, Luke. The vote has to be unanimous, and when it comes to financial matters, I'll always follow Carol's lead."

Luke nodded, then clapped his hands. "Since we all agree on a party, why don't we move ahead with those plans, and take some time to think about the bonuses."

Carol narrowed her eyes. Meaning, take some time for him to *campaign for support for the bonuses*.

"We could reconvene Friday morning," he said, then he cut his gaze to Carol. "If we reached an agreement that morning to pay a bonus, could we have the checks printed in time to give to employees at the party that afternoon?"

Carol pursed her mouth. "*If* we reached an agreement, it would be possible, I suppose."

"Okay," Luke said with a grin. "Let's have a party!"

As the meeting broke up, Carol marveled how everyone gravitated to Luke. He was animated as he spoke to Teresa, the Director of Marketing, whose team handled employee events and would be coordinating the party. Carol flashed back to this morning when she had straightened Luke's tie on the elevator. For a few seconds, she had detected something between them, and for a few moments, had been almost…*excited* about the prospect of seducing him. Standing here, she conceded a little disappointment that even though she knew she'd made the right business decision for her conscience, she would occasionally think about what might have been. Sure, she'd been planning to dump him after the seduction…but it might've been fun along the way…

Then Luke lifted his gaze to hers and over the heads of their peers, the proprietary look in his eyes sent an arrow of longing straight to her sex. She was reminded of the "take no prisoners" Cupid dressed in camouflage because Luke was looking at her as if she were the hill on which he was going to plant his flag.

She knew that look: Luke was planning to change her mind about the employee bonuses. The question was, how far would she let him go to win her over?

By standing up to him, she'd flipped the seduction production. Now who was seducing whom?

chapter four

THE next morning, Thursday, Carol pulled into the parking lot at her regular time, so early that only the security guards were working. But she spied another car in the parking lot—a pewter-colored BMW—and smirked when she saw Luke emerge and hurry in her direction, smothering a yawn. She had to give him points for getting up with the birds to start trying to win her over.

It was a frosty, still morning, cold enough to sting her nose and eyes. Carol lifted her gaze toward the rising sun to find an eerie, reddish hue bleeding over the horizon. The strange color of the winter sky left her with a sense of foreboding that enveloped her this time every year. A shiver skated down her spine. She couldn't wait to put another Valentine's Day behind her.

Her phone chimed to let her know a text message had arrived. She slowed to unclip it from her purse and glanced at the screen. It was from Gabrielle Pope.

Sensing all is not well, hope I'm wrong…let me know if I can help.

Carol squinted. How could Gabrielle possibly know that something had derailed her seduction of Luke?

The man himself bounded up next to her. "Good morning, Snow."

Flustered by the text message from Gabrielle, Carol was further dismayed by the way her vital signs spiked at the sight of Luke in his charcoal gray suit, white shirt, and lime-green-colored tie. Carol vaguely wondered what kind of outdoor activity kept the man so tan and virile-looking.

And when she had become so susceptible to his physical endowments.

"Is that an early morning message from your lover?" he asked, peering at her phone.

She yanked it to her chest. "No."

"No message, or no lover?" he teased.

Carol frowned. "You're early, Chancellor."

He smiled. "That's because I couldn't sleep last night thinking about you, Snow."

She pursed her mouth. "Don't you get tired of using that line?"

His eyes danced. "More specifically, thinking about what you said in the meeting yesterday about your department needing new computers. I might have a solution."

She glanced at him sideways as he held open the door for her. "I'm listening."

"It's better if I show you," he said as they walked to the elevator. When she gave him a suspicious look, he grinned. "Trust me."

Carol averted her gaze. She didn't trust him, or herself. Damn the whole seduction by the book exercise that Gabrielle had proposed. Before the book club, Carol had been content with her sexless life. She'd focused her energy on her career and convinced herself she didn't need a man. But once the idea of seducing Luke had been planted, the sexy man had hijacked her thoughts and her dreams.

As a reminder of his disdain for her, she fingered the crumpled icicle card that she'd left in her coat pocket. If he was being nice to her, it was simply because he wanted her to support the idea of paying bonuses when it came up again at the directors' meeting tomorrow morning.

Men. Could. Not. Be. Trusted.

After they walked onto the elevator, he pushed the button for the basement.

"Where are you taking me?" she asked.

"You'll see," he said with a wink.

He was so casual, so confident. The man never carried a briefcase or a laptop, she noticed irritably. By comparison, she felt like the B student who took every book home every night next to the straight-A student who never studied.

The short elevator ride seemed interminably long. Carol looked up, then down, anywhere to avoid looking at Luke…and noticing the way his suit jacket perfectly outlined his broad shoulders.

"So, did you curl up in bed with a book last night?" he asked.

Her mouth tightened. "Why are you interested in my bedtime reading material?"

"I'm interested in everything about you, Carol, but you're not the easiest person to get to know."

Her head came up and she looked at him. He sounded almost...*sincere*. His gaze was intense. "Forget the books you're reading," he said quietly. "What's *your* story? Why are you so prickly?"

She bristled—who was he to judge her? "Just because I'm immune to your charms, Chancellor, doesn't mean there's something wrong with me."

He leaned in close, until she could see the thick fringe of his dark lashes. "I don't think you're as immune as you let on, Snow. Your lips say one thing, but the color in your cheeks says something else entirely."

"You don't know what you're talking about," Carol said, but her denial sounded thin, even to her ears. Her cheeks flamed. When the elevator doors opened, she practically fell out to escape his company. She willed her pulse to slow, her breasts and thighs to ignore the pheromones the man emitted indiscriminately, like Johnny Appleseed.

"This is where we're having the party, by the way," he said as they stepped into a large open area. At the far end of the space sat offices of personnel who supervised the enormous printers and other pieces of computer equipment housed in the basement. Through their office window, someone threw up their hand and Luke waved back. He seemed to have the run of the place.

Carol followed him as he turned and walked down a dark hallway that seemed to lead nowhere. "Are you planning to off me so the directors will approve bonuses?"

His laughter boomed into the empty space. "No. I have

a better plan." He stopped and flipped on a light that revealed a nondescript door. On a small keyboard, he punched in a code that triggered a click, then he pushed open the door. "After you," he said, rolling his hand to indicate she was to precede him.

Carol was skeptical, but curiosity won out. She stepped toward the large supply room filled with miscellaneous furniture and computer equipment.

And it was *nice* stuff—wood desks and credenzas, glass-front bookcases, flat-screen monitors and CPU towers and sleek laptops. There were leather desk chairs, color printers, scanners, wireless keyboards, web cameras, and more.

She walked inside to survey the rows and rows of furniture and laden shelves. He followed her and the heavy door swung closed behind them.

"What is this place?" she asked.

"It's where leftovers and trade-ins are stored."

"But where did it all come from?"

"Mostly from the sales team in the field."

Her jaw dropped. "Everything in here gathering dust is nicer than the furniture and equipment my employees work on every day! Why didn't I know about his room?"

"You do…now."

She set down her briefcase and purse, gazing around in awe. "What is this, some sort of company secret?"

"I wouldn't call it a secret," he said, hedging. "Technically, all this equipment belongs to the sales department."

She knew better than anyone that sales got the lion's share of the administrative budget—a budget that had gone up steeply since Luke had become director. To attract the best talent, he'd convinced the executive committee to allocate more funds for commissions and perks, like state-of-the-art computers and deep expense accounts. True, the expenditures had proved to be a good investment, but it also left other employees feeling resentful. Carol set her jaw.

"So did you just bring me down here to rub it in?"

Luke turned toward her and she realized suddenly how vulnerable she was with him in here…alone. She wasn't afraid of him, just afraid of her reaction to him. At his nearness, her breathing became shallow, and her nipples budded. She was grateful that her winter coat hid her responses, but the way he looked at her, as if he knew the effect he had on her, was unnerving. His previous comment that her body language betrayed her made her feel even more exposed.

"Where would you like for me to rub it in?" he murmured.

Carol tried to rally an indignant reply, but she couldn't seem to form the angry words. Not even when he planted his hands on either side of her, effectively caging her between the shelf at her back and his big body. Instead, it was as if the will to resist him leaked out of her body. Carol lifted her gaze slowly, over his broad chest and up his crooked tie to the square chin, past the sensual mouth and strong nose to those incredible brown eyes that seemed to pull at her. She reasoned that the equipment in the room must be emitting electrical charges because the scant air between their bodies fairly crackled.

She realized he was going to kiss her, and she didn't want

to stop him. As his mouth moved toward hers and his features softened, she told herself she'd planned to seduce him, hadn't she? What did it matter who was on top and who—

Suddenly Luke pulled back with a blanched expression. "I'm sorry, I—" He straightened and wiped his hand over his mouth. "Carol, I don't know what came over me. It's like—" He looked around the room as if he just realized where they were, then he stepped back and looked her over. "Are you okay?"

She nodded as anger whipped through her. "I'm fine, Chancellor. Is this where you bring all your conquests?"

"What? Of course not. I've never—" He stopped and put out his hands. "I apologize—I lost my head." He cleared his throat and seemed to collect himself. "Are we good?"

Carol burned with humiliation that she'd wanted that kiss so much. She should be grateful that Luke had had the restraint to pull away. Instead she was left with the sensation of having something stolen from her. Old feelings of rejection zoomed to the surface, staggering her. She stuck her shaking hands in the pockets of her coat and found the crumpled card, another reminder that Luke was toying with her, and she'd fallen for it.

"Are you going to tell me why you brought me here?" she said through gritted teeth.

He scratched his temple as if he'd forgotten. "I was going to help you, um, liberate, whatever equipment your department needs."

Carol hesitated. Her first instinct—especially now—

was to refuse anything he offered. But the practical side of her couldn't deny that her employees deserved nice equipment, and she understood office politics. Luke had something she needed and was gifting it to her. She wasn't going to side with him on the matter of the employee bonuses, but why not get something for her people in the meantime?

"Okay," she said. "How do we do this?"

"Today I have to help get things ready for tomorrow's party. Meet me back here after hours?"

Warning bells sounded in her head. After hours... alone...in a confined space. *Danger! Danger!*

Luke lifted his hands. "I promise to be on my best behavior."

"Okay," Carol heard herself say. And that tightness in her chest over his pronouncement to behave himself, was that relief—or disappointment?

chapter five

NO matter how hard Carol tried to keep her mind and hands busy and off the after-hours meeting with Luke, the workday crawled by. Conversely, her body hummed with restless energy. She told herself it was the nervous excitement of doing something unorthodox when it came to shuffling company assets. But Luke's near-kiss this morning had haunted her all day—she could almost taste his lips on hers. Why had he suddenly grown a conscience? Obviously, she was going to have to take control if this seduction thing was going to happen. She would sleep with him once, and because she was now so well-read on erotic love play, she would make sure it was the hottest encounter of his life. And when the moment was right, she'd let him know she knew it was him who'd planted the icicle card and tell him to get lost.

At long last, the clock on her desk flipped to five

o'clock. Already wearing her coat and with briefcase in hand, Carol walked out of her office.

Her assistant Tracy's eyebrows shot up. "You're going home?"

"That's right," Carol said, biting her tongue to keep from telling her assistant she didn't have to explain herself.

"It's only five o'clock. Did someone die?"

Carol pressed her lips together. "No." She handed Tracy the latest version of the memo, this time with four errors circled in red. "Again, please."

Tracy sighed. "Yes, ma'am."

Carol looked to the bullpen where her employees worked on dated computers, some of which were shared. A situation she hoped to remedy soon. Before she turned away, she noticed people glaring in her direction, then exchanging knowing looks with each other. Now that she thought about it, her employees had maintained a wide arc around her all day…

She turned back to her assistant. "Tracy, is there something going on I should know about?"

The young redhead worked her mouth back and forth, obviously weighing whether to be truthful. "Well…word around the watercooler is you're standing in the way of everyone getting bonuses."

Carol's shoulders fell when she realized the collective hostility being directed toward her. She was surprised how much the knowledge hurt, and it made her tone sharp. "I believe a better use of the money is reinvesting in the company. In the long run, we'll all benefit more."

Tracy's mouth tightened into a bow. "I'll have the revised memo on your desk in the morning, Ms. Snow."

"Thank you. Good night."

As Carol walked out, she felt the heat of angry stares boring into her. But as a senior money manager for the company, it was her job to make unpopular decisions. Hopefully the new equipment would help to alleviate ill will.

She braved the notorious Atlanta rush-hour traffic and passed the time taking in the magnificent, brooding color palette of the sky—reds and oranges. An omen of bad weather? Whatever the cause, it was unsettling to her for a reason she couldn't put her finger on.

At home she undressed and redressed slowly, studying her slight curves with a critical eye, something she hadn't done in quite a while. She'd gotten talked into a couple of blind dates in the years since she and James had split, but she hadn't been intimate with anyone. When the moment of truth arrived with Luke, she hoped she remembered what to do.

One thing was certain—she'd be drawing heavily on her recent reading material for the Red Tote Book Club.

The text message from Gabrielle suddenly slid into Carol's mind. She hadn't responded, and now felt compelled to, if only to circumvent the well-meaning woman from interfering. Pulling out her phone, Carol used the touch pad to type in: *Thanks for your concern, but everything going as planned.*

She hit Send and bit her lip at the white lie, but she knew Gabrielle well enough to know that the woman would worry otherwise.

When she drove back to the office at the prescribed meet time, Carol felt like a thief, stealing into the building after most people had gone home. She waved to the guard, then rode the elevator down to the basement. When she alighted, the cavernous space was darker than it had been this morning. Lights in only half of the offices across the way were burning. She could barely see to walk.

"Luke?" she whispered. "Are you here?" She turned and bumped into a wall...with arms. She stumbled backward, but he reached out and steadied her.

"I got you," he murmured close to her ear.

"Why didn't you say something?" she snapped.

"I thought if I was quiet, you might grope around a little."

Her eyes were starting to adjust to the darkness, allowing her to see the light of mischief in his gaze. Her body softened in secret places, leaving her feeling exposed. He was teasing her, and she was bending like putty.

"Shouldn't we get started?" she asked, trying to regain the upper hand.

"Yes," he said, sounding like a little boy who'd been reprimanded. "This way."

He clasped her hand, then led her down the hallway. His fingers felt warm and strong around hers, sending her mind leaping in directions of how it would feel to have his hands on her naked body. Carol felt along the wall with her free hand. "Can we turn on a light?"

"I'd rather not draw attention to our little mission."

She followed him until he stopped. He released her hand to punch in the key code and then a click sounded. Luke reclaimed her hand and guided her into the room, and when the door closed, turned on banks of lights to illuminate the room.

As Carol blinked against the glare, Luke emitted a low whistle. When he came into focus, she realized he was looking at her. "You let your hair down. I like it."

She combed her fingers through the unruly layers self-consciously. "Thanks."

"And wow, I don't think I've ever seen you in anything except a suit, Snow. Nice."

She wore black jeans, black turtleneck, black bomber jacket and black boots. Satisfaction curled in her chest over his compliment, although she tried not to react. "Contrary to popular belief, I have a wardrobe and a life outside the office." She nodded to his clothing. "You look more comfortable than the last time I saw you."

In truth, Luke looked breathtakingly handsome in dark jeans, rugged athletic shoes, and a red V-neck sweater over a white T-shirt. He smiled and nodded, then leaned forward. "Interesting earrings."

"Thanks." Carol reached up to stroke the dangling sterling cylinders that featured channel-set emeralds. James had given them to her.... He'd said emeralds were the "stone of successful love." What a load of manure. She'd worn them tonight as a reminder that men couldn't be trusted. She would use Luke to get what her employees needed, but she had no illusions as to his motivations for helping her.

"Did you bring a list?" he asked.

She pulled a rolled sheaf of papers from her coat pocket. "An inventory of the equipment in my department, and a wish list."

Luke unrolled the pages and scanned them. "Okay, let's start with the wish list. One color laser printer."

At that point, it became a scavenger hunt. The two of them walked the aisles between shelves, looking for something to fit the bill. If one of them found it, they shouted out, and the item got tagged. It was almost fun, Carol conceded. She found herself looking for glimpses of Luke as he moved between shelving units. Damn, the man could wear a pair of jeans.

"So tell me about this life you have outside of work," he called.

She hesitated, but being obscured by the cluttered shelves made her feel safe. "I like to cook."

"Will you marry me?"

She blinked, then leaned into the open aisle. "Huh?"

Down a few rows, Luke leaned into the aisle, too, and flashed a grin. "Kidding." His head disappeared. "Keep going. What do you like about cooking?"

Carol pulled back and toyed with a wireless computer mouse on the shelf in front of her. "I guess I like all the things that go along with it. In the summer I have a small organic plot in the community garden at Piedmont Park."

"Cool. What do you grow?"

"Nothing fancy—corn and beans, peppers and tomatoes."

"Gotta love home-grown tomatoes," came his muffled reply.

"Food seems to taste better when you've grown it yourself," she agreed. "But I like shopping for food, too."

"I make a trip to the Dekalb Farmers Market a couple of times a month," he said.

Impressed, Carol pursed her mouth. "You do?"

"Best selection of international beers in the area."

She laughed. "That's true, I guess."

He appeared at the end of the shelf where she stood. "So, who gets to enjoy the fruits of your labor?"

Caught off guard by his sudden proximity, Carol blinked. "Huh?"

"Who do you cook for?"

She averted her gaze and pretended to scrutinize something higher on the shelf. "Oh…you know—friends and…stuff." Nobody.

"No family close by?"

She shook her head and chanced a glance in his direction. "I don't have any family left. My parents are gone and I'm an only child."

Sympathy flashed in his dark eyes. "I'm sorry."

Carol shrugged. "Thanks, but I've been on my own for a while."

"It makes me feel guilty for all the times I've wanted peace and quiet from my family."

"You have a big one?"

"Three sisters, two brothers, assorted nieces and nephews, and my folks are still alive and well."

Envy coursed through her. "That must make for big holiday gatherings."

He nodded. "It's chaos."

It sounded heavenly to her, but she didn't comment.

He disappeared again, then called out that he'd found another item on the list. Carol crossed it off her copy.

"Ever been married, Snow?"

Her head came up at his question even though from the sound of his voice, he was on the other side of the room.

James's face appeared in her mind and her face burned with shame. "No. You?"

"No. Have you ever been close?"

"Not really," she said. "You?"

"No."

Since he couldn't see her, Carol smirked. Meaning he wasn't serious about the "special lady" he was taking out for Valentine's Day dinner? No big surprise.

Even though he'd brought it up, the topic of committed relationships seemed to have soured him on conversation for a while because he lapsed into silence as he turned on machines to ensure they were operational.

They made multiple trips up and down aisles, opened boxes and sorted through bins of miscellaneous equipment. Over the course of a couple of hours, they were able to find about half the equipment on Carol's wish list, and locate newer computers to replace almost all the machines her employees currently used. They were nearing the end of the list when Luke got chatty again.

"So, Snow," he said from some unseen corner, "tell me about this naughty book club of yours."

Carol squirmed. "It's not 'naughty.' We read and discuss classic erotica."

"I stand corrected—it's even dirtier than I thought."

She couldn't help but laugh. "There's nothing dirty about it."

His face suddenly appeared on the other side of the shelving unit where she stood. "Can you let me have my fantasies?"

Her traitorous body surged with longing. Instead of responding, she lifted a device that resembled a gun and pointed it at him. "I found a handheld scanner."

He put his hand over his heart and pretended to stagger back. "You got me. With me gone, you can do whatever you want with the half million dollars."

Carol sighed, remembering the glares from her own employees. "It's not what *I* want, Chancellor—it's what I think is best for the company."

He nodded, his expression congenial. "As long as you're not opposing the bonuses simply because it was my idea."

And just like that, she remembered what a jerk he was. Anger bubbled in her chest—anger at Luke Chancellor, wunderkind, and anger at all the men out there who steamrolled through life, crushing the hopes and the hearts and the careers of anyone who got in their way—after using that person as a means to their own selfish ends. But she reeled in her temper, remembering her personal and professional goals. Luke would get his.

"No," she said quietly, walking closer to brush dust off the shoulder of Luke's red sweater. It was a casual caress, but the warmth of his body reached through the fibers and seeped into her fingers, making them tingle. "In fact, I've decided to keep an open mind when the directors reconvene tomorrow morning to take another vote."

Luke's gaze followed her hand down his sleeve. "You have?"

"Yes."

"That's great." He grinned. "I appreciate your being flexible."

"I take yoga," she offered with a smile. "I'm nothing if not flexible."

She was feeling smug about throwing him off balance, but then the tip of his tongue appeared to wet his lips, sending Carol's imagination running in a different direction. Her midsection tightened. If only Luke wasn't so…orally gifted.

He was staring at her. "So…what now?"

Carol's pulse spiked. Should she make the first move? Kiss him? Tear off his red sweater? Tackle him? Her mind raced back over the erotic books she'd read…the common theme was women taking control of their sexual experiences.

Still…it had been a long time…

"What did you have in mind?" she asked.

"I was thinking it'll take most of the night."

She swallowed hard. A little cocky, yes, but it was hard not to be impressed by his confidence. "P-probably. My place?" She had stocked up on enough body butter to slide through a keyhole and enough condoms to protect a sorority.

Luke gave a little laugh. "Of course your place. If it's alright with you, I'll supervise."

Carol opened her mouth to agree, then narrowed her eyes. "Supervise?"

"To make sure none of the equipment gets broken." He gestured to the flat-screen monitor behind him. "It would be a shame to move all this stuff to your department only for it to be damaged in transit."

Slowly, she realized that she and Luke were having two

different conversations. For once, *she* had sex on the brain, *he* was thinking depreciating assets.

"You want to move everything tonight?" she asked.

"I think it would be less likely to raise a red flag if the equipment is already in place when your people get in tomorrow, don't you?"

"Probably."

"Go home," he said. "I'll take care of everything. In case someone questions what's going on, I don't want you to get in trouble."

Disappointment that the seduction wouldn't take place tonight was crowded out by an odd feeling—she couldn't remember the last time someone had been *protective* of her. "O…kay."

Warmth and sincerity radiated from Luke's eyes, disorienting her. She'd come tonight with the intention of enticing him, then taking him down a notch. But he'd ruined things by being so…nice. Dammit.

"See you tomorrow?" he said, his eyes crinkling at the corners.

Carol backed toward the door—she had to get away from those crinkles. "See you tomorrow."

Her pulse clicked at top speed on the way back to her car. She raised her coat collar against the cold and rubbed her hands together briskly. She could *not* be falling for Luke Chancellor…she wouldn't let herself. She drove home with hands planted firmly on the steering wheel, determined to regain control of her emotions. When she arrived at her condo, though, one glance in her foyer mirror confirmed her worst suspicions—bright eyes, pink cheeks and a subtle softening of her mouth…she was suc-cumbing to Luke Chancellor's spell. Dammit.

Then she gasped and her hand flew to her ear. One of her emerald earrings was missing. A low moan of anguish sounded from the back of her throat. She frantically back-tracked to her car and looked inside, but didn't find it.

Hot tears flooded Carol's eyes—how fitting that she lose the one nice gift James had given her, the one thing that reminded her to keep her heart in check.

From her belt, her phone chimed to signal an incoming text message. Before she even looked, Carol knew it was from Gabrielle Pope.

Just remember that the best-laid plans often go astray.

Carol closed her eyes. She was obviously the target of some kind of cosmic Valentine's Day conspiracy.

But she would not surrender.

chapter six

CAROL wanted to arrive early the next morning so she could see the looks on the faces of her employees when they saw their new computers, but traffic and the elements conspired against her.

The early sky was angry, a spewing volcano of rolling red clouds that seemed to have an adverse effect on morning commuters. Horns punctuated the air as cars inched toward their destination. On the radio, experts and laypersons offered explanations for the phenomenon. The leading theory suggested the recent drought had allowed an extreme amount of dust from Georgia red clay to accumulate in the atmosphere, accounting for the eerie coloring of the clouds. Regardless of the source, Carol longed for blue skies again.

It was a few minutes past eight o'clock when she pulled into the parking lot. A frigid wind cut through her coat and scarf as she hurried into the building. Atlanta almost never got this cold. It felt…unnatural.

Her heart tripped in anticipation as she rode up on the elevator. It felt good to reward her employees and she conceded that she was even rethinking her position on paying out bonuses. Luke had surprised her last night in the supply room with his warmth and interest…maybe she'd been wrong about him and his motives.

When the elevator doors opened, she smiled at the hum of excited voices. She walked into the area, pleased to see the printers and other peripherals had been installed, and "new" laptops sat on everyone's desks. Tracy, caressing her own new computer, turned a beaming smile in Carol's direction. "Look at all this stuff—isn't it wonderful?"

Carol nodded, then opened her mouth with the intention of saying "You're welcome."

"And we have Luke Chancellor to thank for it," Tracy added with a dreamy sigh.

Carol swallowed her words. "Luke Chancellor?"

"Can you believe it? Apparently he was here all night installing refurbished machines he found somewhere."

Carol's mouth puckered. "Really?"

"Everyone in this department has needed new computers for so long—I know you tried and tried to get them requisitioned. Luke must have pulled a lot of strings to make this happen."

Carol pushed her tongue into her cheek. "He pulled something, all right. How do you know it was him?"

"Everyone knows—it's all over the building. And everyone's excited about the party this afternoon. Apparently, that was his idea, too…along with the bonuses."

Her assistant gave her a wary look, then held up a sheet of paper. "I gave the memo another stab."

"Thank you," Carol said, plucking it from her assistant's hand.

As she proceeded toward her office, Luke's name was in the air. Employees parted in her wake, and their expressions of excitement over their new equipment changed to mild disdain when they looked her way. Their message was clear: *Luke Chancellor will do things for us, but you won't.* If she tried to defend herself at this point, it would only look as if she was trying to take credit to save face.

Luke's words from the previous evening came back to her. *Go home…I'll take care of everything. In case someone questions what's going on, I don't want you to get in trouble.*

And to think she'd believed he was being protective.

Heat infused her body as she set down her briefcase and hung up her coat. He'd made a fool out of her. Not only did everyone know that she was the lone holdout when it came to granting bonuses, but he'd managed to make it look as if he cared about her own department more than she did.

Angry tears scalded her eyelids, but she fought mightily to keep them at bay. She didn't want anyone at work to see her break down. She needed to escape for a few minutes to collect herself before the directors' meeting. Carol considered fleeing to the ladies' room, then remembered she needed to look for the missing earring that she'd most likely lost in the equipment room. She could be alone there.

She backtracked to the elevator and did her best to ignore the accusatory glances from people she passed—apparently word had spread quickly. While she waited for a car to arrive, someone muttered "Ice Queen" under their breath disguised as a cough. A few people tittered. Carol's face burned as she walked onto the elevator, but she managed to lift her chin and keep it together on the short ride to the basement.

When the doors opened, she realized that preparations were already underway for the afternoon party. Red decorations of cupids and hearts abounded. Blowups of some of the company's Valentine's Day cards leaned against the wall, including the "take no prisoners" card she'd seen on her assistant's desk. Cupid looked even more menacing at life-size.

Thankfully, she didn't see Luke among the volunteers…but the people who saw her threw her a look of distaste before turning back to their tasks. Stung, Carol hurried to the stockroom. There she punched in the code she'd seen Luke use and slipped inside.

When the door closed behind her, she leaned against its cool surface for a few seconds, reveling in the quiet. It had been an unsettling week and she fervently wished she could hit the rewind button.

Unfortunately, life didn't come with a remote control.

At length she felt for the light switch and illuminated the room. The shelves were much more bare than yesterday…the equipment scavenged for her department had made a big dent in the inventory. Carol released a pent-up breath and allowed herself the luxury of a few miserable tears.

How had she gotten to this place in her life? She'd thought by now she'd be at the pinnacle of her career, married to a great guy and maybe starting a family. Instead, she felt as if she'd regressed to high school—no matter what she did, no one liked her.

And she was alone. Completely, absolutely, utterly alone.

With no answers at hand, she found a tissue and blew her nose, then began walking up and down the aisles, looking for her missing earring. The longer she walked, the more bitter frustration built up in her chest—frustration toward James, who had so callously toyed with her heart. And toward Luke, who had so easily usurped her authority and conned her with a few probing questions and a handful of compliments.

From the floor, a glint of metal caught her eye. To her relief, it was her silver-and-emerald earring. She knelt to retrieve it from under a shelf, but lost her balance and bumped the shelving unit accidentally. Above her, she heard a scraping noise, and when she looked up, something large was bearing down on her.

Carol didn't have time to put up her hand. Pain exploded in her head, then everything went black.

chapter seven

SOMEONE was shaking Carol by the shoulder.

"Ms. Snow…Ms. Snow?"

She opened her eyes to blink her assistant Tracy's face into view, then winced at the pain that stabbed her temple.

"Oh, thank God—she opened her eyes," Tracy said. "Ms. Snow, are you okay?"

Carol sat up and lifted her hand to her head, where a goose egg had formed. "I think so. I leaned over to pick up an earring I lost and something fell on my head."

"That monitor," a young man said, pointing to a boxy computer screen sitting nearby on its end. "You're lucky you weren't killed."

Carol squinted. "Who are you?"

"My boyfriend, Stan," Tracy said. "He works here in the basement and was walking by when he heard a crash. He recognized you and called me. Should I call an ambulance?"

"No," Carol said, gingerly pushing to her feet. "It's just a bump on the head. I'll be fine."

"Are you sure?"

"Of course I'm sure," Carol snapped. "I have a meeting to go to."

Tracy glanced at her watch. "Actually, the directors' meeting has already started."

Carol brushed off her clothes and straightened her lapel. "Then I'd better be going." She glanced at Tracy's boyfriend. "Thank you for coming to my assistance."

Then she marched out, embarrassed to have been in such a compromising situation. She palpated the tender knot on her forehead. A low, throbbing headache had settled into her crown. The pain brought her near tears again, but she was more determined than ever to stand up to Luke Chancellor. After stopping by the ladies' room to arrange her hair over the reddened bump, Carol proceeded to the room where the directors' meeting was being held and pushed open the door.

Her fellow directors looked up and she could tell not all of them were relieved to see her. Luke Chancellor sat at the head of the table. He smiled up at her. "We were just getting ready to send out a search party for you, Carol."

"I'll bet you were," she said sweetly, then settled into an empty chair. "Sorry I'm late."

"We heard a Good Samaritan delivered new computer equipment to your department this morning," Janet, the art director, said with a smile.

All gazes slid toward Luke. He held up his hands. "It was Carol's idea—I just…facilitated."

She set her jaw—how did he do that? Manage to sound humble and still take credit?

"Have you revisited the issue of bonuses?" Carol asked, pulling the conversation back to the matter at hand. She shot a look of contempt in Luke's direction.

He caught her gaze and confusion registered on his face…what an actor.

"We were just about to," Luke said, then cleared his voice. "I think it's pretty clear that anyone dissenting is following your lead, Carol, so I guess we can cut to the chase by asking if you've changed your mind on the issue of paying out a one-time bonus?"

The weight of a roomful of stares shifted to her. Luke looked hopeful, and Carol knew he was remembering her comment from the previous evening, that she might reconsider her position. But that was when she'd been under the spell he seemed to be able to cast so easily with a handsome face and a few flattering words. That was before he'd made her feel stupid for falling for his caring act, before he'd embarrassed her, turned all her employees against her. This might be her one and only chance to put Luke Chancellor in his place.

"No, I haven't changed my mind. Not about the bonuses, not about a lot of things," she added pointedly.

Disappointment colored Luke's face. His mouth flattened, then he shrugged. "I guess that's that."

"I guess so," Carol chirped, then pushed up from her chair. "If that's all, I really need to get back to work. This party means I have only four hours to get done what I'd normally do in eight."

Luke's mouth tightened. "That's all."

Carol gave him a triumphant look, then walked out. On the way back to her office, she massaged her temples, trying to alleviate the headache that had yet to ease. When she reached her department, she walked the gauntlet of angry stares and closed her office door. There she downed some aspirin and waited for the feeling of vindication to descend. She'd proved to Luke that her opinion still meant something around here…that there was at least one woman he couldn't charm into submission.

But sitting here in the wake of her power, the victory felt strangely hollow. She shook it off, reasoning that she could hardly feel good about anything while nursing a headache. She would savor the success later, in private.

When she was alone. Completely, absolutely, utterly alone.

She pushed away the troubling thought, announced to Tracy through the intercom that she wasn't to be disturbed, then spent the morning plowing through a mountain of paperwork. At some point Carol decided she'd skip the Valentine's Day party and just go home, maybe tuck in with a good book, something she could suggest as a selection for the Red Tote Book Club.

While she was thinking about it, she pulled out her phone and sent a text message to Gabrielle.

Change of plans…seduction OFF.

A couple of minutes later, Gabrielle replied.

Surrender to love, Carol.

Carol frowned at the message. Love? Who said anything about love?

And *surrender?* Never.

A knock sounded at her door, then it creaked open.

"Tracy, I asked not to be disturbed," Carol said without looking up.

"Don't get mad at her," Luke said.

Carol lifted her head to see the man of the hour standing in her doorway. He gestured behind him. "Tracy said you didn't want to be disturbed, but I told her I'd take full responsibility for defying your orders."

He looked handsome in brown slacks and pale blue dress shirt, minus a tie. Her pulse quickened, but she reminded herself that he wasn't to be trusted.

Men. Could. Not. Be. Trusted.

"What do you want, Chancellor?"

"I thought it would be nice if we walked into the party together, a show of solidarity."

She stood and began packing her briefcase. "I'm not going to the party."

He gave a little laugh. "Not going? Why not?"

"Because I'd rather go home, that's why."

"Go home to what?" he asked. "A book?"

At his mocking tone, Carol bit down on the inside of her cheek. "What's it to you?" She looked up and her anger surged to the surface. "I mean, really, Luke, as if you care."

He blinked and visibly pulled back. "That's the thing—I *do* care... Although I'm starting to wonder why."

She rolled her eyes—it was a preposterous statement considering the fact that he'd compared her to an icicle that wouldn't thaw. "Save it, Chancellor. Go." She made a shooing motion. "Go be the life of the party, the company hero, the lady-killer."

She'd spoken with more venom than she'd intended, but once the words were out, she couldn't take them back.

Luke pursed his mouth, then nodded in acquiescence and turned toward the door. She looked back to her brief-case and slammed the lid shut.

"Carol?"

She looked up, surprised he was still standing there. "Yes?"

"I hope you change your mind about the party."

She walked over to her coatrack and shrugged into her coat. "I won't."

"Then maybe fate will intervene." He grinned and strode out.

Carol squinted, then shook her head. Luke could not accept the fact that he couldn't charm her into doing what he wanted.

When she walked out into the lobby area of her depart-ment, only Tracy was still there, sitting at her desk obe-diently, although she glanced longingly at the clock.

"I'm leaving," Carol announced.

"You're not staying for the party?"

"No."

"Is it because your head is hurting?"

At the compassionate tone in her assistant's voice, Carol balked. "Uh…no. But thank you." Then she handed Tracy the perennial memo, riddled with bright red circles. "Six mistakes on this version."

Tracy winced. "Really?"

"Really." Carol gave her a pointed look. "Try again, please."

Tracy bit her lip and nodded. "Be careful driving home. I hear a winter storm is blowing in."

Carol laughed. "I grew up in Atlanta, and none of those so-called 'winter storms' ever materialize. Enjoy the party."

She headed toward the elevator. The offices in every department were empty, with everyone already in the basement for the party. As she rode down to the lobby, Luke's words came floating back to her.

That's the thing—I do care…

Carol shook her head. The man was a master. She knew he was a player, yet she still almost believed him.

The doors opened into the empty lobby. She walked out and headed toward the front entrance. A rumble overhead made her stop. She realized it was a fierce wind shaking the glass of the two-story entryway. The sky looked almost purple—the low-hanging red clouds were brimming with some type of serious precipitation. Rain? Hail?

Neither.

She watched in disbelief as enormous snowflakes exploded from the sky, only to be swept sideways in an almost tornadic wind. Within seconds, the outdoors was enveloped in a thick, impermeable blur of white.

A blizzard in Atlanta…impossible.

And suddenly more of Luke's words came back to her, after she'd claimed she wouldn't change her mind about attending the Valentine's party.

Maybe fate will intervene.

chapter eight

CAROL stood mesmerized by the alien sight of snow falling in Atlanta until she realized that there would be no going home to snuggle up with a good, erotic book. She was stranded at the Mystic Touch office. And she had two choices: return to her office and massage more paper-work…or go to the Valentine's Day company party.

The low throbbing in her temples from the bump on the head she'd received this morning made the thought of scrutinizing spreadsheets unbearable.

The party seemed to be the lesser of the two evils.

So she trudged back to the elevator and rode down to the basement, unwinding her scarf from her neck. She could hear the noise of the party even before the elevator stopped. When the doors opened, the full force of music, laughter and voices blasted her. Her stomach churned—she didn't want to be here, and she couldn't think of a single person who wanted her here.

She stepped off the elevator, feeling self-conscious in her winter coat, thinking she should've returned to her office and dropped her things there. Instead she stood there holding her briefcase awkwardly while everyone else held a glass of pink punch.

A few heads turned in her direction, but after a quick downturn of their mouths, they turned away. The blatant snub sliced through her, but she kept scanning, looking for a friendly face.

She landed on Luke. He caught sight of her and his expression turned from surprise to something else that accompanied a smile. He said something to the person he was talking to, then turned and walked in her direction.

It seemed silly now that she'd dug in her heels about not attending the party. Heat rose in her cheeks as he stopped in front of her.

"Snow," he said with a grin. "What brings you back?"

"Snow," she said matter-of-factly.

"Huh?"

"It's snowing." She pointed to the ceiling. Since the basement had no windows, everyone else was oblivious to the outside conditions. "A blizzard, actually."

"So you're stranded." Then he made a rueful noise. "I'm sorry—you probably don't feel like being here. Tracy told me about the bump on the head. You should've told me that's why you didn't want to come to the party. I would've left you alone."

His concern left her flustered and her tongue suddenly didn't work.

"Let me take your coat," he offered, reaching to help

her out of the heavy garment. "In fact, let's put your coat and briefcase in the storage room."

She followed him slowly, wondering if people were watching them as they disappeared down the hallway. Sadly, though, everyone seemed keen on ignoring her. He unlocked the door of the storage room, then he grabbed her hand and pulled her inside, allowing the door to close behind them.

Her pulse rocketed. "Luke, what are you doing?"

He flipped on the lights, then smiled at her. "Sorry. Overkill, I know, just to give you a Valentine's gift." He hung her coat on a hook, then reached high on a shelf and removed a heart-shaped box of chocolates. When he turned back to her, he looked sheepish.

"It's silly, I guess. I saw this and it reminded me of you."

Carol felt flush with pleasure—until she looked at the box. A large snowflake adorned the top. That was her—cold as ice…like an icicle. The card he'd slipped in her tote bag taunted her. "Very funny," she said, handing it back to him.

His eyebrows drew together. "What do you mean?"

Hurt barbed through her chest. "I get the whole frosty, cold-as-ice thing. I know what people say about me, that they call me Ice Princess." She turned and reached for her coat. "This was a bad idea—I think I'll wait out the storm in my office."

His fingers encircled her wrist. "Hey."

She turned back and looked up at him.

"That's not how I think of you," he said, his brown eyes pensive. "I bought the candy because of the snowflake— get it…? Snow…flake?"

Carol wet her lips. She wanted to believe him…but why would Luke Chancellor buy her candy?

"Sorry if I overreacted," she said. "I'm sure you bought candy for other coworkers."

"No," he said, then pulled her closer. "Just you, Snow."

His mouth lowered toward hers. She expected him to pull back at the last second, but instead, suddenly, his warm lips were on hers. It was jolting, the sense of connection, like she was being plugged into a socket. His tongue swept against hers, sending shock waves of desire coursing through her limbs. It had been so long since she'd felt these sensations that everything seemed new…fresh. Her mind and body reeled from the raw power in Luke's probing kiss.

He lifted his head and looked into her eyes. "I've been wanting to do that for so long."

Her chest rose and fell as she struggled to fill her lungs. She couldn't form words. How could she tell him that he'd just tapped into a deep, still well…unleashed a cataclysmic reaction in her body…awakened a sleeping giant? He couldn't know the depths to which she'd buried her sexual soul…and how amazing it felt to have it resurrected.

He wiped his hand over his mouth. "If you're going to slap me, get it over with."

She lifted her hand, then curled it around his neck and pulled his lips down on hers, hard.

Luke moaned into her mouth and the vibration echoed through her body. He pulled her against him and their hands were frenzied, roaming over each other's bodies. He smoothed his palms down her back and pulled her sex against the hardened ridge of his erection. The physical proof of what they were about to do made Carol dizzy with lust. He picked her up by the waist and set her on a table, then slid up her skirt so she could spread her knees.

"Wait," she said, then nodded to the door. "What if someone knows how to get in?"

He left her long enough to wedge a straight-back chair under the doorknob, then returned to her with a vengeance, wedging himself between her thighs.

Carol's pumps fell off with succeeding thuds. She leaned back on her hands to brace herself, then squeezed his hips with her knees. Her breasts, her sex, her entire body throbbed with anticipation.

"Oh, no," he murmured suddenly, then put a hand to his head. "I don't have a condom. I'm sorry."

She winced, but pulled his mouth back to hers. "Then we'll have to be creative." She was taking a huge risk—she wasn't sexually experienced and James hadn't been particularly adventurous. She'd have to draw on what she'd learned between the pages of the erotic novels she'd read and hope that her enthusiasm would make up for her lack of expertise.

Luke's response was fierce, his tongue stabbing into her mouth, a silent promise to be creative for as long as necessary. He kissed his way down her neck, then plucked at the buttons on her white blouse until it lay open, exposing her lacy bra. Sighing into her skin, he laved the flesh above her bra, until she couldn't bear the suspense anymore and unhooked the front closure.

One breast fell into his hand, the other into his mouth. He licked her nipple, then pulled it into his mouth, leaving her shuddering with pleasure. But they were both too frantic to linger. Luke pushed her skirt to her waist, then rolled down her panty hose and underwear to open her sex to him. When he knelt and flicked his tongue against her folds, Carol dug her fingers into his shoulders. She couldn't think…couldn't speak…could only feel the amazing wonderfulness of having his mouth against her most intimate places. It was a first for her and the sensations pummeling her were almost overwhelming, leaving her languid and elastic.

He suckled the tiny sensitive nub that housed her orgasms, immediately coaxing one out of its hiding place to roam languorously as it made its way to the surface. Carol urged him on with moans and squeezes, riding on pure physical pleasure until the sensations in her womb began to swing with centrifugal force. The circles of liquid bliss grew tighter and heavier, swirling with growing intensity until her body bucked with a deep, intense climax.

Carol bit down on her own hand to muffle the sounds of her release, although the throbbing bass of the party music all but guaranteed that no one could hear them. Luke nuzzled her sex until she quieted, but she was eager to pleasure him, too. She pulled him to his feet, then loosened his belt and unzipped his pants to free his imposing erection.

When she clasped the rigid length of him, he gasped, his eyes hooded with desire. Carol slid from the table to kneel in front of him. She'd never done this before, but from what she'd read, it was hard to go wrong while performing oral sex on a man. She gingerly took his erection into her mouth, surprised by his silky hardness. He groaned with pleasure, his thighs tensing. She could sense his restraint as he allowed her to set the pace, using her tongue and taking cues from his sounds of gratification. She loved pleasing him orally, experimenting, making him feel the way he'd made her feel.

And she reasoned she must be doing it right when he whispered that he was about to come. He withdrew from her mouth and pulled her to her feet, holding her body against his while he stroked his erection. He kissed her neck and shoulder, then tensed and shuddered. She felt his contractions, then the wetness of his release on her stomach. He held her as his breathing slowed, then sighed into her ear.

"Wow," he murmured. "What just happened?"

Carol stiffened. Maybe it was the sound of his voice breaking the spell. Maybe it was the sensation of his seed cooling on her stomach. Maybe it was the realization that they were in a dusty storage room, with all their coworkers mere steps away, probably wondering what they were doing. The weight of remorse staggered her. What had she done?

Luke pulled back, then removed a handkerchief from his back pocket to mop up her stomach. "Go to dinner with me tomorrow night," he urged.

Her mind raced as she straightened her clothes. "Tomorrow…you mean Valentine's Day?"

"Yes."

She turned her back to retrieve her underwear and panty hose, stepping into them as quickly and modestly as she could manage in such a confining space. So Luke didn't mind dumping the "special lady" he already had plans with. So like a man. But she knew what it felt like to be on the other end of that equation…and since Luke had left a string of broken hearts in his wake, she'd be just another conquest. Good grief, for all she knew, this storage room might be his own private place to fool around.

Panic licked at her neck until she realized the situation played perfectly into her original plan to seduce him, then dump him. She turned back and forced a note of casual nonchalance into her voice. "I don't think so. Look, this was just a one-time thing to satisfy curiosity. I'm not curious anymore." She adopted a blasé expression.

Luke pursed his mouth. "Uh…okay."

She slipped her feet into her pumps. "Why don't you go out first so it'll seem less suspicious if anyone is watching."

"Okay." He hesitated, then rechecked his clothing and made his way to the door.

She turned away and closed her eyes. That was close. Having sex with Luke Chancellor might not have been the smartest move, but thinking it meant something would be the biggest mistake.

"Carol."

She schooled her expression, then turned around. "Yes?"

"Whatever he did to you, I'm sorry."

She swallowed. "Who are you talking about?"

Luke shrugged. "I don't know. Whoever it was who hurt you so badly."

Her jaw loosened, but he didn't wait for a reply. He slipped out the door and it closed behind him.

She fisted her hands, shaken by his words…and angered. If she wasn't interested in being swept into Luke's emotional riptide, then she must be damaged. His reaction only reinforced her decision not to have dinner with him, not to foster false hope that a sexual encounter, no matter how explosive, would lead to something more serious.

Carol patted her hair, then realized with some small measure of relief that her headache was gone. She lifted her hand to her forehead to find that the goose egg she'd been nursing was also gone. It was something to be grateful for on an otherwise lousy day.

From the floor, a glint of metal caught her eye—her silver-and-emerald earring. In all the commotion this morning, she'd neglected to take it with her. She knelt to retrieve it from under the shelf, but lost her balance and bumped the shelving unit accidentally. Above her, she heard a scraping noise, and when she looked up, something large was bearing down on her.

Despite the sense of déjà vu, Carol didn't have time to put up her hand. Pain exploded in her head, then everything went black again.

chapter nine

SOMEONE was shaking Carol by the shoulder.

"Carol…Carol?"

The voice was familiar…but out of context. Carol opened her eyes to blink Gabrielle Pope's face into view, then winced at the pain that stabbed her temple.

"Oh, good—you're not dead," Gabrielle said.

"What are you doing here?" Carol asked.

"Just popping in to give you a hand."

"A hand with what?"

"Can you sit up?"

"I think so." Carol pushed up to a sitting position, then lifted her hand to her head, where a goose egg had formed—again. "Ow."

"That looks painful," Gabrielle said. "Maybe I should call an ambulance."

"No," Carol said, gingerly pushing to her feet. "It's just a bump on the head. I'll be fine. I need to get back to work."

"Not yet," Gabrielle said. "First I have to show you something."

"What?"

Gabrielle pointed to a boxy computer screen sitting on the floor nearby. "A memory of Valentine's Day Past."

Confused, Carol watched as the monitor blinked on, then zoomed in on a woman sitting at a restaurant table alone, as if she were waiting for someone.

Carol gasped. "That's me."

Gabrielle nodded.

It suddenly dawned on Carol what she was watching. "I don't want to see this," she said, turning her head away.

"But you must," Gabrielle said gently.

Carol reluctantly pivoted back to the monitor, dread billowing in her stomach. The woman sitting at the restaurant table looked younger...hopeful...in love. Gabrielle leaned forward and turned a volume knob.

A handsome blond man walked up to the table and leaned down to place a kiss on the young woman's temple. "Hi, sweetheart."

Carol's heart squeezed. James...it had been so long since she'd heard his voice, she'd almost forgotten what it sounded like. Music to her heart.

"Happy Valentine's Day," he said, then slid a small gift box across the table.

Carol remembered how her pulse had skipped higher at the size of the box, thinking—hoping—it contained a ring. She had opened the box with shaking fingers, and although her heart had dropped in disappointment at the sight of silver-and-emerald earrings, she had pulled a bright smile out of thin air and gushed over the thoughtful present.

"Emeralds," he said, "are the sign of a successful love."

She put the earrings on and leaned forward to thank him with a kiss. After they ordered drinks, she slipped her gift for him out of her purse. "Happy Valentine's Day," she said, pushing it toward him.

Carol watched her younger self, her stomach taut with nerves.

James opened the box and seemed surprised. "A ring? I love it, darling." He removed the chunky horseshoe ring with small diamonds from its case and slipped it on his finger.

Carol was pleased that it looked classy, yet masculine on his hand.

"Thank you," he said, then leaned forward for another kiss.

She shifted nervously on her chair. "Actually, it's not just a ring."

James's eyebrows shot up. "Oh?"

"Actually…I was hoping…that is, I was wondering…"

"Yes? What is it, dear?"

"James…will you marry me?"

Watching the scene unfold, Carol emitted a mournful sound. She knew too well what was coming next.

James dropped his gaze, then took his time lifting his glass for a drink. Finally, he used his napkin to wipe the perspiration from his forehead. She noticed his pallor had gone gray.

"James?" Carol prompted. "Is something wrong?"

He reached across the table to clasp her hand. "No. I mean…yes. I've wanted to tell you something, but the timing never seemed right."

Carol remembered that at this point, her first worry had been that James was seriously ill. How naive she'd been.

"Whatever it is," she said, "tell me now."

"This isn't easy to say, but…I've been spending time with another woman, and…she's going to have my baby."

Carol watched her younger self, the myriad of emotions that played over her face—disbelief, shock, hurt, anger. She jerked her hand from his as if she'd been burned. "You're lying."

James drained his drink, then set the glass on the table with a thud. "I'm sorry, but I want to do the right thing. She and I are getting married. See you around." Then he got up and walked out of the frame.

Carol had always wondered what she must've looked like that night to other diners…sitting there dressed up, wearing the earrings James had just given her, her face a mask of incredulity. Now she knew. She looked as if she'd been punched in the stomach, or as if she expected James to come back and announce that he'd been playing a practical joke. In fact, she'd sat there and ordered and eaten a meal by herself, just in case James did return.

He hadn't, of course.

Carol's cheeks felt wet, and she realized she was crying. "Other than losing my parents, that was the worst night of my life."

"I know," Gabrielle said quietly. "And I'm sorry to make you relive it. But you need to see that you are not to blame for what James did. His irresponsible and hurtful behavior is his to own. You did nothing wrong."

"I trusted him," Carol said. "That was wrong."

"Trusting James was misguided," Gabrielle corrected, "but it wasn't wrong. It's never wrong to love. It's James's loss that he took advantage of your love instead of returning it."

But Carol's heart still squeezed at the injustice. James had led her on for years, gave her reason to believe they had a future together, all while having an affair and getting another woman pregnant. In hindsight, she wondered if he would've ever told her about the other woman if she hadn't proposed and forced the issue.

When the pain started to suffocate her, Carol turned away from the monitor. "I have to go."

"Very well," Gabrielle said. "But don't forget, it's never wrong to love."

Carol walked to the door of the supply room and let herself out in the hall, shaking her head at what she'd just experienced.

Dreamed, more like it. Walking back to the elevator, she reached up to touch the tender skin on her forehead. Maybe she'd taken a harder hit than she realized.

That would explain her hallucination.

As she approached the elevator, she realized preparations were already underway for the afternoon party.

Carol squinted. But the party had already happened... hadn't it?

Red decorations of cupids and hearts abounded. Blowups of some of the company's Valentine's Day cards leaned against the wall, including the "take no prisoners" card she'd seen on her assistant's desk. Cupid looked even more menacing at life-size.

Thankfully, she didn't see Luke among the volunteers…. She wasn't ready to face him after their encounter during the party.

She stopped and looked back to the party preparations, again disoriented. The workers threw her a look of distaste before turning back to their tasks. Well, even if other events were confused in her head, one thing remained true—everyone hated her for voting against giving the employee bonuses.

On the elevator ride up, Carol did some mental calculations to try to clear her head. She counted backward from one hundred by multiples of nine…she recited the presidents of the United States.

Everything seemed to be in working order.

When the doors opened and she walked into her department, Tracy looked up from her desk where she was playing with her new computer. In fact, everyone was still preoccupied with the new equipment she and Luke had scavenged from the storage room.

"I understand Luke Chancellor was up all night installing these machines for us," Tracy said, her eyes dreamy. "When you see him, give him a big kiss for me, will you?"

Carol blinked. "Excuse me?"

"In the directors' meeting," Tracy said, then glanced at the clock. "You're going to be late."

Carol massaged her temples. "Um, Tracy…what day is it?"

Tracy narrowed her eyes. "Friday, February thirteenth. Are you okay, Ms. Snow?"

"Yes," Carol lied. In truth, a low, throbbing headache had settled into her crown. She stopped by the ladies' room to arrange her hair over the reddened bump on her forehead, then proceeded to the room where the directors' meeting was held. Before entering, she took a deep breath, then pushed open the door.

Her fellow directors looked up and she could tell not all of them were relieved to see her. Luke Chancellor sat at the head of the table. It was the first time she'd seen him clothed since she'd seen him naked. She hoped it wouldn't be awkward.

He smiled up at her. "We were just getting ready to send out a search party for you, Carol."

She settled into an empty chair. "Sorry I'm late."

"We heard a Good Samaritan delivered new computer equipment to your department this morning," Janet, the art director, said with a smile.

All gazes slid toward Luke. He held up his hands. "It was Carol's idea—I just…facilitated."

She set her jaw—how did he do that? Manage to sound humble and still take credit?

And why wasn't he acknowledging—in private glances, at least—that they'd recently shared some very good oral sex?

"We were about to take another vote on the issue of bonuses," Luke said, all business. "I think it's pretty clear that anyone dissenting is following your lead, Carol, so I guess we can cut to the chase by asking if you've changed your mind on paying out a one-time bonus?"

The weight of a roomful of stares shifted to her. Carol glanced from side to side to see if anyone else remembered having this exact meeting at…sometime.

Luke looked hopeful, and Carol knew he was thinking of her previous comment that she might reconsider her position. But that was before he'd turned all her employees against her. Before he'd given her a blinding orgasm in the storage room and made her feel again. This might be her one and only chance…again…to put Luke Chancellor in his place.

"No, I haven't changed my mind," she said carefully, feeling strangely like a doppelganger.

Disappointment colored Luke's face. His mouth flattened, then he shrugged. "I guess that's that."

Carol clapped her hands. "Good. If that's all, I need to get back to work. The party means I have only four hours to get done what I'd normally do in eight." Then she stopped. "There is a party today, right?"

"Right," Luke said, his mouth tight. "And yes, that's all."

Carol's gaze roved over him, recalling the size of his erection, and the sounds the man made when he climaxed.

Or had she dreamed the encounter as well?

"Something else on your mind?" Luke asked.

That little swirly trick you do with your tongue. "Uh…no." She pushed to her feet and left. On the way back to her office, Carol massaged her temples, trying to alleviate the headache that had yet to ease. When she reached her department, she walked the gauntlet of angry stares from her employees and closed her office door. There she downed some aspirin and waited for the feeling of vindication to descend. She'd proved to Luke that her opinion still meant something around here…that there was at least one woman he couldn't charm into submission.

She squinted. But if she'd given him a blowjob, didn't that mean she'd already submitted?

Regardless, sitting here in the wake of her power, the victory of winning the vote felt strangely hollow. She gave herself a mental shake, reasoning that she could hardly feel good about anything while nursing a headache. She would savor the success later, in private.

When she was alone. Completely, absolutely, utterly alone.

She stopped, certain she'd had that thought before—déjà vu?

Carol pushed a button on the intercom and told Tracy she wasn't to be disturbed, then spent the morning plowing through a mountain of paperwork that seemed amazingly simple, as if she'd done it before and already knew all the answers.

But since her headache wasn't letting up, she decided she'd skip the Valentine's Day party and just go home, maybe tuck in with a good book, something she could suggest as a selection for the Red Tote Book Club.

While she was thinking about it, she pulled out her phone and sent Gabrielle an update via text message.

Seduction achieved. Details later.

A couple of minutes later, Gabrielle replied.

Surrender to love, Carol.

Carol frowned at the message. Love? Who said anything about love?

And *surrender?* Never.

A knock sounded at her door, then it creaked open.

"Tracy, I asked not to be disturbed," Carol said without looking up.

"Don't get mad at her," Luke said.

Carol lifted her head to see the man of the hour standing in the threshold. He gestured behind him. "Tracy said you didn't want to be disturbed, but I told her I'd take full responsibility for defying your orders."

He looked just as handsome in brown slacks and pale blue dress shirt, minus a tie, as he had…before. Carol's pulse quickened, but she reminded herself that he wasn't to be trusted. Along with her memory, apparently.

"What do you want, Chancellor?"

"I thought it would be nice if we walked into the party together, a show of solidarity."

She stood and began packing her briefcase. "I'm not going to the party."

He gave a little laugh. "Why not?"

"Because I'd rather go home, that's why."

"Go home to what?" he asked. "A book?"

At his mocking tone, Carol bit down on the inside of her cheek. "What's it to you?" She looked up and her anger surged to the surface. "I mean, really, Luke, as if you care."

He blinked and visibly pulled back. "That's the thing— I *do* care… Although I'm starting to wonder why."

She rolled her eyes—it was a preposterous statement considering the fact that he'd compared her to an icicle that wouldn't thaw. "Save it, Chancellor. Go." She made a shooing motion. "Go be the life of the party, the sales hero, the company playboy."

Once again she'd spoken with more venom than she'd intended, but after the words were out…well, she couldn't take them back…she didn't think…

"Exactly what did I do to make you so angry?" Luke asked.

"Well, for starters, you told everyone I was the reason no one is getting a bonus."

"I didn't tell everyone," he said. "In fact, I didn't tell *any*one. There were eight other directors in that meeting. But, when it comes down to it, *aren't* you the reason no one is getting a bonus?"

Carol slammed her briefcase shut. "I voted no because I think there are better things to do with the company money."

"I know—you said your department needed new equipment, and I helped you get it. And you still voted no."

"That's the other thing. All my employees think you're a hero."

"And that's a bad thing?"

"At my expense."

He gave a little laugh. "Why didn't you tell them that you helped me? You were the one with the wish list, the one who knew what kind of equipment everyone had and what they needed."

She shrugged. "I…I guess I didn't want to feel like I had to toot my own horn."

"I give up." He shook his head and started toward the door. With his hand on the doorknob, he looked back. "I hope you change your mind about coming to the party."

She walked over to her coatrack and shrugged into her coat. "I won't."

"Then maybe fate will intervene." He smiled, then strode out.

Then Carol remembered—the blizzard! Maybe she could get out in front of it. She gathered her things and dashed out of her office. Only Tracy remained in the department, sitting at her desk obediently, although she glanced longingly at the clock.

"I'm leaving," Carol announced as she dashed by. "Here's the memo you need to redo." She tossed the piece of paper in the direction of her assistant's desk.

"You're not staying for the party?"

"No!"

"Be careful driving home," Tracy called behind her. "I hear a winter storm is blowing in!"

Carol sprinted through empty departments toward the elevator. Everyone was already in the basement for the party. As she waited for the elevator, something in particular that Luke said came floating back to her.

That's the thing—I do care…

Carol shook her head. She didn't want him to care. She didn't need the complication of a man in her life who cared. Because even if he cared now, at this precise moment, it would be short-lived.

Frustrated that the elevator was taking so long, she opted for the stairs and took them as quickly as her high-heeled pumps would allow. She burst out of the stairwell into an empty lobby. When she turned toward the front entrance, a rumble sounded overhead. She knew that sound. Sure enough, a bulging purple sky burst open, sending enormous snowflakes to the ground, where they were swept up into a cyclonic wind. Within seconds, the outdoors was enveloped in a thick, impermeable blur of white.

Another blizzard in Atlanta…impossible.

Fate had once again intervened.

chapter ten

CAROL stood mesmerized by the alien sight of snow falling in Atlanta until she realized that there would be no going home to snuggle up with a good, erotic book. She was stranded at the Mystic Touch office. And she had two choices: return to her office and massage more paperwork…or go to the Valentine's Day company party.

The low throbbing in her temples from the bump on the head she'd received this morning made the thought of scrutinizing spreadsheets unbearable.

The party seemed to be the lesser of the two evils…if she could resist Luke.

She trudged back to the elevator and rode down to the basement, unwinding her scarf from her neck. She could hear the noise of the party even before the elevator stopped. When the doors opened, the full force of music, laughter and voices blasted her. Her stomach churned—

she didn't want to be here, and she couldn't think of a single person who wanted her here.

She stepped off the elevator, feeling self-conscious in her winter coat, thinking once again that she should've returned to her office and dropped her things there. Instead she stood there holding her briefcase awkwardly while everyone else held a glass of pink punch.

A few heads turned in her direction, but after a quick downturn of their mouths, they turned away. The blatant snub cut deep, but she kept scanning, looking for a friendly face.

She landed on Luke. He caught sight of her and his expression turned from surprise to something else that accompanied a smile. He said something to the person he was talking to, then turned and walked in her direction.

But he was not looking at her like a man who had intimate knowledge of her choice in underwear.

"Snow," he said with a grin. "What brings you back?"

"Snow," she said matter-of-factly.

"Huh?"

"It's snowing." She pointed to the ceiling. Since the basement had no windows, everyone else was oblivious to the outside conditions. "A blizzard, actually."

"So you're stranded. Let me take your coat," he offered, reaching to help her out of the heavy garment. "In fact, let's put your coat and briefcase in the storage room."

"Um…that's okay…I'll just hang on to them."

"Are you sure? Come with me anyway—I have something to give you."

The box of candy. And she really didn't want their coworkers to see him giving her candy. Carol followed him slowly down the hall, dismayed that her body was already loosening for him, warming, softening. Desire struck her low and hard.

He unlocked the door of the storage room, held it open for her, then allowed it to close behind them.

"You've piqued my curiosity," she offered.

"It's not much," he said, reaching high on a shelf to remove a heart-shaped box of chocolates.

She realized if she didn't act hurt over the whole snow-flake/cold as ice/Ice Princess connotation of the blue snowflake box, then he wouldn't feel compelled to tell her that wasn't how he thought of her, which would lead to her saying he probably bought candy for other coworkers, which would lead to him saying no, only for her, which would lead to the kiss that had been her undoing.

When he turned back to her, he looked sheepish. "It's silly, I guess. I saw this and it reminded me of you."

She opened her mouth to say how much she liked the blue snowflake box, but stopped when she saw instead a pink satin box that read "Kiss Me."

"Kiss me?" she squeaked.

He scratched his head. "To be honest, I'm not quite sure why I bought that one. It just seemed…right."

When his mouth lowered toward hers, she knew she should stop him. Instead, she met his warm lips, rejoicing in the familiar feel of his kiss…the connection…the shock waves. It had been so long since she'd felt these sensations…an entire twenty-four hours ago, at this same point in time. Her mind and body reeled from the raw power in Luke's probing kiss.

He lifted his head and looked into her eyes. "Why do I have the feeling we've done this before?"

"Kismet," she whispered, then curled her hand around his neck and pulled his lips down on hers, hard.

Luke moaned into her mouth and the vibration echoed through her body. He pulled her against him and their hands became frenzied, roaming over each other's bodies. He smoothed his palms down her back, over her buttocks, and pulled her sex against the hardened ridge of his erection. The physical proof of what they were about to do…again…made Carol dizzy with lust.

He stopped, his gaze bouncing around the room, looking for a suitable surface.

Carol pointed to the nearby table. "Take me there."

He picked her up by the waist and set her on the table, then slid up her skirt so she could spread her knees.

"Wait," she said, then nodded to the door. "Can you wedge a chair under the doorknob?"

He did, then came back to stand between her thighs.

Carol's pumps fell off with succeeding thuds. She leaned back on her hands to brace herself, then squeezed his hips with her knees. Her breasts, her sex, her entire body throbbed with anticipation, especially since now she knew what to expect.

"Oh, no," he murmured suddenly, then put a hand to his head. "I don't have a condom. I'm sorry."

Her shoulders fell—damn, she'd forgotten that part.

She pulled his mouth back to hers. "Then we'll have to

be creative." There were still lots of things from the pages of the erotic novels she'd read for the Red Tote Book Club that she wanted to try.

Luke's response was fierce, his tongue stabbing into her mouth, a silent promise to be creative for as long as necessary. He kissed his way down her neck, then plucked at the buttons on her white blouse until it lay open, exposing her lacy bra. Impatient to have his mouth on her, she unhooked the front closure.

One breast fell into his hand, the other into his mouth. He licked her nipple, then pulled it into his mouth, leaving her shuddering with pleasure. But they were both too frantic to linger. Luke pushed her skirt to her waist, then rolled down her panty hose and underwear to expose her sex to him. When he knelt and flicked his tongue against her folds, Carol's toes curled. She couldn't think…couldn't speak…could only feel the amazing wonderfulness of having his mouth against her most intimate places. It felt like the first time all over again. The sensations pummeling her were almost overwhelming, leaving her languid and elastic.

He suckled the tiny sensitive nub that housed her orgasms, instantly coaxing one from its hiding place. But instead of roaming languorously as it made its way to the surface, this one zoomed for air. The speed and intensity took her and Luke both by surprise. Carol bucked against his mouth to ride out a deep, powerful climax.

Carol bit down on her own hand to muffle the sounds of her release, although the throbbing bass of the party music all but guaranteed that no one could hear them. Luke nuzzled her sex until she quieted, but she was eager to pleasure him, too. She pulled him to his feet, then loosened his belt and unzipped his pants to free his imposing erection.

When she clasped the rigid length of him, he gasped, his eyes hooded with desire. Carol slid from the table to kneel in front of him, then took his erection into her mouth as far as she could, reveling in his silky hardness. He groaned with pleasure, his thighs tensing. This time pleasing him orally felt more natural, less awkward. She experimented with nuances in pressure and texture to see how he responded.

And this time when he whispered he was about to come, instead of allowing him to withdraw, she clasped his hips and pulled him deeper into her mouth. When he realized her intention, she sensed his added excitement. Within a few seconds, he tensed and shuddered. She felt his contractions, then the spurt of his release in her mouth.

At length his breathing slowed. He pulled her to her feet and kissed her soundly. "Wow," he murmured. "What just happened?"

Carol steeled herself, but was dismayed when a familiar sense of remorse started to close in. Which only made sense, really. She'd known she and Luke were going to have an empty encounter, and yet she'd gone along with it... again...as if something was going to be different this time around.

But it wasn't.

Luke pulled back. "Go to dinner with me tomorrow night."

Carol straightened her clothes. "Tomorrow…you mean Valentine's Day?"

"Yes."

She turned her back to retrieve her underwear and panty hose, stepping into them as quickly and modestly as she could manage in such a confining space. Once again, Luke didn't mind dumping the "special lady" he already had plans with. Carol knew she should be flattered, but instead all she could think about was the woman who'd been looking forward to a romantic evening relegated to sitting at home. Playing the home version of *Wheel of Fortune* while she watched the show on TV.

Not that she'd ever done that herself.

And this time next year, Luke would have moved on to yet another woman, and she'd be the one dodging him on the elevator or perhaps looking for a new job after a bad breakup.

She turned back and forced a note of casual nonchalance into her voice. "I don't think so. Look, this was just a two-time thing to satisfy…curiosity."

He squinted. "Two times?"

"I mean one-time," she said quickly. "A *one*-time thing to satisfy curiosity. And I'm not curious anymore." She adopted a blasé expression.

Luke pursed his mouth. "Uh…okay."

She slipped her feet into her pumps. "Why don't you leave first so it'll seem less suspicious if anyone is watching."

"Okay." He hesitated, then rechecked his clothing and made his way to the door.

She turned away and closed her eyes. That was close. Having sex with Luke Chancellor…twice…might not have been the smartest move, but thinking it meant something different this time around would be the biggest mistake ever.

"Carol."

She schooled her expression, then turned around. "Yes?"

Luke's expression was pensive. "I have a feeling there's something here between us, but for some reason, you're holding back. But I also have a feeling that this is totally out of my hands."

He didn't wait for a reply. He slipped out the door and it closed behind him.

She fisted her hands, frustrated by a situation that was growing increasingly complicated. How was she supposed to make any decisions when the present double-backed onto the past?

Carol checked her clothing and smoothed her hair, realizing with some small measure of relief that her headache was gone. She lifted her hand to her forehead to find that the goose egg she'd been nursing was also gone. It was something to be grateful for on an otherwise lousy day.

From the floor, a glint of metal caught her eye—her silver-and-emerald earring. She still hadn't managed to get out of here with it. She bent over from the waist to retrieve the earring from under the shelf, keeping her feet firmly planted so as not to lose her balance. She grasped the earring, but when she straightened, she bumped the shelving unit accidentally. Above her, she heard a scraping noise, and when she looked up, something large was bearing down on her.

Despite the overwhelming sense of déjà vu, Carol didn't have time to put up her hand. Pain exploded in her head, then everything went black *again*.

chapter eleven

SOMEONE was shaking Carol by the shoulder.

"Carol…wake up. Carol?"

Gabrielle Pope was back. Carol opened her eyes, and winced at the obligatory pain in her head. "You again?"

Gabrielle nodded. "I'm afraid so."

"Why are you involved in my hallucinations?"

"You have to ask yourself that."

Carol pressed her lips together. She'd have to give it some thought…when she was actually conscious.

"Can you sit up?"

"Unless this bump on the head was worse than the last one." Carol pushed up to a sitting position, then lifted her hand to her head, where a goose egg had formed. "At least it's on the other side."

"Hmm," Gabrielle said. "The fact that the bump is on the other side might mean something."

"What?"

"I have no idea…but you probably do."

"Don't confuse the unconscious girl," Carol said. "Why is this even happening to me?"

"Good question. Some people who suffer an emotional setback bury the memory instead of dealing with it. Once it begins to affect a person's present behavior and relationships, they might choose to see a therapist."

"Or join a book club," Carol offered.

"Yes. But the mind can only deal with so much stress before it has to find a release valve."

"Ergo these little blackouts?"

"Maybe," Gabrielle agreed. "If a person is afraid to process a memory, recalling that memory in a dream or under hypnosis is much safer."

"Like my memory of how James dumped me."

"Right. Similarly, if a person is afraid to try something new, visualization, dreams and hallucinations are a safe way to explore new experiences."

"Like a possible relationship with Luke?"

"Yes."

"What do you have for me today?" Carol asked, gesturing to the monitor lying in the floor on its side.

"A look at Valentine's Day Present—tomorrow, in fact."

Carol watched as the monitor blinked on, then zoomed in on a man stopping at a florist to get a dozen roses.

"That's Luke," Carol said.

On screen, he was knuckle-biting handsome in a dark suit and a light-colored shirt, with a tie.

"Considering how much he hates ties, he must be excited about his date," she offered.

"Wait and see," Gabrielle said.

Carol's heart thudded in her chest…would she be Luke's date? If not, why would Gabrielle be showing her the vision?

Luke walked out with a dozen white roses.

"Nice," Carol agreed. White would've been her choice, too.

The next scene showed Luke driving up to a restaurant and handing his keys to a valet.

"He's at Richardson's," Carol said happily. "That's my favorite restaurant."

Luke got out of the car and walked around to the passenger side to open the door. A woman's legs appeared, then she alighted with Luke's assistance and smiled up at him.

"That's not me," Carol said of the gorgeous, busty blonde.

"I noticed," Gabrielle said drily.

"I don't recognize her, so she's not from the office."

"Let's see," Gabrielle said, turning up the volume.

Luke and the blonde chatted as they entered the restaurant.

"I guess it was my lucky day when I decided to go with my friend to the Steeplechase," the woman gushed. "I never dreamed I'd meet someone like you, Luke."

She leaned in for a kiss and Luke obliged. He seemed attentive, but Carol noticed he had the same look in his eyes as when he was bored in a staff meeting. Still, the blonde looked as if she would be able to keep him entertained after they got past the niceties. A stab of jealousy caught Carol off guard…and she didn't like the feeling. One of the reasons she hadn't dated after James was because she didn't want to be a suspicious, jealous shrew, to make the new man in her life pay for the sins of her ex.

The scene faded and Carol thought they were finished, but then another scene opened onto the interior of a house, and zoomed in on a woman sitting tucked into a corner of a couch, wearing flannel pajamas.

"That's me," Carol said, making a face. Did those pajamas really look so old and ratty?

"Yes," Gabrielle said to her unasked question.

Carol frowned, then looked back to the monitor. She was holding a big bowl of popcorn in her lap. On the table next to her sat a two-liter bottle of diet soda with a giant straw. And next to the soda was the home edition of *Wheel of Fortune*. When the frame pulled back, the show *Wheel of Fortune* was also playing on the television.

Carol's cheeks burned. "It's an educational show," she murmured. Then she looked up. "I get the point."

"I hope so," Gabrielle said. "Because it's time for you to go."

"I know," Carol said, pointing to her suit—the one she'd put on Friday morning and the one she felt as if she'd lived in for a week. "I have a meeting." She stood, righted her clothes, and tossed a few extra things into her briefcase, just in case. Then she walked to the door of the storage room and let herself out in the hall, now more confused than ever. Gabrielle had tried to convince her that her hallucinations had some kind of meaning…but what if they were just a jumble of stored memories and random thoughts?

As she approached the elevator, she noticed that once again, preparations were underway for the afternoon party.

Carol winced. Not again.

Red decorations of cupids and hearts abounded. Blowups of some of the company's Valentine's Day cards leaned against the wall, including the "take no prisoners" card she'd seen on her assistant's desk. Cupid was still just as menacing at life-size.

Your best strategy is to surrender.

The volunteers exchanged eye rolls when she walked by. Apparently everyone still hated her. It was, it seemed, the one thing she could count on.

On the elevator ride up to her floor, Carol lifted one hand in a fist then the other, to make sure they matched, then she stood on one foot at a time.

"Are you okay?"

Mortified, Carol realized she'd performed the exercises in front of an elevator full of her coworkers.

"Fine," she murmured, but secretly wondered if she'd had some kind of stroke—neurological damage would explain the things she'd been experiencing.

When the doors opened and she walked into her department, Tracy looked up from her desk where she was playing with her "new" computer. All around the bullpen, employees were comparing their machines and the peripheral equipment she and Luke had scavenged from the storage room.

"Word is that Luke Chancellor paid for this equipment out of his own pocket," Tracy declared.

Carol frowned. "What did I tell you about watercooler rumors?"

Tracy blanched, then tapped her watch. "The directors' meeting…you should get going."

Carol massaged her aching temples. "Um, Tracy…just checking—what day is it?"

Tracy narrowed her eyes. "Friday, February thirteenth. Are you okay, Ms. Snow?"

"Yes," Carol lied. She was actually getting used to the headache. She stopped by the ladies' room to arrange her hair to cover the angry bump on her forehead, then proceeded to the room where the directors' meeting was held. Being the bad guy was getting easier.

Her fellow directors looked up and once again, she sensed not all of them were relieved to see her. Luke Chancellor sat at the head of the table. Remembering how intimate they'd been only…a while ago…she was unable to keep the secret little smile off her face.

Luke shifted nervously in his chair. "We were just getting ready to send out a search party for you, Carol."

She settled into an empty chair. "Sorry I'm late."

"We heard a Good Samaritan delivered new computer equipment to your department this morning," Janet, the art director, said with a smile.

All gazes slid toward Luke. He held up his hands. "It was Carol's idea—I just…facilitated."

He flashed her a grin. She countered with a knowing smirk, which seemed to throw him off-balance.

"Uh…we were about to take another vote on the issue of bonuses," Luke said. "I think it's pretty clear that anyone dissenting is following your lead, Carol, so I guess we can cut to the chase by asking if you've changed your mind on paying out a one-time bonus?"

The weight of a roomful of stares shifted to her. Luke

looked hopeful, and Carol knew he was thinking of her previous comment that she might reconsider her position. He seemed to have no knowledge of the positions she had already assumed for him, and vice versa. Carol studied her nails, enjoying the suspense.

"No, I haven't changed my mind," she finally announced.

Disappointment lined Luke's face. Carol watched him—was it her imagination or did he seem to take the news worse today than…before?

His mouth flattened, then he shrugged. "I guess that's that."

Carol clapped her hands. "Good. If that's all, I need to get back to work. The party means I have to squeeze eight hours of work into a four-hour day." She glanced at Luke. "There is a party today, right?"

"Right," Luke said, pulling a hand down his face. "And yes, that's all."

Carol felt a pang of concern for him, and stopped short of reaching over to touch his arm. "You okay, Chancellor?"

"Yeah, sure," he said. "I'm just exhausted today for some reason."

She smothered a smile with her hand. "Maybe you're coming down with something."

He nodded. "Yeah…maybe. I don't feel like myself."

"Funny—you feel like yourself to me."

He looked up. "Hm?"

Carol smiled. "Never mind. Hope you feel better." She pushed to her feet and left.

On the way back to her office, her mind swirled. Nothing that had happened today—over and over again—made sense.

What worried her most was that her mind was in some kind of endless loop triggered by trauma, and that her poor body lay in a coma in a hospital bed somewhere, withering away.

Would she be stuck reliving Friday, February the thirteenth forever?

When Carol reached her department, she once again braved the gauntlet of resentment from her employees and closed her office door. There she downed aspirin and waited for the feeling of vindication to finally descend. She'd commanded respect in the directors' meeting this morning in a way she'd never done before. She'd proved to Luke that her opinion still meant something around here…that there was at least one woman he couldn't charm into submission.

She squinted. Okay, strike that, since she'd already submitted to him twice.

Although, did submission count if he couldn't remember it?

Regardless, the victory of winning the vote this morning felt strangely empty. It seemed as if the more times she was able to wield her power, the less appealing it became.

Carol pushed a button on the intercom and told Tracy she wasn't to be disturbed, then spent the first half of the morning zipping through the mountain of paperwork on her desk that now seemed rote. She intended to leave early today—*before* the blizzard hit. Maybe if she could break the cycle of the sequence of events, things would get back to normal.

Midmorning, she began packing up her briefcase, but paused at a timid knock on the door.

"Yes?"

Tracy stuck her head inside. "I'm sorry, Ms. Snow, I know you don't want to be bothered, but I was hoping you'd be willing to help me with this memo that I can't seem to get right."

Frustration spiked in Carol's chest, but at the pleading look on her assistant's face, she caved. "Sure, Tracy, let's have a cup of coffee and I'll answer whatever questions you have."

The sheer relief and happiness on the redhead's face was worth living another day within a day.

As expected, by the time she'd gone through the memo line by line to explain what she expected, it was almost time for the snow squall to descend. Outside the sky was bruised and bloated, the wind picking up exponentially.

While she had a free minute, she pulled out her phone and sent Gabrielle an update via text message.

Here we go again.

A couple of minutes later, Gabrielle replied.

Surrender to love, Carol.

Carol frowned at the message. Another repeat.

A knock sounded at her door.

"Come on in, Chancellor."

The door creaked open and he stuck his head in, his expression quizzical. "How did you know it was me?"

"Uh...I guessed," she said. "What can I do for you?"

She crossed her arms, and surveyed his brown slacks and pale blue dress shirt—minus a tie—thinking he had no idea the things they'd already done for each other.

"I thought it would be nice if we walked into the party together, a show of solidarity."

She worked her mouth back and forth. "Okay."

He blinked. "Okay?"

"Oh, now that I've agreed, you're going to change your mind?"

"Not at all. I guess I'm just surprised, that's all. You haven't exactly hidden your disdain for me and my ideas."

She sighed. "Look, the vote on the bonuses wasn't personal."

"I think it was. I think if any other director had proposed bonuses, you would've at least kept an open mind."

"And if any other director had voted against you, you wouldn't have tried to bribe them with refurbished equipment for her employees."

He pursed his mouth. "Touché. Are you ready to walk down?"

She glanced out the window to see the plum-colored clouds rolling in right on schedule. "Sure."

She picked up her briefcase and coat.

"Don't you want to leave those here?" he asked.

"I'll think I'll keep them close by," she said.

When they exited Carol's office, Tracy was the only employee in the area. The young woman was using the dissected memo as an example as she typed a new one on her laptop. Carol hoped she and her assistant were finally making headway toward a good working relationship.

As she and Luke walked toward the elevator, he jammed his fingers into his hair. "Is it just me, or does this seem like the longest day ever?"

"No," Carol said as she leaned against the elevator wall, "it's not just you."

chapter twelve

THE elevator stopped on the lobby level even though only Carol and Luke were on board and neither of them had pressed the lobby button. When the door opened, Luke stepped forward to press the Close Door button then stopped, staring out the window. "You're not going to believe this—it's a blizzard out there."

She smiled and nodded, not even bothering to look. "Uh-huh."

He stared at her. "But…it *never* snows in Atlanta."

"So they say," she agreed, then pushed the close door button.

She could hear the noise of the party even before the elevator stopped. When the doors opened, the full force of music, laughter and voices blasted her. Her stomach churned, both at the known and the unknown.

A few heads turned in her direction, but after a quick downturn of their mouths, they turned away.

"Ignore them," Luke said. "Hey, why don't we take your coat and briefcase to the storage room? I have something for you."

The candy. Which was connected to the kiss bone. Which was connected to the bone...bone. Carol followed him slowly down the hallway, fighting a groan that somehow turned into a moan.

He looked back at her. "Did you say something?"

"No."

He unlocked the door of the storage room, held it open for her, then allowed it to close behind them while he turned on lights.

"It's not much," he said, reaching high on a shelf to remove a heart-shaped box of chocolates.

"Did you say you feel a cold coming on?" she asked in a desperate attempt to ward off the impending kiss of spiraling lust.

Luke shook his head. "No. Just a little tired for no reason I can put my finger on."

When he handed her the box of candy, his cheeks were tinged pink. "It's silly, I guess."

She opened her mouth to say that, in fact, *she* was feeling under the weather and wouldn't want to spread anything to him through a kiss, but stopped when she saw instead a red silk box that read "Be Mine." Surprise sparkled in her chest at the romantic nature of the gift.

Luke scratched his head. "To be honest, I'm not quite sure why I bought that one. It just seemed...right." He thumped his chest as if trying to self-administer CPR. "Lately I've been having these...fantasies...um, feelings..."

Apparently deciding actions spoke louder than words, he lowered his mouth toward hers. In the wake of his incredibly romantic gesture, Carol's bogus contagion defense went out the window. She lifted her mouth to accept his kiss, knowing what his warm lips would feel like before they even made contact with hers. She sighed through the overlapping of sensations that were both new and familiar. Far removed from their first kiss, her mind and body still reeled from the raw power in Luke's probing tongue.

He lifted his head and looked into her eyes. "Do you believe in déjà vu?"

"Yes," she whispered, then curled her hand around his neck and pulled his lips down on hers, hard.

Luke moaned into her mouth and the vibration echoed through her body. He pulled her against him and their hands became frenzied, roaming over each other's bodies. He smoothed his palms down her back, over her buttocks, and pulled her sex against the hardened ridge of his erection. The physical proof of what they were about to do…yet again…made Carol dizzy with lust.

He stopped, his gaze bouncing around the room, looking for a suitable surface.

Carol pointed to the nearby table. "Take me there."

He picked her up by the waist and set her on the table, then slid up her skirt so she could spread her knees.

"Wait," she said, then nodded to the door. "Can you wedge a chair under the doorknob?"

"Good thinking," he said. After the chair was in place, he came back to stand between her thighs.

Carol's pumps fell off with succeeding thuds. She leaned

back on her hands to brace herself, then squeezed his hips with her knees. Her breasts, her sex, her entire body throbbed with anticipation, especially since now she knew what to expect.

"Oh, no," he murmured suddenly, then put a hand to his head. "I don't have a condom. I'm sorry."

"There's one in my briefcase," she said, pointing. "Top compartment."

She was learning.

There were, after all, lots of things from the pages of the erotic novels she'd read for the Red Tote Book Club she wanted to try that required full contact.

Luke was back with the condom in record time, grinning. "I'm impressed, Snow. And grateful." He kissed his way down her neck, then plucked at the buttons on her white blouse until it lay open, exposing her naked breasts.

This morning she'd skipped the bra entirely.

He cupped one breast in his hand, and suckled the other one, pulling her nipple into his mouth until she shuddered with pleasure. But they were both too frantic to linger. Luke pushed her skirt to her waist, then rolled down her panty hose and underwear to expose her sex.

She loosened his belt and unzipped his pants to free his imposing erection. When she clasped the rigid length of him, he gasped, his eyes hooded with desire. She helped him roll on the condom and position his sheathed cock at her slick entrance.

"Now," she whispered in his ear.

He thrust forward, filling her completely. Carol

wrapped her legs around his waist. She couldn't think… couldn't speak…could only feel the amazing wonderfulness of having his body melded with hers. It felt like the first time all over again. The sensations pummeling her were almost overwhelming, leaving her languid and elastic.

He massaged the tiny sensitive nub that housed her orgasms, looking into her eyes. "Snow, you're so sexy," he murmured, not bothering to hide his surprise. "I'm not going to last long."

His sex talk left her quivering and on the verge of a massive orgasm. He used his thumb to send her over the edge. Carol rode him through a deep, powerful climax, contracting around him. Before she had quieted, he shuddered his own release, groaning against her neck. The throbbing bass of the party music all but guaranteed that no one could hear them.

At length their breathing slowed. He pulled away, then kissed her thoroughly. "Wow," he murmured. "What just happened?"

Carol steeled herself, but felt the dreaded sense of remorse start to nibble away at the pure bliss she'd felt only seconds ago. Part of her felt manipulative, because she'd known what was going to happen, had even prepared for it. Luke, on the other hand, had no idea what was going on, only knew that he was conflicted about her. If he felt the ghost of their intimate encounters, he probably had the sense that his body knew her better than his brain actually did.

It had to be mystifying.

Luke pulled back. "Will you go to dinner with me tomorrow night?"

Carol straightened her clothes. "Tomorrow…you mean Valentine's Day?"

"Yes."

She turned her back to retrieve her underwear and panty hose, stepping into them as quickly and modestly as she could manage in such a confining space. "I thought you already had plans," she chided. "I heard you tell someone that you were having dinner with a 'special lady.'"

He grinned. "I will if you say yes. I haven't made any plans—that's my generic response."

Carol wet her lips, wavering. She wanted to say yes, wanted to go on a bona fide date with Luke, but she was already so…*attached* to him, she was terrified their relationship was already lopsided…and once again she'd be left out in the cold.

The scene of Valentine's Day Present that Gabrielle had played for her had shown Luke with the gorgeous blonde, meaning if Carol said no, he would meet the other woman and think enough of her to ask her to dinner instead.

So despite the great sex—most of which he was unaware of—and his heartfelt invitation, how much could Luke really care about her? She'd suffered enough humiliation in her relationship with James to last a lifetime.

It just wasn't worth the risk.

Carol turned back and forced a note of casual nonchalance into her voice. "I don't think so. Look, this was just a hookup to satisfy curiosity. And I'm not curious anymore." She adopted a blasé expression.

Luke's head went back, as if he'd been slapped. "Uh… okay."

She slipped her feet into her pumps. "Why don't you

leave first so it'll seem less suspicious if anyone is watching."

"Okay." He hesitated, then rechecked his clothing and made his way to the door.

She turned away and closed her eyes. That was too close. Having sex with Luke Chancellor three times might not have been the smartest move, but thinking it meant something emotional this time around would be the biggest mistake ever.

"Luke," she said.

He turned back. "Yes?"

"Thank you for the candy."

He looked as if he wanted to say something, but thought better of it. Instead, he slipped out the door and it closed behind him.

Carol held her breath against the sudden pain squeezing her chest. She had the distinct feeling that her chance to be with Luke had just expired…in every alternate universe.

Wondering how she would get through the rest of the party, Carol checked her clothing and smoothed her hair, realizing with some small measure of relief that at least her headache was gone. She lifted her hand to her forehead to find the goose egg she'd been nursing was also gone. It was something to be grateful for in what seemed like an unending day.

From the floor, a glint of metal caught her eye—her silver-and-emerald earring. She bit her lip. Was it worth one more try to retrieve the stray bauble that James had said was supposed to symbolize "a successful love"?

Carol looked around the room and smiled when she

spied a heavy-duty industrial push broom. No more falling monitors.

She retrieved the broom, then used it to snag the earring and pull it out a safe distance from under the shelf where she could get to it without bumping into anything.

She leaned the broom against the shelving unit, then crouched to pick up the earring. Triumphant, she straightened and pumped her arm.

Which dislodged the broom, sending it sliding along the shelving unit. Above her, she heard a scraping noise, and when she looked up, the end of the broom had nudged something large that was bearing down on her.

Despite the uncannily prophetic sense of déjà vu, Carol didn't have time to put up her hand. Pain exploded in her head, then everything went…well, you know.

chapter thirteen

SOMEONE was shaking Carol by the shoulder.

"Carol…wake up. We still have work to do. Carol?"

Carol resisted opening her eyes because part of her knew whatever "work" Gabrielle had for her would not be fun or pleasant.

"Carol!"

Her eyes popped open, sending a blinding pain through her temple. "*Ow, ow, ow.* What now?"

Standing above her, Gabrielle gave her a tight smile. "You don't have to be so testy, you know. This is your dream, not mine. It's not as if I'm getting paid."

Carol frowned. "It's because of your suggestion to seduce a man that I'm in this dilemma to begin with."

"That was an optional assignment. Let's get you up."

Gabrielle helped her to a sitting position. Carol grimaced. "The pain is worse this time."

Gabrielle made a rueful noise. "A person can take only so many hits."

"Do you think it's a sign that things are about to get worse?"

"Or better."

"Or worse," Carol pressed.

"Or worse," Gabrielle agreed.

"Has this happened to any of the other women in the book club?"

"Not to my knowledge," Gabrielle said.

Carol gestured to the monitor lying in the floor on its side. "Let's get this over with. What is it?"

"A look at Valentine's Day To Come."

Panic flowered in Carol's chest. "How far into the future?"

"Let's see."

Carol held up her hand. "I don't want to."

Gabrielle sat down on the floor next to Carol. "I know. And maybe that's why I'm here."

"What if I see something horrible…like what if I'm not even there?"

"Is that what you're afraid of?" Gabrielle asked. "That you'll die alone?"

Carol tried to think around the pain hammering her head. "Or maybe that I'll die *because* I'm alone."

Gabrielle laughed. "That's not true. When a woman gets married, her life expectancy actually goes down. Besides, you don't have to have a spouse or a lover to have a life rich with family and friends."

"I don't have family."

"I know. I'm sorry. But you could have your own someday."

"And…" Carol swallowed hard. "I don't have friends."

Gabrielle made a disbelieving noise. "Of course you have friends."

"No, I don't. I haven't kept up with childhood friends, and my coworkers hate me."

"That can't be true."

"It is. They call me names behind my back, like Ice Princess."

"You have the women in the book club."

"They don't like me, either," Carol said.

"Of course they do."

"It's why I agreed to the seduction experiment," Carol admitted. "So they would like me. So I would fit in."

"I see." Gabrielle steepled her hands. "Why do you think you have trouble making friends?"

Carol shook her head. "I honestly don't know."

"Then why don't we take a look at the monitor and go from there?"

Carol chewed on a thumbnail while the monitor blinked on. The scene that materialized was a group of five women, perhaps in their eighties, sitting around a table, drinking coffee out of mugs with hearts on them. Carol scanned the faces, looking for herself. "I don't think any of those women are me."

Gabrielle turned up the volume.

"Those were the days," one woman was saying, "when books were actually made out of paper, when you could hold them in your hands and turn pages. Remember?"

The other women nodded, looking wistful.

"Cassie, how do you like your e-book reader?"

Gabrielle and Carol looked at each other. "That's our Cassie!"

"I love it," Cassie said, and when she smiled, Carol recognized the woman's bright blue eyes. "I can carry hundreds of books around with no problem. How about you, Page?"

Gabrielle and Carol laughed when they realized they were looking at the Red Tote Book Club circa fifty years into the future.

"I love it, too," Page said. "What I like best is that I can read the Red Tote Book Club selections on my e-reader and no one makes comments about an old lady reading dirty books!" Page Sharpe's auburn hair had faded, but she was still very pretty—in fact, all of the women had aged well.

As the conversation proceeded, they were able to identify the other women by their voices.

"Oh, my goodness, that's me!" Gabrielle said, pointing. "I'm completely white-headed!"

"But still beautiful," Carol said.

Gabrielle beamed.

Over the course of the next few minutes, they gathered that, amazingly, all the men the women had seduced as part of their book club assignment had become either a husband or significant other—and that all the couples seemed to still enjoy a frisky sex life.

But it became clear that Carol wasn't among the group, and the longer the scene played, the lower her heart hung.

"When was the last time anyone saw Carol Snow?" one of the women asked.

Carol sat forward.

They all made mournful noises and took the opportunity to sip their coffee. "I call her every few months and leave messages," Jacqueline Mays said. "But she never returns my calls."

"Me, too," said Wendy Trainer, still wearing her trademark pixie cut. "I never hear back from her."

"I send her a holiday card every year," Cassie said. "But I never get one in return."

Carol bit into her lip.

"I drove by her place once," the Gabrielle on the screen said. "I knocked on the door, but she didn't answer. Her neighbor said she hardly ever sees her. Says all she does is stay in and watch TV."

"Imagine that," Cassie said. "She still has a television."

"Didn't TVs go out of vogue about the same time as paper books?" Wendy asked.

"Sounds right," Jacqueline said. "God, we're old."

"But at least we have each other," Page said.

"That's right," they all chimed in, clinking their coffee cups.

"I just wish we could reconnect with Carol," Wendy said.

"If you remember," Cassie said, "she was always standoffish."

"Hard to get to know," Page agreed.

"And she didn't really participate that much," Jacqueline said.

"Maybe she likes being alone," Wendy added with a shrug.

In the end, all the women decided that yes, Carol must like being alone. Only the Gabrielle on the monitor said nothing, instead just sipped her coffee as the scene faded to black.

Carol blinked back desperate tears. "See? I'm destined to be alone."

Gabrielle clasped her hand. "You're not destined to be alone. You can control your personal relationships. So, after watching that future scene, why do you think you have trouble making friends?"

Carol sniffed and tried to collect herself. "Because I don't extend myself. Because I don't reach out to people and let them know I care. Because I don't lean on other people for support when I need it."

"All good reasons," Gabrielle said. "And you understand that you're going to have to change those behaviors to attract friends, and maybe lovers?"

She nodded. "Yes. And I will, if I ever get out of this endless loop I'm in."

Gabrielle pushed to her feet. "There's an old truism that says, 'If you keep doing what you're doing, you'll keep getting what you've got.' To break out of your endless loop, maybe you need to do something unexpected."

Carol gingerly stood. "Like what?"

Gabrielle smiled. "That's up to you. It's time to say goodbye."

"I won't see you again?"

The woman smiled wide. "Every week at the Red Tote Book Club as long as you choose to. Good luck with your journey back."

Carol nodded and brushed her hands down the skirt of her Friday suit. Then she walked to the door of the storage room and let herself out in the hallway.

Her feet were heavy as she moved toward the elevator and her hands shook uncontrollably. She didn't want to be the old woman everyone in the scene on the monitor talked about—the recluse whose only pastime was watching TV. The woman who was alone.

Completely, absolutely, utterly alone.

As Carol approached the elevator, she noticed that once again, preparations were underway for the afternoon party. Red decorations of cupids and hearts abounded. Blowups of some of the company's Valentine's Day cards leaned against the wall, including the "take no prisoners" card she'd seen on her assistant's desk.

The volunteers shot unwelcome looks her way as she walked by.

If you keep doing what you're doing, you'll keep getting what you've got.

Carol pivoted and turned back. "Hi," she said to the group of about twenty. "My name is Carol and I work in the finance department. And I was wondering if you could tell me what you'd do with a thousand dollars if it fell out of the sky."

At first the employees were shy about speaking up, but the more probing questions that Carol asked about their families, eventually everyone opened up. She'd expected them to give answers such as a family vacation or a plasma television, not things like medical bills, car repairs, or a new heating unit for their home.

She enjoyed the conversation and appreciated their honesty. When she walked away, she had a better understanding of what kinds of daily financial obligations the average family faced—from school expenses to insurance to caring for elderly parents.

On the ride up to her floor, Carol turned to each person in the elevator and asked them a question about their job. At first, people looked at her warily. That's when Carol realized that people really did see her as cold and uncaring.

And why not? She hadn't given anyone a reason to think anything else—not potential friends and not potential lovers.

Luke's face floated into her mind. That was about to change she just hoped she wasn't too late.

chapter fourteen

WHEN the elevator doors opened and Carol walked into her department, Tracy looked up from her desk where she was playing with her "new" computer. All around the bullpen, employees were comparing their machines and the peripheral equipment she and Luke had scavenged from the storage room the night before.

"Look at all this loot!" Tracy exclaimed. "I assume you had something to do with this. I know you've been trying to get the departmental budget increased for a couple of years now."

"I have," Carol said. "But I can't take credit for any of this. Luke Chancellor pulled strings and had unused machines from sales transferred over to our department. We owe him a huge debt of thanks."

Tracy blinked. "I thought you hated Luke Chancellor."

Carol pulsed with shame—what a bitter person she'd become over the years. James wasn't to blame—she'd allowed herself to get that way. "I'm sorry if I've given you or anyone else that impression. Of everything I know about Luke Chancellor, he's a decent and good man, and he's brought a lot of prosperity to our company."

Tracy angled her head. "Ms. Snow, are you okay?"

Carol gave a little laugh. "I'm a little tired and headachey, but overall, yeah, I'm good."

Tracy winced. "Uh…that would be my fault."

"What do you mean?"

Her assistant pointed to the coffeemaker in the corner. "I accidentally bought decaf coffee. So for the last week— no caffeine…which is probably why you've been tired and getting headaches." She gestured to the bullpen. "In fact, I think it's why everyone around here has been so cranky lately. I'm sorry if anyone has been rude." She cleared her throat. "Including me." She handed Carol a full steaming cup of coffee. "This should give you a boost and get rid of your headache."

Carol reached up to touch her forehead. "Thanks, but there's another reason—" She stopped when she couldn't find the lump that had been there before…many times. "Never mind," she murmured, perplexed anew.

"You're late for the directors' meeting," Tracy said. "Oh, and I revised the memo. You'll have a clean copy on your desk when you get back."

"Great—and thanks for the coffee."

Carol hurried to the room where the directors' meeting was held, but still took time to speak to coworkers along the way. Each time puzzled looks turned to genuine smiles, her mood buoyed higher.

Being the good guy felt…pretty darn good.

When she walked into the room, her fellow directors looked up and even though she sensed not all of them were happy to see her, she offered an apologetic smile to the room, then settled into an empty chair.

Her gaze swung to Luke, who sat at the head of the table. The sight of his handsome face took the breath from her lungs…she was head over heels in love with him. But she had to keep herself in check because as far as he was concerned, the only physical contact they'd had was a near-miss kiss in the storage room.

Luke offered her a friendly smile. "We were just getting ready to send out a search party for you, Carol."

"Sorry I'm late. I hope I didn't hold up the meeting."

"We heard a Good Samaritan delivered new computer equipment to your department this morning," Janet, the art director, said with a smile.

All gazes slid toward Luke. He held up his hands. "It was Carol's idea—I just…facilitated."

"Not true," Carol said. "It was Luke's idea, and he took care of everything. Everyone in my department is very happy, so I'd like to thank Luke publicly."

He seemed surprised by her speech, but pleased. "Okay, moving right along…we were about to take another vote on the issue of bonuses." He looked back to her. "I think it's pretty clear that anyone dissenting is following your lead, Carol, so I guess we can cut to the chase by asking if you've changed your mind about paying out a one-time employee bonus of one thousand dollars?"

The weight of a roomful of stares shifted to her. Luke

looked hopeful, and Carol knew he was thinking of her comment in the storage room last night that she might reconsider her position.

So many things had happened since last night…where to start?

Carol took a deep breath. "As a matter of fact…yes, I have changed my mind. I've had a chance to talk to a small sample of employees and I realize now what a one-time payment of a thousand dollars can do for a family and for employee morale. If we can't afford to reward everyone when we've had a good year, then when can we? I recommend that we approve bonuses immediately."

Luke's eyes widened in surprise, then a smile broke over his face. "All in favor?" It was a unanimous vote. Luke could barely contain his enthusiasm—it endeared him to her that much more. He gave her a little nod of thanks that made her heart squeeze…and scared her a little. How could she feel so close to him in such a short period of time? And would his feelings ever "catch up" with hers?

Carol left the meeting and when she reached her department, everyone was in a celebratory mood—apparently word of the approval of the bonuses had leaked out and maybe the coffee change had helped, too. Her own headache had vanished and her energy level had returned. Carol circulated with her employees as they inspected their new computers. When she made it into her office, she decided to leave the door open to draw on the infectious creative energy of the group.

Carol had another reason to be happy—the red skies were gone. Meaning, there would be no blizzard…which didn't matter anyway because she was eager to go to the company party this time and have fun.

And see Luke.

She had a hard time concentrating on the mountain of paperwork on her desk, even though she had it memorized by now. She was antsy waiting for Luke to knock on her door and ask her to walk down with him to the party. If they got together at the party, he would ask her to Valentine's Day dinner tomorrow night—like all the times before—instead of the blonde she'd seen in her vision. And this time, she'd say yes. Carol kept checking her lipstick in the tiny mirror in her desk drawer, reminding herself she needed to play it a little cool.

While she had a free minute, though, she pulled out her phone and sent Gabrielle a happy update via text message.

Forget seduction—I've surrendered to love.

A couple of minutes later, Gabrielle replied.

Glad you found a way to break the continuous loop.

Carol squinted. "What the?" It was almost as if the real Gabrielle had been privy to…

No, that couldn't be.

A knock sounded at her door.

Her heart surged when she saw Luke standing there, looking gorgeous in his brown slacks and pale blue dress shirt, minus a tie. "Come in."

"Hey, I like your new open-door policy. Wish more directors thought like us."

She warmed under his praise and reminded herself she wasn't supposed to know why he'd dropped by. "To what do I owe this pleasure?"

He crossed to her desk and picked up a ball of rubber bands. "I just wanted to stop by and thank you for reconsidering your position on the employee bonuses. You made a lot of people happy today."

"The credit is yours, Luke. Not only was it your idea, but it's under your leadership that sales has thrived." She gave him a warm smile. "We're lucky to have you."

He stared at her, but his eyes were unreadable. "Thank you."

Suddenly he replaced the ball on her desk and stepped back. "I'd better get going."

"Wait," she said, reaching for her briefcase and coat. "I'll walk down to the party with you."

"Uh, actually…I'm not going to the party."

Disappointment zigzagged through her. "But…the party was your idea."

He nodded. "I know."

She desperately cast around for more excuses to get him to the party. "And…the bonus checks will be given out. I thought you'd want to be there for that."

"I do, but…something came up. I was invited to a Steeplechase and since the weather is so nice this afternoon I decided to go."

Carol swallowed hard. "Steeplechase, huh?"

She had a clear memory of a leggy, busty blonde smiling up at him. *I guess it was my lucky day when I decided to go with my friend to the Steeplechase…I never dreamed I'd meet someone like you, Luke.*

And just like that, Carol remembered the icicle card that Luke had planted in her book club tote bag. That was what he truly thought of her…the Ice Princess who wouldn't thaw. All of this flirtation…all of this buttering up was really to get her support for his bonus program. And now that he had what he wanted, he was pulling back. She could sense it…could see it in his eyes…in the way he avoided her.

"Uh, yeah," he said, then shrugged awkwardly. "You know—horses jumping and…stuff. Sounds…interesting." He couldn't seem to make eye contact.

Carol smiled and nodded, not trusting herself to speak. How ironic that she'd finally opened her heart to a man— and to others because of him—and he didn't want her.

She was two for two. First James, now Luke.

But underneath the hurt and disappointment, there was gratitude. Because without Luke's merciless teasing and prodding, she never would've tried to enact revenge on him…and never would've come to realize how she'd been sporting a Back Off sign on her forehead. That by closing herself off to the hurtful things in life, like loss and rejection, she'd also closed herself off to the good things in life, like love and sensuality.

And even friendship.

So…tomorrow night while Luke was taking Blondie out on the town, Carol would be on the phone, going down a list of old friends that she'd lost touch with and trying to reconnect.

With jerky body language, Luke pointed to the door. "So…we could share an elevator down."

"Sounds good," she said, with the nicest smile she could manage considering her heart was breaking. She'd have to get used to working with him and hiding her feelings. She draped her coat over her arm and picked up her briefcase. They walked to the elevator. Her mind raced to concoct small talk, but she couldn't seem to come up with anything.

Luke pushed the call button, then whistled under his breath, obviously wanting to be anywhere else. Carol felt foolish for suggesting they ride down together. When the car finally came, they walked on, instantly going to opposite sides. He pushed Lobby and she pushed Basement. The doors closed and they started their downward descent.

"So…" Luke alternated looking at the ceiling and at his feet. "I guess the rumor is true."

Carol lifted her eyebrows. "What rumor?"

Luke shrugged. "The reason you're in such a good mood all of a sudden."

She froze. "What reason would that be?"

"Because of a man."

Carol wanted to die on the spot. The only thing worse than pining for a man is him *knowing* you're pining for him. Her mind sprinted ahead—what would the women in the book club advise her to do?

And the answer came to her instantly: *Lie.*

"There *is* a man," Carol admitted, but she was unable to look at Luke—she was afraid he'd see in her eyes that it was him she was crazy about.

"Oh," he nodded. "That's good. Anyone I would know?"

"No," she said emphatically. "You and he would never cross paths." Not a lie, actually.

The doors dinged open to the lobby and not a second too soon. Luke stepped off then turned around. "I'm glad you found someone, Snow. Hope you and your boyfriend have a nice Valentine's dinner."

"Thank you," she said. "Enjoy Richardson's."

As the doors closed, he was squinting and mouthing, "Richardson's?"

chapter fifteen

AFTER her humiliating exchange with Luke about the rumor that a man accounted for her new good mood, Carol was tempted to skip the company party and go home to watch TV shows on her DVR. The only thing that stopped her was the memory of the Red Tote Book Club members as seniors describing her as a recluse. In time the rumor mill would die down. In the meantime, she meant to adhere to her new philosophy of extending herself to coworkers.

She could hear the noise of the party even before the elevator stopped. When the doors opened, the full force of music, laughter and voices blasted her. Her stomach churned, both at the known and the unknown, but with an underlying excitement about the new outlook she had on people and relationships in general. A few heads turned in her direction and Carol extended a smile. When they reciprocated, she moved forward to properly introduce herself.

The party was fun, and a great place to practice her newfound skills. When she spotted her assistant Tracy, she walked over to say hello.

"I didn't get to tell you before you left," Carol said with a smile, "but the memo is top-notch."

Tracy dimpled. "Really?"

"Really. Perfect grammar, spelling, and just a well-written piece of documentation."

"Thank you, Ms. Snow."

Carol touched the young woman's hand. "No, thank you, Tracy, for all the things you do for me and for helping to keep the department running."

Tracy stared at her, then burst into tears.

Carol blinked and patted her shoulder. "What on earth? What's wrong, Tracy?"

"I did something really mean."

Carol shook her head. "I can't imagine you would do something that mean."

Tracy nodded her head like a little girl. "I did it, and I'm sorry."

"What did you do?"

The young woman pressed her lips together, then blurted, "I put a card comparing you to an icicle in one of your bags."

Carol's eyebrows went up. "That was you?"

"I'm so sorry, Ms. Snow. It was a very mean, immature thing to do. I wouldn't blame you if you fired me."

Carol thought back to all the times she'd had nothing but criticism and harsh words for her assistant, and squeezed the redhead's shoulders. "I wouldn't dream of firing you. But thank you for telling me."

Tracy excused herself to repair her makeup, which left Carol alone with a new revelation.

So Luke Chancellor hadn't planted the unflattering card in her tote bag after all. She shook her head. And yet she'd been determined to make that man suffer for something he hadn't even done.

And yes, she was glad to know that he hadn't thought so poorly of her.

She looked in the direction of the storage room, half afraid to go near it, but conceding that one loose end begged to be tied up: her lost earring.

Carol's heart began to thump and she found her feet moving toward the room that still represented so many secrets and mysticisms that she wasn't sure she should go back inside. On the other hand, what kind of nut believed in a time travel portal in the storage room of a greeting card company?

Carol pursed her mouth.

A company named "Mystic Touch."

The hallway leading to the storage room was dark and quiet. The closer she got to the door, the more she felt drawn to the room—compelled to go inside. She punched in the access code and waited for the click, then pushed open the door, walked inside, and flipped on all the lights. Her pulse pounded, on alert for any falling equipment that might take her back to the beginning of this day. Today had been the best version so far, and she wouldn't want to try to top it. Even if Luke had decided not to come to the party.

The door to the storage room clicked, then opened… and Luke stepped inside.

Carol felt her jaw loosen and wondered for a split second if her mind was playing tricks on her again.

"I thought I might find you here," he said.

"I came in to look for an earring I lost last night," she murmured.

"Last night seems…like a long time ago," Luke ventured.

Carol could only nod. "You changed your mind about the party?"

He walked toward her. "Yes. I came back to make a fool out of myself."

Her heart tripped harder against her breastbone. "What do you mean?"

"I know you've met someone," he said, stepping closer. "But…why not me?"

Carol's heart soared. She covered her mouth and tears began to stream down her cheeks.

Luke stood in front of her with an anguished expression on his face as he retrieved a handkerchief from his back pocket. "You have to interpret tears for me. Happy? Sad? Toothache?"

"Happy," she said, laughing and dabbing at her tears. "The man I met, the one who's put me in such a good mood?"

"Yeah," he said warily.

"It's you."

"Me?" His eyebrows drew together and he got a faraway look in his eyes, as if he was trying hard to remember something elusive. "Me," he said, nodding, then pulled his hand over his mouth. "Look, if I've seemed different lately, it's because after that night here in the storage room where

I almost kissed you, I started having these very...*vivid* fantasies and...*feelings*..."

Carol stepped close to him and lifted her arms to loop around his neck. "I think I know what you mean."

Luke kissed her, moaning into her mouth until the vibration echoed through her body. He pulled her against him and their hands became frenzied, roaming over each other's bodies. He smoothed his palms down her back, over her buttocks, and pulled her sex against the hardened ridge of his erection. The physical proof of what they were going to do...again...and again...and again...made her dizzy with lust.

"Let's find your earring," he whispered, "so we can get out of here."

"Never mind," she said, urging him toward the door.

"It must be important to you. Let's do at least one quick pass. If we don't see it, we'll take off."

Since he was determined, she relented. "I have the other earring so you'll know what it looks like."

When she pulled the mismatched one from her briefcase, Luke frowned slightly at her briefcase, as if it seemed familiar to him, then took the earring. As Carol followed Luke up and down the aisles, her nerves jangled. She just wanted to leave. Things were good the way they were... things were perfect, in fact. Why mess with it?

"Is that it?" Luke asked, pointing to the base of a shelving unit. "I think it is." He crouched, down, but Carol couldn't watch. She held her breath, waiting for a crashing noise.

"Carol?"

She opened her eyes to see him dangling the earring in front of her. "Are you okay?" he asked.

She nodded. "Thank you."

"You're welcome, although it bodes well for me, too," he offered. "Emeralds are the symbol of a successful love."

Carol stared up at him, incredulous. "I'd heard that." She palmed the earring. "Let's go. Hurry. Before something… happens."

But at the door, one thing made her turn back. "Aren't you forgetting something?"

Luke frowned. "What?"

"The candy you bought me?"

He squinted at her. "How do you know about the candy?"

"I just do," she said, crossing her arms.

"It's not much," he said, reaching high on a shelf to remove a heart-shaped box of chocolates. When he handed her the box, his cheeks were tinged pink. The red silk box read "I Love You."

Surprise sparkled in her chest at the romantic gesture.

Luke scratched his head. "To be honest, I'm not quite sure why I bought that one. It just seemed…right. I feel like…I know you, Carol…more than I do…"

Apparently deciding actions spoke louder than words, he lowered his mouth toward hers. She lifted her mouth to accept his kiss, sighing through the overlapping of sensations that were both new and familiar. Far removed from their first kiss, her mind and body still reeled from the raw power in Luke's probing tongue.

He lifted his head and looked into her eyes. "Do you believe in déjà vu?"

"Oh, yes," she whispered, then curled her hand around his neck and pulled his lips down on hers, hard.

★ ★ ★ ★ ★

The Harlequin® Blaze™ series brings you
six new fun, flirtatious and steamy stories a month
available wherever books are sold, including most bookstores,
supermarkets, drugstores and discount stores.

Blaze

PLAY WITH ME

leslie KELLY

To loyal romance readers everywhere.
In this economy, I know it's got to be really tough to indulge
in your reading habits. I sincerely appreciate each and every
one of you who keeps buying books so that I can keep
writing them. Thank you so much.

prologue

Columbus Day

"DO you know what your problem is?"

Reese Campbell didn't even look up as the door to his office burst open and the familiar voice of his extremely nosy, bossy great-aunt intruded on what had been a relatively quiet October morning. Because that was one hell of a loaded question.

Hmm. Problem? What problem? Did he have a *problem?*

Being thrust into a job he hadn't been ready for, hadn't planned on, hadn't even wanted? That was kind of a problem.

Being thrust into that job because his father had died unexpectedly, at the age of fifty-five? Aside from being an utter tragedy, that was absolutely a problem.

Battling competitors who'd figured him to be a pushover when he'd stepped in to run a large brewery while only in his mid-twenties? Problem.

Dealing with longtime employees who didn't like the changes he was implementing in the family business? Problem.

Ending a relationship because the woman didn't appreciate that he—a good-time guy—now had so many responsibilities? Problem.

Walking a tightrope with family members who went from begging him to keep everything the way it was, to resenting his every effort to fill his father's shoes? Big effing problem.

"Did you hear me?"

He finally gave his full attention to his great-aunt Jean, who had never seen a closed door she hadn't wanted to fling wide open. He had to smile as he beheld her red hat and flashy sequined jacket. Going into old age gracefully had never entered his aunt's mind. Keeping her opinions to herself hadn't, either.

"I heard," he replied.

"Well, do you know?"

What he didn't know was why she was asking. Because she didn't *want* an answer. Rhetorical questions like that one were always the opening volley in the elderly woman's none-of-your-damn-business assaults on everyone else's private life.

He leaned back in his chair. "Whatever it is, I am quite sure you're about to tell me."

"Cheeky," she said, closing the door. "You're bored."

No kidding.

"You're twenty-nine years old and you're suffocating. For two years, you haven't drawn one free, unencumbered breath."

He remained still, silent. Wary. Because so far, his eccentric, opinionated great-aunt was absolutely, one hundred percent correct.

Suffocating. That was a good word to describe his life these days. An appropriate adjective for the frequent sensation that an unbearable weight had landed on his chest and was holding him in place, unable to move.

As Aunt Jean said, his breath had been stolen, his momentum stopped. All forward thought frozen in place, glued to that moment in time when a slick road and a blind curve had changed everything he and his family had known about their former lives.

"You need some excitement. An adventure. How long has it been since you've had sex?"

Reese coughed into his fist, the mouthful of air he'd just inhaled having lodged in his throat. "Aunt Jean…"

She grunted. "Oh, please, spare me. You need to get laid."

"Jeez, can't you bake or knit or something like a normal great-aunt?"

She ignored him. "Have you gotten any since that stupid Tate girl tried to get you to choose her over your family?" Not waiting for an answer, she continued. "You've got to do something more than deal with your sad mother, your squabbling sisters and your juvenile-delinquent brother."

He stiffened, the reaction a reflexive one.

"Oh, don't get indignant, you know it's true," she said. "I love them as much as you do, we're family. But even apples from the same tree sometimes harbor an occasional worm."

The woman did love her metaphors.

"So here's what you do."

"I knew you would get around to telling me eventually."

She ignored him. "You simply must have an adventure."

"Okay, got it. One adventure, coming right up," he said with a deliberate eye roll. "Should I call 1-800-Wild Times or just go to letsgetcrazy.com?"

"You're not so old I can't box your ears."

A grin tugged at his mouth. "The one time you boxed my ears as a kid, I put frogs in your punch bowl right before a party."

An amused gleam lit her eyes. "So do it again."

Reese's brow furrowed. "Excuse me?"

"Be wild. Do something fun. Chuck this cautious-businessman gig and be the bad-ass rebel you once were."

Bad-ass rebel? Him? The guy most recently voted Young Businessman of the Year? "Yeah, right."

He didn't know which sounded more strange—him being that person, or his elderly great-aunt using the term *bad-ass rebel*. Then again, she *had* just asked him when he'd last gotten laid—a question he didn't even want to contemplate in his own mind.

She fixed a pointed stare at his face. "Don't think I've forgotten who I had to bail out of jail one spring break. Which young fellow it was who ended up taking two girls to the prom. Or who hired a stripper to show up at the principal's house."

Oh. That bad-ass rebel. Reese had forgotten all about him.

"The world was your playground once. Go play in it again."

Play? Be unencumbered, free from responsibilities?

Reese looked at the files on his desk. There was a mountain of order forms, requisitions, payroll checks, ad copy, legal paperwork—all needing his attention. His signature. His time.

Then there was his personal calendar, filled with family obligations, fixing his sister's car, talking to his brother's coach…doing father stuff that he hadn't envisioned undertaking for another decade at least.

All his responsibility. Not in a decade. Now.

It wasn't the life he'd envisioned for himself. But it *was* the life he had. And there wasn't a thing he could do about it.

"I've forgotten how," he muttered.

She didn't say anything for a long moment, then the elderly woman, whose energy level so belied her years, laughed softly. There was a note in that laugh, both secretive and sneaky.

"Whatever it is you're thinking about doing, forget it." She feigned a look of hurt. "Me? What could I possibly do?"

He knew better than to be fooled by the nice-old-lady routine. She'd been playing that card for as long as he could remember and it had been the downfall of many a more gullible family member. "I'm going to leave a note that if I am kidnapped by a troupe of circus clowns, the police should talk to you."

She tsked. "Oh, my boy, circus clowns? Is that the best you can come up with? I'm wounded—you've underestimated me."

"Aunt Jean…"

Ignoring him, she turned toward the door. Before she exited, however, she glanced back. "I have the utmost confidence in you, dear. I have no doubt that when the right moment presents itself, you will rise to the occasion."

With a quickly blown kiss and a jangle of expensive bracelets decorating her skinny arm, she slipped out. Reese was free to get back to work. But instead, he spent a few minutes thinking about what Great-Aunt Jean had said.

He didn't doubt she was right about the fact that he was bored. Stifled. Suffocating. But her solution—to go a little crazy—wasn't the answer. Not for the life he was living now. Not when so many people counted on him. His family. His employees. His late father.

Besides, it didn't matter. No opportunity to play, as she put it, had come his way for a long time. Not in more than two years. The word wasn't even in his vocabulary anymore.

And frankly, Reese didn't see that changing anytime soon.

chapter one

Halloween

IT should have been a routine flight.

Pittsburgh to Chicago was about as simple an itinerary as Clear-Blue Airlines ever flew. In the LearJet 60, travel time would be under an hour. The weather was perfect, the sky like something out of a kid's Crayola artwork display. Blue as a robin's egg, with a few puffy white clouds to set the scene and not a drop of moisture in the air. Crisp, not cold, it was about the most beautiful autumn day they'd had this year.

The guys in the tower were cheerful, the Lear impeccably maintained and a joy to handle. Amanda Bauer's mood was good, especially since it was one of her favorite holidays. Halloween.

She should have known something was going to screw it up.

"What do you mean Mrs. Rush canceled?" she asked,

frowning as she held the cell phone tightly to her ear. Standing in the shadow of the jet on the tarmac, she edged in beside the fold-down steps. She covered her other ear with her hand to drown out the noises of nearby aircraft. "Are you sure? She's been talking about this trip for ages."

"Sorry, kiddo, you're going to have to do without your senior sisters meeting this month," said Ginny Tate, the backbone of Clear-Blue. The middle-aged woman did everything from scheduling appointments, to bookkeeping, to ordering parts, to maintaining the company Web site. Ginny was just as good at arguing with airport honchos who wanted to obsess over every flight plan as she was at making sure Uncle Frank, who had founded the airline, took his cholesterol medication every day.

In short, Ginny was the one who kept the business running so all Amanda and Uncle Frank—now 60-40 partners in the airline—had to do was fly.

Which was just fine with them.

"Mrs. Rush said one of her friends has the flu and she doesn't want to go away in case she comes down with it, too."

"Oh, that bites," Amanda muttered, really regretting the news. Because she had been looking forward to seeing the group of zany older women again. Mrs. Rush, an elderly widow and heir to a steel fortune, was one of her regular clients.

The wealthy woman and her "gal pals," who ranged in age from fifty to eighty, took girls-weekend trips every couple of months. They always requested Amanda as their pilot, having almost adopted her into the group. She'd flown them to Vegas for some gambling. To Reno for some gambling. To the Caribbean for some gambling. With a few spa destinations thrown in between.

Amanda had no idea what the group had planned for Halloween in Chicago, but she was sure it would have been entertaining.

"She asked me to tell you she's sorry, and says if she has to, she'll invent a trip in a few weeks so you two can catch up."

"You do realize she's not kidding."

"I know," said Ginny. "Money doesn't stand a chance in her wallet, does it? The hundred-dollar bills have springs attached—she puts them in and they start trying to bounce right out."

Pretty accurate. Since losing her husband, the woman had made it her mission to go through as much of his fortune as possible. Mr. Rush hadn't lived long enough to enjoy the full fruits of his labors, so in his memory, his widow was going to pluck every plum and wring every bit of juice she could out of the rest of her life. No regrets, that was her M.O.

Mrs. Rush was about as different from the people Amanda had grown up with as a person could be. Her own family back in Stubing, Ohio, epitomized the small-town, hard-work, wholesome, nose-to-the-grindstone-'til-the-day-you-die mentality.

They had never quite known what to make of *her*.

Amanda had started rebelling by first grade, when she'd led a student revolt against lima beans in school lunches. Things had only gone downhill from there. By the time she hit seventh grade, her parents were looking into boarding schools…which they couldn't possibly afford.

And when she graduated high school with a disciplinary record matched only by a guy who'd ended up in prison, they'd pretty much given up on her for good.

She couldn't say why she'd gone out of her way to find trouble. Maybe it was because *trouble* was such a bad word in her house. The forbidden path was always so much more exciting than the straight-and-narrow one.

There was only one member of the Bauer clan who was at all like her: Uncle Frank. His motto was *Live 'til your fuel tank is in the red and then keep on going. You can rest during your long dirt nap when you finally slide off the runway of life.*

Live to the extreme, take chances, go places, don't wait for anything you want, go out and find it or make it happen. And never let anyone tie you down.

These were all lessons Amanda had taken to heart when growing up, hearing tales of her wild uncle Frank, her father's brother, of whom everyone else in the family had so disapproved. They especially disliked that he seemed to have his own personal parking space in front of the nearest wedding chapel. He'd walked down the aisle four times.

Unfortunately, he'd also walked down the aisle of a divorce courtroom just as often.

He might not be lucky in love, but he was as loyal an uncle as had ever been born. Amanda had shown up on his Chicago doorstep three days after her high school graduation and never looked back. Nor had her parents ever hinted they wanted her to.

He'd welcomed her, adjusted his playboy lifestyle for her—though he needn't have. Her father might hate his brother's wild ways, but Amanda didn't give a damn who he slept with.

From day one, he had assumed a somewhat-parental role and harassed her into going to college. He'd made sure she went home for obligatory visits to see the folks. But he'd also shown her the world. Opened her eyes so wide, she hadn't wanted to close them even to sleep in those early days.

He'd given her the sky…and he'd given her wings to explore it by teaching her to fly. Eventually, he'd taken her in as a partner in his small regional charter airline and together they'd tripled its size and quadrupled its revenues.

Their success had come at a cost, of course. Neither of them had much of a social life. Even ladies' man Uncle Frank had been pretty much all-work-and-no-play since they'd expanded their territory up and down the east coast two years ago.

As for Amanda, aside from having a vivid fantasy life, when she wasn't in flight, she was as boring as a single twenty-nine-year-old could be. Evidence of that was her disappointment at not getting to spend a day with a group of old ladies who bitched about everything from their lazy kids to the hair growing out of their husbands' ears. Well, except Mrs. Rush, who sharply reminded her friends to be thankful for their husbands' ear hair while they still had husbandly ear hair to be thankful for.

"Well, so much for a fun Halloween," she said with a sigh.

"Honey, if sitting in a plane listening to a bunch of rich old ladies kvetch about their latest collagen injections is the only thing you've got to look forward to…"

"I know, I know." It did sound pathetic. And one of these days, she really needed to do something about that. Get working on a real social life again, rather than throwing herself into her job fourteen hours a day, and spending the other ten thinking about all the things she would do if she had the time.

Picturing those things, even.

She closed her eyes, willing that thought away. Her fantasy life might be a rich and vivid one. But it was definitely not suitable for work hours.

Problem was, ever since she'd realized just how dangerous she was to men's hearts, she really hadn't felt like going after their bodies.

Her last relationship had ended badly. Very badly. And she still hadn't quite gotten over the regret of it.

"What a shame. Mrs. Rush would have loved your costume."

"Oh, God, don't remind me," Amanda said with a groan.

It was for the benefit of the ladies that she'd worn it. Mrs. Rush had ordered her to let loose on this one holiday trip.

Gulping, Amanda glanced around, hoping nobody was close enough to see her getup. She needed to dart up into the plane and change because while the old-fashioned outfit would have made her passengers cackle with glee, she didn't particularly want to be seen by any of the workers or baggage handlers on the tarmac. Not to mention the fact that, even though the weather was great, it *was* October and she was freezing her butt off.

The Clear-Blue uniform she usually wore was tailored and businesslike, no-nonsense. Navy blue pants, crisp white blouse, meant to inspire confidence and get the customer to forget their pilot was only in her late twenties. Most customers liked that. However, the older women in the senior-gal group always harassed Amanda about her fashion sense. They insisted she would be one hot tamale if she'd lose the man-clothes and get girly.

She glanced down at herself again and had to smile. You couldn't get much more girly than this ancient stewardess costume, complete with white patent-leather go-go boots and hot pants that clung to her butt and skimmed the tops of her thighs.

She looked like she'd stepped out of a 1972 commercial for Southwest Airlines.

As costumes went, it wasn't bad, if she did say so herself. Shopping for vintage clothes on eBay, she'd truly lucked out. The psychedelic blouse was a bit tight, even though she wasn't especially blessed in the boob department, and she couldn't button the polyester vest that went over it. But the satiny short-shorts fit perfectly, and the boots were so kick-ass she knew she would have to wear them again without the costume.

"Now, before you go worrying that your day is a total wash," Ginny said, sounding businesslike again, "I wanted to let you know that the trip was not in vain. I've got you a paying passenger back to Chicago who'll make it worth your while."

"Seriously? A sudden passenger from Pittsburgh, on a Saturday?" she asked. This wasn't exactly a hotbed destination like Orlando or Hartsfield International. Mrs. Rush was the only customer they picked up regularly in this part of Pennsylvania and most business types didn't charter flights on weekends.

"Yes. When Mrs. Rush called to cancel, she told me a local businessman needed a last-minute ride to Chicago. She put him in touch with us, hoping you could help him. I told him you were there and would have no problem bringing him back with you."

Perfect. A paying gig, and she could make it home in time to attend her best friend Jazz's annual Halloween party.

Then she reconsidered. Honestly, it was far more likely she would end up staying home, devouring a bag of Dots and Tootsie Rolls while watching old horror films on AMC. Because Jazz—Jocelyn Wilkes, their lead mechanic at Clear-Blue and the closest friend Amanda had ever had—was a wild one whose parties always got crashed and sometimes got raided. Amanda just wasn't in the mood for a big, wild house party with a ton of strangers.

Being honest, she'd much prefer a small, wild bedroom one—with only two guests. It was just too bad for her that, lately, the only guest in her bedroom had come with batteries and a scarily illustrated instruction manual written in Korean.

"Manda? Everything okay?"

"Absolutely," she said, shaking the crazy thoughts out of her head. "Glad I get to earn my keep today."

Ginny laughed softly into the phone. "You earn your keep every day, kiddo. I don't know what Frank would do without you."

"The feeling is most definitely mutual."

She meant that. Amanda hated to even think of what her life might be like if she hadn't escaped the small, closed-in, claustrophobic world she'd lived in with the family who had so disapproved of her and tried so hard to change her.

She had about as much in common with her cold, repressed parents and her completely subservient sister as she did with…well, with the swinging 1970s flower-power stewardess who'd probably once worn this uniform. When she'd stood in line to get doused in the gene pool, she'd gotten far more of her uncle Frank's reckless, free-wheeling, never-can-stand-to-be-tied-down genes than her parents' staid, conservative ones.

She had several exes who would testify to that. One still drunk-dialed her occasionally just to remind her she'd broken his heart. *Yeah. Thanks. Good to know.*

Even that, though, was better than thinking about the last guy she'd gotten involved with. He'd fallen in love. She'd fallen in "this is better than sleeping alone." Upon figuring that out, he'd tried to *make* her feel something more by staging a bogus overdose. She'd been terrified, stricken with guilt—and then, when he'd admitted what he'd done and *why,* absolutely furious rather than sympathetic.

Making things worse, he'd had the nerve to paint her as the bad guy. Her ears still rang with his accusations about just what a cold, heartless bitch she was.

Better cold and heartless than a lying, manipulative psycho. But it was also better to stay alone than to risk getting tangled up with another one.

So her Korean vibrator it was.

Some people were meant for commitment, family, all that stuff. Some, like her uncle Frank, weren't. Amanda was just like him; everybody said so. Including Uncle Frank.

"You'd better go. Your passenger should be there soon."

"Yeah. I definitely need to change my clothes before some groovy, foxy guy asks me if I want to go get high and make love not war at the peace rally," Amanda replied.

"Please don't on my account."

That hadn't come from Ginny.

Amanda froze, the phone against her face. It took a second to process, but her brain finally caught up with her ears and she realized she had indeed heard a strange voice.

It had been male. Deep, husky. And close.

"I gotta go," she muttered into the phone, sliding it closed before Ginny could respond.

Then she shifted her eyes, spying a pair of men's shoes not two feet from where she stood in the shadow of the Lear. Inside those shoes was a man wearing dark gray pants. Wearing them nicely, she had to acknowledge when she lifted her gaze and saw the long legs, the lean hips, the flat stomach.

Damn, he was well-made. Her throat tightened, her mouth going dry. She forced herself to swallow and kept on looking.

White dress shirt, unbuttoned at the strong throat. Thick arms flexing against the fabric that confined them. Broad shoulders, one of which was draped with a slung-over suit jacket that hung loosely from his masculine fingers.

Then the face. Oh, what a face. Square-jawed, hollow-cheeked. His brow was high, his golden-brown hair blown back by the light autumn breeze tunneling beneath the plane. And he had an unbelievably great mouth curved into a smile. A wide one that hinted at unspilled laughter lurking behind those sensual lips. She suspected that behind his dark sunglasses, his eyes were laughing, too.

Laughing at *her.*

Wonderful. One of the most handsome men she had ever seen in her entire life had just heard her muttering about groovy dudes and free love. All while she looked like Marcia Brady before a big cheerleading tryout.

"Guess I should have worn my bell-bottoms and tie-dyed, peace-sign shirt," he said.

She feigned a disapproving frown. "Your hair's much too short, and not nearly stringy enough." Tsking, she added, "And no mustache?"

The sexy smile was companion to a sexy laugh. Double trouble, either way you sliced it. "I hate to admit it, but I'm not a Bob Dylan fan, either. I guess I really can't turn on, tune in and drop out."

"What a drag! If you say you can't play 'Blowin' in the Wind' on the guitar, I'm afraid I'm going to have to shove you into the engines of that 747 over there."

He held both hands up, palms out. "Peace! I really do dig the threads, sister," he said. "They're pretty groovalicious."

"Ooh, how very Austin Powers of you."

Wincing as if she'd hit him, he muttered, "Do chicks really go for dudes with bear pelts on their chests?"

"Not this one," she admitted with a laugh, liking this stranger already, despite her initial embarrassment. "Obviously, if you own a calendar, you know today's Halloween."

"Yeah, I heard that somewhere. That could explain why I passed a group of Hannah Montanas and SpongeBobs walking down the street on my way here."

"I don't know whether to be more sad that kids have to trick-or-treat in the daytime, or that you know who Hannah Montana and SpongeBob are."

"Nieces and nephews," he explained.

The affectionate way he said the words made her suspect he liked kids, which usually indicated a good nature. One point for the hot guy.

Correction, one *more* point for the hot guy. He'd already scored about a million for being so damned hot.

She also noted that he'd said nieces and nephews…not kids of his own. *Single?*

He glanced around at the other small planes nearby, and the few airport employees scurrying around doing the luggage-shuffle waltz. "So, nobody else got the invite to the costume party?"

Just her. Wasn't she the lucky one? "I was supposed to be picking up a regular passenger and she made me promise to dress up. This is definitely not my usual workplace attire."

"Rats. Here I was thinking I'd suddenly been let in the super-secret club. The *true* reason charter flights are so popular. You're saying it really *is* just to miss the long lines at security, and have some travel flexibility? It's not the hot pants and go-go boots?"

She shook her head. "'Fraid not. But don't forget, you also get to drink more than a half-cup of warm Coke and eat more than four pretzels."

"Well, okay then, we're on."

Amanda suddenly sighed, acknowledging what she'd managed to overlook. For just a minute or two, she had been able to convince herself that some sexy, passing stranger had noticed her and come over.

Passing by on a private, secured tarmac? Don't think so.

He wasn't some random passerby, she just knew it.

"Oh, hell. You're my passenger."

"If you're headed for Chicago, I think I am." He stuck out his hand. "Reese Campbell."

Cursing Mrs. Rush and Halloween and that stupid vintage clothing store on eBay, she put her hand in his. "Amanda Bauer."

Their first touch brought a flush of warmth, a flash of pleasure that was unexpected and a little surprising. The handshake lasted a second too long, was perhaps a hint more than a casual greeting among strangers. And while the exchange was entirely appropriate, she suddenly found herself thinking of all the touches she hadn't had for so long, all the *in*appropriate ways that strong, masculine hand could slide over her body.

Instant lust. It was real. Who knew?

She stared at him, trying to see the eyes behind the sunglasses, wondering if they had darkened with immediate interest the way hers probably had. Wondering what she might do about it if he returned that interest.

Get a grip.

Amanda regretfully tugged her hand away, pushing it down to her side and sliding it over her satin-covered hip. Her fingertips quivered as they brushed against the bare skin of her upper thigh and she suspected her palms were damp.

Forcing herself to take a deep, calming breath, she managed a smile. "Well, thanks for choosing Clear-Blue Air. We…"

"Love to fly, and it shows?"

It took her a second, then she placed the old Delta slogan. Her smile faded. The guy was way too hot to also be quick-witted and flirtatious. She could handle one at a time—it just became a little more distracting when they were all wrapped up in one extremely sexy package.

You can handle him. No sweat. Just stay professional.

Professional. While she was dressed for a love-in with the local beatnik crowd and this guy was both gorgeous and freaking adorable. *Right.*

"It'll be a quick trip," she said, gesturing toward the steps and moving back so he could ascend them ahead of her.

No way was she going in first, not with the length of the damn hot pants. Her cheeks were pretty well covered as long as she remained still. If she walked up the steps with him behind her, however, all bets would be off. He'd get an eyeful, and it wouldn't be of London, *or* France. Because the stupid shorts were too form-fitting to wear even the most skimpy of underpants, unless they were ass-flossers, which she didn't even own.

"Wait," he said, pausing on the bottom step. "Aren't you going to say 'Fly me' or at least 'Welcome aboard'?"

She didn't. The softly muttered word that came out of her mouth was a lot less welcoming. And had fewer letters—four to be precise.

He shook his head and tsked. "Not exactly the friendly skies. Haven't caught the spirit yet this morning?"

"Make one more airline slogan crack and you'll be walking to Chicago," she said.

He nodded once, then pushed his sunglasses up onto the top of his tousled hair. The move revealed blue eyes that matched the sky above. And yeah. They were twinkling. Damn it.

"Understood. Just, uh, promise me you'll say 'Coffee, tea, or me' at least once, okay? Please?"

Amanda tried to glare, but that twinkle sucked the annoyance right out of her. Something irrepressible deep inside made her smirk and order, "Stop flirting. Start traveling."

He immediately got the vague Southwest Airlines reference. "Gotcha." With a grin, he added, "I'm starting to suspect I'm going to experience something pretty special in the air."

She groaned. "You do realize you're a total nerd for knowing all these old slogans."

The insult bounced right off him. "Nerd, huh?" Then he threw his head back and laughed. Innate good humor flowed off this sexy man who, though dressed like a businessman, wasn't like anyone she'd ever shuttled before. "Something tells me this is going to be a trip I won't soon forget," he said, something warm and knowing appearing in those deep blue eyes.

She could only draw in a slow breath as he climbed into the plane, thinking about that laughter and that twinkle, wondering why both of them made her insides all soft. As she watched her passenger disappear into the small jet, she also had to wonder about the trip she was about to take.

Coffee and tea they had, and he was welcome to them. But her? Well, she'd never even considered making a move on a customer before. Talk about unprofessional. Even the original hound dog himself Uncle Frank would kill her. He swore he never mixed business with pleasure.

And yet, how often was it that she actually met someone new, someone sexy and funny and entertaining? Considering her moratorium on anything that resembled dating, maybe a one-night stand with somebody from out of town, somebody she would never see again, was the perfect way to go.

Something inside her suddenly wanted to take a chance, to be a little outrageous. Maybe it was the playful, dangerous holiday—she'd always loved Halloween. It could have been the fortuitous change in passengers from wild old ladies to supremely sexy young man. Maybe it was the costume. The damned hot pants were hugging her open-and-alert-and-ready-for-business sex, the seam doing indecent things to her suddenly throbbing girl bits.

How long since she had done indecent things—or decent ones, for that matter—with a sexy man? Not since before they'd thrown all their energies into expanding Clear-Blue Air, at least. She hadn't had time for a lunch date, much less anything like the lust-fests she'd enjoyed in her younger years. The kind that lasted for entire weekends and involved not leaving a bed except to grab some sort of sensuous food that could be smeared onto—and eaten off of—someone else's hot, naked, sweat-tinged body.

She closed her eyes, her hand clenching tight on the railing. Her heart fluttered in her chest and she tried to make herself move. But she couldn't—not climbing up, but not backing away, either. Not physically, and not in her head.

Was she really considering this? God, she hadn't even looked at Reese Campbell's left hand to make sure he was available. She had no idea if he was actually attracted to her or just an irrepressible flirt. Yet something inside was telling her to take a shot with this complete stranger.

It was crazy, something she'd never considered. Yet right now, at this moment, she was definitely considering it. If he was available…could she do it? Seduce a stranger? Have an anonymous fling with a random man, like something out of a blue movie on late-night cable?

She didn't know, but it sounded good. Given the current craziness of her life—her work schedule, travel, commitment to her uncle and his company, plus her aversion to anything that even resembled "settling down" as she'd always known it, this whole fling idea sounded *damn* good.

The trip to Chicago was a short one, so she had to decide quickly. Really, though, she suspected the decision was already made. And as she put her foot on the bottom step and began to climb up, Amanda suddenly had the feeling she was about to embark on the ride of her life.

chapter two

PITTSBURGH to Chicago was a short, easy trip even on a bad day. Fortunately, aside from the fact that he was taking his first flight in a vehicle that didn't look much bigger than his SUV, today was shaping up to be a very good one. And he wasn't just thinking about the weather, which was cool, crisp and clear.

As they took off, Reese went over the situation again in his mind. One hour in the air—that was good. For a mere sixty minutes, he could trick his brain into believing he wasn't *really* sitting inside an oversize tin can, hurtling across a couple of states.

After that, he faced a short taxi ride to the newest location of a brew-pub chain owned by a wealthy Chicago family, the Braddocks. They had recently agreed to offer Campbell's Lager as a house beer in a couple of their bars. It was a foot in the door, and Reese hoped to grow the account and get them to expand their order to include every one of their establishments. So he couldn't refuse when he got a call from old Mr. Braddock himself this morning, asking him to come to put in an appearance at tonight's opening.

He wouldn't have to stay long—just had to shake a few hands and say a few thank-yous. He should be in and out in under an hour.

And after that...what?

He had intended to hop a commercial flight back to Pittsburgh tonight. The trip had been too impromptu to fly that way this afternoon, but there was one regional jet leaving at 10:00 p.m. that he could undoubtedly find a seat on. If he wanted to.

But ever since he had walked across the tarmac toward the small private plane and seen the woman standing at the base of the steps, he hadn't wanted to. Because one look at her and he'd been interested. One word and he'd been intrigued. And one brief conversation and he'd been utterly hooked.

It wasn't just that she was beautiful. He knew better than to think beauty was ever more than a surface pleasantry. Besides, he was no chauvinist. He had four sisters, three of them unmarried and living at home, the fourth a divorced single mom. Since his brother was only in his early teens, Reese bore the full brunt of female judgment against his sex. The only other adult male in close proximity was Ralph, his black lab, who had lost his claim to maleness at the hands of a ruthless vet when he was just six months old. A female vet.

So, yeah, Reese knew better than to ever judge a woman solely on appearance.

Amanda Bauer's amazing body, her thick reddish-brown hair that hung past her shoulders and her damn-near-perfect face might have stilled his heart for a moment or two. But her smile, her husky voice, the shininess of her green eyes and the snappy humor had brought about the full stop.

So what are you going to do about it?

He needed to decide. And he now had only about forty-five minutes in which to do it.

In any other situation—if they'd met at a business meeting or a local bar—he might not have considered it. He'd been living in a fishbowl for the past two years, with his every move analyzed and dissected by his family. Bringing a woman into the picture was just inviting the kind of microscopic commentary he did not want.

But this was totally different. His pilot was someone he'd never seen before and, after today, probably would never see again. The thought made him suddenly wonder about the ways in which they could spend that day.

Fortunately, thinking about all those things had distracted him from the whole terrifying takeoff business. They'd chatted while she'd prepared for flight, but since the minute the tires had started rolling down the runway, Reese's throat had been too tight to push any words out.

He forced himself to swallow. "So, a full-time pilot, huh?" he asked, knowing the question was an inane one. But it was better than the silence that had fallen between them while she'd been occupied getting them up into the air.

It also beat looking out the window at either the ground, which was getting farther away by the minute, or the wing of the plane, which looked far too small to be the only thing keeping him from a twenty-thousand-foot crash back to mother earth.

He looked away.

"Yep."

"Must be pretty interesting."

"It beats being a kindergarten teacher, which was what my folks wanted me to do."

He barked a laugh. Her. A kindergarten teacher. Right. In his mental list of other careers this woman could have, being a sedate, demure teacher wasn't even in the top gajillion.

Actress. Seductive spy. Rock star. Designer. Sex goddess. Yeah, those he could see. But definitely not teacher.

She glanced back, one brow up, though her tiny smile told him she wasn't truly offended. Reese sat in the first passenger seat on the opposite side of the cabin and their stares locked for just a moment before she faced forward again. "What? You think I couldn't be a teacher?"

"Uh-uh." He quickly held up a defensive hand. "Not that I don't think you're smart enough. You just don't seem the type who'd like working with children."

She did, however, seem the type to be fabulous at the physical act that led to children. Not that he was going to say that to a woman he'd known for less than an hour.

That'd take two, minimum.

"I'm good with kids, I'll have you know," she insisted. "My friends' and cousins' kids love me."

He didn't doubt it. "Because you bring them cool stuff from your travels and you fly an airplane?"

She shrugged, not denying it. Nor did she turn around, keeping her eyes on the sky ahead of her. Which was good. He much preferred his pilot to be on the lookout for any random high-flying helicopters or low-flying space shuttles.

"I'm not knocking it," he said. "I'm the king of doling out loud toys to my sister's kids. I know the gifts will drive her crazy long after I'm gone."

She laughed, low and long, as if reminiscing at some personal memory. Amanda Bauer's warm chuckle seemed to ride across the air inside the cabin and brush against him like a soft breeze on a summer day. He could almost feel it.

Reese shifted in his seat, trying to keep focused on small talk and chitchat. Not on how much he wanted to feel her laughter against his lips so he could inhale the very air she breathed.

"Believe it or not, I think I'd have been a hell of a good teacher."

"Uh-huh. I can hear five-year-old Brittany coming home to tell Mommy she had a hell of a good time learning her ABCs that day."

She still didn't turn around. She didn't have to. Her reaction was made plain by the casual lift of her right hand and the quick flash of her middle finger.

"Hey, both hands on the steering wheel, lady," he said, his shoulders shaking in amusement. His sexy, private pilot had just flipped him off. Damn, he liked this woman. He took no offense. In fact, he was more grateful than anything else that she had already grown so comfortable with him.

It was strange, since they'd just met, but he felt the same way. Oh, not with the fact that he was in a tiny plane far above the ground…but with her. Like he could say just about anything and it would roll off her back. She had such an easygoing way about her. It went well with the adventurous spirit that put her in the cockpit of a plane wearing go-go boots and booty shorts.

Personally, he had the feeling they were going to get along tremendously. He felt more relaxed with her than he had with anyone—including just himself—in months.

Except for the whole being-in-a-small-plane thing. Which he was trying to forget.

"Okay, I apologize," he said. "I'm sure you would have been great. But I think any mother with a brain cell in her head would insist her kid be moved out of your class before the father attended his first parent-teacher conference."

She didn't respond. But the middle finger didn't come up, either.

"Now, back to the subject. Your job. I guess you like to fly, huh?"

Before she could answer, the plane rose suddenly, then dropped hard, though not far, just like a kite being lifted and gently tossed by an unexpected gust. "Jesus…"

"Don't worry, it was just an air pocket. It's completely normal. In a jet this size, we just feel the turbulence a bit more than you're used to."

Why one little pocket of air was any different than the rest of the big, vast atmosphere, he had no idea. He just knew he didn't like it. "Okay, uh, stay away from those pockets, would you please?"

"Sure," she said with a snort and, though he couldn't see it, probably an eye roll. "I'll just watch for the yellow hazard signs and steer around them."

"Your empathy would have been a real help in a job teaching young children."

Instead of being insulted, she snickered, a cute, self-deprecating sound. "Sorry." Then, though she didn't turn completely around, her eyes shifted slightly. Enough to catch a glimpse at his probably tense face. "I like flying better than you, I take it?"

"It's not my favorite thing to do."

"And I bet it's even worse when you're not tucked inside the belly of a huge 747, trying not to catch the mood of all the other nervous flyers who are envisioning the worst?"

"Exactly."

She nodded once, then offered, "Doesn't it help to think something smaller would be easier to keep aloft than some big, monstrous commercial airliner? Just like a feather on the breeze?"

"No," he admitted. "Actually, all I keep thinking about is the whole man/wings thing."

"Relax. I haven't crashed in, oh, a good month at least."

Not appreciating the joke, he stared, his eyes narrowed. "My luck, I get the comedian in hot pants for the pilot."

"Sorry. Just figured if you laugh a little, you might relax."

"Say something that's actually funny and I might." Though, he doubted it. A tranquilizer or a shot of gin might help him calm down. Or this woman's hands. Then again, if this woman's hands ever did land on him, *calm* almost certainly would not describe his mood.

"Why don't you try closing your eyes and just pretending you're somewhere else?"

"Pretend?"

"You know. Fantasize." Her voice melodic, as if she were a hypnotist, she provided a fantasy. "You're in a safe, solid car driving up a mountain pass toward a beautiful old hotel."

"Okay, this isn't helping. I'm thinking Jack Nicholson heading toward that hotel in *The Shining*."

She huffed out a breath. "It's an exclusive ski lodge, glamorous, not haunted. Around you is nothing but pristine, white snow, blue sky, clear air."

"Guys with axes…"

"Don't make me come back there!"

"Okay, okay," he said with a grimace.

Reese closed his eyes and tried to see it. He really did. But he could conjure up no mountain pass. No car. No ski lodge.

A curvy snow-bunny wearing a fluffy hat, skimpy shorts and skis…that was about as close as he could get.

He sighed. Not necessarily because it was a bad thing, but because the vision was so damn hot, it had him a little dizzy.

"Don't use your imagination much, I guess. I should have known."

His eyes flew open. "I have an imagination."

"Uh-huh. Let me guess, most of the time what you imagine is getting through the next sales meeting or closing some big business deal."

Reese shifted a little, not answering. Up until he'd walked up to her on the tarmac, that had been pretty accurate. Since then, though, he'd been imagining a few other things. But to tell her she was wrong meant to spill those thoughts, which he wasn't about to do—again, at least not after a one-hour acquaintance.

Though, two was looking better all the time.

The plane bounced again, quickly, up and down. Reese's stomach bounced with it—at least, on the way up. It didn't go all the way down and settle back into place.

He felt the blood drain from his cheeks. "I think we just ran over a moose. Or a lost skier."

"There's a small fridge between the seats. You look like you could use a drink." She chuckled. "Or a Valium."

"Wow. That is first-class service."

"Kidding."

"Yeah. I figured that," he said, ignoring the offer. He didn't need a drink. He just needed a distraction.

Fortunately, one of the sexiest ones he had ever seen was sitting just a few feet away. As long as he didn't humiliate himself by losing his lunch on the floor of her pristine jet, he fully intended to enjoy spending this flight in her company.

And maybe more than that.

After all, why shouldn't he? He already liked her sense of humor, the competent way she handled the controls, the low laughter. There was a lot to like about this woman beyond her killer legs. Not to mention the rest of the physical package. She was quick and witty, sharp, smart. Lots to like. Lots to want.

And he could like her, want her…maybe even have her, without any of the complications that would arise if he were within fifty miles of home. There, he never felt free to do something for no other reason than the fact that he wanted to. The idea of heaving aside all that responsibility for a little while, of grabbing on to a good thing and enjoying the hell out of it just because he *could,* was incredibly appealing.

"Is this your first time chartering?" she asked.

The plane jiggled the tiniest bit and he instinctively clutched the armrests. "That obvious, huh?"

"You have that first-timers glow."

Huh. Did vampires glow? Because he figured his face was probably as white as one.

"Must be a pretty important trip."

He shook his head. "You'd think so, right? But I'm actually headed to a Halloween party."

She glanced over her shoulder in surprise. Reese waved toward the front, "Keep your eyes on the road, please."

"Don't worry. I'm not about to drive into the back of a slow-moving semi doing fifty during rush hour."

He'd just be happy if she didn't drive into the back of a slow-flying goose. A big Canadian one.

Oh, God, one of those had brought down a huge airliner, hadn't it?

Stop thinking about it.

Right. He had much better things to think about. The way his family business was booming under his management, even in this bad economy. The success of their first nationwide marketing campaign. The house he'd just finished remodeling and considered his private fortress in the middle of his crazy world. The sexy pilot in hot pants whom he now kept picturing on skis, and whose downhill slopes he would very much like to explore. Much better things.

"So, Halloween party, huh?" she said. "If this is you dressing up, what do you regularly look like? I mean, in your real life, are you a biker-dude who usually wears black leather and chains? Only for the occasion, you're dressing up as a boring businessman?"

Reese leaned forward, dropping his elbows onto his knees, and stared at the back of her silky-haired head. "Ahem. Boring?"

"It was a joke. I was just trying to distract you."

Maybe. Or maybe she really did think he looked boring.

He should have felt a little insulted. Reese had been fending off most of the single women in his small hometown since his high school days. *Most* of them. He definitely hadn't fended off all, at least not before two years ago when his life had gotten so out of whack. And he had enjoyed his share of discreet flings through the years. Could've had enough to qualify as a half-dozen guys' shares if he'd felt like it. His sisters were forever cackling over some of the ways in which the hungry local females tried to get his attention.

True, the females in question were no longer the twentysomething party girls who'd gone through his revolving bedroom door a few years ago. They were now career women who saw the steady businessman with a nice income and a reputation as being a great guy who stepped up for his family. But there were still quite a few of them and they definitely wouldn't say no if he *ever* started asking again.

He wasn't the hottest dude in the known universe, and he suspected the money that flowed from his family's successful brewery was partially responsible for the attention. But nobody had ever called him boring before, that was for sure.

Damn, that was harsh.

And damn, she was right. To hell with all the mental pumping about how great business was, and how many women had made plays for him. His personal life was *exactly* what this beautiful woman imagined it to be.

Boring.

Boiled in mediocrity and steeped in sameness, he'd allowed himself to disappear into a daily life that wasn't ever what he'd imagined for himself. Ennui had grabbed him by the lapels of his stuffy suit and forced him to remain in his small box of family, business, responsibility. He hadn't even tried to step outside that box in a long time.

Maybe it was time. Maybe he should heed his great-aunt Jean's advice: live, go a little wild, have an adventure.

It had sounded crazy, impossible a few weeks ago when she'd burst into his office. Now? Not so much. Especially because he'd suddenly found someone he wanted to go a little wild with.

There was, of course, one obstacle.

"Are you single?" he asked, direct and to the point.

Her shoulders stiffened the tiniest bit and she hesitated.

Then, with a small, shaky exhalation he could hear from back here—as if she'd made some decision—she nodded once.

"Yes. Completely unattached. You?"

"The same."

He didn't give it any more thought. She might have thrown the word *boring* at him, but he had seen the look of interest in her eyes before they'd gotten aboard the plane. The tiny hitch in her breath just now, and the sudden tension that had her curvy body sitting so stiffly in her seat told him her thoughts had gone in the same direction as his.

Have an adventure.

Sounded like a good idea to him.

"So how do you like Halloween parties?"

AMANDA HAD TO ADMIT IT…Reese Campbell made one hot-as-blazes 1970s-era airline pilot. Eyeing him from the other side of the backseat of the taxicab, she wondered what strange whim of fortune had sent such a sexy, charming, single man across her path right when she needed one most.

And she definitely needed one. It had been a long time since she'd felt so sure of herself as a woman, so in tune to the sensations coursing through her body. All the late-night blue movies that had played in her mind lately, replacing any semblance of a real love life, had been mere placeholders, no substitute for the great sex she wasn't having.

Those mental movies were going to have a new leading

man in them after tonight. Because she had the feeling that before the night was over, she was going to be saying, "Welcome aboard," and "Fly me," and meaning *exactly* what those old ad execs had wanted passengers to think the sexy stewardesses meant.

She wanted Reese. He wanted her. It was a wild, reckless Halloween night and they were both single and interested.

So why not?

Okay, so she'd never done the one-night-stand-with-an-utter-stranger thing. But her best friend, Jazz, had. She hadn't ended up with a scarlet *A* branded on her chest or any nasty diseases, nor had she needed therapy to get rid of some nonexistent guilt.

Considering she sometimes thought Jazz was the only woman her age in the world who was the least bit like her, or who completely understood her, she didn't figure the example was a bad one to follow.

Besides, Amanda had indulged in short-term affairs before. In fact, considering how badly her last few relationships had ended, a one-night stand sounded just about perfect.

She liked sex. She liked it a lot. This time, she'd just be having it without the two requisite dates—drinks, then dinner—first. Or the worrying about a phone call the next day. Reese would go back to his life in Pittsburgh, she'd stay here, and they'd both smile whenever they thought of the night they'd gotten a little down-and-dirty with a stranger in Chicago.

Best of all…there'd be no crazy fake suicide attempts.

No drunk-dialing complaints that she was a feckless bitch who enjoyed breaking guys' hearts. And Reese wouldn't become the newest member of the Facebook group "Dumped by Amanda Bauer," which had actually been set up by a guy she'd dated during her junior year of college.

God, men could be such fricking babies.

Back to the subject: one-night stand.

Okay. Sounded good. She just had to feel her way around to make sure Reese was on board with it. Judging by the way he'd been devouring her with his eyes since the minute they'd met, she had a feeling that was a big, fat yeah.

"How in God's name did they breathe in these things?" he muttered as he tugged at the too-tight collar of his shirt. "I can't believe there weren't crashes due to lack of oxygen in the pilots' brains."

"It's only a suit, for heaven's sake," she said, rolling her eyes at the typical male grumbling. "It just happens to be too small for you."

They'd found the antique uniform Reese was using as a costume at the airport after landing in Chicago. It hadn't been difficult. Lots of the companies at O'Hare had been around for decades, and Amanda had friends at just about all of them. A few inquiries had put her in the office of a guy who'd worked as a baggage handler since the days when there'd been a Pan in front of American. He'd known where lots of interesting old stuff was kept and had put an only-slightly-musty uniform, complete with jaunty pilot's cap, in her hands within an hour of landing.

It was too tight across Reese Campbell's broad shoulders, but loose around the lean hips and tight buns. Whoever Captain Reliable from the 1970s had been, he definitely hadn't had Reese's mouthwatering build.

"You're going to rip it," she said as he continued to tug. "The thing is flimsy enough."

Brushing his hands away, Amanda reached up to his strong throat, her fingers brushing against the warm, supple skin. A low, deep breath eased in through her nearly closed lips and she suddenly felt a little light-headed. There was such unexpected strength in him, tone and musculature more suited to an athlete than to the boring businessman she'd accused him of being.

Not that she'd meant it. Not at all. The clothes he'd been wearing might have been conservative, but the look in those eyes, the sexy twist to his lips, the suggestive tone of his conversation…none of those things had indicated anything but exciting, intriguing male.

A thin sheen of sweat moistened the throat where the shirt had cut into the cords of muscle. She had to suck her bottom lip into her mouth just to make sure she didn't do something crazy like lean closer and taste that moisture, sample that skin. She ignored the sudden mental command to just *do* it, focusing instead on unfastening the top button and loosening his tie.

Reese said nothing, just stared at her, his expression hard to read in the low lighting of the cab.

When she was finished, she dropped her hands to her lap, twisting her fingers together on top of her long winter coat. It didn't quite match the costume, but despite the mild autumn they'd been having, it had become freaking cold out when the sun went down. She honestly didn't know how the hippest 1970s chicks had stood it.

"So, this client of yours, he's not going to mind you showing up with a…" She considered her words, decided against saying *date* and concluded, "…guest?"

"It's a pub," Reese replied, his sensual lips curving up a little at the corners. "I think they can handle one extra."

"That's some job you've got, *having* to go to pubs for Halloween parties," she said, trying to think about something other than his mouth. How much she wanted that mouth. And *where* she wanted that mouth.

"I don't think it quite stacks up to yours—having to jet off to the Caribbean to ferry the rich around to their sinfully expensive vacations."

"I usually ferry obnoxious, spoiled executives to their sinfully expensive corporate retreats."

He tsked. "I'm sure they consider it bailout money well spent." He hesitated for a split second, then added, "So I guess I should be glad you called me boring rather than obnoxious and spoiled?"

"Not obnoxious," she immediately replied.

A brow went up. "Spoiled?"

Amanda tapped her fingertip on her chin, pretending to think about it. She didn't suspect this man was spoiled in the way some of her clients were. He didn't come off as rich, used to everyone bowing down before him at the first request. And he definitely wasn't the kind of guy who expected a woman to spread her legs at the first mention of something sparkly.

Yeah, she'd met a bunch of those guys. Amanda had always been left wondering what kind of woman would trade a night beneath a sweating, out-of-shape, pasty old man for a pair of diamond earrings.

Reese wasn't like those men, not physically, not mentally. She had the feeling he was successful but he was not financially spoiled.

Spoiled in other ways? Maybe. Something about his self-confidence, his half smile when he'd asked if she was single, told her he was used to getting what he wanted when it came to women. The way he sat just a few inches away—casual and comfortable when she, herself, was tingling with excitement at his nearness—said he was sure of what he wanted to happen and his ability to make it happen.

Sexually confident, yeah. *But spoiled?* No. The guy who'd looked like he was going to lose his lunch during the flight had been adorably sexy and vulnerable. Not one creepy, jerky, I'm-good-and-I-know-it thing about him.

"Not spoiled," she admitted.

"I should hope not. As the oldest of six kids, I learned at a very young age not to count on anything I owned remaining unbroken, unborrowed or unlost."

"Six kids!" The very idea horrified her. One sibling—one perfect, good, just-like-their-parents sibling who did exactly what was expected of her and never stepped off the approved path—was quite enough for Amanda, thank you very much.

"My God. Six. I can't even imagine it," she muttered.

"Oh yeah." A small chuckle emerged from his mouth as he added, "It was never *boring*."

Amanda nibbled her bottom lip before replying, a bit sheepishly, "Sorry I said that earlier. I was just trying to get you to relax."

Reese might dress the part of executive, but no man with those looks, that mouth and that gleam of interest in his eyes could possibly be called boring.

"So how's that strategy work for you?"

Confused, she asked, "What strategy?"

"Throwing insults at guys to relax them. Working out okay?"

Hearing the laughter in his tone—knowing he was laughing at himself, too—she had to admit, she liked Reese Campbell.

Wanted him. Liked him. Two points checked off her mental I'm-no-slut-and-don't-have-one-night-stands list.

Tonight was looking better by the minute.

"It worked on me, by the way." He leaned back farther in the seat, turning a little to stare at her. The dim reflections from streetlights they passed striped his handsome features in light and shadow. His breaths created tiny vapors in the chilly air that couldn't be banished by the car's weakly blowing heater. His voice was low, thick as he promised, "Because I'm looking forward to proving you wrong, Amanda."

Her heart skipped a beat. Just one. Something about the way her name rode softly, smoothly, on his exhalation, thrilled her. But she managed to keep her own breaths even. "Oh?"

He nodded. "There's nothing boring about what's going to happen between us."

A shiver of excitement coursed through her. It started with her lips, which quivered and parted, then moved down her entire body, which suddenly felt so much more…alert, somehow. The cold was more biting, the coat scratchy against her bare thighs. Her breasts tingled under the slick, polyester fabric of her blouse, the sensation sensual against her tight nipples.

Excitement had awakened every inch of her. It had been there, sparking right beneath the surface, for hours, since she'd first spied him on that tarmac back in Pittsburgh. Now the spark had caught and spread into a wildfire of interest and arousal, even though he hadn't touched her.

He knew. He had to know. The very air seemed thick with her sudden certainty of just how much she wanted the man. That certainty must have communicated itself to him with her shallow, audible breaths, the almost imperceptible way she leaned closer to him, irresistibly drawn to his heat. His size. His scent.

The big, strong hand sliding into her hair and cupping her head came as no surprise. She smiled in anticipation as he turned her face, tilted her chin up, then bent toward her. Their breaths mingled in the cold evening air and an almost tangible sizzle of excitement preceded the initial meeting of their lips.

A heartbeat later, the cold air disappeared. Nothing separated them at all.

Their first kiss was no tentative brush of lip on lip, nor

was there any hesitation, or even a gasp at the thrill of it. It was instead strong and wet. Sensuous. Confident and hungry, Reese parted his lips and slid his tongue against hers, tasting deeply, thoroughly, with enjoyment but not desperation.

Enjoyment could easily lead to desperation, she had no doubt. But despite the fact that they were in the backseat of a random cab, and had a one-man audience, courtesy of the rearview mirror, Amanda didn't care.

She wanted this. Craved it. So she didn't resist or even hesitate. Instead, she reacted with pure instinct, wrapping her arms around his neck. Tilting her head to the side, she silently invited him deeper. She moaned at the delights provided by his soft tongue, tasting him and exploring the inside of his mouth.

He was warm and solid, the spicy, masculine smell of him filling her head even as his heat against her body chased away any last remnants of chill.

Finally, he ended the kiss, slowly pulling away far enough to stare down into her eyes. She saw want there. And something else—excitement. Pleasure.

His lips quirked. And she saw even more: self-confidence. He confirmed it with a broad, satisfied smile.

"This is going to be so much fun."

"The party?"

He shook his head. "You and me."

chapter three

ALMOST from the moment they'd met, Reese had known he was heading in one direction: toward Amanda Bauer's bed.

They were going to have sex. Soon.

Reese knew it. Amanda knew it. The two of them were savoring that knowledge, building the anticipation as the evening wore on.

He'd done his bit for the business. Then, when old Mr. Braddock and his family had left for the night, he'd taken off his official Campbell's Lager title and gone back to being Reese, the man who'd picked up his sexy personal pilot.

Every look asked and answered the same question. Every smile was a seduction, each casual word a hidden code and every brief brush of hand on hand had become the most sensual foreplay. The way they intentionally tried *not* to touch more intimately increased the incredible tension, each non-caress promised unimaginable pleasure when they finally did come together.

Reese couldn't remember a time in his life when he'd been more excited by a woman. He just knew, as he stared at her across the crowded bar, that he'd never desired one more.

They hadn't kissed again since that brief encounter in the cab. They hadn't needed to. The want they were both feeling had been building by the minute.

When they'd danced, and his hand cupped her hip, or her thigh slid against his, the anticipation of how this night was going to end had nearly sent him out of his mind.

It had also sent him in search of something to try to calm down his body's heated reactions.

"So, are you supposed to be, like, the president or something?"

Reese didn't bother glancing over at the vapid little redhead dressed as a sex kitten—one of at least a dozen in the packed-to-bursting bar. She'd been trying to engage him in conversation for a full minute, but he was busy focusing on the dance floor. And frowning.

Because there, in the middle of a writhing crowd full of zombies and witches, mad scientists and vampy angels, was his sexy stewardess…dancing with another guy. He'd made his move when Reese had gone in search of a cold shower, but had had to make do with a cold glass of water.

"Or, like, a James Bond spy?"

Right. 'Cause James Bond always wore stupid navy blue uniforms and captain's wings on his lapel.

"You're way too hot to be an accountant or something."

"Pilot," he mumbled, barely paying attention. All his attention was focused on Amanda.

She looked better than any woman in the place as she shook her stuff with a man Reese recognized as one of Braddock's low-level employees. Steve something or other.

Reese had never had a problem with him—at least not until he'd realized Steve was seriously moving in on his date.

Steve hadn't been able to keep his covetous eyes off Amanda since the minute they'd arrived. Reese had figured the hands-off-she's-here-with-someone-else code would prevent the other man from actually doing anything about it. But when Steve's hand accidentally brushed Amanda's luscious ass for a second time, Reese realized he was either too drunk, or too hot for her, to even remember the code.

He tensed, ready to stride out there and do something that could cost his company a major customer, depending on how much Mr. Braddock liked Steve, even as he wondered what this crazy, unfamiliar jealousy was all about. But before he could do anything, the redheaded feline jiggled around in front of him, purring, "Dance with me?"

She didn't wait for an answer, just grabbed his arm and tugged him forward. He wasn't the first man she'd been gyrating up against tonight. An hour ago, she'd been wrapped around some guy dressed as a caveman, complete with fur loincloth. Captain Caveman was now groping a woman in a Little Red Riding Hood costume cut so low it barely covered her nipples.

Was there a law somewhere that said Halloween costumes for twenty-something-year-old women had to be
slutty? God, he hated parties like this. How could he
possibly have forgotten?

The only good thing about tonight's was the moment
he and Amanda had hit the dance floor themselves. After
he'd officially gone "off duty" they'd had a couple of
drinks. Drifting into the crowd, they'd danced not to the
loud music, but to the intimate, primal beat that had been
thrumming between them for hours.

He should never have left her alone. He should have just
lived with the hard-on, trusting that the crowd on the
dance floor would ensure nobody else knew he was dying
to rip his date's hot pants off and screw her into incoher-
ence.

"C'mon, it's a party, in case ya haven't noticed!"

The redhead was the one who wasn't too observant. She
obviously didn't notice that every ounce of his attention
was focused on another woman. Or else she just didn't care.
He figured that was it because she had dragged him to
within a few feet of Amanda and Steve, then proceeded
to pole dance against his thigh, rubbing so hard he could
feel the heat of her crotch through both sets of their
clothes.

Nasty.

Grabbing her shoulders to push her off, he grimaced
when she reached up and clasped onto his hand. Holding
tight, she then turned her head and tried to suck his thumb
into her mouth.

Repeat:You hate Halloween parties. And he was so far over

the bar scene, he honestly couldn't remember why he'd once enjoyed it.

Before he could disentangle himself, he glanced over and met Amanda's stare. Her eyes narrowed and hardened. Her pretty lips compressed as she saw the strange young woman practically riding him, the pouty suction-cup mouth trying to simulate a sex act on his thumb.

He knew how it must look—as if he was pulling the bimbo closer rather than pushing her away. Amanda obviously saw it that way, because she rolled her eyes and grimaced, her jaw rock-hard and her slim form straight and tense. Considering she had been fending off the groping hands of one of Reese's customers, she had every right to be angry as hell.

Reese was on the verge of just sacrificing his thumb to death-by-the-jaws-of-drunk-ho and pushing over to Amanda's side. He needed to explain, and to get her the hell out of there. But she suddenly changed the game. With a look that verged between anger and challenge, she wrapped her arms around Steve's neck. She slid closer to him, swaying slowly to the pounding music that had everyone else gyrating and bouncing. Steve all but stumbled as her beautiful mouth came close to his neck. Over the other man's shoulder, her stare sought out Reese's and she lifted one brow in a deliberate taunt.

Damn. She was tormenting him. His sexy pilot had claws much sharper than this intoxicated little cat who was still trying to use his thigh as a scratching post and, now, his neck as a lump of catnip.

He should have been annoyed—he'd never liked women

who played games. But somehow, as his heart started thudding hard against his rib cage and all his blood again rushed to his cock, he realized he was incredibly excited by Amanda Bauer instead.

Their stares locked, intense and hot. She licked her lips, and Steve tugged her closer, as if he'd almost felt that sweet, wet tongue. But her attention wasn't on Steve, it was entirely on Reese. Her eyes sparkled, as if she knew he was torn between wanting to laugh at her for trying to make him jealous or pick her up, throw her over his shoulder and out-caveman the guy in the loincloth.

Reese lifted a questioning brow, silently asking her how far she was going to take this. In response, she leaned toward Steve's ear and whispered something. The other man froze, dropping his arms and watching as Amanda turned away from him. She eased through the crowd, winding a path across the dance floor, heading toward a back hallway that led to the restrooms. A number of men turned to watch her go, and she earned more than a few glares from their dates. Just before she slipped down the short hallway, she cast one more glance over her shoulder. Her half smile taunted Reese, daring him to follow.

Reese spun the horny little cat around and pushed her toward the still-frozen Steve, who appeared almost shell-shocked. When he met Reese's eyes, he flushed, then mumbled, "Sorry, man."

Whatever Amanda had said, it had worked. He should have known she needed no help in taking care of herself. Still, he couldn't help smiling tightly and saying, "I think my date and I will be leaving now. Before you do something that requires me to break your jaw."

Not waiting for a reply, Reese moved in the same direction Amanda had gone. Easier said than done, as the dance floor swelled when the deejay put on a campy version of the "Monster Mash." He couldn't find an inch of clear space and had to push his way through couple after couple.

Finally, though, he reached the short hallway. A woman had just disappeared into the ladies' room, and a guy in a toga passed him as he left the men's. Stepping into a corner to wait, he started when he felt a hand on his shoulder.

"I knew you'd follow me," a throaty voice whispered.

Amanda.

She'd appeared from the shadows of a storage room, ignoring the Private: Employees Only sign. Standing in the doorway, she watched him with heat in her green eyes and a pant of audible hunger flowing across her moist lips.

"I knew you wanted me to."

He didn't resist when she tugged him inside the small room, dark, damp, smelling of yeasty beer and booze.

"Your girlfriend isn't going to come after us, is she?" Amanda whispered as she pushed the door shut behind him, trapping them inside.

He made sure everyone else was kept out by twisting the lock on the knob. "My girlfriend?"

She reached up and ran the tip of one index finger over his bottom lip, hissing lightly when he nipped at it. "Uh-huh. She looks very *catty*." Leaning up on tiptoe, she pressed her wet lips to his throat, swiping her small tongue against the hollow. "I don't usually go after other girls' guys but the way you've been looking at me all night has me feeling a little reckless."

He got into the spirit of her game. "She's not the one I want." Reese stared down at her, able to see her beautiful face more clearly as his eyes adjusted to the glimmer of moonlight spilling in from a small window. He leaned into her, knowing by her groan that she felt his raging erection pressing into the juncture of her thighs. "She's not the one who's had me hard and desperate for the past six hours." Being honest now, he added, "You're a stranger and yet I'm dying for you."

She lifted one slim leg, tilting toward him so his cock nested against the warm seam of her silky hot pants. He swallowed hard, desperately wanting to yank down his zipper, tear her shorts off and thrust into her hard, fast and deep. But a bigger part of him wanted it slow and hot, erotic as hell, with every sensation building upon the last, until the tension of anticipation had them both ready to explode.

"Sex with a stranger is a very enticing fantasy, isn't it?" she asked. "How lucky that we saw each other across the bar and both knew exactly what we had to have."

Wicked. Erotic. So damned sexy.

"Aren't you afraid your boyfriend is going to come looking for you?" He was half-curious about what she'd said to the other man before abandoning him. But not curious enough to ask, or do anything that might distract them from what was happening right here, right now.

"I don't care," she mumbled, her fingers tugging at his

tie, slipping the top button of his shirt open. "He can't satisfy me."

Her fingertips brushed his bare chest and he hissed at the sensation of skin on skin. "No. He can't. But believe me, I'm going to."

Hearing the sexy confidence in Reese Campbell's voice, Amanda melted a little. Okay, a lot. Coming from another guy—like the drunk ass she'd just ditched on the dance floor—the pronouncement might have come off as arrogant. But to her ears, Reese's certainty about the pleasure he intended to give her was utterly intoxicating. There was no conceit in it; he simply knew, as she did, that their chemistry was enough to take them both to places neither of them had ever gone before.

"One thing we have to make clear up front," she said, staring up at him, dropping the game for a moment.

"Yes?"

"This is just a one-night stand."

Instead of taking offense, he laughed softly. "Why don't you wait until after you've actually tasted something off the menu before deciding whether or not you want dessert?"

"I suspect you're going to fill me up very nicely the first time," she said, trying to sound seductive but knowing that had come out almost prim.

His continued laughter confirmed it.

She nibbled her bottom lip, her heart beating in excitement at all the ways she wanted to taste him. But the demands of her job, her travel, her commitment to the company and her allergy to anything resembling a relationship made her persist.

"I'm not looking for anything serious or long-term. No entanglements."

Sounding almost relieved, he replied, "Then we're on the same page. My life is so full of people right now, the Health Department is gonna cite me for overcrowding."

She hammered the point home. "So we're clear. One night, then it's done. We'll just enjoy ourselves because it's a holiday and we're both unattached and we want each other. We play all night and then walk away in the morning?"

"Sure," he said with a half grin that promised he didn't really mean it. But she had the feeling it was as close to a promise as he intended to give her.

"Okay. Good…perfect."

He stared at her in the darkness, running the tip of his index finger across her cheek. "Yeah. Perfect. That's exactly the word I'd use."

For her? For them? For this moment and this night and this wonderful, unexpected interlude? All of the above?

Who gave a damn?

"I want you, stranger," she said, feeling bold, crazy, wild with need and want. "I want you *now*."

He groaned, sinking his hands into her hair, tugging her face to his to capture her mouth in a deep, hard kiss. Without breaking away, he maneuvered her around so her back was to the door, and he crowded her there. Every inch of her body was enveloped by his, every curve, angle and point, and she whimpered and writhed at the feeling of being so utterly in his control.

She wasn't used to the sensations, had never been so enslaved by a person, a feeling, a need. She felt powerless, immobilized, able only to enjoy what he was doing to her, give herself over completely to his every sensual whim.

Somehow, she just didn't care. Maybe because she had gone for so long without any kind of physical connection. Or because it was Halloween and she was dressed in a crazy costume. Or that she had never played sexy, sultry games like they were engaging in tonight and had suddenly discovered she liked them. Or simply that she found Reese more attractive and exciting than any man she had ever met. It didn't matter.

This mattered. Just this.

"Please," she whispered, not even sure what she was asking for.

Moving his mouth to her jaw, he pressed hot kisses to her even hotter skin. He tasted her neck, before traveling on to her pulse point and licking lightly. "Have I told you that I really like your costume?"

That mouth moved lower, down to her nape, and he scraped his teeth across her collarbone, ever so lightly. She shivered. Ever so lightly.

"I do, too," she admitted, meaning it. Arching against him, she groaned at the feel of her own silky blouse against her hard, sensitive nipples. The hot pants had never felt so tight, and the seam did wonderfully wicked things to her highly sensitized clit.

"I think I'll like it even more when it's on the floor." His strong hands moved down, brushing her shoulders, sliding the length of her arms. His fingertips brushed hers in a caress so light and delicate she shivered with the need for more.

He cupped her hips, holding her in place. Pressed against him, she almost cried with the need to see, feel, taste and be filled by the massive erection pressed into her groin.

"Don't you think we should hurry before somebody comes looking for us?" she asked, helpless and desperate for him to go faster. Harder. Now.

"Nobody's going to come looking for us."

She wasn't giving up. "Not even your girlfriend?"

He smiled a little, his white teeth gleaming in the low lighting. "Oh, we have a very open relationship. She told me to come back here and have a fabulous time with you, then tell her all about it."

God, he was so sexy, tempting her with all that was forbidden and hot. He was still playing, but changing the rules of the game to suit his whim. He made it more taboo, more erotic.

"So does that mean you like handling two women at the same time?" she asked, intentionally trying to inflame him. She wanted him to go faster, give her more, *immediately*.

She should have known better. Reese merely continued to kiss her mouth, her jaw, her earlobe. "I'd like to have two yous."

"Why don't you have one me first before deciding whether you want a double portion?"

Though he chuckled, Reese continued to take his time, dragging this out. He was going to torture her with a slow, seductive ignition rather than just making her explode in a hot, sexual inferno the way she wanted him to.

"You evil man," she muttered.

Reese moved his mouth back to her throat, kissing his

way down, licking, nibbling. Amanda could only wriggle and moan as sensations washed over her. When his rough cheek brushed the upper curve of one breast, she instinctively arched toward him, wanting a much more intimate connection.

Reese complied, rubbing his cheek against the silky blouse as he moved his mouth to her nipple. He breathed over it, hot and anticipatory, then covered the taut peak and sucked her through the material.

"You wonderful man," she groaned.

Her legs going weak, she sagged against him. His body in front of her and the door at her back seemed to be the only things holding her up.

As much as she wanted him to, he didn't pull her blouse open and suckle her bare breast, seeming content to torment her through her clothes.

"Reese, touch me, please," she whispered.

He *was* touching her, gripping her hips, his fingertips digging lightly into her bottom. But she wanted so much more.

Reese's strong hands traveled up her sides in a slow, deliberate slide. The palms nestled in the indentation of her waist, cupped tenderly, then rose to her midriff, right beside her breasts.

"Beautiful," he murmured as he tightened his hands, plumping her breasts up so the top curves almost spilled free of the blouse. Then the ancient top button gave way, popping open. He took immediate advantage, lowering his face and nuzzling against her, even as he worked the next button free, and the one below that.

When the silky blouse fell off her shoulders, Reese stepped back so he could look down at her, his appreciative stare turning into one of pure, raging hunger. This time, she didn't have to ask him to touch her, taste her. Instead, he immediately bent down, covering a nipple with his mouth and sucking hard.

She tangled her hands in his hair, holding him there, feeling every deep pull right down to the quivering spot of sensation between her thighs. Tweaking her other breast with his hand, he rolled the tip between his fingertips. A firm pluck brought a shaky cry to her lips. Reese moved his mouth over to kiss and suck away any twinge of pain, though he knew—he had to know—that what she felt was utter pleasure.

Desperate for skin-on-skin contact, she yanked at his shirt, pulling it apart, not giving a damn that a few buttons went flying. He didn't seem to care, either. He simply shrugged out of it, continuing the lovely, erotic attention to her breasts.

Then, once he, too, was bare from the waist up, he moved back to her mouth and kissed her deeply. Their tongues tangled and played as their bare chests sizzled against one another. She didn't know that she'd ever felt anything as delicious as the crisp hairs on his chest scraping across her moist nipples.

Except, perhaps, for his mouth. And his hands. And, she suspected, just about anything else he chose to press against her in the next fifteen minutes.

They didn't end the kiss, not even when they each reached for the other's waistbands. His deft fingers easily unfastened her hot pants, and his costume was so loose on him, she only had to unbutton, not unzip, before she was able to push the trousers down over his lean hips.

He'd had something on under his clothes—boxer briefs that strained to contain an erection that literally made her suck in a shocked, delighted breath.

All that hugeness. All hers. At least for tonight.

Before he let the pants fall away, he reached into the pocket. "I hope you don't think I was taking you for granted, but I bought this from a machine in the men's room."

She saw him tug the condom from his pocket and grinned. "My purse is over there. And if you look inside, you'll see that I stopped at the airport gift shop and bought an entire box. So I think I'm the one who could be accused of taking you for granted."

"Anytime, anywhere, beautiful."

She liked the way he called her that, liked the way he silently repeated it with his eyes as he stared at her. His gaze was covetous as he stepped back enough to look down at her middle, her hips, the juncture of her thighs.

That look was so hungry, she should have been warned about what he was going to do. But she wasn't. It took her completely by surprise when he dropped to his knees on the bare cement floor and pressed his mouth to the hollow just below her pelvic bone. Then his soft, seeking tongue was dipping low, licking the moisture off her damp curls.

Oral sex was, to quote the song, one of her favorite things. But she had never gotten it quite so quickly from a man. Or quite so....

"Oh, God," she groaned when he moved lower, sliding that warm, sweet tongue between the lips of her sex and swirling it around her throbbing clit. "That's fantastic."

She sagged against the door, helpless to do anything else under the onslaught of such intense pleasure. And she didn't make a sound of protest when he encircled one of her bare limbs with a big, strong hand. Without a word, he guided it over his shoulder, tilting her sex even closer to his hungry mouth.

"Reese, you don't have to…"

"Yeah, actually I do," he mumbled, continuing what he was doing.

She looked down at him, seeing her own booted foot resting against his back. Only now it looked incredibly hot and sexy, the ultimate do-me boots from the original era of free love.

She suddenly felt like the girl she'd been portraying. Like she was some sexy stewardess having a crazy closet interlude with a pilot, just because she *wanted* to. No explanations, no questions, no regrets. Live in the moment and love the one you're with.

Sounded pretty damn fine to her.

"Stop thinking. Let go," he ordered, not looking up.

Amanda did what he asked, giving up any effort to pretend she didn't want him to finish what he'd started.

Finish it he did. Within moments, she felt the sparking, zinging waves of heated delight that had been focusing tightly in on her clit turn around and explode outward. They rocketed through her entire body, wave upon wave, delighting her to the tips of each strand of hair.

Amanda cried out, rocking her hips. He stayed with her, continuing to taste her as she rode the orgasm out, milking it and squeezing her muscles tight to wring out every last bit of sensation. And only after it was over did he slide out from under her leg and ease his way up her naked body.

She was panting and nearly desperate by the time his face was level with hers. His eyes gleaming, he licked at his moist lips and whispered, "Definitely want to keep ordering off this menu."

Dying for him now, needing to be filled, she grabbed two handfuls of his hair and pulled his face to hers for a deep, drugging kiss. This time, she was the one who lifted her leg. Wrapping it around his thighs, she tilted her groin against that thick erection still covered by his briefs.

"Off," she ordered, mumbling the command against his mouth.

He moved a few inches away, far enough to strip out of the last of his clothes. Far enough for Amanda to look down and take measure of the delightful present that was headed her way.

Whoa. As she'd suspected, Reese's "present" was far greater than any she'd ever seen before. She nearly panted with the need to have all that male heat slamming into her, filling the hollow core that had practically grown dusty with disuse.

"Damn. I wasn't exaggerating," she whispered.

He didn't even glance up, tearing the condom open with his teeth and rolling it onto his cock as he mumbled, "Hmm?"

"I told that jerk on the dance floor that if he thought

he could measure up to you, he obviously needed to get a new ruler because his had to be broken."

He barked a laugh, but that immediately faded when he moved between her thighs. Amanda lifted her leg again, opening for him, arching toward the massive tip and rubbing her body's natural juices over it.

He put a hand on the door behind her head, palm flat, his strong arm just above her shoulders. She turned her head for a moment, wanting to taste his wrist, feel his blood pounding in his veins. She did so, licking the sweat off him, feeling the strength of his pulse against her tongue. His excitement merely fueled her own as she looked back up into his face, losing herself in those blue eyes.

Their stare never broke as he eased into her. He moved slowly, with utter restraint. Amanda's mouth fell open with a tiny gasp at the feel of him as he went deeper, inch by inch. He was solid and thick, stretching her, making a place for himself within her body.

A temporary one, she knew that. But she also knew it was one she would never *ever* forget. This was the one-night lover every woman fantasized about at least once in her life. And for tonight, he was hers.

"Perfect," he said, echoing his earlier claim.

This time, she knew what he was talking about. Knew as he slid home, burying himself to the hilt inside her, that he meant their connection was perfect. Being joined with him felt about as wonderful as anything on this earth possibly could.

"You okay?"

She nodded, unable to speak. Sensations battered her,

his smell, the heat of his skin against hers, his warm breaths against her cheek. She even felt his heartbeat, realizing at once that its rhythm was perfectly matched to her own, as if they shared one single organ.

"Perfect," she finally agreed.

As if he'd been waiting for her, to make sure she was really okay with his incredibly deep possession, Reese finally began to move. He dropped his hands to her hips, holding her still as he slowly withdrew, then slid into her again, making her feel so damn good she let out a tiny sob.

The next thrust was a little harder. The one after that harder still. Each wrung a louder groan from her throat.

"More," she ordered, digging her hands into his broad shoulders, still stunned by the strength of the body he'd hidden beneath that conservative suit.

"You got it."

He lifted her, his hands holding her bottom, controlling every thrust, every move, every sensation. Wrapping her legs around his hips, Amanda kissed his cheeks, stroked his hair and held on while he brought her to another intense orgasm.

It rocked her, hard. She threw her head back and cried out, banging into the door but not really caring. Nor did she care when Reese seemed to lose whatever remnants of control had been restraining him. As if her cries of pleasure had stripped away his every thought, he drove into her mindlessly, until finally, with a cry that was twice the volume of her own, he climaxed, too.

He held her there for a long time, still inside her, his breath sounding ragged and his heart pounding crazily against hers. Finally, though, he let her down to stand on her own two shaky legs.

He didn't let her loose entirely, keeping his arms draped around her shoulders. Finally, after a few minutes during which her pulse dropped back from the red zone to orange, he lifted a hand to her face and cupped her chin.

"Amanda?"

"Yeah?"

"Where do you live?"

"I have an apartment not too far from here."

He nodded, then disentangled himself from her with one last, regretful caress. "Let's get dressed. Or, get as dressed as we can given the missing buttons." He stared at her intently, as if he were looking for some clue to her mood. "If you really meant it, if we've only got one night…"

Her heart skipped a beat. She knew what he was asking. Did she *really* want to stick to that original condition?

Oh, God, was she tempted to tell him to forget what she'd said. Having had him once, it seemed almost inconceivable that she wouldn't have him again after tonight.

But a small voice inside her head—the one that kept reminding her of just how badly every one of her previous affairs had ended—wouldn't let her do it. So she said nothing.

He nodded once, then pressed a hard kiss on her lips.

"Got it." He handed her her clothes and began pulling on his, as well. "Let's hurry up, then. If we've only got this one night, I want to spend as much of it as I possibly can in your bed…making love to you."

Her hand shook a little. Because with those words, those sexy, tender words, a sneaking suspicion crossed her mind. One night was not going to be enough.

chapter four

Veterans Day

From: mandainflight@hotmail.com
To: Rcampbell@campbelllagers.com
Sent: Tuesday, Nov 10, 2009
Subject: One more time?
Reese—
Another holiday…whaddya say? Want to meet me for a Veterans Day game of captured enemy soldier vs. ruthless interrogator?
Manda

From: Rcampbell@campbelllagers.com
To: mandainflight@hotmail.com
Sent: Tuesday, Nov 10, 2009
Subject: One more time?

Affirmative. Where. When.

R.

PS: Tell me I get to be the ruthless interrogator.

BEING interrogated had never been so much fun.

Lying in bed in the Cleveland hotel room, Reese watched as the sexiest woman he knew emerged from the bathroom. She was wrapped in a white towel, her skin slick and reddened from the steamy hot shower she'd just taken. It was probably also that way because he'd been touching her, tasting her, adoring her all afternoon. And though he'd already spent almost as many waking hours today inside her body as he had out of it, he already wanted her again.

He still couldn't quite believe this had even happened. Not the sex—God, yes, that was bound to happen whenever the two of them were in a room with a flat surface. But them being together again at *all*.

He'd tried calling Amanda a couple of times after they'd said their goodbyes in Chicago the morning after Halloween. She hadn't responded. Nor had she returned his e-mails.

Finally, he'd had to accept the fact that she'd meant it—one night only. He'd have to live for the rest of his life with the knowledge that the most desirable woman he'd ever met, and the best sex he'd ever had, were both in his past.

He'd tried to get his mind back into his real life. So much needed his attention: the business, the family, his own house. Responsibilities seemed to weigh heavier on his back every time he answered the phone or opened his front door.

Then, out of the blue, this morning, her message.

He hadn't hesitated. Inventing an out-of-town meeting, he'd thrown a few things in a bag, dropped his dog off at a buddy's and headed to Cleveland. He'd needed no further details than the name of the hotel and the time she'd be there.

There was nothing that could have prevented him from making the trip. Absolutely nothing that would have stopped him from accepting her invitation to sin.

And oh, sin they had.

"You know, I might have been lying about where the top-secret orders were hidden. They might not really be inside Jimi Hendrix's guitar at the Rock and Roll Hall of Fame. Maybe you should torture me again to get the truth out of me," he offered.

Reaching for her purse, Amanda grabbed a hairbrush from within it, and turned to face the mirror. She caught his eye in the reflection as she began to brush the wet strands. "Sorry. Not buying it. I don't think anybody could have held out against that last round of—" she licked her lips "—questioning."

God. He began to harden again, just at the thought of it. That last round of *questioning* had been unforgettable.

Well, to be honest, the whole afternoon had been un-forgettable.

She'd been playing her role from the minute he'd walked through the door of the hotel room. He was her prisoner and he had to do what she said. He'd gone along, liking the wildness in her. She was aggressive, demanding. So damned sexy.

Amanda had insisted that he strip. Threatening to punish him if he didn't cooperate, she had then instructed him to sit in a chair right beside the head of the bed.

Half curious, more than half turned-on, he'd agreed to her terms. He wanted to see how far she would go, just what she had in mind. So he'd given his word he would not rise from that chair, no matter what she said or did.

He'd been certain he could do it. Absolutely positive. He'd told himself he wouldn't get up, not even if the room caught fire.

Then it did. Or, at least, she'd made it *feel* that way, filling the place with so much intense heat he'd thought his skin was going to peel off his bones.

It took every bit of his strength to remain still, just an observer. Because with pure wickedness in her eyes, Amanda had slowly slid out of her clothes and gotten comfortable on the bed, directly in front of him. There she'd proceeded to thoroughly pleasure herself.

Seeing her hands move over that amazing body, being an observer, unable to participate, had been *exactly* the torture she'd anticipated. He'd begun to sweat, to pant, to strain and to clench his fists in a quest for control.

Not content to just run her hand across her bare breast or delicately stroke her long fingertips over her gleaming slit, she'd actually pulled out a vibrating sex toy. He'd had to sit there, silent, nearly dying, while she'd used it to bring herself to orgasm three times.

Then, still ordering him to stay still and leave everything in her control, she'd climbed on top of him and slid down onto his shaft, taking him deep inside her body, controlling their every move, every thrust, every stroke. At one point she'd even turned around to ride him like a cowgirl, all while smiling at his reflection in the same damn mirror she was using now.

He was pretty sure he'd come at least a gallon when she finally did let him go over the edge with her. And that had been only the beginning.

"You're incredible."

"Must be Stockholm Syndrome," she quipped. "You're infatuated with your captor, right?"

"Uh-huh." *Infatuated.* Good word. Maybe even on the verge of obsessed.

"Don't worry, it'll pass."

He very much doubted it. "I don't think so."

Her smile faded a little at his intense tone, and her eyes shifted as she busied herself finishing her hair. He suddenly wondered if he'd touched a nerve.

"You might say you like all of me, but I bet there are certain parts you like better than others." She pursed those lips, reminding him of everything else they'd done so far today. Amanda's second round of torment had involved her luscious mouth.

He had loved giving her oral sex their first time. But Reese had never even contemplated how mind-blowing it would be when she wrapped her lips around his cock. Again and again, she'd brought him to the very edge, taking him as close to orgasm as she could get him, then backing off, cooling things down.

He'd held out as long as he could, liking this reckless, wild side of her. Not to mention loving the feel of her lips and tongue sucking him into oblivion. Finally, though, it had gone too far and he knew he couldn't wait much longer. So he'd played his role in the game, giving her the "information" she had been asking for.

But instead of ending it, pulling him down on top of her so he could finish things in the sweet channel between her legs, she'd ended the game with her mouth. She hadn't even given him the chance to do the polite guy thing— or the standard porn movie one—and pull out before reaching the end of the countdown.

Wild. Erotic. Intense.

She was his every fantasy. And about as far from his real life as a woman could possibly be.

He forcibly pushed that thought away. Because, though they'd done almost no talking so far today, he didn't imagine Amanda's feelings about what they were doing— and what they were going to do in the future—had changed. A one-night stand had evolved into a holiday affair. He just didn't know how far out on the calendar she'd want to go. She might be his Thanksgiving feast or his ultimate Christmas present. If fate was kind, perhaps she'd be the one coloring his Easter eggs.

Or they might have tonight and nothing else. Ever.

Not knowing drove him crazy, in both a good way and a bad one. The possibility that this might be all made him desperate to have and take and possess her as much as he could.

It's not all. It can't be all.

"I'm hungry," she said.

Thrusting away his thoughts of tomorrow, he knew he had to focus on tonight. He rolled over to sit up on the edge of the bed. One thing was sure—he needed to eat in order to have the strength to spend the rest of the night the way he wanted. "Me, too. Please tell me I've been cooperative enough to get more than bread and water."

"How's cold gruel sound?"

"Uh-uh. I need protein. Let me take you out to dinner."

Her mouth fell open, but quickly snapped closed again. After a hesitation, she murmured, "I don't know…"

"I've got to keep up my strength. How else can I hope to resist you?"

Her head turned a little and she averted her gaze. "Resist me? That's what you call resisting?"

"Come on, cut me a break. It's kinda hard to say no to a woman when she has your cock in her mouth."

Amazing. They'd done the most intense things to one another, but he'd swear a slight flush rose in her face at his words. And she still wouldn't look at him.

Embarrassment? That seemed crazy, given all they'd shared. Besides, her unease hadn't started with his crass comment, but when he'd suggested that they go out to eat. Or maybe a few minutes before that when he'd admitted to being infatuated with her.

"Let's stay in. We can order room service," she insisted.

She'd play sex games with him all afternoon, but didn't want to go on anything resembling a date?

Interesting.

Reese stood and walked up behind her, dropping his hands to her hips and pressing a kiss on her nape. "Room service for breakfast," he whispered. "Tonight, though, let's get out of here for a little while."

She still looked uncertain. As if, now that the game was over, now that they were played-out and talking about something as simple as food, she didn't know what to say, how to act.

Or who to be.

"We both know that's not what this is about..."

"Look, I'm not proposing, okay?" he said, forcing a non-committal laugh. "It's dinner. Eating together, not any kind of a declaration. Sharing a meal doesn't elevate this to anything more than the two-night stand you've decided we can have."

Her eyes flared in surprise, as if she hadn't guessed how easy she was to read.

Reese shrugged. "I'm not stupid, okay? I know what you want, and what you don't. I accepted that when I showed up here today."

She still hesitated.

"No pressure, no hidden meanings, just food," he said, coaxing her as carefully as he would a wild bird with a piece of bread. "You can choose where we go. As long as it's someplace that serves red meat, I'll take it."

She nibbled her bottom lip, than finally said, "Do you consider pepperoni red meat? Because I could really go for some pizza."

He almost breathed a sigh of relief. Both that she'd said yes, and that she wasn't a woman who liked to nibble on a few carrots and pieces of lettuce and call it a meal.

"Perfect."

She managed a weak smile. "You say that a lot."

"You *are* that a lot."

He met her stare in the mirror. Amanda didn't exactly pull away at the gentle push into more personal, intimate territory that fell out of the boundaries of their sexy games. But the muscles beneath the silky skin tensed ever so slightly. Enough to warn him to back off.

He did. "Give me ten minutes to grab a shower."

Gently letting her go, he walked toward the bathroom, figuring she needed a chance to pull herself back together. Hell, so did he. Because in the past few minutes, it had hit him—hard—that despite being more intimate with the woman than he'd ever been with anyone in his life, he didn't know much about her.

Sure, he knew he liked her. Knew she had a great sense of humor, was smart and hardworking. Knew that right before she came, she emitted this adorable little high-pitched sound from the back of her throat.

Beyond that—not so much. He'd been to her place, in an old downtown Chicago highrise, but even seeing where she lived hadn't offered many answers about her personal life. She had no pets, no plants, no pictures, nothing that personalized her apartment at all. Entering it, he'd immediately known it was just a place for her to eat, sleep and chill—not really what anyone would call a home.

So maybe this time-out for dinner, with no play-acting, no innuendo…no sex…would be a good thing. Maybe it was time to take a step back, drop the pretense and actually get to know the real people playing the games.

She might not like it, she might not want it. But Reese did. Because he had the feeling the woman behind the wild seductress was someone he really wanted to get to know better.

As THEY WALKED INTO a nearby Italian restaurant recommended by the hotel's maitre d', Amanda found herself starting to sweat. And not just because Mr. Hotness was walking so closely behind her, his hand resting possessively on the small of her back.

This was too much like a date. Way too much like a date. And while she liked Reese Campbell a lot, dating him hadn't been part of the deal. Dating made this too real, when all she'd set out for from the beginning was a fantasy. A one-night stand that had somehow segued into two.

And only two. This was it, tonight *had* to be the end of it. Her life was just too complicated, and Reese was too incredible a guy for her to get any more involved with. He was too stable, too solid, too nice.

She…wasn't. Amanda wasn't dating material. She was sex material, oh, yes, she was good for flings and wild affairs, even if she'd had no time for any in recent months.

But dating? Romance? Relationships?

Uh-uh. She was the bitch who broke hearts. The one who panicked and took off whenever anybody got a little too serious or tried to tie her down in one place, instead of letting her live her life in flight, as she'd done for the past ten years.

This isn't a date. Just food so we can build up more energy to have lots more anonymous, no-strings sex.

"Would you relax?" Reese murmured as they followed the hostess, a fiftyish brunette in a full-skirted dress who'd yelled something in Italian as they passed by the swinging door to the kitchen. "It's just pizza, for God's sake."

Amanda drew in a long, shaky breath, trying to force

the stiffness from her spine. Although, that was hard to do when his fingers were branding her.

"Is this all right?" the older woman asked as she reached a small, intimate table set for two.

"Just fine," Reese murmured.

Thank heaven he didn't say *perfect*. That word coming off his lips just had too many associations. Sometimes it made her incredibly horny, sometimes nervous as hell.

With its red-checked tablecloth, and an old Chianti bottle plugged with a candle and dripping wax, their table looked like the one where Lady and the Tramp had shared a romantic plate of spaghetti. All they needed was a pair of Italian singers with an accordion and a violin to serenade them.

God, this was *so* a date.

She almost bolted. If he hadn't already pulled out her chair and gently pushed her down into it, she probably would have done so.

It wouldn't have been the first time. One guy she'd been involved with had, despite all her warnings, told her he was in love with her. And she'd run to the airport, hopped on a flight to Paris and stayed away for two weeks.

No wonder he still drunk-dialed her.

But maybe this time could be different. Because he's different.

Reese was so different. So fun and sexy and playful. Daring and imaginative. He made her feel unlike any other man had before.

She sighed heavily, forcing those thoughts away. The way he made her feel couldn't possibly be a good thing.

Not when it left her so confused, off-balance, unsure. Completely un-Amanda-like.

"Thank you," Reese said as he took the seat opposite her and smiled up at the hostess. Despite being at least twenty years his senior, she preened a little, as would any woman under the attention of a man as handsome as her companion.

Companion. Not date.

"So are you locals?" the woman asked.

Reese shook his head. "Just visiting."

"Excellent! Contrary to what you might think, Cleveland is a wonderful vacation spot. Very romantic," the woman said with a wag of her eyebrows. "Lots for a young couple in love to do."

Amanda opened her mouth to respond, lies and denials bubbling to her lips. They were just playing here…just two wildly compatible people playing naughty games. Nothing more to it.

But before any could emerge, Reese reached for her hand and clasped it in his on top of the table. Their hostess nodded approvingly, then turned away to greet some newcomers standing in the entranceway.

"You were going to make up some outrageous story, weren't you?" he asked, casually releasing her hand, lifting a napkin and draping it over his lap.

"How do you know?"

"Are you denying it?"

"Of course not. Just wondering how you know."

"Oh, believe me, I'm starting to understand how your

mind works. Romance, love…those words aren't in your vocabulary, right?"

She nodded once. "Right."

The hostess had left a basket of bread sticks on their table, and Amanda took one, nibbling lightly on the end, not elaborating even though she knew he probably expected her to. That kind of talk was for dates. This was just a…nutrition break.

"So what kind of story were you going to tell?" He sounded genuinely curious.

"I don't know." Thinking about it, she tapped her finger on her chin. "You're a witness against the mob in protective custody and I'm your bodyguard?"

"You're obviously not a very good bodyguard if you go around blabbing about me being a witness."

"I didn't say I was a good one. Maybe I'm a too-stupid-to-live one, like in one of those really bad movies."

"Hmm, possible." He looked around the restaurant, at the tables full of people who all looked much like their very-ethnic hostess, Rosalita. "But that might not be such a good idea in this place. I think half the diners in here are one generation out of Sicily. You might get me whacked."

"Got any better ideas?"

"Playboy bunny and mogul?"

"Keep dreaming." Giving him an impish look, she added, "Besides, I don't think you'd look very good in bunny ears."

He laughed out loud. Before he could reply, though, a busboy came over and filled two glasses of water, leaving them beside their untouched menus. A not-uncomfortable silence fell once the bored-looking teen had walked away.

Finally, Reese broke that silence. "So, why don't we just go with a pilot from Chicago hooking up with a business-man from Pittsburgh?"

She snorted, forcing herself to remain casual when her first reaction to the idea of just being who they really were more resembled panic. "Boring."

"You keep using that word...I do not think it means what you think it means."

Delighted that he'd quoted one of her favorite movies, *The Princess Bride,* complete with Spanish accent, she said, "Well done."

"Wow, we have something in common? A movie we've both seen?"

She gestured toward the table and the candle. "If we had the same taste in movies, you'd know just how terrified I am that some Italian dude is going to come up and start singing 'Bella Notte.'"

"At least tell me I'd get to be the Tramp in that one."

Something about his put-upon tone, plus the fact that he knew exactly what she was talking about, made her relax and offer him her first genuine smile since they'd arrived. "I'm a pain in the ass, I know. I doubt you'd understand."

"I might. Why don't you try me?"

She thought about it. But how could she? How, exactly, did you go about telling your lover—*no, not lover, sex partner*—that you had a reputation as a bitch, that men faked suicide attempts because you couldn't love them, that you'd rather just not be bothered with the whole romance thing anymore? It wasn't exactly ladylike to admit you didn't want a guy who'd bring you chocolate and flowers and had long ago realized you were much more the fuck-buddy than the girlfriend type.

She couldn't say those things. And suddenly, she didn't want to. Not to him.

Why the very thought of it bothered her so much, though, she honestly didn't know.

When she didn't respond, he finally prompted, "Sometimes it's just easier to pretend than to be who you really are?"

"Yeah, something like that."

He shook his head ever so slightly, either disapproval or disappointment visible in the tightness of his mouth.

"Hey, you agreed to the terms."

"I agreed to a one-night stand." His eyes sparkled as he added, "You *changed* those terms with your e-mail."

He had a point.

"So maybe it's time to renegotiate."

Wary, she asked, "How so?"

"Maybe we should agree to at least one open, honest conversation, without any, uh, embellishments."

Figuring great sex would make him forget that idea, she licked her lips. "I don't see why you're complaining. I thought you were pretty happy about how things turned out this afternoon."

"As I recall, so were you. At least three times."

She licked the tip of her bread stick. "Mmm…six."

Reese crossed his arms over his chest and leaned back in his chair, eyeing her steadily. "I'm not counting the ones I wasn't involved in."

"Oh, honey, you were most definitely involved."

A brow arched over one blue eye. "Oh?"

"Mmm-hmm. And you've *been* involved every other time I've played with that little toy in the past two weeks."

He dropped his crossed arms onto the table, leaning over it, closer to her. Close enough that she saw the way his pulse pounded in his throat. "Is that so?"

"Yes."

He reached for his water, bringing the slick glass to his mouth. As he sipped, the muscles in his neck flexed. And when he lowered the glass, his lips were moist, parted. "Did that happen often?"

"Probably more than it had in the past year."

A masculine expression of self-satisfaction appeared on his incredibly handsome face. "You thought about…"

"Everything," she purred. "I thought about it a lot."

"Ditto."

She swallowed, immediately knowing what he was admitting. "I don't suppose you had any toys to play with?"

"'Fraid not. Had to go the old-fashioned route."

Squirming a little in her chair as she thought of him needing to gain some relief because he'd been thinking about her, she echoed his question. "Did that happen often?"

He lowered his eyes, gazing at her throat and the soft swell of cleavage rising above her V-necked sweater. "What do you think?"

Realizing she'd bit off a little more than she could chew, and that images of Reese pumping that long, thick shaft into his own tight fist were going to intrude on the rest of her meal, she cleared her throat and bit hard on the bread stick.

Reese didn't let it go, however, going right back to

where he'd been headed before that detour into Lustville. "So what happened, your little toy was no longer enough so you decided to break your own rules and come back to order something else off the menu?"

She opened her mouth to answer, but before she could, a chirpy voice intruded. "Something else? Wait, has somebody already taken your order? Gosh darn it, I told her I was coming right over!"

Amanda bit her lip in amusement at the realization that a young waitress, whose name tag said Brittani, had overheard part of their conversation. Of course, she'd obviously misinterpreted it. Thank God.

The girl was probably only about seventeen, and she looked extremely annoyed that someone else had been poaching on her table. She apparently feared losing her tip. Considering they'd been left sitting here unattended for a good ten minutes, she was apparently the optimistic type.

"It's okay," Reese said, "we were talking about something else."

Amanda couldn't resist being a little mischievous. "Oh, yes. Definitely something else. Just reminiscing about something we ordered off a menu in Milan last week."

The girl's jaw opened far enough to display the chewing gum resting on her tongue. "You been to Australia? For real? Did you see any koala bears?"

Amanda managed to hide either a laugh or a sigh at Brittani's less-than-impressive geography skills.

"No koalas," Reese interjected smoothly. "Just a few dingoes. Now, if you don't mind, I think we're ready to order."

They did so, asking for the pepperoni pizza she'd been craving since they'd first talked about food back in the hotel room. Their perky waitress, whose mood had picked up once she realized nobody was horning in on her table, nodded and sauntered away, not even asking if they wanted anything other than ice water to drink.

The ice water that was just about gone.

When they were alone again, Reese said, "To be sure I've got it, let's clarify. Honest conversation is just as forbidden on your planet as actual dinner dates, right?"

Damn, the guy was tenacious. "Depends on the conversation."

"Can we talk about sports?"

She wrinkled her nose.

"Movies?"

"Sure. Though I haven't seen a new one in a theater in at least two years."

He shrugged. "Me, either. Moving on. Politics?"

"Only if you're a right-down-the-middle moderate like me."

"Progress. We have one thing in common."

Grinning impishly, she said, "I think we have more than one."

"Touché."

She lifted her glass and drained the last few drops of water from it, then sucked a small piece of ice into her mouth. "I think there's another thing we can safely agree on. Brittani's tip is getting smaller by the minute."

"I think we can also agree that world geography should be a required course in high schools."

She snickered, liking his deadpan sense of humor. Liking so much about him. Too much.

Maybe…

No. She wasn't going to go there, not even in her own head. She wasn't going to evaluate the possibility that this thing between them might be about anything more than having fun and incredible sex.

She'd take fun and incredible sex over angsty emotional dramas and minefields of feelings any day.

Despite her best efforts, for a few minutes Amanda let herself actually converse with the man. Nothing too heavy, definitely no sharing of past relationships or deepest fears. He got her to admit she'd once had a mad crush on every member of the Backstreet Boys, and he'd come clean about his secret desire to be a drummer for a rock band, even though he'd never held a drumstick.

"Backstreet Boys never had a drummer," she pointed out.

"Too bad. To think we could have started all this fun fifteen years ago."

"Fifteen years ago, we would both have been seriously underage."

"But think of all the interesting things we could have learned together."

Frankly, she was learning lots of interesting things from the man, right here and now. At fourteen, still the rebel trying to survive in good-girl wonderland, she didn't think her heart could have taken meeting someone who excited her like Reese Campbell.

Well, her heart probably could have. Her parents, however, would have lost their minds.

Their light chatting seemed to satisfy Reese, at least for now, and he didn't try to steer her toward any more personal subjects. That was fortunate. Amanda honestly didn't know if she'd have been able to explain her aversion to such things. Not without giving him all the information he was looking for in the process. Her past heartbreaks, her rigid upbringing, her bad reputation for being a little too foot-loose and coldhearted…all explained who she was today. But none were topics she particularly cared to talk about. Teenage fantasy was about as intimate as she wanted to get.

"Okay, here you go. Enjoy!"

Brittani had returned with their pizza right on time—before Reese could slip through any conversational back doors she might have inadvertently left open. She was so anxious that it remain that way, she grabbed a slice and bit into it right away.

Bad move.

"Ow!" she snapped when the gooey cheese burned the roof of her mouth.

Reese immediately scooped a piece of ice out of his own water glass and lifted it toward her. Dropping the pizza, Amanda gratefully parted her lips, sucking the cube he offered into her mouth. Her tongue swiped across his fingertips as she did so, and suddenly the pain wasn't so bad. Seeing the way his eyes flared at the brush of her tongue against his skin, she had to acknowledge it wasn't so bad at all.

"Watch it. Don't want any injuries that could cut short our two-night stand," he teased. Then, looking at his own pizza, he added, "I think I'll wait a while for this to cool off. I have definite plans for my mouth tonight."

She quivered in her seat at the very thought of it. Because oh, the man did know how to use his mouth. And there were such wonderful things he could do with it that did not involve the conversation she suspected he would want to get back to as soon as they finished eating.

She thought about it. Stick around here and deal with lots more talking? Or just seduce the man back to their hotel room?

No-freaking-brainer.

"Reese?" she said, speaking carefully, the ice now just a small sliver on her tongue.

"Yeah?"

"Can we please take this to go?"

He stared at her, as if gauging the request, and her motivation for making it. She didn't have to feign her interest in getting back to where they'd been a couple of hours ago: in a hotel room bed. But she did have to hide the fact that her motivation was at least partly to get out of having to talk anymore.

Something that looked like understanding crossed his face, though she would swear she saw a hint of frustration there, too. "You're sure?"

"I think you need to kiss this better," she said, pushing him just a little more. She swiped her tongue across her lips to punctuate the point.

He shook his head, smiling ruefully. "I guess I should be thankful just to have found out you're a political moderate who doesn't go to the movies. That's more than I knew two hours ago."

"And don't forget—not a sports fan."

"We're really getting somewhere."

"Now let's get somewhere else," she insisted, leaning across the table. This back-and-forth conversation was reminding her of how much she liked his quick wit, his easygoing personality. Physically, she'd been attracted from the get-go. Now she knew there was so much more about him that interested her.

But only until tomorrow.

Unless…

Only until tomorrow!

"Please," she whispered. "We only have until morning and I really don't want to waste it sitting here waiting for the pizza to cool off."

Apparently hearing her sincerity, he no longer hesitated. He waved to their waitress, then murmured, "But I do reserve the right to ask you if you've read any good books lately on the ride back to the hotel."

"Books. Okay, I can do that."

And she could. Books were fine. So were movies and politics and sports and anything else that didn't really require intimate conversation.

He just couldn't ask her about her past relationships, her family background or her footloose lifestyle. She wouldn't share details of her aversion to small towns, home, hearth, wholesome values or anything else resembling the world in which she'd grown up.

And she definitely didn't want to talk about her slightly hardened heart. Or the fact that some people didn't even seem to think she had one.

chapter five

Thanksgiving

"SO, I've been meaning to ask you, how'd your folks take you not coming home for the holiday weekend?"

Sprawled back in a comfortable, cushy chair in the rec room of her friend Jazz's parents' house, Amanda resisted the urge to unsnap her khakis. After the two full plates of Thanksgiving dinner, plus the pumpkin pie and the teensy sliver of pecan that she'd simply had to taste, she should be glad the snap hadn't just popped on its own.

"Manda? Were they upset?"

Tryptophan kicking in, she yawned and shook her head. "Actually, I think they were relieved."

Jazz, who supervised the mechanics who kept Clear-Blue Air flying, curled up in her own chair, her head barely reaching the top of it. She was petite, five-foot-four, but you'd never know that by the way she ran her mechanics' shop or the magic way she coaxed the best performance out of an airplane.

The two of them were hiding down in the converted basement. They'd finished dinner a few hours ago and Jazz's big family had just begun saying their goodbyes. Neither of them being the air-kisses type, Amanda and Jazz were waiting out the big huggy scene downstairs. Once the coast was clear, they would go back up and let Jazz's mother make a big fuss out of loading up plates of left-overs for the "single girls" to take home.

It was becoming a tradition. Somehow, hanging out with Jazz's big, loud, crazy family on holidays was easier than going home and sticking out like a sore thumb in her own small, quiet, proper one.

"Relieved why?"

"You know Abby got engaged?"

Jazz nodded with a big roll of her dark eyes. She'd met Amanda's younger sister last year when Abby had come to the city for a spring shopping trip.

Abby was okay, at least when their parents weren't around and she didn't have to play Miss Perfect. But the stick up her ass only ever came out so far, and Jazz was not the type around whom Abigail Bauer would ever let down her guard.

Jazz was an exotically beautiful, loud-mouthed, crass, wild-child. Abby was a demure, classically beautiful, prodigal one. Oil and water.

Which made Amanda, what…the vinegar to their Good Seasons salad dressing?

Yeah, tart and sour.

She thrust that thought away, preferring to think of herself as flavorful and zesty.

"How do you like her fiancé?"

"He's a douche."

Back to tart and sour.

Jazz snorted, sipping from the glass of wine she'd smuggled down from the kitchen. "Figures."

"He's as cold as my father and as reserved as my mother. And he comes from a family of people just like him. His parents invited my folks over for a prewedding holiday meal today."

"Gotcha. No bad girls allowed, huh?"

Amanda lifted a brow, feigning offense. "Look who's talking."

Jazz bent her head and smiled into her glass. "I'm not the one flying off tomorrow to have a weekend of illicit sex with a guy I barely know."

Sucking her bottom lip between her teeth, Amanda reached for her glass of water. Because damn it, yes, she was doing exactly that.

She'd left Cleveland absolutely certain she'd never see Reese Campbell again. She'd felt sure she'd gotten him out of her system. They'd had a great time, built some incredible memories. Plus they'd done just about everything two people could do together sexually.

Okay, that was a lie. She could think of about another four or five things she'd like to do with the man. Or five dozen.

The point was, they'd had amazing sexual encounters twice now, and twice was once more than the one-night stand she'd intended. So how crazy was she to go for number three?

Third time's the charm.

She'd been unable to resist. Hearing his voice on her voice mail the other day, she'd gotten shaky and weak all over again. When he'd asked her if she wanted to meet him in Florida to see if they could get kicked out of a theme park for having hot sex in public, she'd been unable to say anything but yes. She hadn't even insisted that he promise to put on any mouse ears.

She had something else in mind for the fantasy part of their sensual weekend. Something a little more risqué than a theme park.

"Where are you meeting him?"

"Daytona."

"Warm. Sounds good. So, uh, when are you going to let me meet this guy?"

"Never."

Her friend pulled a hurt look. "Come on, I introduce you to all my boy toys."

"He's not my boy toy. He's…"

"He's what?" Jazz asked, leaning forward and dropping her elbows onto her knees.

Good question. She couldn't really call Reese a stranger anymore. They not only knew and had explored every inch of each other's bodies, they'd also spent time together doing nonsexual things. Damn it, she'd gotten roped into pillow talk that last time.

Even worse, they'd actually chatted about his family the morning after. Mainly because his teenage sister had called him at the butt-crack of dawn to ask him to intervene with their mother for permission to go to some party.

Even adorably tousled and sleepy, Reese had been kind and patient with the girl, whose loud voice Amanda could hear from the other side of the bed. She'd watched him during the conversation, seeing the great guy, the caring brother.

He'd told her a little about his family after the call. That his father had died, that he'd taken over as head of the family business. He hadn't had to tell her he'd taken on his father's role in his younger siblings' lives, too. She'd heard it in the tender—and a little overwhelmed—tone when he talked about them.

Those were about a half-dozen more details than she had ever intended to learn about him. Especially because every one of them just made him that much more appealing.

She absolutely should have steered well clear after that. So how dumb was she to have said yes to this weekend's get-together? Extremely. And yet, she was already almost breathless with excitement when she thought about the fact that she'd be with him again in under twenty-four hours.

"I guess he's just a pretty big distraction right at the moment," she finally admitted.

"I'm glad," Jazz declared. "It's about damn time."

"I know. Now I don't have to give up my membership card to the sexually alive club."

"I don't mean that." Jazz finished off her wine, then got up and crossed to a well-stocked bar, digging around in a fridge for another bottle. She held it up questioningly, but Amanda shook her head. She'd had one glass with dinner. That was her max, considering she was flying the next day.

"So what did you mean?" Amanda asked, once her friend returned to her seat.

"I mean, it's about time you stop thinking about what that creepazoid Dale said to you when you dumped his sorry ass. You're not cold, you're not ruthless and you're no heartbreaker."

Amanda couldn't help humming a few bars of the Pat Benatar song under her breath.

Jazz ignored her. "He was a tool."

True.

"And that fake-overdose shit also proved he was one taco short of a combination plate."

Also true. But he wasn't the only man she'd ever let down. Something her loyal friend was apparently trying to ignore.

"Face it," Amanda said, "moss doesn't grow under my feet. In thirty years, I'm going to be like Uncle Frank. I'll be the one flying off to the Bahamas to hook up with some hot divorcée for the Thanksgiving holiday."

Hell, she was already like Uncle Frank. Suddenly, she wished she could have that second glass of wine.

"If you're swinging that way in thirty years, I might just have to be the hot divorcée."

Amanda snorted with laughter, as Jazz had obviously intended her to. Because the girl was about as flaming a heterosexual as she'd ever known. Jazz often said her favorite color was purple-veined penis.

"Give yourself a chance," Jazz murmured, her smile fading and her tone turning earnest. "Don't decide what this is before you have the opportunity to really find out."

Amanda opened her mouth to respond, but didn't quite know what to say. So she said nothing and simply nodded.

They fell silent for a minute or two. Then, from upstairs, they heard the tromping of feet and the slam of the back door, which meant that Jazz's mother was ushering out the rest of her guests. They'd managed to successfully avoid the big so-great-to-see-you-let's-do-this-more-often goodbye. The two of them lifted their glasses in a silent toast.

To hiding out when the going gets tough, and avoiding emotional entanglements.

She just had to keep reminding herself of that thought for the next couple of days. And not think about the silent promise she'd just made to her best friend.

As HE DROVE HIS RENTAL CAR closer to the beachfront hotel where Amanda awaited him, Reese had sex on his mind. Wild sex. Steamy sex. Crazy, never-thought-it-could-be-this-good sex.

That had been on his mind for days. Ever since he'd driven away from that Cleveland hotel room, unsure of whether he would ever again see the beautiful woman who'd slept in his arms the night before.

This time, he'd played it a little smarter. He hadn't called or e-mailed her right away. Despite how much it killed him, he'd let a full of week go by before he'd tried to contact her.

And it had paid off. Amanda had let her guard down enough to admit she missed him and wanted to see him again. She'd agreed that Thanksgiving weekend in Florida sounded like a perfect holiday.

He should have known it wouldn't stay entirely perfect. Nothing ever did, right?

"Damn it," he muttered, seeing a blue light come on behind him, and hearing the brief trill of a siren.

He was a good driver. But when it came to these getaways with the most exciting woman he'd ever known, even his foot got excited and pressed down a bit too hard on the gas pedal.

He could see their hotel, an older place with a sign showing a blue dolphin leaping through the waves. The thought that Amanda was waiting behind the door of one of the rooms, while he was going to have to spend the next fifteen or twenty minutes just a few yards away dealing with a ticket was frustrating in the extreme.

He put the car's emergency flashers on and pulled into the hotel parking lot, praying the cop was in a good holiday mood. Considering it was Black Friday, however, and he'd probably been chasing credit-card-crazy shoppers clamoring to make it from door-buster to door-buster, Reese somehow doubted he'd be that lucky.

The cop who'd pulled him over spoke from a few feet away as Reese lowered the window. "License and registration?"

Reese started at the female voice, glancing over and seeing the shapely woman standing beside the car door. She was dressed in a formfitting uniform, and wore dark sunglasses even though it was just after sunset. She stared down at him, not taking them off.

"Good evening, Officer," he said slowly. "Is there some kind of problem?"

"You were doing forty in a twenty-five."

"Really? Are you sure about that?"

She bent down into the open window. "You saying I'm wrong?"

"Not wrong. Just maybe…mistaken?"

"You have a smart mouth. Maybe I should haul you in."

He offered her his most charming smile. "I'd really appreciate it if you didn't. I've got a busy night planned."

She fisted her hands and put them on her shapely hips. "You think your night's more important than the safety of everyone else on the road?"

He hesitated, giving it some thought.

"Step out of the car," she snapped.

Reese didn't argue but did as she ordered. Removing the keys from the ignition, he opened the door and stepped out into the thick Florida night. Despite the fact that it was November, heat assaulted him. Though it was already evening, the air was still heavy and hot, with that not unpleasant smell found only in the south. A mixture of citrus, flowers, paper mills and suntan oil.

And spicy, sultry female cop.

"Don't you think we could come to some kind of arrangement, Officer? Can't you get me off…excuse me, I mean, let me off, with a warning or something?"

Her lips tightened. "I don't think a warning will do."

He lifted both his hands, palms up. "There must be some kind of arrangement we could reach. Something I could do for you so you'd feel comfortable forgetting about my speeding?"

She rubbed her hand on her slim jaw, her lips pursed. Then, as if she'd come to some decision, she slowly nodded.

"Okay, then. Maybe you can sweet-talk me into not writing you a ticket."

"Talk?" he asked, moving closer, until the tips of his shoes touched hers and the fabric of their pants brushed. "You sure that's all you want from me? Conversation?"

She swallowed visibly, her throat moving with the effort. Reese lifted his hand, tracing the tip of his index finger from her full bottom lip, down her chin, then her throat, her neck. All the way to the top button of her blouse.

This time, her hard swallow was preceded by a shaky sigh.

"Which room?" he asked, urgency making his voice weak.

She lifted a shaky hand and pointed to the nearest one, on the end.

"Key?"

Tugging it out of her pocket, she handed the key card to him, then put her hand in his and let him lead her across the parking lot. Just before he opened the door, he glanced back at the car, and the motor scooter—obviously a beach-side rental—sitting directly behind it.

Smirking, he said, "Not even a real motorcycle? It's not terribly intimidating."

"Maybe not," she said with a wicked smile. Then she reached into her pocket and pulled out something…something metal. Something that jangled. "But these are definitely real."

Handcuffs. Oh, yeah. They were real. And they were most definitely intimidating.

He just wondered what his sexy-lover-playing-cop was going to say when he got the upper hand and used them on *her*. She might think she was in charge this time, but she'd played that role in Cleveland. It was his turn.

"Okay, Officer Bauer. I guess I'm your prisoner."

At least for a few minutes. As soon as he could gain the upper hand, he'd be the one calling the shots, leaving her vulnerable and helpless against every bit of pleasure he could possibly give her.

AMANDA DIDN'T KNOW WHAT happened. One second, Reese was lying on the bed, his shirt off, pants unfastened, arms upstretched toward the headboard. The next, *she* was flat on her back and wearing one of the sets of handcuffs.

She sputtered. "What are you doing?"

He didn't answer at first, too busy double-checking the cuffs that attached her left hand to the headboard. The other set was lying on the bed, but instead of reaching for it, he hesitated. "We don't have to use both…if you're not comfortable."

She had fully intended to use both sets on him, wanting him totally at her mercy. How wonderful Reese was to take it just far enough, but then pause to make sure she was okay with what he was doing.

Not a lot of men would do that. Of course, not a lot of women would say 'to hell with it' and offer up her other wrist for restraint, either.

But they weren't exactly your average couple.

"Go for it," she said with a sultry smile as she twisted on the sheets, suddenly so aroused she could barely stand it.

He reached across the bed, fastening her other hand, then came back to center, brushing his mouth against hers.

"I've wanted you since the last time I saw you," she told him.

"I know."

He wasn't being arrogant, she realized. He knew because he felt the same way.

"Okay, you've got me, big guy. Now what are you going to do?"

Reese had been almost undressed when she tried to take over, but Amanda hadn't removed so much as her shoes. Which would probably present a bit of a problem when it came to her top. But she trusted him—he was a very resourceful kind of guy.

And it buttoned up the front. Thankfully.

"I'll think of something." He frowned down at her. "So, madam police officer, are you used to trading sexual favors for legal ones?"

"Only in very special circumstances."

He rose to his knees, reaching for her waistband, and unfastened her pants. Amanda lifted up a little so he could slide them down over her hips and bottom, feeling the slow glide of his fingertips down to her very bones.

"What circumstances would those be?"

"Well, when I haven't had a man in a very long time." She licked her lips. "And I stumble across one who looks like he could satisfy me."

He tsked. "Didn't we have this conversation in a beer closet once? Is there any doubt that I can satisfy you?"

Giving him an innocent look, she asked, "A beer closet? Why, I don't know what you mean."

He reached for her tiny panties, catching the elastic and

pulling them off the way he had her pants. This time, she didn't help. She let him work them down, liking the way he couldn't take his eyes off her body as he revealed it.

Those blue eyes darkened as he stared at her hips, her pelvis, the curls at the top of her sex. But he didn't touch, seeming content to drive her mad with just a stare.

He could set out to be as slow and deliberate as he wanted. Amanda knew, however, that his strength would only last so long.

She'd been there, done that, and brought home the orgasms to prove it.

Bare from the waist down, she casually lifted one leg, letting her thighs fall apart so he could see the glistening effect he'd already had on her.

He hesitated for a second, then, as if unable to resist, he reached for her. Tracing her pelvic bone with his fingertips, he finally slid them down to swirl over her clit.

Amanda jerked, her hips lifting off the bed. He didn't go any faster, or further, he just continued to toy with her, to pluck her like a fine instrument, until she was gasping. Then he moved his hand away and reached for the bottom button of her blouse. He unfastened it, pressing his mouth to the bare skin of her belly. The next button—and that wicked, wonderful mouth moved higher.

By the time he reached her midriff, his tongue was involved and he was taking tiny tastes of her, as if he was nibbling delicately on some luscious dessert. She twisted beneath him, arching toward that questing mouth and those careful fingers.

For the first time, she got a sense of just how difficult

this being restrained was going to be. Because she desperately wanted to twine her hands in his hair, to caress his handsome face, cup his strong jaw.

She also wanted to pull him up a teensy bit faster. Her breasts were throbbing with need, her nipples scraping almost painfully against the rough, starched blouse—part of her phony uniform. And having his mouth on her skin, his breaths blowing hotly against her, all she could think about was how incredible his tongue felt on other parts of her anatomy.

But she could do nothing: couldn't hurry him, couldn't touch herself to provide some relief. She could only lie there, silently begging with every quiver of her body.

"What's wrong?" he asked, and there was laughter in his voice.

She faked it. "Not a thing."

"Uh-huh. Sure."

He moved up again. One inch closer to where she needed him to be. Or one inch farther from where she needed him to be. She honestly couldn't decide.

Well, of course she could. She wanted both. Wanted him sucking her nipples and also giving her the kind of mind-blowing oral sex that she'd had erotic dreams about for weeks.

"Please…"

He moved again, this time his slightly roughened cheek scraping the bottom curve of her breast. His lips followed, kissing away the irritation, and she flinched with the close contact to her sensitized nipples.

Finally the right button. He looked down on her and

shook his head. "No bra? Is that standard uniform attire, Officer?"

She twisted, trying to push her nipple toward his mouth, needing him to suck and squeeze and twist.

"Your breasts are a work of art," he mumbled, dropping his aloof act.

She didn't totally agree, always feeling at least a cup size less adequate than most women. But they were pretty, nicely shaped and high. Plus her nipples had so many nerve endings it was a wonder she didn't come when she wore a silk blouse.

"Suck me, Reese," she begged.

"That an order?" He pulled farther away, deliberately tormenting her.

"Let's call it a polite request."

"Well, since you're being polite."

He said nothing else, gave her no warning, merely bent to capture the taut tip between his lips. He sucked her once, then deeper, reaching up to catch the other mound in his hand.

She cried out, her hips instinctively jerking toward his jean-covered legs. Twisting her thigh over his, she tugged him closer, gaining satisfaction from the brush of his jeans against her sex.

She was all nerve endings, all sensation, and between the deep, strong pulls of his mouth on her nipple and the rub of his strong, masculine thigh between her legs, she felt herself begin to climax. The wave began, and she let out a hitchy little cry.

Reese moved suddenly, removing all that physical connection. He covered her mouth with his, swallowing down the sound with a kiss. And the orgasm dissipated like morning fog baked away by the rising sun.

"Not yet," he whispered. "Not just yet."

Oh, God. She was going to kill him. "Paybacks are hell," she snapped.

"Yeah, I know." He moved his mouth to her neck, sucking her skin into his mouth and biting her lightly. "Consider this a payback for November 11th."

Oh. Yeah. The day she'd kept him on the brink of climax but hadn't let him go over the edge until she was good and ready.

"Can I just cry uncle, say you win and take my orgasm now, please?"

"Nope."

Damn. She'd been afraid of that.

Reese was as good as his word. For the next hour, he tormented her, delighted her, toyed with her, thrilled her. There was magic in the man's hands and heaven in his mouth. And he used those hands and that mouth on every last inch of her.

Her shoulders became sore from twisting around on the bed while her arms were restrained above her head. But, to be honest, Amanda didn't mind. There was something incredibly freeing about being at the sexual mercy of someone she trusted completely. There was no quid pro quo, no reciprocity. She just had to lie there and let him give her pleasure, just take, take, take and not feel one bit of guilt about it.

It wasn't until she was sobbing with the need to come

that Reese finally decided to grant her an orgasm. He'd been moving his mouth and tongue across her groin, her upper thighs and the outer lips of her sex, but not lingering long enough. Finally, though, perhaps hearing the sobs of pleasure mingled with frustration, he did linger.

Oh, did he linger.

Swirling his tongue over her clit, he flicked and sucked, then upped the intensity by moving a hand to her swollen lips. He wet his finger in her body's moisture, then slid it into her. Then another, moving slowly, deeply.

"Oh, yes," she said. "More, please."

He gave her more. More pressure, more suction, more delicate stabs of his tongue. And he began to withdraw his fingers, then plunge them in again, filling her as best he could until he could use the part of his anatomy she really wanted.

"Oh, God, finally!" she cried as the waves of pleasure erupted. Nothing could have held them back this time. Her body had reached its very peak of sexual arousal and the explosion that rocked her seemed to last for a solid minute. She almost had an out-of-body experience, she was so in its grip.

By the time it finally released her, she realized Reese had moved away long enough to strip out of his clothes. His erection was enormous, looking bigger somehow, as if seeing her so entirely lost had aroused him more than he'd ever been before.

He paused only long enough to pull on a condom, then moved between her splayed thighs. Amanda immediately tilted up to greet him, wrapping her legs around his hips, wanting him as deep as he could possibly get.

They knew each other now. Knew what they wanted, what they liked, what they could take. So there was nothing tentative, no gentle easing like there'd been the first time, when he'd almost seemed worried he might hurt her.

This time, Reese drove into her in one thrust. Though she was dripping wet and took him easily, Amanda let out a little scream of pleasure. He filled her thoroughly, stretching out a place for himself, making her wonder how she withstood the emptiness when he wasn't inside her.

She wanted her hands free, wanted to wrap them around his neck and hold on tight. But he was too hungry for her to consider asking him to pause to find the keys.

Oh, what the hell.

Amanda didn't even think about it. She easily slid her hand out of the left cuff, twisted the right and tugged that one free, too. Reese had been so tender and sweet about it, not wanting to hurt her, that he hadn't fastened the damn things tightly enough.

His eyes flared in surprise when she lifted her hands to his thick, broad shoulders. "Sneaky woman."

"You don't have to be gentle," she told him, not just referring to the cuffs.

"I know." His eyes glittered as he withdrew, then slammed back into her, hard, deep, almost violent.

Nothing had ever felt so good. Nothing. Not ever.

Amanda raked her nails across his back. Wanting even more, she tilted farther until her legs were so high, he took them and looped them over his shoulders.

"Yes, yes...."

Smiling down at her, Reese bent to catch her mouth in another hungry kiss. His warm tongue thrust deeply against hers, catching the rhythm of his thick member moving in and out of her body. She matched both movements, taking everything, giving it back again. Until finally, in a lot shorter time than he'd allowed for hers, he came close to reaching his own ultimate level of fulfillment. She knew, by his hoarse groans and the strain on his face, that he was almost there.

Not willing to be left behind, yet not wanting to give up one centimeter of that deep possession, she reached down between their bodies, rubbing at her most sensitive spot with her fingertips. Reese looked down, and she followed his stare. It was incredibly erotic, seeing her fingers tangled in her curls, and below, his big, thick cock disappearing into her.

The sights, the sounds, the weight of him, the smell of him, and, oh, the feel of his body joined with hers…all combined to drive her up to that ledge again. And once he saw she was right there with him, Reese brought them both as high as they could possibly go…and then just a little bit further.

THOUGH THEIR PREVIOUS encounters had, literally, been one-nighters, this trip to Daytona was actually going to last two. Amanda had booked the hotel room through Sunday, and Reese wasn't about to ask her why. She again wanted to change the terms of their…whatever it was. Well, that was just fine with him. Double the pleasure, double the fun.

Problem was, by Saturday afternoon, he could see she was beginning to regret it. Her smiles were forced. She kept averting her gaze during their brief talks. And whenever he began any kind of real conversation, she tried to seduce him.

Not that he minded being seduced. Seriously. But he was only human and while the mind was willing, his dick was just about worn-out after six or seven rounds of cops and robbers.

Amanda had even resisted going out to eat, having filled the small fridge with food before his arrival. He knew without asking that she was remembering their dinner at the Italian place in Cleveland. Her aversion to anything that looked, smelled or sounded anything like a date had come through loud and clear. He didn't know why she felt that way—how could he?—but the message had definitely been received.

Still, he'd had enough of grapes and cheese. Not to mention enough of her skittishness about doing anything that didn't involve some part of his anatomy connecting with some part of hers. And that was why, at three o'clock Saturday, he put his foot down, insisting they get out of the hotel room and actually see the ocean they could hear pounding right outside their window.

"I didn't bring a bathing suit," she muttered as he nudged her toward the door.

"I didn't, either. The water's not exactly swimming temperature, is it?" Though, judging by the clear blue sky and blazing yellow sun he could sort-of see through the tired, smudged windows, he figured it had to be as hot as a typical summer day in Pittsburgh. "A walk on the beach doesn't require special clothing. And I might be lucky enough to find a hot dog vendor or something. Because if I have to eat nothing but cheddar cheese for the rest of the day, I'm going to fly to Vermont and shoot someone."

Though a grin pulled at her mouth, she visibly subdued it. With her brow tugged down, she looked like someone trying to get out of some difficult chore. "Fine. We'll walk."

"You know, if I hadn't already seen just how daring you can be, I'd have to conclude you were a total chickenshit."

Her eyes flared wide in surprise. "What did you call me?"

"You heard me," he said with a shrug.

"I'm not afraid of the beach," she insisted.

He'd lay money she intentionally misunderstood. "I didn't say you were."

"Then what are you saying?"

Putting a hand on her elbow, he led her out the door while she was distracted being all pissed off. "I'm just wondering something. Are you scared that if you take your hands out of my pants for too long, you might actually start to like me?"

Her face flushed, but, as he'd figured, she kept on walking, now challenged more than anything else.

It took a full minute for her to respond. As they crossed the wooden planking over the dunes and stepped down onto the sandy beach, she finally muttered, "I don't dislike you."

"Progress."

She fell silent again while they stopped to kick off their

shoes. As he'd suspected, it was blazingly hot out, at least fifty degrees warmer than it had been yesterday in Pittsburgh. While he definitely could appreciate the warmth, he honestly didn't think he'd ever actually enjoy living someplace like this. Wearing shorts while watching football on Thanksgiving day just sounded wrong on all kinds of levels.

Carrying their shoes, they made their way down toward the water. They skirted the pasty-skinned sunbathers, on vacation from cold northern cities, who were sprawled on colorful towels and slathered with lotion. Only when the warm ocean surf lapped at their feet did they turn and proceed north.

Heading away from the hotels, the beach grew less and less crowded. Soon the voices of shouting kids, radios and gabby teenagers had disappeared. There was nothing but the churning of the waves, the hiss of the breeze and the squawk of overhead seagulls. And the very loud silence of his companion.

It was probably a good ten minutes before Amanda said a thing. When she did, it was in a whisper he could barely hear above the strong lapping of the surf against his ankles.

"I actually like you a lot, Reese."

He said nothing, just reached for her hand and laced his fingers through hers. He'd touched her in so many ways, but this was, as far as he could recall, the first time he'd simply held her hand.

Amanda had such a strong, confident personality, he sometimes forgot how feminine she was. Her slender hand, delicate fingers and soft palm reminded him that, despite the swagger and the attitude, she was still vulnerable. More than she'd ever want anyone to realize.

"I probably like you too much already." She sounded as though she'd just admitted to liking tuna-and-peanut-butter sandwiches.

"I wish I could say I understand why that's such a bad thing."

"I told you I didn't want anything serious."

"Who said liking each other meant we were about to exchange rings?"

She stopped, but didn't pull her hand away. Tilting her head back to look up at him, she pushed her sunglasses up onto the top of her thick hair, as if wanting to ensure he understood what she was about to say. He did the same, seeing confusion in her green eyes.

"Here's the thing. I am poison when it comes to men and relationships. My name might as well be Ivy."

He didn't laugh, knowing she was dead serious. She really believed what she said. "Why do you think that?"

"Because I've been *told* that. I break hearts and hurt people, Reese."

"Intentionally?"

Her brow furrowing in confusion, she shook her head slowly. "No, I suppose not. But what difference does that make?"

Leaning down, he pressed his lips onto her forehead, kissing her tenderly. There was nothing sexual in it, just warmth and a bit of consolation for this beautiful woman who seemed to see herself so differently than the way he saw her.

"It makes all the difference in the world," he murmured.

She remained stiff, unyielding. "Not to the guys whose hearts I've broken."

"Armies of them, I suppose?"

She wasn't teased out of her dark mood.

"Platoons?" Reese put his arms around her shoulders, tugging her against him, making her take the support and connection she tried so hard to resist. "Squads?"

"I don't know how big those things are," she mumbled into his shirt, her voice sounding a little watery.

He didn't tease her, didn't pull back to see if those really were tears dampening the front of his shirt or just the misty spray off the ocean.

"I don't, either. And I honestly don't care."

He meant it. He was a grown man, and she'd warned him from the get-go. He could take care of himself.

He only wondered if she was really as tough as she tried to make herself out to be, or if all these protestations and fears were more about protecting her own heart than anyone else's. Not that he was about to say that out loud. Not when she had, at last, seemed to let down her guard, at least a little bit.

"Let's just go with this—no more rules, no more walls. And see where it takes us. Okay?"

No answer. Instead, quietly, slowly, she relaxed against him. After a few moments, she even slid her arms around his waist, holding him, if not tightly, at least comfortably.

They stood that way for a long while, on the edge of the water, with the waves splashing against their legs. And in the quiet stillness of the moment, he felt the tension leave her, felt her give up some of the control she'd been trying so very hard to maintain.

And finally she murmured, "Okay."

He didn't respond or react in any way, knowing the decision had been a difficult one for her to make. He also knew they'd just agreed to something that could end up not working at all.

Because what was happening between them was unpredictable, as uncontrollable as the currents sending the salty ocean water splashing over their feet. He didn't know where they were going or how long it would take to get there. Or how long they'd stay.

He was just glad Amanda had finally appeared to decide to continue the journey with him.

chapter six

December 7

SEEING the number on her caller ID as it rang very late
one weeknight, Amanda almost didn't answer the phone.
Not because she didn't want to talk to Reese, but because
she *did* want to…a little too much.

They hadn't spoken since they'd parted at the airport the
Sunday after Thanksgiving. Yes, they'd exchanged a few
e-mails, but neither of them had pushed it, both realizing
things had changed during their walk on the beach.

Amanda hadn't yet decided how she felt about that
change. Going from a holiday fling to a long-distance relationship was such a big step. An enormous one, at least for
her. So the cooling-off period had seemed like a very good
idea. Mentally, she'd been hoping her common sense would
slowly edge out her libido and she'd somehow find the

strength to tell him she had changed her mind and it was over.

Not seeing him again was the best course of action. They hadn't gone too far yet. At this point, he couldn't decide to hate her and blame her for leading him on. Couldn't accuse her of taking his heart and crushing it beneath the heel of her boots when she left.

Logically, she knew all that. But as the days had dragged on, she'd begun to realize how much she missed him. She missed *everything* about him. She wanted to hear the laughter in his voice, and the sexy way he said her name. She missed the whispers about how much he wanted her when they made love. She even found herself missing the way he kept trying to get her to talk about her past, her family and her lousy romantic track record.

She missed his touch.

Third ring. Fourth. She swallowed hard, twisting in her bed, the covers tangling around her legs. Her muscles flexed, the blood rushing a just bit harder through her veins. Her senses perked up, the scratch of the sheets on her bare skin, the image of his face, the thought of his hands and his mouth.

She hadn't reached for her little sex toy in a few weeks, and if she answered the phone, she had the feeling she would need it. Hearing his voice, wanting him but not having him, would take the low, edgy need throbbing deep inside her and push it up like lava rising in a volcano.

Of course, not answering would still leave her needing it. So she might as well enjoy it. "Hello?"

"Do you realize that today is National Cotton Candy Day?"

She chuckled, wondering how the man could amuse her when she was suddenly so damned horny. "Funny, I had figured you were calling because it's Pearl Harbor Day." She had half thought about it herself, sticking to their holiday theme.

"That's too somber," he said. "Cotton candy's a lot more cheerful. It's very pink."

"I'm not a pink kinda girl."

He didn't even pause. "It can also be blue."

"An expert at cotton candy, are you?"

"Let's just say I'd like to become better acquainted with it. Especially with what I'm picturing right now."

She settled deeper into the pillow, the phone nestled in the crook of her neck. "What are you picturing?"

"You. Wearing nothing but a lot of fluffy cotton candy."

Laughing softly, she said, "Sounds sticky."

"Sounds delicious."

"You really think you could eat that much?"

"I could dine on you for days, Amanda Bauer."

Okay, definitely gonna need the vibrator tonight. Sighing in utter pleasure at the sound of his need for her, she kicked the covers totally off. She bent one knee, letting her legs fall apart, barely noticing the cold night air. The heat of his whispers warmed her enough.

"Where are you?" he asked, his voice thick, as if he'd suddenly realized she was no longer thinking light and flirty thoughts, but deep and sultry ones.

"I'm in my great big bed, all by my lonesome."

"Mmm. And what are you wearing."

"Not a blessed thing."

"Hold it…ahh, now you are. I see you. All wrapped in blue fluff just waiting for me to eat it off you."

Amanda licked her lips, then slid her hand across her stomach, tracing her fingertips along the bottom curves of her breasts. "Where are you?" she asked.

"In bed. Of course, I don't have as much privacy. I'm not alone like you are."

She stiffened, though realistically she knew he wouldn't be calling if he had a woman with him. Especially because he knew if he did, she'd fly to Pittsburgh and punch him.

"Get down, Ralph."

Hearing a low woof in the background, she realized who he was talking about. "Ahh. Your dog."

"Out you go, buddy," he said. She heard the click of a door as the dog apparently got sent out of the bedroom for the night. Then Reese admitted, "He's not as cuddly as you are."

Cuddly? Her? Ha. "I'm as cuddly as a porcupine."

His soft laugh told her he didn't believe her instinctive protestation. "You're very nice to hold, Manda. I can't decide which I like better—holding you in my arms while you sleep, or just watching you."

"You watch me sleep? Why?"

"You're soft when you're asleep," he explained simply.

Soft. He didn't mean her skin, or her hair. She knew what he meant, that he had seen her with her guard down, emotionally vulnerable, no barriers. And he sounded happy about it.

Her heart twisted a little. Then she kicked her legs restlessly. "Get back to the cotton candy," she ordered, preferring sexy talk to the gentle, tender stuff. It was safer. Less risky.

"God, you're so predictable."

Gasping, she snapped, "I am not!"

"Yeah, babe, you are. You wanted to reach for your sex toy and let me whisper you through an orgasm and I went and got sappy on you."

Okay. So she was predictable. She didn't reply at first, nibbling her lip, finally asking, "Does that mean no phone sex?"

"Are you kidding? Hell yeah to the phone sex." His voice lowered, all amusement fading from it as he admitted, "I'm lying here with my rock-hard cock in my hand, just thinking about all the places in your body I want to fill with it."

"Oh, my," she whispered, a few of those places reacting instinctively. Her mouth went dry, her sex very wet. She moved her hand in a long, slow slide down her bare stomach until she reached her hip. "Tell me more."

He did, speaking in a hoarse whisper. "I want to take you in every way a man can take a woman."

She closed her eyes, the very word *take* making her quiver. Amanda was not one to give up control. But oh, how she had enjoyed it that Friday night in Daytona. Giving herself over to him, knowing he wouldn't hurt her and only wanted to give her pleasure had been one of the most exciting sexual experiences of her life.

"But first we'd have to get rid of all that cotton candy."

"You want to take a shower together?" she teased.

"Not right away. No, first I want to lie on my back and pull you up on top of me."

Her pulse pounded, her breath became shallow.

"I want you sitting on my chest, your legs open for me so I can lick all that sugar off the insides of your creamy thighs."

Amanda's legs clenched reflexively. She moved her hands to the curls between them, sliding her fingertip over her clit, hissing at how hard and sensitive it was. Every word he uttered was an invisible caress, the mental picture he created almost drugging in its sensual intensity.

"It'll be soft and fluffy at first. So sweet. But the closer I get to you, the more pure sugar I'll find. Because you'll be so hot and wet it will already have melted."

"Oh, Reese." She arched on the bed, stroking her clit harder, then sliding her finger between the lips of her sex. *Hot and wet* most definitely described what she felt.

"Do you know how much I love having my tongue on you…in you?" he asked. "How good you taste to me?"

She reached for the sex toy in the drawer beside the bed. Now, more than ever, she wished she had a big, thick rubber one rather than just the thin plastic vibrator. She wanted to be filled. *Taken.*

"Manda?"

"I'm here," she whispered as she flipped the switch and moved the device right where she most needed it. Then she clarified, "Actually, I'm not here…I'm almost *there.*" Hearing his deep breaths, she knew she wasn't alone. "Tell me what happens next. After you've licked away every bit of sweetness."

"You tell me," he countered.

"Easy. I'll slide down your body. Slowly. Tormenting you."

"No fair. I didn't torment you."

He was tormenting her now. Giving her fantasy when she wanted reality. But fantasy would have to do, at least for now.

"But I wouldn't be able to hold out," she conceded. "I'd be so desperate to have you inside me, the second I felt the tip of your cock against me, I'd slide down onto it, welcoming you in one deep thrust."

He groaned. Hearing that deep, primal sound of pleasure, recognizing it from all the times Reese had come inside her, Amanda pressed the vibrator a little harder. The waves of her climax rolled up. Higher. Faster. She couldn't speak anymore, couldn't listen, couldn't even think. She could only feel as the pleasure exploded in a hot rush, filling her body.

But it was short-lived. Very short. Not nearly the kind of satisfaction she got in Reese Campbell's arms.

Silent and spent, gasping on the bed with the phone still beside her ear, she had to admit it, if only to herself. She'd become addicted to him.

And she knew, without a doubt, she'd do just about anything to be with him again. For as long as she could have him.

Christmas

SOME YEARS, THE CELEBRATION of Hanukkah coincided with Christmas. Fortunately, however, this year was not one of them.

Which meant two real holiday getaways in December.

They'd spent the first one in a room in a New York City hotel. Reese had met Amanda there, not sure what she had up her sleeve for them. The venue had been far different from the place in Florida where they'd spent Thanksgiving weekend.

Not that he'd complained. Just wanting to be with her again, he really hadn't cared where they went. That desire had grown exponentially after their Cotton Candy Day phone sex, and he probably would have agreed to meet her in the middle of a war zone if that was the only way he could get her.

So, yeah, anyplace would do, as long as it had a bed and was far away from the real world where nobody knew them. A place where Amanda could relax and forget she wasn't the settling-down type, that she didn't want a relationship, was just fine with him.

Especially since, whether she liked it or not—whether she would admit it or not—they *had* a relationship.

Far from a beachfront dive, the Manhattan high-rise had been all about luxury and indulgence. He'd understood her reason for choosing it when she'd finally revealed herself…and the game. Reese had nearly had a heart attack when she'd snuck out of the closet in their room, dressed all in black from head to toe. She was playing the part of a cat burglar who'd just been caught in the act.

He'd really liked the way she'd taken possession of his most valuable jewels.

He'd liked it just as much that she hadn't resisted when he'd whisked her out of the hotel for dinner at an upscale restaurant. And that she'd given him a loud, smacking kiss when he'd presented her not with tickets to a Broadway show but with ones to a hard-rock concert at the Garden.

During the trip, she'd been relaxed—sexy as always, but not so guarded. She'd laughed easily, talked more. It was as if she'd done some thinking after their walk on the beach, and had decided to just go with this for as long as it lasted.

His Easter eggs were looking brighter already.

The thought of it made him smile. Especially since he was going to be seeing her again so soon.

"I still can't believe you're taking off for Las Vegas on Christmas. That's so mean!"

Ignoring the disgruntled tone of his teenage sister, Molly, he forced his thoughts off tomorrow's trip—technically, the day *after* Christmas—and turned them back to the matter at hand: the board game which was set up on the kitchen table. Playing games after Christmas dinner had been a Campbell family tradition since he was a kid.

That his father had been the game fanatic made the ritual one everyone seemed to want to keep alive. Including Reese, even though, on any other day of the year, he'd rather eat moldy fruitcake than play Risk.

Then again, it could be worse. There had been those Pretty, Pretty Princess marathons all those years ago when his sisters were young and got their way most of the time.

Hmm. Not that much had changed. Even though he wasn't the pushover his dad had been when it came to the Campbell girls, they still managed to get what they wanted for the most part.

Like now.

"Wahoo! I just took over Australia! You keep thinking about the chick you're hooking up with in Vegas, big brother, and I'll keep taking your countries."

Reese frowned at his sister Debra, nine years his junior and halfway through her second year of college. She smirked, lifting a challenging brow, daring him to deny what she'd said.

"What?" Molly asked, her eyes widening. "You're meeting someone? Who?" The sixteen-year-old, who hadn't yet figured out that the world didn't revolve entirely around her, pouted as she added, "Is that why you won't take us, even though you *know* how much I'm dying to go to Vegas? Because you want to hook up with some girl? Talk about shitty."

"Watch your mouth," he said, the reply automatic. Funny, considering when he was sixteen, his bad language had prompted their mother to squirt a bottle of dish detergent all over his dinner one night. But he figured it's what Dad would have said.

"Why would *you* want to go, anyway? All you'd do is shop for clothes and text with your friends, just like you do here."

That was the longest sentence Reese had heard out of his kid brother Jack's mouth all day. The fourteen-year-old had eased up on his I-hate-everyone-because-I'm-a-teenager schtick a little bit today, and for him, the remark was downright chatty. He even went on to add, "Who's the girl, Reese?"

As pleased as he was that his sullen brother, who'd been only twelve when their father had died, was actually interested in having a conversation, that was one talk he didn't want to have. "Ignore her. She's trying to distract you so she can take over Southeast Asia."

"Is she hot?"

Incendiary. "Are we playing or are we talking?" He glanced at his watch. "Because it's almost eight and I'm outta here at nine whether I control the entire world or not."

Jack wasn't put off. Neither were his sisters. Like three dogs sniffing after a bone, they stayed on the subject. He was just lucky his other two sisters—Tess, a hard-assed, divorced man-hater right now, and Bonnie, the bleeding heart who wanted to save the world—were in the other room watching Tess's kids play with their new toys.

"Is your new girlfriend the reason you went away for Thanksgiving weekend?" asked Molly, that whine in her voice making his eye twitch.

"Friend," he clarified.

Molly rolled her eyes. "Does she live far away?"

"Chicago," Debra said.

Reese gaped. "How the hell do you know that?"

"Aunt Jean told me," she said with a broad, self-satisfied grin. Debra had outgrown any teenage whininess and now just loved playing her role of family shit-stirrer.

Reese didn't ask how Aunt Jean knew. The old woman had spies watching her spies. Besides, if he wanted to know, he could ask her himself. She should be here soon; they would be the last stop on her around-Pennsylvania visits to all her nieces, nephews and distant family members.

But he didn't want to know. In fact, he didn't want to see her at all, knowing she'd take one look at him and crow with triumph. Obviously, if she was telling his kid sister about his trips to meet Amanda, she knew damn well he'd taken her advice—well, her order—to go out and live a little.

Nobody said "I told you so" like an old woman who really *had* told you so. With any luck, he'd be gone before she got here to say it.

"Why hasn't this 'friend' come to meet us?" asked Molly.

"Maybe because you'd scare her into the next state."

"Oh, a real Miss Priss, huh?" the sixteen-year-old said with a tsk. "No balls?"

Jack grunted. "I sure hope not. If Reese switches sides and starts tea-bagging, I'm giving up on this family for good."

His jaw hanging open, he stared at his kid brother. "If I start *what?*"

"You know, it's when you…"

Reese threw a hand up, palm out. "Enough. I know what it is." Glancing at his sisters, who made faces ranging from ewwwy to grossed-out, he saw they knew what it was, too.

Jesus, how had his father ever stood it? Teenagers were a damned nightmare.

"What's her name?" Molly asked.

"None of your business."

"None of Your Business Campbell. Has a nice ring to it," said Debra, her pretty eyes dancing with laughter. She was the mischief-maker of the bunch, playing that middle-child role like she'd invented it. "You can name your kids Go Away and Bite Me."

"Go away," he mumbled, closing his eyes and rubbing at them with his fingers.

"Bite me," she said sweetly.

"That's not very polite, young lady."

His eyes flying open, he looked up to see his great-aunt Jean standing in the doorway. Surveying the scene, she looked matriarchal, though her lips twitched with amusement. He suspected she'd been there for a while.

His sisters both rose from the table to greet their aunt who, though an eccentric one, was also everybody's favorite. He suspected that was partly due to the fact that she always came loaded for bear with presents.

"Help me unload my car, will you? I brought a few goodies."

The girls raced toward the door so fast the Risk board almost went flying. Which would have been fine with him.

"Gonna help them, bro?" Reese asked Jack, who had slouched down in his seat, not wanting to appear eager or excited about anything. Around the immediate family, he'd lowered his defenses for a little while today. Aunt Jean's arrival had put that guarded look back in his eyes.

Reese's heart twisted. The kid had once been a happy-go-lucky, smiling Little Leaguer. But not anymore. Fourteen was bad enough. With the weight Jack had been carrying around for two years, it was a lot worse.

The boy shrugged. "Whatever."

As his brother got up and walked by, Reese couldn't help offering a small, encouraging nod, and a slight squeeze of his bony shoulder. *Be a kid. Just for tonight, even. Tomorrow's soon enough to go back to being mad at the world.*

Jack didn't smile in return. But his spine might have

straightened a little and his trudging footsteps picked up. It was something, anyway.

"He'll be all right," Aunt Jean murmured, her eyes softer than usual as they watched Jack walk out the back door.

Reese sincerely hoped so.

"Now, let's talk about *you*."

He had known that was coming. "I hear you already have been. Thanks a lot. I really love getting the third degree from my sisters."

"And a merry Christmas to you, too."

Curiosity won out over embarrassment. "So how'd you know?"

She merely shrugged, guarding that mysterious, all-knowing, all-seeing reputation. Then, glancing at her diamond watch, she shook her head. "Hadn't you better be heading home for the night? It's a long trip to Las Vegas." She shrugged. "I'm afraid I don't have very much for you in the car, because I think I've already given you a big enough gift this year."

Well, he supposed her urging him to go out and have an adventure for himself did count as a gift. Because, whether he wanted to admit it or not, the past few months had been the best he'd had in a long, *long* time.

Reese's mouth widened in a smile and he crossed the room to kiss her powdery, paper-thin cheek. "Thank you, Aunt Jean."

"You're welcome. Now, go. Have fun. Be wild." She waved a hand, gesturing around the kitchen. "This domestic bliss will all be here waiting for you when you get back."

Whether that was a promise, or a threat, he didn't know. Nor did he really want to think about it. Because he already had other things on his mind.

He had the rest of a holiday to celebrate. And a woman he was crazy about to share it with.

AMANDA WASN'T MUCH of a Christmas person. Her parents had not believed in spoiling her or her sister, so the season had never really entailed presents or parties. The holidays comprised a lot of volunteer work, the requisite Bing Crosby songs, quiet dinners and church. Some years, they hadn't even gotten a tree, her frugal father finding the expense excessive.

The Christmases she'd spent with Uncle Frank had been completely different. Big parties, lots of drinking, dancing, jetting off to some hot spot for New Year's. There had definitely been no popcorn stringing or chestnuts roasting.

The closest she ever came to a normal American family holiday were the years she'd stayed in Chicago and had gone to Jazz's parents' house. But she'd always felt a bit like an outsider. She didn't quite get the lingo, had never felt completely comfortable receiving socks and bras from Jazz's mom, who treated her just like one of her own.

Christmas, she had long ago decided, just wasn't her thing.

So when Reese Campbell walked into their hotel room with a suitcase full of presents for her, she didn't know what to think. "Oh, God, are you kidding? I only got you one small gift!"

A small, sexy gift. A small, sexy, *funny* gift.

But she didn't think the men's velvet boxers with the Rudolph head—complete with blinking red nose—was quite equal to the ten or so packages he pulled out and tossed onto the big bed.

"I'm so bad at this," she groaned, not elaborating. He knew what she meant: this whole *girlfriend* thing. No, they weren't using the word, but it was about the only one she could come up with. And as girlfriends went, she totally sucked the big one.

Metaphorically speaking. Well, literally speaking, too, but thinking about that wasn't going to help right at this particular moment.

"I don't care. Christmas isn't about getting, it's about giving."

"You're giving me a guilty conscience," she wailed, staring at the brightly wrapped boxes.

Funny, a few months ago, her first instinct would probably have been to give in to the tightness squeezing her chest, turn and walk out the door. She'd always wanted to visit London during the winter. Prague sounded good. Amsterdam.

No. You're not doing that. Not this time. Not to him.

She'd come here this weekend knowing full well what it meant. After their conversation in Florida, she knew the terms had changed yet again. Their New York trip had been fun, but Christmas and a whole week in Vegas together added up to something more. And while she'd managed to convince herself nothing would be really different, that this was just another sexy holiday getaway, deep down she'd known Reese might treat it as a genuine one between two people who were involved.

And she'd shown up with damned fuzzy Rudolph boxer shorts.

Tart, sour and heartless. That was her.

"Don't even think about it," he warned, obviously seeing something in her eye.

She didn't need his warning. Because even without it, she'd already kept her feet planted on the floor.

The pressure in her chest gradually eased until she could breathe normally again. Then, instead of frowning and accusing him of taking things too seriously, getting her gifts like they were some kind of real couple, she couldn't help but smile.

"You're serious? All these are for me?"

"Well," he admitted as he threw himself down on the bed, "some of them are for me, too." He wagged his brows suggestively as he rolled onto his side, resting on his bent elbow. "I think a fashion show is in order."

She bit the inside of her cheek to keep from laughing. "Okay, but only if you promise to do one, too, with what I got you."

"You're on."

Oh, boy, was he going to regret that one. But Amanda could hardly wait.

Well, giving it some thought, she realized she could wait. There was a way to salvage this situation. "Listen, let's hold off on the presents until tomorrow, okay? Give me a little time to at least come up with an ugly tie, a bowling ball or a bottle of Hai Karate for you to open."

He snorted a laugh. "You just described every one of my father's Christmas mornings. But, bad news. I don't bowl."

"Okay. Maybe I can come up with something else."

He sat up, reaching for her hand and tugging her forward until she stood between his legs. "You really don't have to."

"I know." She wanted to. Suddenly, the idea of giving her lover a real Christmas gift sounded like exactly the right thing to do.

There was something else she wanted to do, as well. Something that had been on her mind for days, ever since she'd realized they were going to sin city. She had a fantasy in mind, one she suspected he was going to enjoy sharing.

"You do realize today is a holiday, too. It's Boxing Day."

"I'm not into boxing, either," he said, his eyes twinkling.

"It's a big deal in some countries." She shimmied out from between his strong legs. "What I'm trying to say is, I would very much like to *play* with you on this holiday."

He nodded slowly, the twinkle turning into a gleam of interest. Hunger.

"So here's what I want you to do." She dug a piece of paper out of her pants pocket and shoved it toward him. "Go to this address and wait for me. I'll be there in an hour."

He glanced at it. "Is it a restaurant or something?"

She shook her head. "No. Just wait outside."

Still appearing puzzled, he rose to his feet. But he didn't leave immediately, pausing to cup her chin and tug her toward him for a soft, slow kiss goodbye.

She almost relented, giving up on the fantasy for some good, old-fashioned, lovely sex. But she'd been thinking about this for a long time. After showing up without any presents for him, the least she could do was try to give him the kind of fantasy he would never forget.

And just about every man in the world had one fantasy when it came to Vegas. Reese's was going to come true.

Pushing him toward the door, she said, "Go. One hour."

He lifted his hand in mock salute. "I can hardly wait."

The minute he was gone, Amanda raced to her suitcase and began yanking clothes from it. She'd done a little more eBay shopping, looking for another costume. Not a stewardess this time, she was going for someone quite different.

She intended to transform herself completely. And fifteen minutes later, when she looked at her reflection in the mirror, she knew she had succeeded.

"Hot damn," she whispered, smiling as she checked herself out from bottom to top.

The boots were even more kick-ass than her Halloween ones. Black leather, spiked, coming all the way up over her knee. They were wicked and screamed sex.

Above them was a large expanse of fishnet-covered thighs. And finally a few inches of hot pink miniskirt that barely covered her ass. It was made out of something that felt like cellophane and crinkled when she walked.

The teensy, tie-front white top covered her shoulders and her breasts and not much else. And the short, platinum-blond wig completed her transformation from Amanda Bauer, professional pilot, to Mandy the hooker.

After all, what guy hadn't fantasized about being picked up by a sexy call girl in Vegas?

"Whatever the customer wants, that's what he's going

to get," she whispered, smiling as she headed for the door to the room. She paused only to grab her long coat off the back of a chair. Not only because it was chilly out, but also because there was no way she wanted any hotel employees to see her entire costume. The place was five star all the way, and the *Pretty Woman* look probably wouldn't be welcome in the lobby.

"Okay, sweet man, get ready, because here I come," she said under her breath as she descended in the elevator. Every minute ensured her certainty of one thing.

Reese Campbell had no idea what kind of night he was in for.

chapter seven

Boxing Day

SHOWGIRL or stripper? Paid escort? Call girl?

Reese wasn't sure which Amanda was going to show up tonight. He only knew that whichever woman met him here on this slightly seedy corner, one block off the northernmost end of the Strip, she was going to blow his mind. Just like she always did.

"Come on, it's been over an hour," he muttered, glancing at his watch as he leaned against a light post. She'd better show up soon, or one of the real working girls might decide he was looking for some company.

She'd been adorable when pushing him out of the room back at the hotel. Had she really thought he didn't know, that he couldn't figure out what kinds of games she'd want to play in Las Vegas? Seriously, what could be more obvious?

Still, maybe it wasn't as clear to her as it was to him that he knew her so well. Better than he'd ever imagined when they first met. Better than she'd ever wanted him to, that was for sure.

He was even beginning to understand why. Despite those careful walls she'd kept around herself in the beginning, during their last couple of get-togethers, she had started to reveal bits and pieces of herself.

She'd talked a little about her family back home, hinting at a lack of connection that saddened him on her behalf. His own family might drive him crazy, but he'd been raised in a house filled to the brim with love.

He suspected Amanda had never been assured of that emotion from her parents.

She'd also asked about his upbringing, and in her slightly wistful tone, he'd heard much more than she was willing to say out loud. He'd known, somehow, that despite how much she claimed not to need anyone, a part of her might actually wonder what such connections might be like.

One thing she hadn't talked any more about was her past love life. But, hell, she didn't need to. He knew she'd had a few rocky relationships. He also knew they'd ended badly, and that she still kicked herself about it.

She was human, wasn't she? Human and only in her late twenties. Who the hell didn't do dumb things in their twenties, things they regretted for a long time after? Amanda simply hadn't realized yet that she wasn't much different from anybody else. Including him.

"Hey stranger, you lookin' for some company?"

Call girl.

Excitement washed over him as he turned to stare at the

woman who'd spoken from a few feet away. She stood just outside a puddle of illumination cast by the streetlight, and he couldn't see her well. But he'd know her anywhere. That voice, that scent. The very air seemed filled with static electricity, snapping with the excitement that always surrounded her. He reacted to it on a visceral level, as he had since the moment they'd met.

"Maybe," he admitted. "Are you offering to keep me company?"

"I might be willing to do that. If you offer me enough… incentive."

She sauntered closer, into the light, and Reese had to suck in a surprised breath. Good thing he'd had that moment of instant recognition, all his other senses confirming her identity. Because for a brief second, when he saw her, he feared he'd been mistaken. At first glance, she looked like a completely different woman. An incredibly sexy woman. A woman he wanted with every cell in his body.

"Wow," he muttered.

Her wig was short, blond, curling just past her chin. The style emphasized the heavy makeup she wore. Amanda's face was already lovely, but with the added coloring—the thick mascara, the ruby-red lips—she looked exotic and oozed sex appeal.

The clothes, however, took the sex appeal from oozing to gushing.

Her long, black overcoat clung to the very edges of her shoulders. Completely unbuttoned, it gaped open to reveal the skimpy outfit beneath. What little of it there was.

Her white top was not only incredibly tiny, plunging low to tie beneath her breasts, it was also thin, nearly sheer. Even in the low light, he could make out the dark, puckered nipples and hunger flooded his mouth. It had been too long since he'd tasted her, touched her. He should have insisted on at least a few minutes back at the hotel to satisfy the raging need he'd been feeling ever since they'd parted ways in New York.

Her midriff was entirely bare, down all the way past her stomach. The skirt, which didn't even reach her belly button, merely pretended to clothe her hips, and was so tight he could see the line where her thighs came together underneath. And oh, those fishnet-clad thighs beckoned him, tempting him to taste the tiny squares of supple skin revealed between the black, stretchy bits of fabric.

The boots were, without a doubt, his favorite part of the whole thing. And he already knew he was going to rip those hose off her body so she could leave the boots on to wrap around him as he pounded into her.

"So, whaddya say, mister?"

"To what?"

"To a date?"

"A…date? With you?" he asked, pretending reticence he in no way felt.

"No," she said with a definite eye roll. "With that light post holding you up."

He still didn't move.

"Come on, admit it. Haven't you fantasized about spending a night with a girl like me?"

He couldn't answer that. Not truthfully. Because if he

answered in the game, as if she were really a call girl, he'd have to say no. He'd never even thought about being with a prostitute.

If he answered as himself, the real Reese Campbell talking to the real Amanda Bauer, then the response was unequivocally yes. He wanted to go out with *her,* be a half of a couple with her—Amanda—almost as much as he wanted to take her back to the hotel and do her until she screamed with pleasure.

"I promise you, I'll let you do things to me that your nice little wife or girlfriend back home has never even heard of."

Interesting. The corner of his mouth lifted in a half smile. "I think I might need to hear more about these things before I make a decision."

She moved closer, her gait slinky, the sway of her hips exaggerated. When she reached his side, she lifted her hand to his chest. "Let's just say you can do anything you want to me. Absolutely *anything*. And I'd let you."

He shook his head, feigning confusion. "I'm still not sure I know what you mean."

She lifted her chin and her eyes narrowed as she heard the challenge in his voice. Then, with a smile of pure wickedness, she leaned up on her toes, coming close enough for her beautiful lips to graze his cheek. With a nip on his earlobe, she told him one *very* naughty thing she wanted him to do to her.

Damn. Heat and excitement flared and he slid his hands into her coat, cupping her waist. Without a word, he turned her around, so her back was to the light pole, then bent down and kissed her. Licking his way into her mouth, he met her tongue with his and thrust lazily. Their bodies melded and he heard her tiny groan when she felt how hard he already was for her. She pressed against him, grinding her groin against his erection, wrapping one long leg around his to cup him more intimately between her thighs.

They were on a public street and it was only ten o'clock at night. Fortunately, though, the cool weather had people staying inside the closest casino gambling, not outside cruising the block. So as far as he could tell, they didn't have an audience.

That was good. Because he couldn't stop. No *way* would he stop. Not when her lips were so sweet and her body so willing. Not when she'd whispered such wanton, erotic desires in his ear, promising their fulfillment with her dreamy-eyed stare.

When he finally ended the kiss, lifted his head and looked down at her, he saw the dazed look of pure want on her face. Her lids half covered her green eyes and most of her lipstick had been kissed off. She looked sensual and awakened, ready for sin and sex and more of everything they'd ever done together. And some things they hadn't.

He had to have her. *Had* to.

"Let's get out of here," he muttered, already stepping toward the curb to flag down a taxi.

"Absolutely," she whispered, her voice shaking.

Traffic wasn't heavy, and not a cab was in sight. Figured. When he saw one crossing the next block, Reese stepped off the curb onto the street, whistling loudly. But before he could see whether the cabbie had heard him and made a last-minute turn, he was startled by a shout that split the night air.

"Stop, thief!"

Reese froze, jerking his head to stare in the direction of the voice. The cry had sounded like it was coming from the closest building, which had a sign identifying it as a pawn shop.

He was a split second slow in reacting. If he'd been thinking more clearly, he would have immediately jumped back up onto the sidewalk, grabbed Amanda and shoved her safely behind him. In his surprise, though, he hadn't done it.

So she was right in the path of the black-cloaked figure that came hurtling out from behind the building.

"Manda!" he cried, seeing the shape emerge from the darkness.

Before she had time to react, the running man barreled into her. They stumbled around together for a second, their legs and coats tangling.

"You son of a bitch." Reese dove toward them, knocking the man off her, but falling, himself, in the process. "You're dead," he snarled.

The thief, obviously realizing there was only one thing that would stop Reese from chasing him down and beating him to a pulp, whirled around toward Amanda and shoved. Hard.

The blow sent her careening toward the street. Those high-heeled boots wobbled, making it impossible for her to catch her balance. Right before she fell off the curb into the path of the cab, which had indeed turned and was rapidly cruising up the block, Reese lunged to his feet and grabbed her around the waist, hauling her back to safety.

"My God, are you okay?"

She nodded, though her whole body was shaking, especially as a taxi screeched to a stop right where she would have landed in the street.

"That rotten bastard," Reese snapped, his feet nearly in motion to go after the man in black. The thief had just darted down the next alleyway, heading across a debris-laden, abandoned construction site that separated this road from the north strip.

"No, Reese," she insisted, holding on to his arm. "I'm fine, really. And you are *not* going to go chasing after some robber. You could get hurt."

"He was a scrawny runt."

"Who might be armed. You're staying right here."

Before he could reply, a heavyset, balding man with flaming red cheeks jogged up to them. "Did you see him? Did you get a good look? Rotten thief robbed my shop!"

"I saw him," Amanda replied, sounding weary.

The shop owner peered at her, narrowed his eyes and sighed heavily. "Oh, that's just *great*."

The man's sneer toward Amanda, whom he obviously took for a real lady of the evening, tempted Reese to let the guy deal with his own problems. But his rage toward the thug who'd so callously tossed her into the street was greater. So he admitted, "I saw him, too. Now why don't you go call the police so we can give them a description."

He tightened his arm around Amanda's shoulders. "And hurry. We've got things to do tonight."

OF ALL THE WAYS she'd envisioned spending their first night in Vegas, standing in a dingy pawn shop, talking to two officers from the LVPD, hadn't been in the top thousand. Especially because said cops had spent the first ten minutes of their interview trying to figure out whether they needed to arrest her for prostitution and Reese for solicitation.

Talk about a convincing costume. She and Reese had finally had to come clean about what they were up to, showing their credentials, including Amanda's pilot's license. Ever since, the younger police officer had been trying to hide a smile and was casting quick, sneaky glances at Amanda whenever he thought he could get away with it. The older one hadn't even tried to hide his amusement. She'd swear she heard him mumbling something about how much he wished his wife would wear thigh-high boots.

That so didn't help.

"Okay then, miss, sir, I think I've got everything I need," said the older officer, who'd introduced himself as Parker. Standing in the well-lit entranceway of the shop, they'd just finished answering all his questions. "You did a good job remembering details about this guy."

Amanda didn't think she would soon forget the pale, pockmarked face of the man who'd so readily shoved her toward what could have been her death. His glazed brown eyes and long, greasy blond hair weren't going to leave her mind anytime soon, either.

"The owner of the shop says the thief got away with some valuable diamond jewelry," Parker added. He snapped his notebook closed and tucked it into his uniform pocket.

Reese glanced around the small, nondescript shop, which was a little dusty and unimpressive. "Really?" he asked, sounding doubtful. "It doesn't look exactly top shelf."

"You'd be surprised," offered the younger officer, whom the older one kept calling Rookie. His voice low, he looked around for the owner, who'd disappeared into the back to do yet another check on his inventory. "A lotta these places are mob-owned, legit businesses where money goes to get nice and clean."

"Would you shut yer yap?" said Parker. With a glare, he explained, "We're really not in the habit of making un-founded comments about members of our local business community."

The younger guy snapped his mouth shut and didn't say another word.

"If we're finished, are we free to go?" Reese asked.

"Sure thing." Smiling, Parker tipped his hat at Amanda. "Hope you two enjoy the rest of your visit to our fair city. And might I suggest that next time you, uh, confine your field trips to the lobby of your own hotel?"

Though she'd been embarrassed at first, now all Amanda could do was chuckle. Parker seemed like a nice guy, and, really, it was either laugh or cry. Laughing seemed the much better option.

"You bet," she said. Winking, she added, "And if you

get your wife a pair of these boots, be sure to get one size larger than she usually wears. They're pretty painful."

He threw his head back and guffawed. "If I came home with a pair of those things for her, she'd use them to kick my ass."

With a polite nod, Reese led Amanda out of the shop by the arm. She was still chuckling as they emerged outside, knowing she was going to have to share this whole story with Jazz. Her friend would love it.

So would Uncle Frank, if she was ever able to get over the whole embarrassment factor and tell him, too. But it was the kind of situation that would horrify her parents, and reinforce their firm belief that she was a reckless wanton who cared nothing for her own reputation. Or theirs.

Caught up in thought, she didn't notice that a small crowd had gathered outside the pawn shop. About a dozen people milled around on the sidewalk, likely drawn by the flash of the police lights and the whispers of a robbery in the neighborhood.

"Hey, what happened?" somebody asked.

"You'll have to let the police fill you in," Reese said, sliding a hand around her waist as he tried to lead her through the crowd.

It was only when she felt the warmth of his fingers against her very bare skin that she realized she hadn't re-buttoned her coat, which she'd unfastened in the heat of the store. Gaping open, it revealed her costume in all its glory to the wide-eyed strangers. She reached for the edges of it, intending to yank it closed. But before she could, a male voice called, "Hey, sweet thing, how late you working tonight?"

Another one added, "Got a business card?"

Though she knew she should be absolutely mortified, and maybe even a little nervous, more laughter bubbled up inside her. The size of the crowd, the presence of a few normally dressed women and tourists, and the two police officers right inside the closest building eased her hint of fear.

And the embarrassment? Hell, she was so far past that, she couldn't even remember what it felt like.

Beside her, Reese made a small sound. Worried, she glanced over and saw his lips twitch. Relief flowed through her. His anger and concern had finally eased up and he was beginning to see the humor in the situation, too.

"Sorry, guys, she's retired," he said, tugging her closer to his side.

"Since when?"

Following his lead, she sidled closer to Reese. Glued to his side from ankle to hip, she slipped her arm around his waist, too. Dropping her head onto his shoulder and simpering a little, she pointed toward a small white building across the street. "Since I roped myself a man tonight at that wedding chapel over there. Jeez, what's a girl gotta do to enjoy her wedding night?"

The two potential clients groaned, but the others surrounding them started to laugh and call out congratulations. They were probably going to go back home and tell their friends and family they'd stumbled into a real-life version of *Pretty Woman*.

Reese, wicked amusement dancing in his eyes, took full advantage, playing to the crowd. Without warning, he tugged her closer, turning her so their faces were inches apart, then he caught her mouth in a deep, intimate kiss.

She forgot about everything for a full minute. The robbery, the thug, the cops, the onlookers. When Reese kissed her like this, all hot and wet, with delicious strokes of his tongue, everything else just ceased to exist.

When they finally ended the kiss, it was to the sound of applause. "Way to go, girlfriend!" someone yelled.

She didn't have to force the note of breathless excitement as she asked, "Can we please get outta here, hubby-cakes?"

"You got it, sugar-britches," Reese replied, compressing his lips, trying so hard not to laugh.

He amazed her. From sexy playmate, to hero who'd literally saved her butt, to serious witness, to passionate lover, and back to the most playful, good-humored, self-confident man she'd ever known, all in the span of an hour.

She'd known before tonight that Reese Campbell was a great guy. But as she let him lead her away, holding her protectively, lovingly, like a new husband with his bride, she had to acknowledge that he was even more than that.

He was special. Very special. The kind of man women read about in romance novels and dreamed about actually meeting.

He was, to use his favorite word, just about perfect.

Perfect for her? Well, that she wasn't ready to concede, at least not in the long term. But for right now, there was simply no place else she'd rather be...and no one else on earth she'd rather be with.

New Year's Eve

THEY SPENT THE ENTIRE holiday week in Las Vegas. And this time, after that first night when their game playing had nearly gotten them into legal trouble, they'd let all the other identities fade away. It was just Reese and Amanda, spending every minute of the day together.

They gambled, they saw a few shows, they walked the strip and shopped. They laughed over pizza dinners and shared a bucket of popcorn as they went to see a movie, which neither of them had done for so long.

And finally, eventually, they even talked.

"You're sure you don't mind leaving before midnight?" Amanda asked as they reentered their room at around eleven-thirty on New Year's Eve.

"My ears have been ringing all week from the sound of the slot machines. Add a few thousand voices screaming 'Happy New Year' and I might go deaf." Before he'd even reached back to lock the door, he drew her into his arms and kissed her cheek. "In other words, no, I most definitely do not mind sharing a quiet celebration with you."

Though he had never seen her drink much, Amanda had enjoyed a couple of glasses of champagne at the hotel's holiday party downstairs. Though not drunk, he'd have to describe her as slightly tipsy. Her eyes sparkled and her always beautiful smile flashed a little wider. Though nobody would ever call her giddy, when she kicked off her shoes and spun around the room with her arms extended straight out, she looked pretty darn close.

She also looked damn near adorable—young and

carefree. Her black cocktail dress was tight to the waist, but flared on the bottom and it swirled prettily around her bare legs.

"I love New Year's," she admitted once she stopped twirling.

He never had understood the appeal of the holiday himself, having grown up hearing his father calling it amateur night: the night normally smart, rational people drank too much then drove drunk. In their line of work, they knew way too much about it. The Campbells had always stayed home on New Year's Eve.

"It doesn't sound like the kind of holiday your family would be into," he said, his tone careful, as always, when the subject of her family life came up.

Amanda laughed out loud. "Are you kidding? Hell no, they weren't into it." Her voice lowered and her brow pulled down in a deep frown. "'This holiday is just an excuse for people to use poor judgment and do things they know are immoral and indecent. No daughter of mine is going to participate in public drunkenness or lewdity.'"

The imitation had to be of her father, though, honestly, he couldn't imagine this woman having grown up with someone like that. "Not exactly Mr. Tender Loving Care?"

She snorted. "I don't think he knows the meaning of any of those words." She thought about it, then clarified. "Well, *mister* he gets very well. He has kept my mother in her place since the minute he proposed to her. But *tender, loving* and *care* just aren't part of his vocabulary. Not toward her, not toward *anyone*." She yawned widely, as if she were discussing something mundane rather than utterly heartbreaking. "And I guess living with him all these years has rubbed off. Because my mother is about as warm as a guppy, too."

He glanced away so she wouldn't see the sudden flash of sympathy—and even anger—in his face. There was no malice in her. This wasn't an adult kid blaming her poor, unknowing parents for some imaginary slights. She didn't even sound resentful. She'd simply accepted their frigidity as a fact and moved on.

How much of their coldness had she unintentionally absorbed? How deeply had it affected her own life, her choices, the face she showed to the world? Seeing her like this, hearing the truths she'd been trying to hide from him since the very beginning, he understood so much more…and he liked her all the more for it. Even though he knew she would probably resent any sympathy he tried to offer.

He forced the thoughts away, as well as the unpleasant subject of what her parents had or hadn't given her in her childhood. Not wanting her to even think about it anymore, he changed the subject. "So when did you become a New Year's convert?"

She plopped down onto the edge of the bed. "In college. My freshman boyfriend took me to my very first New Year's Eve party and I got completely caught up in everyone else's excitement and good mood."

He hid his interest in the "boyfriend" part.

"I loved all the resolutions, the anticipation of a clean slate, a fresh start. And I suddenly saw it as a chance to reevaluate, figure out what went wrong in the past year and plan on how to make it right in the coming one."

Interesting. He had to wonder what she had evaluated and planned on this particular holiday. But he knew better than to ask. He shrugged out of his suit jacket and tossed it aside, then sat in a chair opposite the bed, eyeing her. "What did you decide that first year?"

"To dump my boyfriend."

Caught off guard, he had to chuckle. While that subject had been taboo up until now, Amanda laughed, as well. "He was a creeper," she admitted.

"A…creeper?"

"He had moist hands and he was sneaky, always touching me. That was when I was only nineteen, and still a virgin."

She'd held on to her virginity longer than most girls he knew. Considering her family background, he wasn't entirely surprised. He doubted there had been much dating or teenage partying in her household.

"So we have the creeper," he murmured, lifting his index finger to count off. "Who was next?"

Probably because she'd had a couple of drinks, Amanda didn't immediately freeze him out and change the subject. Instead, she threw herself back on the bed, her brow scrunched as she thought about it.

"I dated around when I was a sophomore. Kind of a lot." The way she nibbled her lip told him what that meant. She'd lost that pesky virginity and had gone for a walk on the wild side.

"Then I hooked up with a guy named Scott for several months. I broke up with him when I caught him copying the answers from my take-home exam for a class we had together. After that came Tommy…he drove a Porsche and

I think I liked the car more than I liked him, which he eventually figured out."

"Completely understandable," he pointed out.

She ignored him. "Rick was nice, but the first time we slept together and I realized he was lousy in the sack, I stopped taking his calls."

Again, completely understandable, at least for a college-aged kid. Not that he intended to interrupt her again, not now, when she seemed to really be getting to the nitty-gritty.

She was now the one with her fingers up. Mumbling under her breath, she lifted another, then another, and then moved on to her next hand. Up came the index finger. The middle one, then a third…which she quickly put back down. "Wait, Josh doesn't really count."

"Why not?" he asked, amused by this frank, open Amanda talking about her past. Even if she was only being that way because she'd had one too many sips of champagne.

"Because I was just a beard. I found out he was in the closet on our second date, but kept going out with him just 'cause he was a nice guy. Plus he had a crush on my roommate's boyfriend, who I hated, and it made me laugh to keep him around." Sitting up quickly, she gave him a stricken look. "Oh, that was bitchy, wasn't it? I *told* you."

"Yeah, yeah, you're cast-iron, babe."

So far, from what he could tell, she'd had about the same number of boyfriends as his twenty-something-year-old sisters. The difference being, from what he had pieced together in the past, that she had always been the one to walk away.

That refrain repeated in his mind. *She always walked away.*
He should have taken that as a warning sign, proceeded with caution. But he hadn't…mostly because he
wasn't at all convinced Amanda was as anti-love-and-
commitment as she claimed. She'd just never been
involved with the right man. Whether that was pure hap-
penstance, or by design—since her upbringing had to
have soured her on the whole idea of personal relationships—he didn't know.

"Come to think of it, I don't feel so bad," she suddenly
said with a firm nod. "I didn't break his heart or anything,
so he had no business joining that Facebook group." Her
voice lowered. "No business at all."

"What group?"

She hesitated, the finally admitted, "The 'Dumped by
Amanda Bauer' group."

He threw back his head and laughed…until he saw that
she wasn't smiling. Instead, her eyes held a hint of moisture
and her bottom lip quivered. The tough girl actually
looked vulnerable. Hurt.

Mentally kicking himself, he got up and joined her on
the bed, pulling her into his arms. She burrowed into his
chest, sniffing a tiny bit, and he suddenly had the urge to
hunt down the pricks who'd formed the mean little club
and made her cry.

Talk about ridiculous—holding on to some bullshit
college gripes and sharing them with the world years later,
no matter who you wounded. It was one way in which
the Internet age definitely had not improved life.

Amanda let herself relax against him for a minute or two,

then she began to tense, shifting uncomfortably. He recognized the signs and knew what she was thinking: too much emotion, too much talking, too personal, too dangerous.

He released her, forcing a smile. "It's almost midnight."

She didn't smile back, her beautiful face still wearing that same sad, stricken expression. Amanda stared at him for a long moment, her green eyes revealing her every thought as her gaze traveled over his face, as if to memorize him for the not-too-distant future when she wouldn't see him anymore.

"He wasn't the last one," she admitted.

"You don't have to do this...."

She ignored him. "The last guy I dated decided if I wouldn't just *give* him my undivided attention and devotion, he'd take it from me."

He didn't like the sound of this, not one bit.

"We had a fight, I broke it off, then he called in the middle of one night saying he'd just swallowed a bottle of pills."

Oh, God. Whether she wanted it or not, he had to hold her, tightly, giving her the support and tenderness she never asked for. He kissed her hair, whispering, "It wasn't your fault...."

She immediately shook her head. "No, he didn't die or anything."

Thank God.

"Because he was lying. The whole thing had been a setup, just to play on my emotions."

"What's his name?" he snarled, ready to kill a guy he'd just been thankful hadn't died.

"It doesn't matter. It's all over, all in the past. The point is…" She hesitated, then, with a voice as shaky as her slowly indrawn breath, whispered, "Don't love me, Reese."

His heart broke a little. For the pain of her past affairs, for the heartbreaks, and for the cold family life she'd endured. They'd combined to create a beautiful, extremely lovable woman who didn't think she was capable of returning the emotion.

She was wrong. She wouldn't admit it, not now, maybe not for a long time. But he knew Amanda Bauer had feelings for him, deep ones. Just as he did for her.

Reese was no fool, however. So he said nothing, merely nodded slowly, as if agreeing to her command.

The bedside clock glowed red, catching his eye as the numbers shifted from 11:59 to 12:00. And suddenly it was a whole new year. A new future had opened up and the mistakes of the past seemed destined to be washed away, with only good things coming toward them.

"Happy New Year, Manda," he whispered, leaning close to brush his lips against hers. "I hope this upcoming year is one neither of us will ever forget."

Her soft lips parted and she kissed him back, sweetly, tenderly. In that kiss she said all the things she would not say out loud—that she wanted more, but was afraid to let herself ask for it.

She'd changed a lot in the two months he'd known her. The hard shell had started to crack, whether she liked it or not. One day, sooner or later, Amanda was going to realize she was capable of a lot more than she gave herself credit for. She was capable of loving, and of being loved.

He only hoped she let him stick around until that day came.

chapter eight

Groundhog Day

"HONEY, why don't you just fly to Pittsburgh and see him?"

Amanda averted her eyes, not wanting to hear another lecture from Ginny, their administrative assistant, who stared at her from across her paper-laden desk. The older woman had figured out months ago that Amanda was involved with someone. She had finally gotten her to talk about Reese after the holidays. Probably because Amanda had walked around with a constant frown on her face since she'd arrived home.

As she'd flown back to Chicago on January 2, she'd wondered if it was time to end the affair. The intimate conversation she'd shared with Reese, and the way he'd made such sweet, tender love to her afterward, had convinced her she had to at least call a time-out, if not quit the game altogether.

Damn the man for slipping past her defenses, breaching her outer walls. Somehow, he'd worked his way into her previously brittle heart. That could be the only explanation for why she'd opened up to him the way she never had to anyone else before.

She'd told him such dark, ugly things about herself, it was a wonder he hadn't run screaming into the night.

It wasn't that she minded so much that she cared for him. The problem was, caring for him meant she wanted to be with him, to keep going with this thing that had sprung up between them. And that, she greatly feared, would not be good in the long run…for Reese. Having feelings for the man meant she didn't want to see him hurt. And she especially didn't want to be the one doing the hurting.

But it was inevitable, wasn't it? Just a foregone conclusion? When the going got tough, Amanda hit the skies.

"Would you talk some sense into her?" another voice said.

Jazz had come into the office, wearing a pair of her mechanic's overalls. A smear of grease on her cheek and the sweat on her brow made her hard labor obvious, but didn't diminish her earthy beauty one bit. "I swear to God, Manda, if you don't call the dude, I'm gonna leave a wrench in your aft engine and just let you fall out of the sky and put us all out of your misery."

Amanda rolled her eyes, feeling very much ganged-up on. "I saw him on Martin Luther King day, and I talk to him every few days."

The government holiday had been a busy one, and a weekday. She hadn't been able to take time off for any out-of-town tryst. But she had arranged for a three-hour layover at the Philadelphia airport. Reese had driven all the way there…and spent those three hours doing incredible things to her in the cockpit of her plane.

She thrust away the warm, gooey feeling those memories inspired. "It's not like I've ended it."

"Uh-huh. But you're planning to," Jazz said knowingly. Ginny nodded in agreement. "Definitely."

She glared at both of them. "It was never meant to be serious. My God, we live in two different states."

"And you fly a plane for a living," Jazz retorted. "An air trip from Pittsburgh to Chicago would probably take less time than commuting in from the suburbs on the El every day."

That was crazy talk. Jazz almost made it sound like she thought Amanda could actually *move* to Pittsburgh and live with Reese. Make something permanent out of what was just a holiday fling.

Wouldn't that be nice? Her, Amanda Bauer, the heart-break queen of Chicago living a couple of blocks away from Reese's perfect, all-American family with a house full of siblings who adored him and would absolutely hate her guts.

I don't think so.

She stood abruptly, silently telling them the conversation was over. Jazz and Ginny exchanged a frustrated look, but they didn't say anything else, knowing her well enough to know she was already mentally halfway out the door.

Glancing at the clock, she said, "It's late. Time for all of us to call it a day, right?" Forcing a laugh, she added,

"Wish that stupid groundhog hadn't seen his shadow this morning. I don't know if I can stand another six weeks of winter."

Jazz muttered something under her breath. Something that sounded like ice-queen, but Amanda ignored her.

Ginny, a little less blunt, walked over and put her hand on Amanda's shoulder, squeezing lightly. "We love you, honey. We just want you to be happy."

Love. Happy. Two words that hadn't even been in her vocabulary for the first eighteen years of her life. One of them still wasn't.

Not true. Not entirely, anyway. She did love. She loved Jazz and Ginny and her uncle Frank. She loved her sister, if in a somewhat pitying way. She supposed she even loved her parents, because for all their inattention and coldness, they were still her mother and father, after all.

How crazy was it to imagine she might widen that circle and actually let herself love a man? One man?

Maybe it bore consideration.

"I know," she finally replied, giving Ginny a brief hug. Normally not demonstrative, she knew the impulsive act had probably taken the older woman by surprise. Jazz's wide eyes said she felt the same.

"I'll see you guys tomorrow."

Grabbing her keys and her bag, she left them and walked through the quiet office wing of the airport where Clear-Blue Air was housed. As always, it took a while to make her way to the car, and even longer to drive to the city and park in the garage by her building. The entire time, she tried to pull her thoughts into order, to focus and make sense of everything that was going on and how she felt about it.

Feelings and all that stuff so weren't her thing. She just didn't know what to *do* with them.

"Hell," she muttered as she got out of her car, stepping into the frigid Chicago night. It was very dark out, and even inside the parking garage, the wind whipped wildly off the nearby lake. Its gusts made eerie whistles through the openings of the structure, making her freeze for a second before locking up and heading toward the elevator.

As she punched the button and waited for it, an unnerving sensation began on the back of her neck. She glanced side to side, then turned to look behind her. Nobody was around, not a single car moving. She'd gotten home after most commuters but before the club crowd started hitting downtown.

"Okay, cool it," she told herself, knowing she was imagining things. Still, she didn't drop her key chain into her bag, keeping it in her hand with long, sharp keys protruding between her fingers. Just in case.

The elevator arrived and she quickly scanned it to make sure it was empty before stepping inside. She remained close to the control panel, ready to jab the open button if somebody she didn't like the look of suddenly came out of nowhere and joined her. But nothing happened, not a sound, not a soul.

She breathed a sigh of relief, laughing at her own foolishness as the doors began to slide closed.

That's when she saw him. A man stood a few yards away, not far from her own car. Fully visible beneath an overhead light, he must have intentionally moved toward it because he had not been there a few seconds ago.

She caught a good look at his face right before her door shut, blocking the view. That glimpse was enough to capture a few quick impressions. Short, compact body clothed in black. Longish, stringy blond hair. Dark-eyed glare.

And suddenly, she remembered him.

"No way," she muttered, her hand tightening on the keys.

But she knew it was true. She'd just seen the thief, the guy who'd mown her down back in Las Vegas.

"You rotten bastard," she added, wishing the door hadn't closed before she'd identified him. Because her first impulse was to go after him and punch his lights out for shoving her into the street.

Then, of course, the wiser head that had kept Reese from doing that very same thing back in Vegas whispered wisdom in her brain. He could be armed, and he'd already proven himself dangerous.

Within seconds, the door reopened on the ground level of the garage. There was no way he could have beaten her here, not unless he'd sprouted wings and flown. He'd been far away from the stairs and the other elevator was clear on the opposite side of the deck. So she wasn't nervous as she stepped outside. Merely very curious. And worried.

"What are you doing here?" she whispered.

It couldn't possibly be a coincidence. The guy had tracked her down, come all the way to Chicago for some reason. But instead of confronting her, he'd played a sneaky game of hide-and-seek, trying to scare her.

But why?

Right outside the garage, people passed by, a nearby bar already swelling with regulars. She put her keys away, though she kept very focused, constantly looking around as she walked the few yards to her building. The doorman offered her a pleasant nod, and once she was inside, she breathed a small sigh of relief.

Not that she was truly frightened. Creeped out, that was a much better way to put it.

"Thanks, Bud," she said to the doorman as she headed toward the elevator. Before she'd reached it, however, she heard a distinct ring. Her cell phone. Grabbing it, she answered with a distracted, "Hello?"

"Is this Amanda Bauer?"

The voice was unfamiliar and throaty, as if the person were trying to disguise it. "Yes, who is this?"

"Long time, no see. You look a little different without the wig."

It was him. The guy from Vegas…the one from the garage. Tense, she stepped into a corner, not wanting to be distracted by the voices of people coming in behind her. "What do you want?"

"I want what's mine. That night when I bumped into you, I dropped a bag of my stuff. The police report says they didn't recover it, which means only one thing. *You* kept it."

"Bullshit," she said with a snort.

He hesitated, as if surprised she wasn't quivering with fright. Which only made her more convinced he was nothing to be afraid of. If he'd had any kind of a weapon, and had the guts to use it, he would have grabbed her in the parking deck and forced her to take him to his so-called loot.

"I'm calling the cops."

She could almost hear his sneer. "What are you going to tell them? That the guy you stole the jewelry from is after you?"

"Oh, I stole your merchandise, huh?"

"Yeah, you did. And I want it. More important, the people I work for want it."

People he worked for? What was there some ring of thieves in Vegas led by a modern-day Fagin and the Artful Dodger? Ludicrous.

"Look, you're crazy. I don't have any jewelry and you've just wasted a trip to Chicago," she said, feeling more annoyed than fearful. "Maybe you should go back and check all the storm drains or something. It probably fell down one when you tried to kill me."

"Drama queen."

"Psycho asshole."

He hesitated, as if at last realizing he wasn't scaring her one little bit. "Then your boyfriend has it."

She stiffened, suddenly wary. If he'd tracked her down, he might have done the same thing with Reese. "No, he doesn't."

Her tone must have betrayed her tension, because Mr. Robber's voice got a tad more confident. "Oh, he has it, all right. I think I'll have to make a trip to Pittsburgh now."

Damn it. "How did find out who we are?"

"You're famous, lady, don't you know that?"

She had no idea what he was talking about.

"Plus, the people I work for have a few friends in the LVPD. Your names and contact information were right on the police report."

That didn't exactly inspire confidence in the Las Vegas Police Department. She suddenly had the urge to call Parker and tell him to stop worrying about his wife's footwear and start looking for dirty cops.

"I guess I'll be seeing ya," he muttered with a laugh.

"Wait, he doesn't have them, I swear to…"

But she was talking to dead air. The creep had hung up on her.

She quickly flipped back to her caller ID, not surprised that the last incoming call had been from an unavailable number.

Nine-one-one? Officer Parker? Who to call first?

Of course, the answer was neither of those. Without hesitation, she thumbed to her address book, highlighting Reese's contact information on the tiny screen.

She started with his cell number. "Come on," she said when it rang and rang. When his voice mail came on, she didn't bother leaving a message, just moved on to the next one on the list, his house. Again, she got the same result.

"Damn it, where are you?"

The elevator had come and gone a couple of times, and it returned again with a loud ding, letting off a couple who lived on her floor. She smiled impersonally, bringing the phone up to her face to avoid any conversation.

The elevator door remained open and she stared at it. She was in the lobby of her own building, a few floors down from her apartment. But she suddenly found herself unable to walk through the open door and take the short ride upstairs.

An entire evening of trying to track Reese down, to warn him about the crazy thug from Vegas, sounded unbearable. And Jazz's claim about how quick the commute was between Chicago and Pittsburgh kept repeating itself in her head.

She gave it about ten seconds' thought. Then she turned and strode toward the exit. "Bud, would you flag me a cab?" she asked, knowing she couldn't go back for her own car. El Creepo could still be lurking around, and she didn't want him knowing she was heading to the airport, going to warn Reese.

"Sure, Ms. Bauer," the doorman said.

A few minutes later, as she got into the taxi, Amanda had to smile. Because, as usual, when in crisis mode, she was taking off, hitting the skies. This time, though, instead of running away, she intended to fly *toward* the very person who'd been filling her head with confusion and her heart with turmoil.

Trouble could be heading Reese's way. But she fully intended to get to him first.

WHEN SOMEONE knocked on his front door at ten o'clock that night, Reese immediately tensed. The reaction was instinctive. Even now, two years later, the ring of a phone awakening him out of a sound sleep, or an unexpected knock on the door this late brought him back to the moment when his whole world had changed.

He'd been the one who'd answered the door when the uniformed police officer had come to inform his mother of his dad's accident.

He thrust the dark thoughts away. His family was just fine. He'd left them a half hour ago, happily eating birthday cake at Aunt Jean's mansion, where they'd been celebrating her seventy-whatever'th birthday. Nobody was entirely sure how old she was since she'd lied about the number for so many years.

The only other person he truly cared about was Amanda, and nobody even knew they had any connection. So it wasn't like anybody would be coming to him if something had happened to her.

Besides, he had no doubt she was just fine. Right about now, she was probably in her bedroom, wearing something plain but incredibly sexy, staring at the phone. She would likely be having a mental debate about whether to call and entice him into some serious phone sex, or to continue to try to be strong and resist him, showing them both she didn't *really* need him…at least until she just couldn't help herself.

God, the woman drove him crazy. In a good way, as well as a bad one. And oh, how he adored her for it.

The doorbell rang, then rang again, as if his visitor had become impatient. He forced himself to relax and headed over to answer it, reminding himself not to worry. Still, he couldn't deny his pulse sped up when he turned the knob and pulled the door open.

Seeing who stood there, he jerked in surprise. "What are *you* doing here?"

His four sisters, his brother, his mother, his young niece

and nephew and his great-aunt all pushed their way into his house, babbling a mile a minute, all talking over one another.

Reese froze, trying to make his brain process what was happening.

A gaggle of insane people had just turned his quiet respite into a loony bin. Ralph, smart dog that he was, got the hell out, dashing toward the laundry room, probably to snuggle between the dryer and the wall, his favorite hiding spot when he'd done something bad.

"My God, Reese, how could you be so damned irresponsible? How am I supposed to raise my kids to make good choices when their uncle does something so incredibly *brainless?*"

"Reese, are you okay? I'm so sorry if you felt you couldn't share this with us."

"Oh, I've failed you. What would your father say? How could you do such a thing? Where did I go wrong?"

"Were you ever going to tell us, you sneak? I can't wait to meet her."

"Man, wait'll I tell the guys. They're gonna shit bricks."

"How could you! I'll never be able to show my face at school again!"

"When I said to have an adventure, dear boy, I didn't know you'd take it quite *that* far."

All the voices swelled, a chorus of them, but one comment, his sister Debra's, pierced through the cloud of confusion.

"Wait. *Her* who?" he asked, staring at his second-to-youngest sister.

"Reese, are you listening to me?" his mother asked, waving a hand in front of herself, as if to fan away a hot flash. She was red-cheeked, and appeared a bit woozy, although that could have been from the brandy Aunt Jean had been shoving down her throat before Reese's departure.

"Do go sit down before you faint," said Aunt Jean, pushing his mother toward Reese's leather couch. "Molly, take the little ones into the kitchen and get them a snack. They weren't happy that they didn't get to finish their cake."

The sixteen-year-old cast a furious glare at everyone, then grabbed Reese's young niece and nephew and marched them toward the kitchen.

"Jack, why don't you go find Ralph. I'm sure he's scared to death at all of us barging in like this," Aunt Jean said.

Jack frowned darkly. "I'm not a kid."

"No, you're not, which is why you are mature enough to recognize that a poor animal is hiding and frightened in the other room and you should go help him," Aunt Jean said.

Jack had always been a sucker for animals, and he really loved Ralph. Sometimes he came by just to play with the dog, throwing a stick for him, bringing a toy. So the quiet request worked like nothing else would have.

Finally, when it was just the older females of his family, and him, the lone man—Lord, talk about painful torture: estrogen poisoning—Reese repeated his question. "Which *her* are you talking about? What the hell is going on here?"

"Don't act all innocent. The truth is out. Oh-ho, is it out, in a major way," said Tess, the oldest of his siblings.

She was the mother of the two kids who were probably right now whining that they had to make do with dry crackers because Uncle Reese didn't have any cookies or good snacks in his pantry.

Seeing Reese's open laptop on the coffee table, since he'd been checking his e-mails before bed, hoping for one from Amanda, Tess grabbed it and began punching letters on the keyboard. "Talk about irresponsible. And stupid!" she snapped, as always, voicing her opinion and not caring how anyone else felt about it.

"Will someone *please* talk to me?"

His mother sniffed, then waved a hand toward the computer screen. Reese turned his attention toward it, wondering why in the name of God everyone was so worked up about a YouTube video.

Then the video started.

"Hey, sweet thing, how late you working tonight?" a male voice said from off camera.

The voice was unfamiliar, but the words rang a bell, though he couldn't place them right away. Nor could he make much out in the dark, grainy image.

Then the focus kicked in, the picture brightened and cleared. And another voice said, "Got a business card?"

"Sorry, guys, she's retired."

That voice he recognized. "Oh, hell," he muttered, unable to believe it, but knowing what he was looking at. Especially now, as the image got nice and sharp and the screen filled with an easily identifiable couple.

Him. And "Mandy" the hooker. In all her wicked glory.

He glanced away, scrambling to remember everything

they'd said and done, wondering if the sly videographer had caught the sexy kiss. Or, worse, the line about…

"…I roped myself a man tonight at that wedding chapel over there. Jeez, what's a girl gotta do to enjoy her wedding night?"

He leaned back in his seat, dropping his head onto the back of the couch and staring up at the ceiling.

This couldn't be happening. It just couldn't.

"You're married?" his mother cried. "How could you get married and not tell us?"

"Worse, how could you marry a poor, down-on-her-luck prostitute? Do you know anything about her? Where is she? Did you abandon her?" asked Bonnie, his twenty-four-year old sister, who shared the middle-child title with Debra but was extremely empathetic and had never seen a tree she didn't want to hug.

"Look," he said, not even sure what he was going to say. "It's not what you think."

"Then what is it?" Tess asked. "Did you or did you not either go temporarily insane or get roofied, and marry some trashy Vegas whore?"

That made him sit straight up and snap, "Watch your mouth." He cast his sister a stare so heated she actually drew back a little. Her mouth remained shut, her lips compressing tightly.

Beside her, watching like the proverbial cat that swallowed the canary, was his aunt Jean. Her mouth was tightly shut, too, only it wasn't because she was trying to control her anger. The wicked old woman was instead trying desperately not to laugh. It was a wonder she didn't hyperventilate from lack of oxygen as she held her breath, trying to contain her merriment.

She was loving every minute of this. Probably taking full credit for pushing Reese completely over the edge.

"I'm just *thrilled* that you're so happy," he said, his voice dripping sarcasm.

She sucked her bottom lip in her mouth, then finally let out a whoosh of air. Rushing toward the kitchen, she said, "I think I'll go check on Molly and the children."

Well, that was one for the record books, a red-letter moment. The ballsiest woman he knew had cut and run. Add that to the rest of this funfest and this might just go down as the strangest night of his decade.

"So tell us, brother dear, what's the story?" asked Debra as she leaned back in a chair and lifted her feet onto the coffee table. She looked to be enjoying this almost as much as Aunt Jean had, but she didn't race for the kitchen in an effort to hide it. "When do we get to meet our new sister-in-law?"

He didn't reply. Instead he stared again toward the computer screen. The video had ended, but he wasn't focused on that, anyway. No, what had drawn his eye was the small counter that indicated how many people had viewed it.

Thousands. Many of whom had left five-star reviews and salacious comments.

He could only shake his head in disbelief.

"Well?" prompted his mother. "Don't you have anything to say for yourself? Not a single explanation?"

Hmm. Which would be worse? Letting his family

believe he'd married a hooker during a wild night of partying in Vegas? Or admitting that, for months, he'd been traveling all over the country to play naughty, sexy role-playing games with a woman he was falling head over heels for?

He wasn't sure what he was going to say. Truth or consequences? Either way, he came out looking like a total jackass.

Before he could figure it out, he was, quite literally, saved by the bell. The *ding-dong* was the perfect sound effect for the insane situation in which he'd found himself.

"Good heavens, who can that be?" asked his mother.

"Not a clue," he replied, hearing an almost cheerful note in his own voice.

"Who on earth would simply show up here unannounced at this time of night?" she added.

"Can't imagine. Rude, isn't it?" he muttered, certain the sarcasm would go over her head.

Reese didn't know who had landed on his doorstep this time. He only knew he was grateful to the bastard for giving him an excuse to get up and walk away from the inquisition.

Maybe he'd get lucky and it would be a fireman saying the whole neighborhood had to be evacuated due to a gas leak. Maybe he'd get even luckier and just blow up with it. Anything to escape having to share embarrassing fiction or even *more* embarrassing truth with his nosy, incredibly obnoxious family was a-okay with him.

Whatever he'd been imagining, though, it didn't even come close to reality. He thought he'd been surprised to find his family barging in twenty minutes ago? Hell, that was nothing compared to the shock he got when he opened the door.

Of all the times he'd imagined Amanda Bauer coming to his home, being part of his real world, it sure hadn't been under circumstances like these. Yet there she was, staring at him with uncertainty in her eyes and apologies on her beautiful lips.

"Reese, I'm sorry to just show up like this, but I need to see you and it's not just to jump your bones, even though that's exactly what I'd like to…" Her words trailed off as she looked past him into the house, obviously seeing a bunch of wide-eyed, openmouthed females who'd heard her every word. Her babbling nervousness segued into a momentary horrified silence.

Gee. The night just got better and better.

"Oh, man, *please* tell me you're having a late-night Pampered Chef party, and that's *not* your entire family sitting over there," she said in a shaky whisper.

"'Fraid I can't do that." He forced a humorless smile, stepped back and extended an arm to beckon her in. "Welcome to the asylum."

To give her credit, she didn't run. A few months ago she probably would have. But tonight, she took one tentative step inside, and then another, her curious stare traveling back and forth between him and the women watching wide-eyed from a few feet away.

The silence lengthened, grew almost deafening, and finally, the sheer ludicrousness of the whole situation washed over him. This was like something out of a movie—a romantic comedy where the hapless hero went from one humiliating situation to a worse one, constantly looking like an idiot in front of the smart, witty heroine.

Fortunately, this smart, witty heroine had a couple of skills that could come in really handy right now. First, she wasn't the type to pass judgment. Second, she was really good at adapting to new situations, as evidenced by her aptitude at role-playing. And finally, she had one hell of a sense of humor. So, with laughter building in the back of his throat, he squeezed Amanda's hand and drew her toward the others.

He opened his mouth to make a simple introduction, trusting that she looked different enough from the woman in the video to be unrecognizable.

He should have known better. Eagle-eyed Tess leaped out of her seat, hissing, "She's the one—it's her!"

Amanda flinched, obviously having no clue what the other woman was talking about. Reese kept a strong, comforting arm on her shoulder. And then, though he didn't really plan to say the words until they left his mouth, he introduced her to the judgmental women watching them with expressions ranging from pure curiosity to horror.

"Amanda, this is my family." He draped an arm across her shoulder and tugged her against him. "Campbell family, meet the little woman."

chapter nine

TEN hours later, the shock of the previous night still hadn't sunk in. Amanda felt dazed whenever she thought about it.

"I just can't believe you did that. Your family must hate me," she said as she walked into Reese's bathroom the next morning. She'd spent the night, of course, having nowhere else to go and not a single piece of luggage.

She now wore one of his T-shirts, which barely skimmed her thighs. Not that she'd needed anything to wear last night. Oh, no, he'd kept her quite warm while making love to her until just a few hours ago, when they'd finally fallen into an exhausted sleep.

She liked the feel of the shirt, liked that his smell clung to it, and she felt perfectly comfortable intruding on him in the bathroom, hopping up to sit on the counter,

Strange that they were already so comfortable with each other, like longtime lovers. Strange, but nice.

"Don't worry about it," Reese said, glancing at her in the mirror. He stood over the sink, shaving, amusement warring with lazy sexual satisfaction in his eyes. "I'll tell them the truth and they'll fall all over themselves apologizing."

The truth? That she was his holiday mistress who'd had him play-acting all across America since Halloween? Oh, lovely.

"But you told them I was your wife."

"No, they told *me* you were my wife and waved their 'evidence' in front of my face to prove it."

The damned video. She still couldn't believe it. Someone had been videotaping them that night, possibly with a cell phone, and they'd never even realized it. Heaven help her if any of their corporate clients stumbled over the clip.

At least she hadn't been *too* easily recognizable. Unlike Reese, who'd been completely uncostumed.

"But you confirmed it. My God, Reese, what were you thinking?"

"Well, I was thinking that my family is composed of a bunch of nosy busybodies and they deserved a little payback." Grinning, he swiped his razor along one more strip of lean jaw. "If my aunt Jean hadn't ducked out the back door before you arrived, I would have seriously considered dropping a pregnancy bombshell, too."

"Whoa, big boy," she said, knowing she sounded horrified. She leaped off the counter and backed out of the bathroom, both hands up in a visible "stop" sign. "That's not even funny."

He didn't look over, that half smile still playing on his

mouth as he shaved around it. Ignoring her dismay, he said, "You didn't meet my aunt Jean."

No, she hadn't. Nor did she think she wanted to. She'd met quite enough of the clan last night and didn't care to expand on, or to repeat, the experience.

She slowly shook her head. "I should have denied it."

"I'm glad you didn't."

He could laugh. He wasn't the one being mentally murdered by a group of women who thought she'd either trapped or drugged their brother and son.

Yeah. Denial would have been the way to go. But she'd been so surprised by Reese's claim, she could only watch in silence as his shocked family quietly rose and headed for the door. She'd said nothing when they'd murmured their apologies to Reese for the intrusion and left the house, giving her looks that ranged from disgust to pity. They'd been gone within five minutes of her arrival.

Something else she could have done—followed them out. It would have been even better to have just stayed home in Chicago and kept trying to call Reese all night long rather than flying off to play superhero and protect him from the bad guy.

Superhero my ass. She'd come in person because she'd wanted to see him. That was all there was to it. Excuses about Vegas thugs be damned.

She'd stayed for the same reason. Stayed despite the crazy lie, despite the sheer misery it had been to come face-to-face with the women in his family, playing the girlfriend—no, *wife*—role as if she had some actual right to it. Stayed after facing down the women who all thought she had sex for money.

She felt like throwing up.

Backing up, she stopped only when her legs hit the edge of his enormous bed, then slowly sat down on it. What the hell had she gotten herself into? And she wasn't even referring to the fact that an angry robber had followed her halfway across the country and could be parked outside Reese's door right now, just waiting to break in.

Not that Reese seemed to care. In fact, when she'd told him what had driven her here last night, he'd spent about five minutes being utterly enraged and the next thirty muttering all the ways he intended to punish the guy if he actually had the nerve to show up.

She'd just wanted to call the police. Which was exactly what they were going to do in a couple of hours, once they'd made up the time difference in Vegas and had a good chance of catching Officer Parker on the job.

In the meantime, she didn't quite know what to do with herself. She'd already called Ginny and had her rearrange her schedule. Fortunately, the week looked pretty light and Uncle Frank was able to pick up today's trip. A part-time pilot they contracted with when they were extra busy was on for tomorrow.

Not that she intended to spend another night here. Uh-uh. She had no clothes, and she was already itching to get back to her real life, away from Reese's admittedly beautiful house and ultranormal one.

She wasn't ready to play the role of domestic goddess, or even live-in girlfriend. No matter how nice it had been to wake up in his bed this morning and watch *him* sleep for a change.

Time to run, girlfriend.

But she couldn't leave just yet. Not until they'd reached Officer Parker and found out what he wanted them to do about their unwelcome stalker. They might need to get in touch with the local police. Or she might have to go right back and report to the Chicago ones. She just didn't know.

"Forget it," Reese said, watching her from the doorway of the bathroom. He wore a white towel slung around his lean hips and looked so utterly delicious she wished she'd said yes when he'd offered to share his shower.

"Forget what?"

"You're not going home, not until we've dealt with this guy."

"So, what, I'm supposed to just move in here?"

He shrugged, a non-answer, but the quirk of his lips said he didn't mind the idea.

She forced away the flash of pleasure that gave her, knowing she couldn't let herself be distracted by the realization that Reese really wanted her to stay. "I don't have any clothes."

"It's not the Magnificent Mile, but we do have stores here in Pennsylvania."

She ran a hand through her hair, which she hadn't even brushed yet this morning. "I have a job."

"Your plane's sitting at the airport, isn't it? Who's to say you can't fly from here to go pick up your passengers?"

That was a good point, and was, in fact, exactly what she would have done if she hadn't been able to get coverage for today and tomorrow. But she wasn't ready to give up. "I really shouldn't."

"Yeah. You really should."

The sexy, cajoling smile widened and he walked toward her. She swallowed as that hard, muscular form stopped in front of her, and she couldn't resist reaching out to rub her fingertip along the rippling muscles of his stomach.

"What's more, you really want to," he whispered, stroking her hair and then her cheek.

Amanda leaned closer, wanting to taste that hot skin. She pressed her mouth to the hollow right below his hip, which was uncovered by the low-slung towel. "How will I spend my time?" she asked, brushing her lips across him, toward the long, thin trail of dark hair that led from his flat stomach down into the white terry cloth.

The fabric began to bulge toward her as he hardened right before her eyes.

"Mmm."

He lifted his other hand and twined those fingers in her hair as well, but he didn't guide her closer, didn't force her anywhere she didn't want to go.

She was capable of deciding that all on her own.

A quick flick of her fingers and the towel fell to the floor. His rock-hard erection jutted toward her, and she blew on it lightly, hearing him hiss in response.

She knew what he liked, knew how to please him. But she also knew how to draw out the pleasure. So instead of opening her mouth and sucking him in, she continued to press those featherlight kisses on his groin, letting her cheek brush against his shaft, knowing every soft caress sent his tension—his want—skyrocketing.

"Manda…" he muttered, already sounding near the edge of control.

She moved her hand, sliding it across his strong thigh, one goal in sight. When she cupped the delicate sacs in her palm, handling them carefully, Reese jerked toward her. Only then did she open her mouth and lick at the broad tip of his cock.

"More?" she asked.

His hands tangled a little more in her hair, but he still didn't take what he wanted, merely accepting what she chose to give him.

And what she chose to give him was the pleasure of sinking that throbbing maleness into her mouth. She took as much of him as she could, then tilted her head to take a little more. Using her tongue and soft, gentle suction, plus the careful strokes of her hand between his legs, she soon had him groaning in pure sexual pleasure.

She was ready to go all the way, loving the taste of him and the power of knowing how much he loved what she was doing. But he suddenly pulled back, gently pushing her off him. Then he lifted her under the arms and tossed her back onto the bed, following her down.

He didn't say a single word, didn't kiss her, or stroke her, seeming beyond all capacity to do anything except have her.

It didn't matter. Because when he plunged into her, she was creamy-wet, completely ready for him.

She arched up, taking everything, meeting him thrust

for thrust, not even minding that he began to reach his climax long before she was ready for him to. Especially not when he muttered, "I'm sorry. I swear, I'm going to make you come so many times tonight that you won't remember what it feels like not to be having an orgasm."

That sounded like a pretty okay deal to her.

Then he couldn't say anything else, he could only groan as he exploded in a hot rush inside her. Having long since gone on the pill so they wouldn't have to use condoms, she savored every sensation, loving that there was nothing separating skin from skin. Having this man empty himself into her body made her feel connected to him in a way she'd never been with anybody before.

Or maybe it was more than that. Perhaps it was the knowledge that, for the first time in her life, she hadn't just opened her legs to a man.

She had begun to suspect she'd opened her dusty heart to him, as well.

HIS FAMILY KEPT their distance for the next few days. Reese didn't get a single phone call, not one e-mail, and didn't have to endure any fact-finding trips disguised as casual dropping-by-the-brewery-to-say-hello visits.

That was fine. Just fine. No, he wasn't still furious at them for barging in on him the other night, whether they thought they had the right or not. But he just didn't want to deal with that part of his life right now.

Not when the rest of it was going so very well.

Amanda might not be his wife, she might not even be ready to admit she loved him, but she was sleeping in his bed at night. She was sitting across his table for breakfast each morning, and curling up on the couch to watch a movie with him during the evening. She used his tooth-paste and she slept in his undershirts, her shopping trip that first day not including a stop for a nightie.

She'd even done as he'd first suggested and gone back to work from here, flying in and out of Pittsburgh. Her origination point didn't really matter, considering she picked up people all over the country and shuttled them where they wanted to go. So it wasn't a difficult adjust-ment—he took her to the airport in the morning and picked her up at night.

They were playing a whole new game: normal couple. And he'd never enjoyed anything more.

The only imperfection in the whole thing was that they were playing this game because some sleazy criminal from Vegas might be after her. There hadn't been much progress in the case, though they kept in touch with Officer Parker, a detective from Chicago and a local cop, all of whom were monitoring the situation.

Parker had been furious to learn the thief had been able to access police records to track down the witnesses against him. And their first conversation with him had been quickly followed up by one with someone from the Internal Affairs office.

There was one bit of good news: they'd at least identi-fied the guy. Parker had had a few leads on suspects, and when he found out about the thug's visit to Chicago, he'd narrowed them down even further, focusing on any who had left Vegas. A faxed mug shot later and they'd both iden-

tified their man as one Teddy Lebowski, age thirty-six, oc-
cupation petty thief and all-around scumbag.

Hearing the criminal was loosely connected with one
of the Vegas crime families hadn't made their day. But the
fact that he had never been charged with a violent crime,
and that Parker considered him little more than a blowhard
who didn't have the balls to actually try to hurt anyone,
brought a hint of relief.

Sooner or later, the bastard would be caught. Reese half
hoped he was stupid enough to show up in Pittsburgh.
He'd sincerely like the chance to beat the guy to a pulp
for what he'd done to Amanda, both in Vegas and when
he'd stalked her in Chicago.

"Hey, you," she said, interrupting his thoughts as he
finished locking up his desk for the night. She hadn't had
to fly today, and had agreed to come to the brewery for a
few hours this afternoon, to see where he worked.

The afternoon had stretched into evening, as a crisis had
arisen with one of their distributors. But Amanda hadn't
appeared bored, insisting she'd enjoyed touring the place,
inspecting the enormous vats and watching the plant
workers running the equipment and observing the bottling
line.

She'd done a tasting, declaring their amber lager the best,
then had sat quietly in a corner while Reese dealt with
putting out the fires. Now that the last phone call was
done, he stood and wearily rubbed at his temples.

"You look like you could use a massage," she said, rising
from the couch that stood against one wall of his office.

"Mmm. You want to play massage therapist now?"

"I think that could be worked into my repertoire," she said flirtatiously.

Arm in arm, they walked outside. A few night workers remained within, but Reese paused to lock up. Then, taking her arm again, they headed for his car.

They hadn't even made it down the outside steps when he saw a familiar vehicle pull into the parking lot.

"Oh, hell."

Beside him, Amanda tensed, going on alert. "What is it?"

"More like *who* is it." The Caddy came to a halt directly in front of them. "You're about to meet my great-aunt Jean."

"Oh, terrific. I can hardly wait for this one," she said, her tone saying exactly the opposite.

He had a lot to say to his great-aunt, both for her leading the charge over to his house the other night—which he had no doubt she did—and for the way she'd slunk out the back door after getting everyone completely stirred up.

The door opened and the elderly woman stepped out of the driver's seat, into the shadows of the parking lot. Then she walked around the luxury auto, approaching them without a hint of wariness, her obnoxious red-leather cowboy boots clicking merrily on the blacktop.

He was about to open his mouth to warn her against saying anything out of line to the woman at his side when Amanda made a small, confused sound. "Mrs. Rush?"

"Hello, Amanda my dear," the old woman said as she reached the steps and walked up them. She leaned over to press a kiss on Amanda's cheek. "I can't tell you how happy I am to see you here." She wagged her drawn-on brows at Reese. "And under such delicious circumstances."

Reese couldn't move, couldn't speak, couldn't put a thought together. He could only stare, wondering how in the name of God his great-aunt knew his lover.

"I don't understand," said Amanda, sounding a little dazed.

But Reese did. Or he was beginning to. "Damn it. You manipulative old…"

His aunt waved aside his anger, as if it were a pesky odor, then lifted her cheek for his kiss.

He didn't give it to her. "You set this up. This whole thing."

"Oh, no, of course I didn't."

"Wait," Amanda said, finally catching on. "*You're* really Reese's great-aunt Jean?"

"Guilty as charged," said the woman.

"Son of a bitch," Amanda muttered, taking the words right out of his mouth.

"Oh, you two, please stop acting as though I had anything at all to do with this fine mess you've gotten yourselves into." She tsked and shook her head, though her lips twitched with merriment. "I merely pushed you in each other's direction. Arranged for your first meeting after I'd planted a few suggestions in Reese's mind—" she turned toward Amanda "—and made sure you were suitably dressed and loosened up for the occasion, thinking you were going to be part of my in-flight costume party."

Her Halloween costume. His last-minute flight. All a setup.

The light dawned. "You called old Mr. Braddock and had him call me to get me to come to Chicago that day."

Her bracelets tinkled as she clapped her hands, as if

pleased he'd put it together so quickly. "Yes!" Then she made a cross-my-heart motion and said, "But that was all. Everything else is all on your heads." She almost beamed at them, so wrapped in approval and self-satisfaction she could barely contain herself. "Oh, my, playing such wicked games in Las Vegas." She tapped her fingertip against Reese's chest. "You're a naughty one, Reese Campbell."

He crossed his arms, almost forgiving her, considering she had, in fact, done him one of the biggest favors of his life. But he wasn't quite there yet. "Did you have anything to do with that video clip showing up on YouTube?"

She shook her head hard. "Absolutely not." Then, averting her gaze, she admitted, "Though, I must admit, it was one of my friends whose daughter spotted you in it and sent me a link. I fear that video has gone, what do they call it, viral? You're right smack-dab in the middle of your own fifteen minutes of fame."

Lucky him. And he'd had absolutely no clue. One more reason he wasn't so crazy about the Internet age.

"Let me guess. You just had to show it to the rest of the family after I left the other night."

"Yes. I would say I'm sorry, but you know I'm not."

Of course she wasn't. The woman had never been truly sorry for anything she'd done. Damn, she must have led his great-uncle on a merry chase.

"So, all's well that ends well!"

"No, it's not," he protested. "In case you've forgotten, my family is convinced I'm married to a hooker."

She waved an unconcerned hand. "No, they're not. I straightened that all out."

Almost not sure he wanted to know, he asked, "How?"

"I told them you were flamingly angry and embarrassed that you and Amanda had been caught on camera at a New Year's Eve costume party in Las Vegas. That it was all a joke and you were punishing them for assuming the worst of you."

It wasn't a bad story, come to think of it.

His aunt reached over and pinched Amanda's cheek, apparently not noticing that she'd been almost completely silent. "I knew you'd be perfect for him…and that *he'd* be perfect for *you*. Do forgive an old woman's meddling. It's just that when I see two wounded people who so obviously belong together, I can't stand not doing something about it."

Without waiting for a reply, she turned around and skipped down the steps like a woman one-third her age. She gave them a cheery wave before getting back into her car and driving away, leaving them staring after her in silence.

He didn't move for a long moment, just stood there absorbing the fact that he'd been completely manipulated by a family member. How much worse must it be for Amanda? God, she barely knew his great-aunt, who, apparently, from what they'd said, was one of her regular customers.

He should have known, should have suspected when his aunt simply insisted he take her place on the private flight to Chicago on Halloween.

"Amanda?" he finally murmured. "Are you all right?"

She hesitated for a moment, then, tilting her head

sideways, with her brow furrowed, she replied, "Your family is freaking nuts, you know that, right?"

Startled, relieved, he could only nod and grin. "Yeah."

"I mean, certifiable."

"I repeat…yeah."

She paused again, shaking her head, still staring off down the road where his elderly relative's car had disappeared. When she spoke again, her confusion was gone. So was any hint of anger. "You know, I like that crazy old woman."

"I do, too, when I don't want to strangle her."

"We really have to plan our revenge."

His heart getting lighter by the minute, he nodded in agreement. Plotting together made it sound like she planned to stick around for a while.

Which sounded just about perfect to him.

chapter ten

AFTER they'd left his office, Reese insisted on taking Amanda out for a late dinner. It was after eight, they were both wiped and a steak was the least he could offer her considering she'd just come face-to-face with the person who'd been pulling her strings for months, even though she hadn't known it.

They went to one of his favorite places, not too far from home. It was low-key with good food and great service. There was no play-acting, not even a whisper of suggestion to be anything other than who they were. He didn't mention it, not wanting Amanda to think for a minute that disappointed him.

On the contrary, he couldn't be more pleased that she continued to drop those walls, let down her guard and just be herself...the woman he had fallen in love with.

He knew she didn't want to hear it, and that she'd warned him against it, but there was no hiding the truth, especially not from himself. He'd fallen hard for the woman. Fallen head over heels into the kind of love he had seen in others—like his parents—but hadn't had time to consider he might find for himself.

By the end of the meal, they were laughing as they tried to outdo each other with extreme revenge plots against Aunt Jean. He had also promised her a dozen times that if and when she met his family again, they were going to be falling over themselves to make up for their assumptions and their coldness toward her.

That would happen even if he had to order, blackmail and browbeat everyone in his family to make absolutely sure of it.

Once they were finished eating, they walked to the car. Night had grown deeper, and she shivered in the frigid air.

"You okay?" he asked, dropping an arm over her shoulder and tugging her closer.

She nodded, clutching her coat tighter around her body. "How can it be colder here than in Chicago?"

"It isn't."

"It sure feels like it."

"I'll warm you up," he offered.

She glanced at him from the corner of her eye. "I'm counting on it."

Once inside the car, Reese watched as Amanda fastened her seat belt, then he put the key in the ignition. But he didn't turn it right away. Instead, he glanced over at his companion, wondering what she was really thinking, wondering if her good mood was covering up any last, lingering resentment over his aunt's confession.

Finally, he just asked. "Are you *sure* you're okay?"

"Uh-huh. I'm about as fine as somebody being chased by a crazy Vegas mobster and mistaken for a prostitute can be." Shaking her head woefully, she added, "It's really not fair that I can be accused of being a hooker and not have the sordid experience to show for it. And called a thief and not have any jewels."

Any final threads of tension evaporated, and Reese had to admire the way she'd taken everything that had come her way in the past several days in stride. Just like she did everything else.

Some women would have left that first night, after she'd been treated so harshly by his pushy family members. Others might have resented being moved around like a pawn on a chess board by a rich old busybody who liked getting her own way.

But Amanda just went with it, laughed and never complained about what she couldn't change. He found that incredibly attractive.

He also really liked the way she teased him about it as they drove back to his place, asking what his sweet old aunt would think if she knew the wild things he'd done to her the night before. As if wanting to remind him, she put her hand on his thigh. Then she began sliding it up, inch by inch.

Suddenly, though, when she went too high, whispering something about making the ride home more enjoyable, he dropped his hand on hers and squeezed, shaking his head in silence.

He didn't have to say anything. She immediately understood. Sucking in an embarrassed breath, she pulled away. "Oh, Reese, I'm sorry."

"It's okay," he murmured, knowing she understood why he was such a careful driver.

There were some games he'd never play, some risks he would never take. No matter what. He'd learned that lesson all too well.

"I'm an idiot." She sighed heavily. "An insensitive twit." She curled up one leg, wrapping her arms around it and resting her chin on her upraised knee, staring pensively out the windshield at the oncoming traffic. With a hint of wistfulness in her tone, she added, "He must have been a wonderful man for you to have turned out to be such a great guy yourself."

"Yes, he was."

He fell silent, not elaborating at first. Talking about his father was probably as difficult for him as talking about hers was for Amanda. Not for the same reasons, of course. Her wounds were old and scarred, and she no longer felt the ache. His were fresh and raw, and he just didn't feel like poking at them and starting the bleeding all over again.

But he could tell by the continued silence that she felt like crap for even suggesting they fool around while he was behind the wheel. The last thing he wanted to do was make her feel worse. So he began to speak.

"His name was Patrick, and he died way too young."

She turned her head to look at him, wide-eyed and tentative. "You don't have to…"

"It's okay. Actually, it's kind of nice to be able to say his name without someone bursting into tears."

She wasn't crying, but he could tell, even in the low lighting of the car, that her eyes were moist.

"He'd worked late, as usual. And he was driving too fast, trying hard to make it to one of Jake's basketball games. He'd missed the last few because of work, and they'd had a big fight about it the day before. He'd promised he'd make the next one. Only…he didn't."

"Oh, God, poor Jake," she whispered, immediately grasping the situation. "That's a lot of weight for a kid to bear."

"Tell me about it. He's been the one I've been most worried about. He's angry at the world, sometimes mean and rebellious, sometimes still just a lost kid wondering what happened."

Amanda reached across for his hand, this time lacing her fingers through his in a touch that was all about sweetness and consolation. And because she didn't ask any questions, didn't pry at all, just letting him say whatever he wanted, he felt okay about saying it.

He told her about that night. About the nights that followed. About how fucking hard it had been to pick out a casket and decide on a headstone and keep his mother upright and his sisters from sobbing and the business functioning and his brother from blowing his whole life out of guilt, and still maintaining his own sanity amid his own deep, wrenching grief.

It was like someone had pulled a plug on all the words that had gone unsaid for two years. And it wasn't until he'd let them out that he realized just how much he'd needed to say them. Being the strong one, the stoic one, the steady

342   LESLIE KELLY

one had also left him the one who'd never been able to release the anger and the heartbreak that had been locked inside him.

By the time he finished, they were sitting in his driveway, and had been for several minutes. They were silent, neither of them even looking at each other, or moving to get out of the car. But finally, once he'd taken a deep breath and realized the world hadn't ended just because he'd admitted to someone else that he sometimes resented his life and his family and even his father, he looked over at her and saw the kind of warmth and kindness Amanda Bauer probably didn't even know she possessed.

"It's all right," she whispered. "Everything you're feeling is completely understandable." She lifted his hand to her mouth, pressing a soft, gentle kiss on the backs of his fingers. "I'm sorry you and your family had to go through that, Reese. So damn sorry."

"Thank you," he said, rubbing his knuckles against her soft cheek. He opened his mouth to continue, to both thank her and to tell her she needn't feel sorry for him. He also felt an apology rise to his lips, feeling bad for dumping everything on her like that. But before he could say a thing, something caught his eye.

A shadow was moving around the corner of his house.

He stiffened, leaning over to stare past her, out the window, but saw nothing. Thinking about what he'd seen, he knew it hadn't been Ralph. He never left the dog out if he wasn't home. Nor had the shape looked like any other kind of animal.

It had been man-size.

"Stay in the car and lock the doors," he ordered, reaching for the door handle.

"Huh?" She swung her head around to see what he'd been looking at. She figured it out almost immediately. "Is it him? Wait! Don't you dare…"

But he had already stepped out into the cold night, quietly pushing the door closed behind him. Maybe that bastard Lebowski didn't know he'd been spotted.

Reese paused for one second to glance back at Amanda, who watched wide-eyed from inside the car. Making a dialing motion with his hand, he mouthed, "Call 911," then crept across his own front lawn.

Though Parker had said the thief wasn't considered dangerous, Reese wasn't taking any chances. As he passed by the front flower bed, he bent over and grabbed the ugly ceramic gnome one of his sisters had given him as a gag housewarming gift. The thing had weight, it was solid in his palm. And if knocked against somebody's skull, he suspected it would hurt like crazy.

It'd do.

The night was moonless and cold, wind whipping up the few remaining dead leaves still lying in the yard. Reese moved in silence, approaching the corner of the house, carefully peering around it before proceeding.

He spotted Lebowski immediately. The robber was trying to use a credit card to jimmy the lock on the side door leading into the utility room. Muttering curses under his breath, the robber appeared clumsy and not terribly quiet, as if he'd gotten spooked when he'd heard them pull up in the driveway and was now on the verge of panic.

Reese suspected the man had been at it for a while. The fact that the guy hadn't been scared off when he and Amanda had returned said a lot about how desperate Lebowski was to get whatever he thought Reese and Amanda had.

The guy might be sly, but he wasn't much of a criminal. He didn't even notice Reese moving up behind him, jerking in shock when Reese pressed the pointed tip of the gnome's hat against the small of his back. "Make one move and you're dead."

"Aww, shit, man," the guy whined. "No, don't shoot, please don't. I wasn't gonna hurt anybody. I just wanted to get what's owed me and get outta here before you got back!"

"Yeah, so why'd you feel the need to threaten my girl-friend?" he asked, digging the point a little harder into the bastard's back.

"Are you kidding me? I didn't threaten her. The crazy bitch is hard-core, she ain't afraid of nothin'. *She* scares *me!*" The other man risked a quick peek over his shoulder, paling a little more when he saw the obvious rage in Reese's face. "Sorry."

"I most certainly am not hard-core," a voice said, cracking through the cold night as sharp and forceful as a whip.

He was going to kill her. "I asked you to stay in the car." He had to push the words through tightly clenched teeth.

"I did. I called the police, they'll be here any minute. When I saw you had things under control, I thought I'd come back and see if you could use this." She held out her hand, extending the long waist-tie to her overcoat.

Smart thinking. He'd gotten Lebowski to remain still, but hadn't thought ahead to how to keep him that way until the cops came. If the little toad figured out he was being held in place by a ceramic gnome's head, he might not be in the mood to stick around and wait to be arrested.

"Fine. Tie him up."

She moved closer, carefully. "Put your hands behind your back."

"I swear, I just wanted my jewelry. I owe some money to some of my colleagues and if I don't come up with it, they're gonna kill me."

"Well, hopefully they won't be able to get to you in a jail cell," Amanda said, sounding distinctly sour and a little bit pleased at the thought. Not that the guy didn't deserve it.

As she tied Teddy Lebowski's hands behind his back, yanking the fabric so tight the other man winced, she also said one more thing.

"And you can call me the biggest bitch in the known universe. But I am *not* crazy."

REESE HAD NEVER TOUCHED her more tenderly, more lovingly than he did that night after they'd watched Teddy Lebowski being taken away by the local police. They'd walked upstairs with their arms around each other's waists, her head dropping onto his shoulder in utter weariness.

But once they'd slipped out of their clothes and met in the middle of his bed, sleep had been far from Amanda's mind. And from Reese's.

He'd spent hours stroking her, tasting every inch of her

skin, teasing her with soft kisses and slow, deliberate caresses. Every brush of their lips had included a sweet whisper, each embrace a sigh of delight.

Even as he aroused all her senses, bringing her every nerve ending to its highest peak, he'd made her feel...cherished.

Adored.

There had been absolutely no frenzy. They exchanged long, slow kisses that didn't prompt any urgency, didn't make them want to go faster or hurry on to whatever came next. They were delightful just for how good they felt, how intimate and personal and right.

Kissing *was* an incredibly intimate act, she saw that now. She'd always considered it more a prelude to other things, but in Reese's arms, under his rapt attention where every touch brought waves of sensation, she gained a whole new appreciation for a simple kiss.

She'd never experienced anything like it. Never dreamed that emotional tears would fill her eyes as a man slowly slid into her body. She hadn't ever pictured every slide becoming a declaration and each gentle thrust a promise.

Nor had she ever imagined that when it was nearly over, when she'd lost herself to climax after climax, and had known he was reaching his, too, she'd actually feel her heart split in half at the sound of the words he'd softly whispered in her ear.

I love you.

He'd done it—the unthinkable. The thing she'd warned him not to do. He'd fallen in love with her. And he'd told her so.

Part of her wondered why she hadn't already left, slipping out the minute he'd fallen asleep. The old Amanda would have headed for the hills or the plains or another continent where she didn't have to deal with someone else's feelings that she simply didn't return.

She didn't have to wonder for long. The answer was simple, really. She *did* return them.

And that broke her heart even more.

Lying in Reese's arms after he'd fallen asleep, Amanda couldn't stop thinking about that moment she'd been sitting in the car, when she'd watched him disappear around the corner of the house. She'd heard the expression about your heart going into your throat when terror had you in its grip. But she'd never experienced it…until then.

It didn't matter what Parker had said, or that he'd been right in pegging Lebowski as a cowardly punk who didn't have the nerve to commit real violence. There'd been no way to be sure of that. As the seconds had passed, when her ears had still rung with his sad, grief-stricken whispers about his father, whom he had so loved and lost, she could only imagine the worst.

Losing him, something happening to him…she wouldn't be able to stand it. And though she had no real liking for his family yet, given their behavior the other night and the fact that his mother had looked at her like she was something that had crawled up from out of a toilet, she suddenly felt boatloads of sympathy for them.

The pain of losing someone you deeply loved had to be unimaginable. Which was, perhaps, one reason she'd never wanted to experience the emotion.

Too late. She, the stone-cold, heartbreaking bitch had fallen in love. Completely, totally, irrevocably in love. The ice had melted, her heart had begun beating with renewed energy and purpose. And the man she'd fallen in love with was incredibly sexy, smart, funny, loyal…and great.

Yet instead of that realization filling her with joy, she could only lie here in the dark and wonder just how long it would be before she screwed it up.

What would be the first callous thing she'd say to start piercing at his feelings for her? What trip would she take, what birthday would she forget, what need would she ignore, what promise would she not keep? How soon before she felt constricted, restrained, and just needed to *go?*

Because those things were inevitable. That was her M.O. No, she'd never gone as far as falling in love before, but it didn't matter, did it? She always let men down, always hurt them, always bailed.

She was just like Uncle Frank. Feckless, reckless, lovable but unreliable Uncle Frank. Everybody said so.

She suddenly wanted to cry. Because how badly did it suck to finally fall in love, *really* in love, and realize you liked the person too much to inflict yourself on him?

Reese was too good, way too good for her. She didn't want him hurt.

Not only that, he had a million and one things on his plate, was obviously at the end of his rope in terms of all the demands placed on him by everyone around him. So how could she add to that, become one more thing for him to worry about, one more weight on his shoulders?

Funny, when he realized she was gone, he would probably think it had something to do with his family, his responsibilities, his ties that bound him so tightly to this place and these people. All the things he'd told her about on the ride home tonight.

In fact, none of that really mattered. She'd told herself she never wanted to be stuck in place, living the same kind of life her parents had lived. But it didn't take a genius to see she didn't have to. She'd been in Reese's house for almost a week, and the world hadn't come to an end. She'd kept going to sleep each night and getting up each day. Kept breathing in, then out. Kept working, kept flying, kept living.

They *could* make this work.

If only she weren't so damned sure it wouldn't last.

It was that certainty that drove her out of bed just after dawn. For a moment, the thought of just leaving, heading for the airport, occurred to her. It had been her standard operating procedure in the past.

But Reese didn't deserve that kind of treatment. Besides, she wasn't that person anymore. Cowardice and immaturity had led her to make those decisions in the past. Now, she wasn't afraid, and she was looking at this through calm, adult eyes.

They couldn't work. Not in the long term. So *he'd* be better off getting out in the short one.

Sitting at his kitchen table, with Ralph—sweet dog, she was going to miss him, too—at her feet, she sipped a cup of coffee and waited for the chill of morning to leave her bones.

It didn't. Not one bit. She just sat there cold and sad, waiting for him to come down.

Finally, he did. When he walked into the kitchen, she could only stare at him. He wore low-riding sweatpants, no shirt, and she gazed at the strong arms that had held her during the night, the rough hands that had brought her so much pleasure. The broad chest against which she'd slept.

God this was hard. Love was hard.

He knew before she said a word that she was leaving.

"Do you need a ride to the airport?" he asked, not meeting her stare.

"Reese…"

He waved off her explanation. "I know. Game's over. Bad guy's caught. It's not even a holiday, so there's no reason for you to stay."

There were a million reasons for her to stay, but one really good one for her to go. All the men in the Dumped by Amanda Bauer group could attest to that. She just wasn't cut out for a serious, loving relationship.

"I did the unthinkable," he added, sounding so tired, and looking so resigned, her heart twisted in her chest. "I fell in love with you when I told you I wouldn't."

He finally met her stare, watching her closely. He seemed to be looking for something—a sign, a hesitation, a hint that she was happy he loved her.

It took every bit of her strength not to give it to him.

Finally, with a short nod that said he'd gotten the message, he broke the stare. "So, do you need a ride?"

"I can get a cab," she murmured.

"Fine. Goodbye, Amanda."

He didn't say anything else, merely turned and walked

back out of the kitchen. His footsteps were hard as he walked up the stairs, and from above, she hard the slamming of the door as he went into the bathroom.

The shower came on. It would undoubtedly be a long one. He didn't have to tell her he hoped she'd be gone when he got out. That was a given.

She followed him up, quickly threw her new clothes in the shopping bags they'd come in. Not really thinking about it, she crossed the room, walking toward the bathroom door. She lifted her fist, half tempted to knock. But her hand unclenched and flattened. She pressed it against the wood, fingers spread, almost able to feel the steam-filled air on the other side of it. Closing her eyes, she leaned her forehead against the door, picturing him in the shower, already hurt by her when it was the very last thing she'd wanted to do.

Better now than later.

Her eyes opened. Her hand dropped. She picked up her bag. Then Amanda Bauer walked out of Reese Campbell's bedroom and out of his life for the last time.

chapter eleven

Valentine's Day

REESE wished the one day of the year set aside for lovers took place in March. It would help him out a lot if he could talk Saint Valentine into switching places on the calendar with Saint Patrick, just this once. Maybe Hallmark wouldn't appreciate it, or the flower or chocolate industries, but he could really use an extra month before the big day meant for romance and love—all the stuff he'd had a couple of days ago, before Amanda had walked out of his house.

All the stuff he intended to have again. With her.

It had been hell watching her go. But the minute he'd walked into the kitchen and seen the sad, resigned expression on her face, he'd known she was leaving. He could do nothing but let her, not because of that "If you love something set it free" bullshit, but because he knew her well enough to know there was no point trying to talk her out of it.

As he'd gone upstairs, he'd briefly hoped that seeing how calmly he'd taken it—even though inside he'd been a churning mass of anger, frustration and want—she would realize she was making a mistake and change her mind. Hearing her come up to gather her things, he'd waited in the bathroom, not in the running shower, but standing right on the other side of the closed door. Half wondering if she'd knock. Pretty sure she wouldn't.

She hadn't.

As strong as she was, Amanda wasn't the type to make important decisions on the spur of the moment. She was the retreat–consider–evaluate–then–cautiously–edge–forward type.

He only wished he was able to give her more time to sit in Chicago considering, evaluating, before edging back in his direction. That's why it would have been better if Valentine's Day were a month away. With one month to think about it, he knew—without a doubt—that she'd be calling, e-mailing or showing up on his doorstep.

Maybe not for emotional reasons. Not for commitment and marriage and a lifetime together. It could be just because she *wanted* him, and would send him an invitation to come to D.C. to play a game of senator and naughty aide. Sex. Not love. She was as sexually addicted to him as he was to her, and within thirty days, she'd be jonesing for the kind of hot, wild intimacy the two of them had shared from day one.

So, yeah. She'd call, or write or text.

And he'd go.

It was okay. She could use him to satisfy her deepest needs, because he knew he'd be filled with the same hunger for her. And their game would begin again.

Mainly, however, he'd go because deep down, he knew that one of these days, she was going to finally figure out she loved him, too.

She did love him, of that he had no doubt. Amanda just hadn't acknowledged it yet. Or else she had come up with a million reasons why it couldn't work and had decided not to *let* herself love him.

That was okay, too. He didn't need her to say the words. Sex was enough to intertwine their lives until she was ready, and in a month, she'd be dying for it.

"Curse you for being born in February, St. Valentine," he muttered.

Because while thirty days would have done the trick, five might not be enough. In the short time since she'd left, she might have gotten just a little edgy, but she was stubborn. She could probably hold out longer than that, no matter how incredible the sex between them had been during those nights when she'd slept in his bed.

He had no choice, though. It was February 14, and the romantic in him just couldn't let the day pass without at least giving his best shot at seduction. For the first time in his life, he was in love with the right woman on Valentine's Day. He had to do something about it.

And that was why he was sitting on a plane that was right now landing at O'Hare Airport. He'd booked the best room he could get on such short notice at an exclusive

Chicago hotel. Tonight, he would either be there with her, reminding her she'd made the right choice in showing up.

Or he would be sitting in it alone, tossing a box of chocolates into the trash, watching the rose petals strewn all over the bed wilt, and wishing he hadn't wasted a case of champagne by pouring it into the bathtub. Not to mention regretting the oysters he'd already ordered from room service.

He was definitely hoping for option A.

Fortunately, he had an accomplice in his plan to whisk Amanda away for a night of sexy romance. As much as he'd hated to do it, he'd gotten in touch with Aunt Jean and asked her who at Clear-Blue Air would be the best person to ask for inside info on Amanda's schedule. This Ginny woman she'd recommended had been extremely helpful, either because she liked his great-aunt, or she loved her employer. Maybe a combination of both.

From what the woman had said, he had a few hours before Amanda returned to Chicago from her day trip to Cincinnati. A few hours to check into the room, set the scene, then call her and ask her if she had the nerve to see him again this soon.

Asking her probably wouldn't do it. Daring her just might.

All those things churned through his mind as he followed the long stream of passengers off the plane and into the terminal. One more thought occurred to him, too: if this didn't work, he might just have to come back next month and check out the green river and a few Chicago pubs. Amanda would look cute as hell in a leprechaun hat. Or sexy as hell if it was all she was wearing.

Smiling at that thought, he headed not for the taxi stand,

but rather toward the offices of Clear-Blue Air. He'd told Ginny he would come by when he arrived, just to touch base and make sure Amanda's schedule hadn't changed. He probably could have called for the information, but he suspected the woman wanted to check him out.

Speaking of calling...*phone*. As he walked, he tugged his cell phone out of his pocket and turned it on. A quick glance at the bars confirmed he had no reception. So maybe Ginny wasn't sneaky and a hopeless romantic, just used to spotty service inside the airport. Though, it could be both.

Making his way through Security, who had his name on the list of authorized visitors to the office wing, he followed the directions Ginny had given him. The airport was huge, he'd always known that. But he'd never imagined the amount of space the public never saw. The hallway seemed to go on for blocks.

Of course the Clear-Blue office was at the end of that hallway. His steps quickened as he realized what time it was. He'd figured this errand would take a few minutes.... It had been thirty since he'd stepped off the plane.

When he was finally within a few feet of the door, he saw it open from the inside. He stepped out of the way to let the person out, not really paying attention. At least, not until a woman emerged. The very woman he did not want to see, at least not until tonight.

"Oh, hell," he muttered as all his plans went up in smoke.

Amanda stared at him, wide-eyed, wide-mouthed, not saying a word. She probably feared he'd turned into some psycho stalker.

"Hey," he said softly, wondering if she'd duck back into the office and avoid him altogether.

Instead, she did something far more shocking. Something that rocked him where he stood.

Without a single word, Amanda dropped the small overnight case she'd been carrying, stepped toward him, threw her arms around his neck and kissed him like she hadn't seen him in at least…a month.

HE WAS HERE. She couldn't believe he was really here, that he'd come to Chicago for her for Valentine's Day.

Kissing Reese, feeling the warmth of his body, inhaling his scent and reliving all the pleasures of his mouth, she found tears rising to her eyes. She loved him, she'd missed him. And she had finally found the man who might give her the freedom to fly when she needed to, but would always be waiting for her when she got back. Or else he'd simply come after her.

Finally, their kiss ended and she smiled up at him. "You came."

"Of course I came." Shaking his head and narrowing his eyes in confusion, he said, "You're supposed to be in Cincinnati."

A quick stab of worry made her ask, "Oh, God. You didn't expect me to be here? You didn't come here to see me?"

He threw back his head and laughed, tightening his arms around her waist. "Crazy woman, of course I came here to see you. But I had this big seduction plan all worked out and you didn't give me as much as an hour to get over to the hotel and set it all up."

"There's a couch in my office," she said, her tone dry. "For you and me, that's about all it would take."

"True." He leaned down and kissed her forehead, murmuring, "But I want to give you more than that."

She sighed, turning her face up so her soft cheek brushed his rough one. "I guess that's okay, then. Ginny's desk *is* right outside my door."

"Hotel it is."

Sounded just fine to her. Anxious to go, to be alone with him somewhere so she could tell him about all the wild thoughts that had gone on in her head, and the wilder feelings that had her ready to burst emotionally, she slipped out of his arms and bent down to grab her overnight bag. He took it from her, slinging it over his shoulder with his own.

She didn't argue—it wasn't much of a burden, because there wasn't much in it. A silky red teddy, a pair of thigh-high stockings. Just the necessities. Not what she typically packed for working trips, because she most definitely had not been on her way to Cincinnati when she'd run into him. Ha! No wonder Ginny had kept looking at the clock and stalling her with inane questions. She'd been worried Amanda would fly to Pittsburgh while Reese was flying here.

"So why aren't you somewhere in or over Ohio?" he asked as they began walking toward the terminal, his arm around her waist, their hips and thighs brushing with every step.

"I had someone else take my flight," she told him. "Too flipping cold in Ohio."

Even as he laughed at that, given the fact that it had to be ten-below-cold-as-shit here in Chicago, he jiggled the overnight bag. "So where *were* you headed?"

There was a hint of amusement in his voice, as if he knew the answer. Well, of *course* did. He knew she'd been coming to see him. He hadn't realized it before he'd arrived here, obviously, but once he'd seen her, once she'd thrown her arms around him and kissed him with all the love she felt for the man, how could he not know she'd want to be with him on *this* of all holidays?

"Where do you think, hotshot?"

"Daytona? It's certainly warmer."

"Not as hot as Pittsburgh."

He stopped when she confirmed it, turning her in his arms so he could kiss her again. This time it wasn't sweet and soft, but deep and hungry, as if he'd been thinking about her since the minute she'd left his house, wanting her all that time.

Or maybe she was projecting how she'd been thinking and feeling. Whatever. All she knew was the man's sweet mouth was covering every millimeter of hers and she never wanted it to end.

Finally, though, because a nearby office door opened and voices intruded, it did.

"Let's get out of here," she whispered, looping her arm through his and leading him back toward the terminal. "I think we have some talking to do."

But not yet. She didn't want to have any deep, important conversation as they walked through the public area of the airport. It was filled with travelers frantic to make their destinations and groaning their way through the long lines at Security.

Since "I'm sorry, I was stupid and I love you" was out, she used the time to fill him in on something a little less personal.

"You're not going to believe the phone call I got this morning." She had intended to tell him about it when she saw him at his place tonight. At least, as long as he let her in the front door.

Not that it would have stopped her if he hadn't. She already knew one of his windows didn't lock right—thank goodness their visitor from Las Vegas hadn't realized it.

"From who?"

"Officer Parker. I guess he was really curious why a sleazy thug would follow us all the way to Chicago, and then Pennsylvania, if he hadn't *really* dropped the jewelry he'd stolen."

Reese eyed her in interest. "Did he have any theories about what happened to it?"

"Yep. Turns out the store owner was apparently just as sleazy. Our friend Teddy *had* dropped his bag of goodies that night—right outside the door of the shop. The owner found it, hid it, then filed a false insurance claim. Parker got him to confess the whole thing."

Reese nodded, appearing as relieved as she had been at the news. "So no more worrying about Mr. Lebowski."

"Correct." Smiling, she added, "Which means you don't have to update your garden gnome for a .357 Magnum."

He chuckled, and a companionable silence again fell between them. It continued as they reached her car and got in it, neither saying much of anything once he'd given her the name of the hotel where they were staying. It was as if he already knew she had a lot to tell him, and didn't want that conversation to start until they were completely alone. She wanted no distractions caused by nosy onlookers, or the need to keep her hands on the wheel.

Besides, a little silence was good. She needed the drive time to put everything into words.

She'd figured she'd have a few hours before arriving on his doorstep in Pittsburgh, armed with a coffee can in one hand, and a teabag in the other. "Coffee, tea or me?" had seemed like a good opening line. Getting him to smile might ensure he didn't slam the door in her face for being such a cowardly bitch and running out on him the other morning without giving him the courtesy of an explanation.

Finally, they arrived at the hotel. She whistled as they walked into the lobby, duly impressed. The man was going all out for this little holiday getaway.

"Don't get too excited," he murmured as they approached the front desk. "I just made the reservation yesterday. They're probably desperate to take advantage of every holiday sucker they can get, so we might end up sleeping in a tiny bed stuck inside a janitor's closet."

She laughed, but honestly didn't care. As long as they could be alone, and a bed was in the vicinity, that was just fine with her.

A few minutes later, when they arrived at their room, she realized Reese needn't have worried. Neither of them were laughing as they walked inside and looked around. Despite the last-minute reservation, the room was beautiful, with a huge, plush bed, elegant furnishings and enormous windows that looked down on bustling Michigan Avenue. She didn't doubt he'd paid several times the rate it would have been on any other night of the year.

"Not bad," he conceded.

"It's amazing," she whispered, not really talking about the room, but about one spot in it.

He had obviously been specific with his requests, because spread all over that plush, turned-down bed were what looked like hundreds of red rose petals.

"What game are we playing here?" she asked, suddenly a tiny bit cautious and wary.

This looked like wedding-night stuff. And while she'd mentally acknowledged she could not let Reese go without giving the feelings they had for one another a chance, she was in no way ready for rings and white veils.

Liar.

Okay, maybe the thought *had* crossed her mind. But only in a "someday, possibly" kind of way. Definitely not soon.

He accurately read her expression. "Don't worry, if I wanted to play honeymoon, I would have whisked you off to one of those places in the Poconos with the heart-shaped beds and the raised, champagne-glass bathtubs."

She punched him lightly in the arm, instinctively replying, "We are not spending our honeymoon in Pennsylvania!"

Only after the words had left her mouth did she realize what she'd said. And acknowledged the implications.

Seeing the warmth in his eyes, she put a hand up. "Wait. That's not what I meant. I'm not saying…"

"Would you shut up?" he asked, sweetly, tenderly. He lifted a hand to her face, brushing his thumb across her cheek. "Just stop thinking about it, stop talking about it and love me."

It was as simple as that.

She nodded, rising on tiptoe to press her lips against his. Just as sweetly, just as tenderly. When the kiss ended, she kept her arms around his neck and stared into his handsome face. "I do love you."

"I know."

She kissed him again. "I shouldn't have run out the other day without admitting it."

"I understand why you did."

Her brow furrowing, she lowered her arms and slowly sat down on the edge of the bed, careful not to disturb the flower petals. "You do?"

He pulled a chair closer and sat opposite her, bending over with his elbows on his knees, hands dangling between his parted legs. His expression was serious as he said, "All the difficulties you're sure we have can be dealt with. My family, your family, our jobs, our homes. That whole geography thing they no longer teach in schools."

He didn't have to go on. She had already realized none of those problems really mattered. They could be worked out. In fact, she'd already talked to her uncle about modifying her work schedule so she could, as Jazz had suggested, commute out of Pittsburgh.

Uncle Frank had been incredibly supportive once he'd found out why. Urging her not to let his own bad example lead her to a life as lonely as his, he'd offered to do whatever it took to accommodate her.

"Reese, I…"

"Let me finish, please." The corner of his mouth lifted in a half smile as he completely bared his heart to her.

"I love you. And after we talked the other night in the car, I realized life is just too damned precarious not to be with the person you love."

She understood. Those very same thoughts had crossed her mind the other morning…only she'd taken the cowardly way out of having to deal with any future pain, loss and heartache. She'd cut and run. Reese was far more daring, willing to risk whatever happened tomorrow for the good things they could have today.

That kind of emotional bravery at least entitled him to the whole truth. "I didn't leave because I was scared for myself, but because I was afraid for you."

"What?"

"I don't want to hurt you, Reese. I love you too much. I've just grown used to the idea that I'm destined to hurt men because I'm not cut out for relationships."

He shook his head. "That's crazy, you wouldn't…"

"I know that now. Sitting at home for the past few nights, going over it in my mind, I realized all those failed relationships I *wasn't* cut out for had one thing in common."

"What's that?"

"They weren't with you."

He pulled her off the bed into his arms, settling her into his lap. Amanda cuddled against him, sucking up his heat and his essence, then said, "How can any loving relationship work if only one person is actually in love?"

"It can't."

"Exactly. And once I realized that, once I acknowledged that I have never been in love with *anyone* until now, I was finally able to let it go. The guilt, the regret, the shame."

He squeezed her. "You have nothing to be ashamed of."

"Tell that to Facebook," she mumbled. But she quickly thrust the thought aside. No room for darkness now, there was only light and happiness, passion and possibility. Love.

"There's nothing wrong with me," she admitted, to both of them. "I just don't fall in love easily."

"Neither do I."

"Which means neither one of us is going to fall out of it easily, right?"

He kissed the top of her head, vowing, "Neither one of us is going to fall out of it at all."

He couldn't know that. No one could know such a thing. But she believed him. With all her heart, with every instinct she owned, she believed him.

"I can't promise not to be insensitive and self-absorbed sometimes," she warned. "Can't say I'll never do something selfish and hurt you."

"Well," he replied after giving it some thought, "I can't say I'll always remember to put the toilet seat down or not squeeze from the middle of the toothpaste tube."

She laughed softly.

He thought about it some more. "I can't promise to let you handcuff me the next time we play cops and robbers... but I might agree to a few silk scarves."

Her laughter deepened, as she knew he'd meant it to. Then Reese got more serious.

"I can't say I'm never going to work late. Or that I won't sometimes just need to be alone with my thoughts. Some days of the year my mood will be dark and I won't want to talk about it."

Hearing that hint of sadness she'd heard in his voice the other night, she understood that. Completely.

"Okay. But I can't promise I'm not going to try to kidnap you away from work once in a while so I can fly us to Aspen to do a little skiing."

He grinned. "That sounds great. Especially because *I* can't promise we won't have one or another of my PMS-ing sisters calling in the middle of the night because she had a fight with her boyfriend and needs a ride."

His family was part of his life. She knew that. The way he cared for them was one thing she loved best about him. Still, the memory of their first meeting intruded. Nibbling her lip, she asked, "Do they all hate me?"

"No! Not one little bit. In fact, two of my sisters showed up at my place last night asking me why I hadn't left yet to come here and win you back."

She breathed a sigh of relief. Though she hadn't wanted to admit it, the idea of a wedding had, indeed, flitted around in her mind once or twice. She'd immediately done her Amanda-thing and started worrying about how she could handle having bridesmaids who hated her guts in her wedding party.

Plus Jazz. Plus her sister, Abby. Oh, Lord.

Not thinking about that now.

"You should also know, my mother called to apologize and asked me to tell you that despite her behavior that first night, she would not be a Monster-In-Law. Which is true—she's sad lately, but she's never been pushy or tried to interfere in my life before. I've been the one hovering."

"That's because you're a good man," she whispered.

A really good, funny, *sexy* man.

A man she deserved.

For the first time, she allowed herself to believe it was possible. She *could* make the right man happy. She *did* deserve him.

Reese was that right man.

Though the rose petals beckoned, and she truly wanted to slip out of her clothes, and get him out of his, so they could express their love in the most elemental, sensual way possible, she had to add one more thing. One more promise, that she intended to keep.

"I won't ever run from you, Reese."

"Sure you will." He smiled tenderly. "But I'll always follow."

★ ★ ★ ★ ★

The Harlequin® Blaze™ series brings you
six new fun, flirtatious and steamy stories a month
available wherever books are sold, including most bookstores,
supermarkets, drugstores and discount stores.

Blaze

THE CHARMER

kate HOFFMANN

For all my readers, everywhere!

prologue

Angela@SmoothOperators.com
January 6, 5:30 a.m.
Heading out for my 7:00 a.m. interview on Daybreak Chicago. Hope you all remember to tune in. I'm a bit nervous, but excited at the same time. Call in with questions! I'll post more later.

ANGELA Weatherby glanced up at her image in the video monitors, squinting into the bright television lights that illuminated the studio. She looked worried. Quickly, she pasted a cheery smile on her face.

The chance to make an appearance on *Daybreak Chicago* had seemed like a good idea when it had first been offered. But now, faced with the prospect of airing her dirty romantic laundry, Angie wasn't so sure.

With her Web site, SmoothOperators.com, she could be anonymous, just another jilted lover with a score to settle.

But on morning television, for all of Chicago to see, she might come off looking like a first-class bitch, out for revenge.

She glanced over at Celia Peralto, her Web master and best friend, who stood next to one of the cameramen. Ceci grinned and gave her a thumbs-up.

A sound technician approached her from behind and clipped a microphone to her collar. "Just tuck the wire under your hair," he advised, "and set the pack on the chair next to you." With trembling fingers, Angie did as she was told.

"Thirty seconds," the producer called.

"Just relax," the host said as she took her place in the opposite chair. "This isn't the Spanish Inquisition. Just a fun segment on single life in Chicago. And it's great publicity for your Web site—and for the book you're planning to write."

The book. Her publisher was expecting the manuscript in three months and though she had gathered all sorts of anecdotal research from her Web site, the book still had to be written.

"Good morning, Chicago! I'm Kelly Caulfield and I'm here with our next guest. About two years ago, Angela Weatherby founded a Web site called SmoothOperators.com and it has become a national sensation. What began as a way for single girls in Chicago to network over their dating horror stories has evolved into something akin to the FBI's most-wanted list for naughty men."

"I wouldn't put it that way," Angela said. "These men aren't criminals."

"I suspect some Chicago bachelorettes would disagree. Through the Web site, women are helping each other avoid those men who make dating miserable for all of us. And the trend is spreading—the site adds new cities every week. So, tell us, Angela, what gave you the idea for your Web site?"

Angie shifted in her chair, then drew a deep breath. If she just focused on answering the questions, her nerves would eventually calm. "After a series of not-so-nice boyfriends, I felt there had to be a way for me to avoid guys who weren't interested in an honest and committed relationship. I started blogging about it and before long I had over a thousand subscribers. They added their stories and my friend and Web master, Celia Peralto, put their comments into a database. Now, you can check out your date before you even step out the front door. As of last night, we have files on almost fifty thousand smooth operators in cities all over the country."

"Don't you think this is unfair to the men out there? An ex-girlfriend might not be the most objective person to provide commentary."

"You'd check out the plumber you wanted to hire or the doctor you planned to visit, right? We offer information and leave it to our visitors to decide the truth in what they read. And I think we're doing a service. We've even unmasked a number of cheating husbands."

Kelly leaned forward in her chair. "Well, I looked up my cohost, Danny Devlin, and he wasn't very well reviewed on your site. Your rating system goes from one to five broken hearts, with five being the worst. And he's rated a four. Care to comment?"

Angela opened her mouth to reply, then snapped it shut. A glib answer here might turn the interview in a different direction. "Mr. Devlin is always welcome to defend himself. We're open to differing opinions. We just require that the discourse be civilized."

Kelly flipped to her next note card. "Well, that leads us to the book you're writing. Tell us about that."

Angela drew a deep breath and focused her thoughts. She'd practiced her pitch more than once in the mirror at home. "I hope the book will be a guide to the different species of smooth operators out there. Most of these men fall into one of ten or twelve categories. If women can learn to spot them quickly, maybe they'll save themselves a bit of heartbreak."

"And what professional credentials do you bring to the table?" Kelly asked.

"I have an undergraduate degree in psychology, a masters in journalism and experience as a freelance writer. And I've dated a lot of very smooth operators myself," Angie replied, allowing herself a smile. "I'm curious as to why they behave the way they do, as are most women."

"Let's take a few questions from callers," Kelly said. For the next three minutes, Angie jousted with a belligerent bachelor, commiserated with two women who'd just been dumped and fended off the evil glares of Danny Devlin, who had wandered back onto the set. When the six-minute segment was finally over, she sat back in her chair and breathed a sigh of relief.

"You were wonderful!" Kelly exclaimed, hopping out of her chair. "We'll have to have you back again."

"The switchboard went crazy," the producer said as she walked onto the set. "The most calls we've ever had in this time slot. Let's book another interview for next month. Maybe we can do a longer feature segment when the book comes out."

Angie stood up and unclipped the microphone. "That would be lovely," she murmured as she handed it to the sound technician. "Thank you. Is there anything else I need to do?"

"Get that book written," Kelly said. "And personally, I think Danny Devlin deserves five broken hearts. He dumped me by e-mail."

Angie crossed the studio to Ceci, then grabbed her arm and pulled her along toward the exit. "Let's get out of here," she said, tugging her coat on. "Before Danny Devlin corners me and demands that I take his profile off the site."

The early morning air was frigid and the pavement slippery as they walked through the parking lot. When they reached the relative safety of Ceci's car, Angie sat back in the seat and drew a long, deep breath. It clouded in front of her face as she slowly released it. "So, how was I? Tell me the truth. Did I come across as angry or bitter?"

"No, not at all," Ceci said. "You were funny. And sweet. And just a little vulnerable, which was good. You were likeable."

"I didn't seem judgmental? I want people to look at the Web site as a practical dating tool. Not some organization promoting hatred of the opposite sex." She glanced over at Ceci. "I really do like men. I just don't like how they treat women sometimes."

Ceci smiled as she started the car. "Sweetie, if we didn't like men so much, we wouldn't waste our energy trying to fix them. Someone has to hold these guys accountable."

"Did you get through to Alex Stamos?" Angela asked, turning her attention to the next bit of research for her book. "He's been ducking my calls for a week now."

"I got his assistant. She says he's out of town for the next few days on business, but he'll be sure to get back to me when he returns. She also mentioned that she had a few stories of her own about the guy."

"You made it clear that this interview would be anonymous, didn't you?" Angie asked.

"I said that you wanted to give him a chance to set the record straight," Ceci said. "But I think getting an in-depth profile of each of these types might be kind of tricky. Especially once they've seen the site."

"Maybe I shouldn't do the interviews and go with my original plan."

"Absolutely not," Celia cried. "I think having a conversation with each of these types makes them real. Just move on to the next guy on your list and catch up with Stamos later."

Angie had been working as a freelance writer ever since she got out of college. It had been a hit-and-miss career and there were times when she barely had enough to pay the rent. The blog had just been a way to exercise her writing muscles every day, but once it took off, she was able to attract advertisers and make a reasonably constant paycheck from the Web site.

She sighed. Her parents, both college professors, had wanted her to become a psychologist, but when she finished her undergrad studies at Northwestern, she'd decided to rebel and try journalism.

This book would give her instant credibility as a journalist—and it might appease her parents as well as open a lot of doors. The advance alone was nearly gone, lost to car repairs and computer upgrades. Right now, every Tom, Dick and Mary was a blogger. But not many people could say they were a real author.

"You're right," she said. "I can work on Charlie Templeton. Or Max Morgan." But would they be willing to talk? She'd have to readjust her strategy. If the men weren't going to be identified in the book, then maybe a bit of subterfuge to get their stories wouldn't be entirely out of line.

chapter one

ALEX Stamos peered into the darkness, the BMW's head-lights nearly useless in the swirling snow. He could barely make out the edge of the road, the drifts causing the car to fishtail even at fifteen miles per hour.

He'd done a lot of things to boost business at Stamos Publishing and as the new CEO, that was his job. But until now, he'd never had to risk life and limb to get what he wanted. His cell phone rang and he reached over to pick it up off the passenger seat. "I'm in the middle of a blizzard," he said. "Make it quick."

"What are doing in a blizzard?" Tess asked. "I thought you were leaving for Mexico tonight."

He had decided to put off his midwinter vacation for a few days. Business was much more important than a week of sun and windsurfing at his family's oceanside condo. "I have to take care of this business first. I'm leaving the day after tomorrow."

"Where are you?"

"The middle of nowhere," he said. "Door County."

"Isn't that in Wisconsin?"

"And you failed geography, little sister. How is that possible?"

Tess groaned. "That was in eighth grade."

"There's a new artist I need to see. He hasn't been return-ing my calls, so I decided to drive up and pay a personal visit."

"Well, I thought you'd want to know. *The Devil's Own* got a great review in *Publisher's Preview,*" Tess said. "And the distributors have been calling all afternoon to increase their orders. At this rate, we're going to have to go back for the second printing before the first is out the door, so I just wanted to let you know that I'm going to put it on the schedule for later next week."

Tess was head of production at Stamos Publishing. She and Alex had been working together on his new business plan for nearly a year and this was the first sign that it was about to pay off. Until last year, Stamos Publishing had been known for it's snooze-inducing catalog of techni-cal books, covering everything from lawnmower repair to vegan cookery to dog grooming. But as the newly ap-pointed chief executive officer, Alex was determined to move the company into the twenty-first century. And that move began with a flashy new imprint for graphic novels.

From the time he was a kid, walking through the press-room with his grandfather, he'd been fascinated by the family business. While most of his peers were enjoying their summers off, he'd worked in the bindery and the production offices, learning Stamos Publishing from top to bottom.

His dream had been to make Stamos Publishing the premier printer in the comic book industry. That way, he could get all the free comic books he wanted. But as he got older, Alex began to take the business more seriously. He saw the weaknesses in his father's management plan and in the company's spot in the market and vowed to make some changes if he ever got the chance.

The chance came at the expense of his family, when his father died suddenly four years ago. His grandfather had come back to run the business, but only until Alex was ready to take over. Now, nearly all the extended Stamos family, siblings, cousins, aunts and uncles, depended upon him to keep the business in the black.

"I'm going to run forty thousand," Tess said. "I know that's double the first run, but I think our sell-through will be good."

"I guess we were right about the graphic novels," he said, keeping his concentration on the road. Though they weren't comic books, they were the next best thing. The edgier stories and innovative art had made them popular with readers of all ages. And Stamos was posed to grab a nice chunk of the market. "What else?"

"Mom is upset," Tess said. "One of her bridge club ladies showed her that Web site. The cool operators site."

"Smooth operators," he corrected. "What did she say?"

"That a nice Greek boy won't find a nice Greek wife if he acts like a *malakas*. And she also said the next time you come to Sunday dinner, she's going to have a conversation with you."

"Great," Alex muttered. A conversation was always much more painful than a talk or a chat with his mother. No doubt he'd be forced to endure a few blind dates with eligible Greek girls, handpicked by the Stamos matriarch.

"Some people think that any P.R. is good P.R. I don't happen to agree, Alex. I think you need to do some damage control and you need to do it fast. I'm looking at your profile on this page right now and it's not good. These women hate you. Heck, I hate you, and I'm your sister."

"What do you suggest? I'm not about to talk about my love life in public."

"Who suggested that?"

Alex cursed beneath his breath. "The owner of the Web site called to interview me. Angela…I can't remember her last name. Weatherall or Weathervane."

"She wants to talk to you?"

"I guess. Either that, or she wants to yell at me. But I'm almost certain I've never dated her." He cursed softly. "What makes her think I'm the one at fault here? Some of these women are just as much to blame. They were ready to get married after three dates."

"You have had a lot of girlfriends. Listen, Alex, I know you're a nice guy. So why can't you find a nice woman?"

The car skidded and he brought it back under control, cursing beneath his breath. "I'll figure this out when I get back."

"So this artist must be pretty good for you to drive through a blizzard to see him."

"A little snow is not going to stop me," he replied. "And this guy isn't just good, he's…amazing. And oddly uninterested in publication. The novel came through the slush pile and I figure the reason he's avoiding me is because he's got another publisher interested."

"So, you're just going to drive five hours in the snow and expect he'll want to talk business?"

"I'm a persuasive guy," Alex said. "My charm doesn't just work on the opposite sex. Besides, if I'm his first offer, then I have a chance to get a brand-new talent for a bargain-basement price. I'm not leaving without a signed contract."

The car skidded again and Alex dropped his phone as he gripped the wheel with two hands. He gently applied the brakes and slowed to a crawl as he fished around for the BlackBerry. But he couldn't find it in the dark. "I have to go," he shouted, "or I'll end up in the ditch. I'll call you after I check in."

"Let me know when you're settled," Tess replied.

Alex found the BlackBerry and tucked it in his jacket pocket, then turned his attention back to the road. He knew Door County was well populated, at least in the summer. But in the middle of a Wisconsin winter, the highway was almost desolate between the small towns, marked only by snow-plastered signs looming in the darkness.

Was he the only one crazy enough to be out during a blizzard? Alex leaned forward, searching for the edge of the road through the blowing snow. A moment later, he realized he was no longer in control of his car. Without a sound the car hit a huge drift and came to a silent stop in the ditch.

This time, Alex strung enough curse words together to

form a complete sentence, replete with plenty of vivid ad-jectives. He wasn't sure what to do. The car wouldn't go forward or backward. Even if he got the car back on the road, it was becoming impossible to see where the road was. He didn't have a shovel, so there wasn't much chance of getting himself out of the ditch.

Alex grabbed his gloves from the seat beside him and pulled them on. If he could clear some of the snow from beneath the wheels, he might be able to get back on the road. If not, he'd call the auto club for a tow. He grabbed a flashlight from the glove box, then crawled out of the car, his feet sinking into a three-foot drift.

Even with the flashlight, it was impossible to see through the blowing snow. Blackness surrounded him as he dug at the snow with his hands. But for every handful of snow he pulled away, two more fell back beneath the tire. Alex knew the only safe option was to wait in the car for help.

He pulled out his phone to call for a tow, but his gloves were wet and his fingers numb from digging in the snow. The BlackBerry slipped out of his fingers and disappeared into the snowdrift. "Shit," he muttered. "From one bone-headed move to the next." Was it even worth searching for the phone?

He decided against it, figuring the BlackBerry would be ruined anyway. As he struggled back to the door, head-lights appeared on the road. For a moment, he wondered if the car would even see him in the blinding snow, but to his relief, the SUV stopped. He waded through the drift as the passenger-side window opened.

"Hi," he called, leaning inside. "I'm stuck."

A female voice replied. "I can see that."

Alex could barely make out her features. She wore a huge fur hat with earflaps and a scarf wound around her neck, obscuring the lower part of her face. In truth, she was bundled from top to toe, except for her eyes. "Can you give me a ride into town?"

"No," she said. "I've just come from town. The road is nearly impassable. I'm on my way home."

Her voice was soft and kind of husky...sexy. He felt an odd reaction, considering it was the only thing that marked her as a woman. "I'd call for a tow, but I lost my cell phone."

"Get in," she said. "I'll take you to my place and you can call from there."

"Let me just get my things from the car." By the time Alex retrieved his duffel, his laptop and his briefcase from the BMW, he was completely caked with snow. He crawled into the warm Jeep and pulled the door shut. "Thanks," he said. He glanced over his shoulder to find two dogs in the backseat, watching him silently, their noses twitching. The larger of the two looked like a lab mix and the smaller had a fair bit of terrier in him.

"What are you doing out on a night like tonight?" she asked.

"I could ask the same of you," Alex said with a grin. "I'm glad you were as brave as I was."

"Stupid is more like it. And I'm not driving a sports car," she said.

"It's not a sports car," he said. "It's a sedan." He glanced over at her. It was impossible to tell how old she was. And the only clue to her appearance was a lock of dark hair that had escaped from under her hat. "Do you live nearby?"

"Just down the road."

He settled back into the seat, staring out at the swirl of white in front of them. He couldn't see the road at all, but she seemed to know exactly where she was going, expertly navigating through the drifts. Before long, she slowed and turned off the highway onto what he assumed was a side road and then a few minutes later, into a narrow driveway, marked by two tall posts, studded with red reflectors. The woods were thick on either side, so it was easy to find the way through the trees.

A yard light was visible as they approached and, before long, Alex could see the outline of a small cabin made of rough-hewn logs. She pulled up in front and turned to face him. "The front door's unlocked," she said. "I'm just going to put the Jeep in the shed."

Alex grabbed his things from the floor and hopped out, then walked through another knee-deep drift to get to the front steps. As he stamped the snow off his ruined loafers, the dogs joined him, racing through the darkness to the porch.

He opened the door a crack and the animals pushed their way into the dimly lit interior. The cabin was one huge room, with a timbered ceiling and tongue and groove paneling. A stone fireplace covered one wall and windows lined the other. The décor was like nothing he'd ever seen before, every available space taken with bits and pieces of nature—a bird's nest, a basket of acorns, a single maple leaf in a frame on a bent-willow table.

He kicked off his shoes and stepped off the rug, but then froze as the dogs growled softly. They'd seemed so friendly in the car, but now they watched him suspiciously as he ventured uninvited into their territory.

"The phone is over there."

He turned to see her standing in the shadows on the other side of the kitchen. "Do they bite?" he asked.

"Only if I tell them to," she murmured. There was a subtle warning in her tone. It wasn't surprising, considering she just allowed a stranger into her home. For all she knew, he could be some deranged psycho—driving an expensive European sedan and wearing ruined Italian loafers.

"I won't make any sudden moves," he said.

She shrugged and walked out of the room, her heavy boots leaving puddles of water on the floor. Alex slipped out of his coat and tossed it over a nearby chair, then kicked off his shoes. When the two dogs approached, he held his breath. They sniffed at his feet, then each picked up a shoe and retreated back to the sofa with their prizes.

"Give those back," he pleaded. "No, don't do that. You can't eat those." Alex heard footsteps behind him and he spun around, coming face-to-face with a woman of peculiar beauty. He glanced around the room. "Hello," he said.

He slowly took in the details of her face. She wore dark makeup on her eyes and her shoulder-length hair was cut in a jagged way, with streaks of purple in the bangs. Was this the woman who had rescued him? He'd imagined the face that went with the voice, speculated about the body, but this wasn't at all what he'd expected.

"They eat shoes," she said, grabbing the loafers and handing them back to him.

Only when he heard her voice was Alex certain. This *was* the woman who had rescued him. But the instant attraction he felt was rather disconcerting. She was the exact opposite of women he usually pursued. He liked blondes, tall and willowy, surgically enhanced and trainer-toned. This girl was petite, with an almost boyish figure, and a quirky sense of fashion.

"Put them in the closet," she said, pointing to a spot near one door. "They don't know how to operate a doorknob…yet. They're still working on tearing strangers limb from limb."

Alex smiled, but she didn't return the gesture. She continued to regard him with a cool yet slightly wary stare. After he'd dropped his shoes in the closet, he surveyed his surroundings. "Nice place. Do you live here alone?"

"No," she said. "There are the dogs. And two cats. And I have two horses down in the barn."

"A regular Noah's Ark," he teased. She gave him an odd look and he decided be more direct. "So, you're not married?"

"Are you?"

"No," he said, chuckling. Crossing the room, he held out his hand. "I'm Alex Stamos." He waited, growing impatient with the long silence between them. "Now, you're supposed to tell me your name."

"Tenley," she said, refusing his gesture.

"Is that your first or last name? Or both. Like Ten Lee?"

She shook her head. "I haven't had dinner yet. Are you hungry?"

"I could eat, Tenley," Alex said. Odd girl with an odd name. Yet, he found her fascinating. She didn't seem to be interested in impressing him. In truth, she didn't seem the least bit fazed by his charm.

Strange, Alex thought to himself. Women usually found him utterly mesmerizing from the get-go. He slipped out of his jacket and draped it over a nearby chair. His pants were damp and his socks soaked through.

"You should probably call for a tow. Or your car is going to get covered by the drifts. The phone is over there."

"I'll call the auto club." He paused. "I don't have the phone number. It's on my BlackBerry, which is in the snowbank."

"I'll call Jesse. He has the garage in town." She walked over to the phone and dialed. Alex watched her from across the room, studying her features. She really was quite pretty in an unconventional way. Alex drew a slow breath. She had a really nice mouth, her lips full and lush.

When she turned to face him, he blinked, startled out of a brief fantasy about the body beneath the layers of winter clothes. "He won't be able to get to you for a while," she said. "Maybe not until the morning."

"Did you tell him that wasn't acceptable?"

This caused a tiny smile to twitch at the corners of her mouth—the first he'd managed. "No. He's busy. There are more important people than you stuck in the snow. You're safe and out of the storm. Your car can wait. Now, if it's acceptable to you, I'll make us something to eat."

Alex cursed beneath his breath. He hadn't gotten off to

a very good start with Tenley. And hell, spending the evening in her company, sharing an intimate dinner, was far more intriguing that sitting alone in his room at the local bed-and-breakfast. "Can I give you a hand?" he asked, following her to the kitchen.

HE SAT ON A STOOL at the kitchen island, his elbows resting on the granite counter top, his gaze following her every move. The tension between them was palpable, the attraction crackling like an electric current.

What had ever possessed her to bring this man in from the storm? She thought she was doing a good deed. He probably would have survived just fine on his own. She could have come home, called the sheriff and let law enforcement ride to the rescue. But now it looked like she'd be stuck with him for the rest of the night.

Tenley was accustomed to a solitary existence, just her, the dogs, the cats, the horses and those occasional demons that haunted her dreams. Having a stranger in the house upset the delicate balance—especially a stranger she found so disturbingly attractive.

In truth, she wasn't sure how to handle company. Since the accident almost ten years before, she'd made a habit of isolating herself, always maintaining a safe distance from anything that resembled a relationship. It was just easier. Losing her brother had sapped every last bit of emotion out of her soul that she didn't have the energy or the will-power to engage in polite conversation. And that was what people expected in social situations.

"Stop staring at me." Tenley carefully chopped the

carrot, focusing on the task and trying to ignore Alex's intent gaze. She felt her face grow warm and she fought the urge to run outside into the storm to cool off.

There was work to do in the barn; the horses had to be fed. She didn't have to stay. But for the first time in a very long time, Tenley found herself…interested. She wasn't sure what it was, but his curious stare had her heart beating a bit quicker and her nerves on edge. From the moment he'd offered his hand in introduction, she'd felt it.

Maybe it was just an overreaction to simple loneliness. She had been particularly moody this winter, almost restless. In years past, she'd been happy to hide out, to take long walks in the woods, to spend time with her animals, indulging in an occasional short-lived affair. But this winter had been different. There had been no men and the solitude had begun to wear on her.

She handed him a carrot to munch on, using the opportunity to study him more closely. Alex Stamos. For some reason, the name sounded familiar to her, but she couldn't put her finger on why. He was here on business. Maybe he was one of those real estate developers from Illinois, interested in building yet another resort on the peninsula. She'd probably seen his name in the local paper.

And she didn't understand this sudden attraction. Tenley was usually drawn to men who were a little rougher around the edges, a bit more dangerous. She usually chose tourists who were certain to leave at some point, but she had indulged with a number of willing single men from some of the nearby towns. Her grandfather called them "discardable," and Tenley had to agree with his assessment.

Tenley looked down at her vegetables. There weren't many women who'd kick Alex Stamos out of their bed.

Tenley glanced up again, to find him still staring. She drew a deep breath and met his gaze, refusing to flinch. For a long time, neither one of them blinked.

"I like this game," he said. "My sister and I used to play it when we were kids. I always won."

"It makes me uncomfortable," Tenley said. "Didn't anyone ever tell you it wasn't polite to stare?"

He shrugged and looked away. "Yeah, but I didn't think that applied in this case. I mean, it's not like you have a big wart on the end of your nose or you've got two heads. I'm staring because I think you're pretty. What's wrong with that?"

"I'm not pretty," she muttered. She grabbed an onion and tossed it at him, then shoved the cutting board and knife across the counter. "Here, cut that up."

She didn't invite this attraction. In fact, over the past year, she'd done her level best to avoid men. The last man she'd invited into her bed hadn't been just a one-night stand. She'd actually found herself wanting more, searching for something that she couldn't put a name to.

She knew the risks. Physical attraction led to sex which led to more sex which led to affection which ultimately led to love. Only love didn't last. It was there one day and gone the next. She'd loved her brother, more than anyone else in the world. And when he'd been taken from her, she wasn't sure she'd ever recover. She wasn't about to go through that again.

"I'm wondering why you wear all that makeup. I mean, you don't need it. I think you'd look prettier without it."

"Maybe I don't want to look pretty," Tenley murmured.

Alex chuckled at her reply. "Why wouldn't you want to look pretty? Especially if you are?"

The question made Tenley uneasy. She didn't tolerate curious men, men who wanted to get inside her head before they got into her bed. What business was it of his why she did what she did? He was a complete stranger and didn't know anything about her life. Why bother to act as if he cared?

She turned and tossed the chopped carrots into the cast-iron pot on the stove. Maybe the town's speculation about her would come true. She'd slowly devolve into an eccentric old spinster, living alone in the woods with only her animals to talk to.

"Do you like peppers?" she asked, turning to open the refrigerator.

"Do you ever answer a direct question?"

"Red or green? I prefer red."

"You don't answer questions," Alex said. "Red."

Tenley gave him a smile. "Me, too. They're sweeter." She handed him the pepper, then grabbed a towel from the ring beneath the sink. Bending over the basin, she quickly washed the makeup off her face, wiping away the dark liner and lipstick with dish soap.

When she opened her eyes again, she found an odd expression on his face. "Better?"

"Yeah," he said softly, his gaze slowly taking in her features. "You just look…different." He paused. "Beautiful."

She swallowed hard, trying to keep herself from smiling. "Thank you," she murmured. "You're beautiful, too."

The moment the words were out of her mouth, she wanted to take them back. This was what came from spending so much time alone, talking to herself. She expressed her thoughts out loud without even realizing it.

He opened his mouth, then snapped it shut. "Thanks."

"I'm not just saying that. You are. Objectively, you're very attractive." Oh, God, now she was just digging a deeper hole. "I just noticed, that's all. I'm not trying to…you know."

"I don't know," he said. He picked up the pepper and walked around the island to the sink, then rinsed it off. "But you could try to explain it to me."

There was no going back now. "The way you're looking at me. I just get the feeling that you're…flirting."

He turned and leaned back against the edge of the counter. "I am. Is there something wrong with that?"

"It's not going to work. I—I'm not interested in…that."

"What?"

"Sex," she said.

He frowned, then shook his head. "Is that what you think I'm doing? I was just having some fun. Talking. I didn't mean to—"

"I didn't want you to think that I was—"

"Oh, I didn't. I guess, I'm just used to—"

"I understand and I don't mean to—"

"I do understand," he said softly. He took a step toward her and she held her breath.

This was crazy. She wanted him to kiss her. With any other man, she would have already been halfway to the bedroom. But Alex was different. All these strange feelings stirred inside of her. She longed for his touch, yet she knew how dangerous it would be. Need mixed with fear and she wasn't sure what to do.

But then Alex took the decision out of her hands. He smoothed his hand over her cheek and bent closer. An instant later, his lips met hers and Tenley felt a tremor race through her body. He lingered over her mouth, taking his time, waiting for her to surrender.

With a soft sigh, Tenley opened beneath the gentle assault. A delicious rush of warmth washed through her body. Lately, she hadn't felt much like a woman. It was amazing what one kiss could do to change all that.

She pushed up on her toes, eager to lose herself in the taste of him. It didn't matter that they'd just met. It didn't matter that she knew nothing about him. He made her feel all warm and tingly inside. That was all she cared about.

He drew back slightly, his breath warm against her mouth. "Maybe we should get back to dinner," he suggested.

With a satisfied smile, Tenley stepped out of his embrace. They did have the entire night. With the blizzard raging outside, there was no way he'd be able to get into town. "There's white wine and beer in the fridge and red wine in the cabinet above. Pick what you want."

"What are you making?" He stood over her shoulder and peered into the cast-iron pot steaming on the stove. "It smells good."

"Camp supper," she said. "It's just whatever's at hand, tossed into a pot. There's hamburger, potatoes, peppers, carrots and onions. I think I'll add some corn."

It wasn't gourmet. Cooking had never been one of her talents. In truth, Tenley wasn't really sure what she was good at. Right about the time she was ready to find out, her life had been turned upside down. Her grandfather was an artist and so was her father. And her mother was a poet, so creativity did run in her veins.

But like everything else in her world, she'd been too afraid to invest any passion in her future for fear that it might slip through her fingers. So she chose to help her grandfather further his career by running his art gallery. At least she knew she was good at that, even though it was more of a job than a passion.

Alex retrieved a bottle of red wine from the cabinet and set it on the counter. She handed him a corkscrew and he deftly dispatched the cork and poured two glasses of Merlot. "This is a nice place," he said.

"It belonged to my grandparents. My great-grandfather built it for them as a wedding gift. After my grandmother died, my grandfather moved into town, and I moved here."

"What do you do?"

"I was just going to ask you the same thing," Tenley said, deflecting his question. "What brings you to Door County in the middle of a blizzard? It must be something very important."

"Business," he replied. "I'm here to see an artist. T. J. Marshall. Do you know him?"

Tenley's breath caught in her throat and for a moment she couldn't breathe. This man had come to see her grand-father? How was that possible? She was in charge of her grandfather's appointments and she didn't remember making one for— Oh, God. That was where she knew his name. He'd left a string of messages on her grandfather's voice mail. Something about publishing a novel. Her grandfather already worked with a publisher and he didn't write novels, so she'd ignored the messages. "I do. Everyone knows him. What do you want with him?"

"He sent us a graphic novel. I want to publish it."

Tenley frowned. Her grandfather painted landscapes. He didn't even know what a graphic novel was. She, however, did know. In fact, she'd made one for Josh Barton, the neighbor boy, as a Christmas gift, a thank-you for caring for her animals. "Do you have it with you?" she asked, trying to keep her voice indifferent.

"I do."

"Could I see it?"

"Sure. Do you like graphic novels?"

"I've read a few," she replied.

"This one is incredible. Very dark. The guy who wrote this has got some real demons haunting him. Or he's got a great imagination. It's about a girl named Cyd who can bring people back from the dead."

Alex walked across the room to fetch his briefcase. Tenley grabbed her glass of wine and took three quick gulps. If this was her work, how had it possibly gotten into Alex's hands? Perhaps Josh had decided to start a career as an artist's agent at age fourteen?

Alex returned with a file folder, holding it out to her. "The story is loaded with conflict and it's really edgy. It's hard to find graphic novels that combine great art with a solid story. And this has both."

Tenley opened the folder and immediately recognized the cover of Josh's Christmas gift. She sighed softly as she flipped through the photocopy. What had he done? He'd raved about the story, but she'd never expected him to send a copy to a publisher. It had been a private little gift between the two of them, that was all. Josh had shared his love of the genre with her and she'd made him a story of his very own. She'd never intended it for public consumption.

Tenley had always had a love-hate affair with her artistic abilities. Though establishing her own career in art might make sense to the casual observer, Tenley fought against it. She and her brother had always talked about striking out on their own, leaving Door County and finding work in a big city. She'd wanted to be an actress and Tommy had been interested in architecture.

But after the boating accident, Tenley had given up on dreams. Her parents had been devastated and their grief led to a divorce. There was a fight over where Tenley would live and in the end, they let her stay in Door County with her grandparents while they escaped to opposite coasts.

They still encouraged her to paint or sculpt or do anything worthy with her art. But putting herself out there, for everyone to see, made her feel more vulnerable than she already did. There were too many ways to get hurt, and so many expectations that could never be met. And now, the one time in years that she'd put pen to paper had brought this man to her door. What were the odds?

"This is interesting," she murmured. "But I think

someone is messing with you. T. J. Marshall paints land-scapes. This isn't his work."

"You know his work?"

"Yes. Everyone does. He has a gallery in town. You must be looking for another T. J. Marshall."

"How many are there in Sawyer Bay?" he asked.

Two, Tenley thought to herself. Thomas James and Tenley Jacinda. "Only one," she lied.

"And you know him. So you can introduce me. Tell me about him. How old is he? What's his background? Has he done commercial illustration in the past?"

What was she supposed to say? That Tenley Jacinda Marshall was the T. J. Marshall he was looking for? That she was twenty-six years old, had never formally studied art or design, and had spent her entire life in Door County? And that she'd never intended anyone, outside of Josh Barton, to see her story?

"I know this will sell. It's exactly what the market is looking for," Alex continued. "A female protagonist, a story filled with moral dilemmas and great pictures."

Was he really interested in paying her for the story? It would be nice to have some extra cash. Horse feed and vet care didn't come cheap. And though her grandfather paid her well, she never felt as if she did enough to earn her salary. Still, with money came responsibility. She liked her life exactly the way it was—uncomplicated.

"I think I'll make a salad," she said.

He reached out and grabbed her arm, stopping her escape. "Promise you'll introduce me," Alex pleaded, catching her chin with his finger and turning her gaze to his. "This is important."

"All right," Tenley said. "I will. But not tonight."

He laughed. "No, not tonight." He bent close and dropped a quick kiss on her lips, then frowned. "Are you ever going to tell me anything about yourself?"

"I don't lead a very exciting life," Tenley murmured, as he smoothed his finger along her jaw. A shiver skittered down her spine. His touch was so addictive. She barely knew him, yet she craved physical contact. He'd come here to see her, but somehow she knew that revealing her identity would be a mistake—at least for the next twelve hours.

"You rescued me from disaster," he said. "I could have frozen out there."

"Someone would have come along sooner or later," she said.

They continued preparations for dinner in relative silence. But the thoughts racing through Tenley's mind were anything but quiet. In the past, it had always been so simple to take what she wanted from a man. Physical pleasure was just a natural need, or so she told herself. And though she chose carefully when it came to the men who shared her bed, she'd never hesitated when she found a suitable sexual partner.

This was different. There was an attraction here she'd never felt before, a connection that went beyond the surface. He was incredibly handsome, with his dark hair and eyes, and a body that promised to be close to perfection once he removed his clothes. He was quite intelligent and witty. And he seemed perfectly capable of seducing her on his own.

It might be nice to be the seduced rather than the seducer, Tenley thought. But would he move fast enough? They only had this one night. Sometime tomorrow, he'd find out she was the artist also known as T. J. Marshall. And then everything would change.

"Would you like some more wine?" Alex asked.

Tenley nodded. "Sure." The bottle was already half-empty. Where would they be when it was gone?

THEY HAD DINNER in front of the fire. The sexual tension between them wasn't lost on Alex. By all accounts, the setting was impossibly romantic—a blazing fire, a snow-storm outside and the entire night ahead of them. With any other woman, he could have turned on the charm and had her within an hour. But there was something about Tenley that made him bide his time. She wasn't just any woman and she seemed to see right through him.

In the twelve years he'd been actively pursing women, Alex had honed his techniques. He'd found that most women were turned off by a man who wanted jump into bed after just a few hours together. Though he usually felt the urge, he'd learned to control his desires. He never slept with a woman on the first date. Or the second. But by the third, there were no rules left to follow.

Now he was finding it difficult putting thoughts of se-duction out of his head. He wasn't sure he was reading the signs correctly. Though he found Tenley incredibly sexy, he wasn't sure they were moving in that direction. One moment she seemed interested and the next, she acted as though she couldn't care less.

Though the conversation between them was easy, it wasn't terribly informative. He'd learned that Tenley had lived in Door County her entire life and that the cabin had belonged to her grandparents. Her father was an artist and her mother, a poet. Though she didn't say for certain, he gleaned from her comments that they were divorced. When he asked where they lived, she'd quickly changed the subject.

She kept the conversation firmly focused on him, asking about his business, about his life in Chicago, about his childhood. She seemed particularly interested in the market for graphic novels and his interest in publishing them.

"My grandfather started the company in 1962," Alex explained. "He used to do technical manuals, then started a line of how-to books, right about the time everyone was getting into home improvement. He retired and my father expanded our list to include other how-to titles. *How to Groom a Poodle, How to Make a Soufflé, How to Play the Ukulele.* Real page-turners."

"And then you came along with an idea for graphic novels."

"I've read comic books since I was a kid. But they're not just comic books anymore. They're an incredible mix of graphic art and story. They've turned some of the best ones into movies, so they're starting to move into mainstream culture."

"And this book by T. J. Marshall? Why do you like it?"

"It's…tragic. There's this heroine who, after a brush

KATE HOFFMANN

with death, discovers she can bring people back to life. But she's forced to choose between those she can save and those not worthy. The power only works for a short time before it's gone again. And there's this governmental agency that's after her. They want to use her powers for evil."

"And you liked her—I mean, *his* art?"

"Yeah," Alex replied. "The drawings have an energy about them, a rawness that matches the dark emotion in the story. I find it pretty amazing that someone could be such a great writer and an incredible artist, too."

"So you just want to publish it? Just like that?"

Alex shook his head. "No. There are some things that need to be addressed. The story needs to be expanded. There's a subplot that has to be fleshed out. I've got minor questions about the character, some inconsistencies in the backstory. And we'd want to explore a story arc for a sequel or two, maybe make it a trilogy."

She frowned. "A trilogy?"

"Yeah. We'd want to publish more than one novel. The real success in publishing is not in buying a book, but in building a career."

"So it pays a lot of money?"

"Not a lot. It would depend on how the books sold. But we have a great marketing department. I think they'd do really well. Well enough to provide a comfortable living for the artist."

Tenley quickly stood and gathered up the remains of their dinner. He got to his feet and helped her, following her into the kitchen with the empty bottle of wine. Though he hadn't quite figured out her mercurial mood changes, he was finding them less troublesome. She just moved more quickly from one thing to the next than the ordinary person, as if she became bored or distracted easily.

"Can I help you with the dishes?" he asked, standing beside her at the sink.

"Sure," she murmured.

He reached across her for the soap, his hand brushing hers. The contact was startling in its effect on his body. A current raced up his arm, jolting him like an electric shock. Intrigued, he reached down and took her hand in his, smoothing his fingers over her palm.

"You have beautiful hands," he said, examining her fingers. It was as if he knew these hands, knew exactly how they'd feel on his face, on his body. Her nails were painted a dark purple and she wore several rings on her fingers and thumb.

Alex slowly pulled them off, setting them down on the edge of the sink. It was like undressing her in a way, discovering the woman beneath all the accoutrements. He drew her hand up to his lips and placed a kiss on the back of her wrist.

Her gaze fixed on his face, her eyes wide, filled with indecision. Alex held his breath, waiting for a reaction. He kissed a fingertip, then drew it across his lower lip. The gesture had the desired effect. She leaned into him and a moment later, their mouths met.

Unlike the experiment that was their first kiss, this was slow and delicious. She tasted sweet, like the wine they'd drunk. He pulled her close, smoothing his hands over her back until her body was pressed against his. Kissing her left him breathless, his heart slamming in his chest.

He ran his hands over her arms, then grasped her wrists and wrapped them around his neck. A tiny sigh slipped from her throat and she softened in his embrace, as if the kiss were affecting her as much as it was him.

Alex had made the same move with any number of women, but it had never had this kind of effect on him. What was usually carefully controlled need was now raw and urgent. He wanted to possess her, to get inside her soul and find out who this woman was. She was sweet and complicated and vulnerable and tough. And everything about her drew him in and made him want more.

Maybe that was it. He'd learned well how to read women, to play on their desires and to make them want him. But Tenley was a challenge. She didn't react to his charm in the usual ways. Yet that wasn't all he found so intriguing. She lived all alone in the woods, with a bunch of animals. Where was her family? Where were the people who cared about her? And how did a woman as beautiful as Tenley not have a boyfriend or a husband to take care of her?

He sensed there was something not right here, something he couldn't explain. Alex felt an overwhelming need to reveal those parts of her that she was trying so hard to hide. She'd rescued him out on the road, but now he suspected that she was the one who needed saving.

The diversion was short-lived. The phone rang and, startled by the sound, Tenley stepped back. Her cheeks were flushed and her lips damp. "I—I should get that."

Alex nodded as she slipped from his embrace. She hurried

to the phone and picked it up, watching him from beneath dark lashes. He leaned back against the edge of the counter and waited, certain they'd begin again just as soon as the call was over. But when she hung up, she maintained her distance.

"Jesse towed your car into town," she said.

"Good."

"But not before the snowplow hit it. He says it's not real bad. It'll need a new back bumper and a side panel. And a taillight. And a few more things."

Alex groaned. "Can I still drive it?"

"No. I don't think so."

"Great," he muttered. "How the hell am I going to get around?"

"I guess I'll have to drive you," Tenley said. "You're not going to be going anywhere tonight anyway, so it's not worth worrying about. Jesse says the wind is just blowing the roads closed right after they plow them." She crossed back to him. "I—I should go out and check on the horses."

"I'll come with you," Alex suggested.

"It's late. You're probably tired. You can have the guest room. It's at the end of the hall. There are towels in the closet outside the bathroom. Just help yourself."

With that, she fetched her boots from a spot near the back door, then pulled on her jacket. A moment later, she stepped out into the storm. Alex opened the door behind her and watched as she disappeared into the darkness. The cold wind whipped a swirl of snow into his face and he quickly closed the door and leaned back against it.

What had begun as a simple business trip had taken a rather interesting turn. But he wasn't sure whether he ought to take his chances and hike into town, or spend the night under the same roof as this utterly captivating and perplexing woman.

He grabbed his duffel and walked to the guest room. When he finally found the light switch, he was surprised to find two cats curled up on the bed. The two calicos were sleeping so closely, he couldn't tell where one ended and the other began. Neither one of them stirred as he dropped the bag on the floor. But when the dogs came bounding into the room, they opened their eyes and watched the pair with wary gazes.

"Time to go," he said, picking them each up and gently setting them on the floor. They ran out the door, the dogs following after them.

Alex shut the door, then flopped down on the bed. He closed his eyes and let his thoughts drift back to the kiss he'd shared with Tenley. Though he hadn't had any expectations of further intimacies, he wished they hadn't been interrupted. With each step forward, he found himself curious about the next.

Though he'd enjoyed physical pleasure with lots of women, this was different. Everything felt…new. As if he were experiencing it for the first time. He groaned softly. He wanted her, in his arms and in his bed. But wanting her was as far as he would go. He was a guest in her house and wasn't about to take advantage, no matter how intense his need.

He'd come here to do a job, to sign T. J. Marshall to a publishing contract. It wouldn't do to get distracted from his purpose.

chapter two

THE water was so cold and black. Even with her eyes open, she couldn't see her hand in front of her face. *Stay awake, stay awake.* A voice inside her head kept repeating the refrain. Or was it Tommy? Was he saying the words?

Her nails clawed at the fitting on the hull of the boat as it bobbed in the water. *Stay with the boat. Don't try to swim for shore.* Though she wore a life jacket, Tenley knew that sooner or later her body temperature would drop so low it wouldn't matter. She wouldn't drown. She'd just quietly go to sleep and drift out into the lake.

"Tommy!" She called his name and then felt his hand on hers. "I'm sorry. I'm sorry." She grasped at his fingers, but they weren't there. He wasn't there. He'd decided to swim for it, ordering her to stay with the boat. "I'll be back for you," he called. "I promise."

How long had it been? Minutes? Hours? Tenley couldn't remember. Why was she so confused? She called his name again. And then again. Over and over until her voice was weak and her throat raw.

The sound came out of nowhere, a low rumble, like the engine of a boat. It was Tommy. He'd come, just as he'd promised. But as the roar came closer, Tenley realized it wasn't a boat at all but a huge wave, so high that it blocked out the moon and the stars in the sky. She held her breath, waiting for it to crash down on top of her. Where had it come from?

A ton of water enveloped her, driving her deep beneath the surface. The breath burned in her lungs and she struggled to reach the cold night air. Maybe it was better to let go, to stop fighting. Was that what Tommy had done? Was he safe at home, or had the black wave taken him as well? No, she wouldn't. She couldn't. She—

Tenley awoke with a start, sitting upright in her bed, gasping for breath. For a moment, she wasn't sure where she was. She rubbed her arms, only to find them warm and clad in the soft fabric of her T-shirt. She was safe. But where was Tommy? Why wasn't he—

A sick feeling settled in her stomach as she realized, yet again, that Tommy was gone. There were times when she had such pleasant dreams about their childhood. They'd been the best of friends, twins, so much alike. As the only children of a poet and an artist, they'd grown up without boundaries, encouraged to discover all that nature had to offer.

Back then, they'd lived on the waterfront, in the apartment above her grandfather's studio. The sailboat had been a present from her grandfather for their thirteenth birthday and every summer, she and Tommy had skimmed across the harbor, the wind filling the small sail and the sun shining down on them both.

But as they got older, they became much more daring. Their adventures had an edge of danger to them. Diving from the cliffs above the water. Wandering into the woods late at night. Sailing beyond the quiet confines of the harbor to the small islands just offshore.

They'd both known how quickly the weather could shift in the bay and how dangerous it was to be in a small boat when the waves kicked up. But they both loved pushing their limits, daring each other to try something even more outrageous.

A shiver skittered through her body and Tenley pulled the quilt up over her arms. It had been her idea to sail out to the island and spend the night. Even though the wind had been blowing directly into shore and they'd gotten a late start, they'd tacked out, the small Sunfish skimming over the bay at a sharp angle.

But sailing against the wind had taken longer than she'd anticipated and by the time they'd reached open water, it was nearly dark. Tommy had insisted that they head back toward the lights, but Tenley had been adamant, daring him to go on. A few minutes later, a gust of wind knocked the boat over.

It was usually easy to right the boat in the calm waters of the harbor, but in the bay the currents worked against them, exhausting them both. Tenley could see the outline of the island and suggested they swim for it. But in the dark, it had been impossible to judge how far it was. In the end, Tommy had left to get help.

They'd found her clinging to the boat, four hours later. They'd found his body the next morning, washed up on a rocky beach north of town. Tenley shook her head, trying to rid herself of the memories. It had been nearly a month since she'd last dreamt of him. In many ways, she'd longed for the nights when the dreams wouldn't haunt her. But sometimes, the dreams were good. They were happy and she could be with her brother again.

She threw the covers off her body and stood up beside the bed, stretching her arms over her head. The room was chilly, the winter wind finding its way inside through all the tiny cracks and crevices in the old cabin. Outside, the storm still raged.

Tenley rubbed her eyes, then wandered out of the bedroom toward the kitchen. She rarely slept more than four or five hours at night. For a long time, she'd been afraid to sleep, afraid of the nightmares. But she'd learned to cope, taking the good dreams with the bad.

The dogs were curled up in front of Alex's door and they looked up as she passed. Tenley stirred the embers of the fire and tossed another log onto the grate. As she watched the flames lick at the dry birch bark, her mind wandered back to the kiss she'd shared with Alex in the kitchen.

She'd been tempted to let it go on, to see how far he'd take it. The attraction between them was undeniable. But she wasn't sure she wanted to act upon it. She preferred uncomplicated sex and Tenley sensed that sex with Alex might be like opening a Pandora's box of pleasure.

Restless, she got up and began to pace the perimeter of

the room. She had no idea what time it was. Tenley had given up clocks long ago, preferring to let her body decide when it was time to sleep and when it was time to wake up. Besides, since Tommy's death, she'd never slept through an entire night so what was the point of a schedule?

Tenley grabbed a throw from the back of the leather sofa and wrapped it around her, then slowly walked down the hall to the guest-room door. Dog and Pup were still asleep on the floor, pulling guard duty, defending her safety. Perhaps the dogs knew better than she did about the dangers that lay beyond the door.

"Up," she whispered, snapping her fingers softly. They both rose, stretched, then trotted off to her bedroom. Holding her breath, Tenley opened the door and peeked inside.

Alex's face was softly illuminated by the bedside lamp and Tenley crossed the room to stand beside the bed. His limbs were twisted in the old quilt, a bare leg and arm exposed to the chilly air in the room. Tenley let her gaze drift down from his handsome face and tousled hair, to the smooth expanse of his chest and the rippled muscles of his belly.

An ache deep inside her took her breath away and she felt an overwhelming need for physical contact, anything to make her feel again. She'd pushed aside her emotions for so long that the only way to access them was to lose herself in pleasure. Until now, all she really required was a man who wouldn't ask for anything more than sex. But now, watching Alex sleep, she yearned for a deeper connection, a way back from the dark place where she'd lived for so long.

Was he the light she was looking for? Tenley rubbed her eyes with her fingers. Then reaching out, she held her hand close to his skin, surprised at the heat he generated. If she were warm and safe, she could forget the dream, forget the guilt. All she needed was just a few minutes of human contact.

A shiver skittered through her and without considering the consequences, she lay down beside him, tucking her backside into the curve of his body. Tenley felt him stir behind her and she closed her eyes, waiting to see what might happen.

He pushed up on his elbow and gently smoothed his hand along her arm. She glanced over her shoulder to find a confused expression on his face. Slowly, she rolled onto her back, their gazes still locked. Then, Tenley slipped her hand around his nape and gently pulled him closer, until their lips touched.

The kiss sent a slow surge of warmth through her body as he gently explored her mouth with his tongue, teasing and testing until she opened fully to his assault. With a low moan, he pulled her body beneath his. They fit perfectly against each other and Tenley arched into him, desperate to feel more.

The memories of the nightmare slowly gave way to a tantalizing pleasure. Alex ran his hand along her leg and beneath the T-shirt, then stopped suddenly, as if surprised that she wore nothing beneath. Giving him permission to continue, she slipped her fingers beneath the waistband of his boxers, searching for an intimate spot to explore.

But as the touching grew more intense, the clothing they

wore seemed to get in the way. Frantic to feel his naked body against hers, Tenley sat up and tugged her T-shirt over her head, then tossed it aside. She heard his breath catch and she smiled. "It feels better without clothes."

He grinned, then skimmed his boxers off, revealing the extent of his arousal. Unafraid to take what she wanted, Tenley wrapped her fingers around his hard shaft and gently began to stroke him. The caress brought a moan from deep in his throat and his fingers tangled in her hair as he drew her into another long, deep kiss.

"Am I awake or am I dreaming?" he asked, his lips soft against hers, his voice ragged.

"You're dreaming," she whispered.

"It doesn't feel like a dream," he countered. He cupped her breast with his palm and ran his thumb over her nipple. "You're warm and soft. I can hear you and taste you."

"Close your eyes," Tenley said. "And don't open them until I get back."

She crawled off the bed, but he grabbed her hand to stop her retreat. "Don't leave."

"I'll be right back. I promise. Close your eyes."

He did as he was told and Tenley hurried out of the room to the bathroom. She rummaged through the cabinet above the sink until she found the box of condoms, then pulled out a string of plastic packets. When she returned to the room, he was sitting up in bed, waiting for her. She held up the condoms. "I think we might need these."

He chuckled. "All of those?"

Tenley felt a blush of embarrassment. It had been a

while since she'd had a man in her bed. Once might not be enough. "Yes," she said. "All of them."

"I think you might be overestimating my abilities," he teased.

"And you might be underestimating mine," she replied.

When she got close to the bed, he grabbed her hand and yanked her on top of him. "Tell me what you want. I'll do my best to comply."

She wanted to lose herself in the act, to let her mind drift and her body take flight. She wanted to forget the past and the present and future and just exist in a haze of pleasure. She wanted the warmth and touch of another human being. And most of all, she wanted that wonderful, exhilarating feeling of release with a man moving deep inside her.

She tore a packet off the strip and opened it, then, with deliberate care, smoothed it down over his erection. Without any hesitation, Tenley straddled his hips and lowered herself on top of him. When he was buried to the hilt, she sighed. "This is what I want," she murmured, her eyes closed, her pulse racing.

"Me, too," he whispered.

ALEX HADN'T BEEN prepared for how good it would feel. Maybe because it had all been so unexpected. He'd always taken his time charming a woman, knowing that once he got her to bed, his interest would soon wane. But from the moment Tenley had lain down beside him, Alex knew something remarkable was about to happen.

This wasn't some game he was playing, a diversion that

he found interesting until something better came along. This was pure, raw desire, stripped of all artifice and expectations. He closed his eyes and sighed, reveling in the feel of her warmth surrounding him.

He didn't care what it meant or where it would go after this. All he knew was that he wanted to possess her, even it if was just for an hour or two on a snowy January night.

His fingers tangled in her hair and he drew her to his mouth. Though she didn't possess any of the attributes he normally found attractive in a woman, he couldn't seem to get enough of her. Her skin was pale, but incredibly soft. And her breasts, though small, were perfect. She was everything he'd never had before—and never wanted. Alex smoothed his hands over her chest and down her torso to her hips. Then he sat up, wrapping her legs around his waist and burying his face in the curve of her neck.

Tenley moved against him, her head tipped forward and her eyes closed. Her hair fell across her face and he reached up and brushed it aside, watching as desire suffused her features. Though he wanted to surrender to his own passion, Alex found it far more fascinating to watch her.

The intensity of her expression made him wonder what was going through her mind. She seemed lost in her need, searching for release in an almost desperate way. He reached down between them and touched her. A soft cry slipped from her lips and Alex knew he could give her what she wanted.

Her breath came in deep gasps and he focused on the sound, trying to delay the inevitable. And then, she was there, dissolving into spasms, her body driving down once more, burying him deep inside her.

It was all Alex could take, watching her orgasm overwhelm her. He surrendered to the sensations racing through his body and a moment later, found his own release.

Tenley nestled up against him, her arms draped around his neck, her lips pressed to his ear. "Oh, that was nice," she whispered.

"Umm," he replied, too numb to put together a coherent sentence. "Very nice."

She drew back, a wicked smile curling her lips. "You want to do it again?"

"No, not quite yet," he said with a chuckle. "Just let me catch my breath for a second." Alex wrapped his hands around her waist and pulled her down beside him, dragging her leg up over his hip. "This is a nice way to spend a snowy night." She shivered and Alex rubbed her arm. "Are you cold?"

Tenley shook her head. "Would you like some hot chocolate? I feel like some." She crawled out of bed and walked to the door, naked. "Are you coming? It makes a really good nightcap."

With a groan, Alex rolled out of bed. First, incredible sex and then hot cocoa. He didn't know much about her, but she was a study in contradictions. Grabbing the quilt off the bed, Alex wrapped it around himself and followed her to the kitchen.

The room was dark, lit only by the flames flickering in the fireplace. She opened the refrigerator and he stood and stared at her body, so perfect in the harsh white light. "You are beautiful," he said.

"No," Tenley replied. "You don't have to say things like

that to me. I don't need reassurance. I wanted that as much as you did."

"I'm just telling you what I think," Alex said. "You don't take compliments well, do you?"

"No," she said. "They make me…uncomfortable."

"Personally, I love compliments," he teased.

She poured milk into a pan and set it on the stove. The burner flamed blue and she turned it to a low simmer. "I think you have nice eyes," she said. "And I like your mouth."

"Thank you," he replied. "I like your mouth, too."

"Thank you," she said.

"See, that wasn't so bad."

"The key to making good hot chocolate is in the chocolate. You have to use real cocoa and sugar, not those powdered mixes."

He sat down on a stool and wrapped the quilt more tightly around him. "I was always of the opinion that marshmallows were the key. You can't use the small ones. You have to use the big ones. They melt slower."

Tenley opened a cabinet above the stove and pulled out a bag of jumbo marshmallows, then tossed them at him. "I totally agree. Bigger is better."

"Oh, another compliment. Thank you."

She giggled. "You're welcome." Tenley turned back to the stove and Alex got up and circled around the island to stand behind her. He wrapped the quilt around her, pulling her body back against his. Just watching her move had made him hard again.

She tipped her head as he pressed his lips to her neck. "Why do you smell so good? What is that?"

"Soap?" she said. "Shampoo."

"I like it." The women he'd known had always smelled like a perfume counter. But Tenley smelled clean and fresh. He closed his eyes and drew a deep breath, trying to commit the scent to memory. "I'm glad you came into my room," he whispered.

She turned to face him, then pushed up on her toes and gently touched her lips to his. "It's too cold to sleep alone." Tenley brushed his hair out of his eyes and smiled. "Cocoa. I need cocoa."

After she'd retrieved a container from a nearby cabinet, Tenley measured out the cocoa and stirred it into the milk, before adding a generous handful of sugar. Then she picked up the pan and poured the steaming drinks into two huge mugs that were nearly full of marshmallows.

"Let's sit by the fire," she said, grabbing the mugs.

Alex followed her, spreading the quilt out on the floor in front of the hearth. She seemed just as comfortable naked as she did clothed, stretching out on her stomach and offering him a tempting view of her backside.

"What are you doing here?" he asked.

She took a sip of her hot chocolate, then licked the melted marshmallow from her upper lip. "Relaxing?"

"That's not what I meant. I meant, here, all alone, in this cabin. Why isn't there someone here with you?"

She rolled over and sat up. "Like a roommate?"

"Like a man," he said.

"I like being alone. I don't really need a man." She paused. "Not that I don't enjoy having you here."

The words were simple and without a doubt, the truth.

"I can always head back out into the storm, if you'd rather be alone," he offered.

"No. It's nice to have company every now and then."

"Someone to talk to?"

"Someone to touch," she said. Tenley reached out and placed her hand on his chest. "Aren't there times when you crave physical contact?" She paused. "Never mind. I suppose you just go find a woman when that happens, right? Men have it easy. No one questions your need for sex."

"And they question yours?"

"Not they. Me. I guess that comes with being a female. We aren't supposed to want it like men do."

"And do you want it?" Alex asked.

"I'm not afraid to admit that I enjoy it," she said. "Sex makes me feel...alive."

"Good to know," Alex said. He took her mug from her hand and set it down on the floor, then cupped her face in his hands. "You are the strangest girl I've ever met."

"Weird strange?"

"Fascinating strange," he replied.

He gently pushed her back until she lay on the quilt. Tenley stretched her arms over her head, her body arching sinuously beneath his touch. Taking his time, he traced a line from her neck to her belly with his lips.

He knew how to bring a woman to the edge and back again, and he wanted to do that for Tenley. His fingers found the damp spot between her legs. She responded immediately, her body arching, her breath coming in shallow gasps.

And when his mouth found that sensitive spot, she cried

out in surprise. But Alex took his time. He'd always been a considerate lover, but sex had been about his pleasure first. It wasn't that way with Tenley. He wanted to make it memorable for her.

After he was gone, Alex needed to know he would be the standard by which other men in her life might be judged. It was silly, but for some strange reason, it made a difference to him. He wanted her to remember what they shared and continue to crave it.

Her fingers slipped through his hair and he felt her losing control. Alex slowed his pace, determined to make her feel something that she'd never experienced before. Her drew her close, tempting her again and again. She whispered his name in a desperate plea to give her what she wanted.

The sound of her voice was enough to arouse him and to Alex's surprise, he found himself dancing near the edge. He shifted, the friction of the quilt causing a delicious frisson of pleasure to race through him. Gathering his resolve, Alex brought her close again. But this time, it was too much for her.

When he drew back, she couldn't help herself. Tenley moaned, her body tense. An instant later, her orgasm consumed her, her body trembling and shuddering. It was enough to drive him over the edge. Startled, Alex joined her.

He rolled over on his back. This was crazy. He felt like a teenager, with nothing more than his imagination and a little friction standing between him and heaven. Throwing his arm over his eyes, he waited for the last of his own spasms to subside.

"That was a surprise," he murmured. Alex rolled to his side and kissed her hip.

"I've never really liked surprises, until now."

Alex knew how she felt. From the moment she'd rescued him from the snowbank, he'd learned to expect the unexpected from Tenley. He closed his eyes and pressed his face into the soft flesh at her waist. Forget the vacation. Spending time with Tenley was all the adventure he needed.

TENLEY OPENED her eyes to the early morning light. An incessant beeping penetrated her hazy mind and she pushed up on her elbow to survey the room.

After making love in front of the fire, they'd wrapped themselves in the quilt and fallen asleep on the floor. She couldn't remember the last time she'd slept so soundly and for such a long stretch of time.

She sat up and glanced over her shoulder at Alex. He was a beautiful man, tall and lean and finely muscled. And he knew what he was doing in bed—and on the floor, too. A shiver skittered through her as she remembered the passion they'd shared.

She'd never experienced anything quite so powerful. Usually she used sex to forget. But she remembered every little detail of what she'd shared with Alex, from the way his hands felt on her skin to the taste of his mouth to the soft sound of his voice whispering her name. She felt safe with him, as if she didn't need to pretend.

It had taken so much energy to keep her emotions in check and now, she finally felt as if she might be able to let go, to find a bit of enjoyment in life…in Alex. Tenley didn't know what it all meant, but she knew it felt right.

As she studied his features, she wondered about the women he normally dated. A man like Alex Stamos wouldn't lack for female company. There were probably hundreds of women waiting outside his door, hoping to enjoy exactly what she had last night.

The beeping continued and she crawled around him to find his watch lying on the hearth. Tenley picked it up and, squinting in the low light, tried to turn off the alarm. But when she couldn't find the right button, she got to her feet and carried it into the kitchen. With the soft curse, she opened the refrigerator door and put it inside.

This is exactly why she hated clocks. Simple, inanimate objects in control of a person's life! Was there anything more obnoxious? Well, maybe television. She didn't own one of those either. She preferred a good book. Although, there were times when she wished she could watch a movie or check out the weather station.

Rubbing her arms against the cold, Tenley returned to their makeshift bed, ready to slip back beneath the covers and wake him up slowly. It was so easy to relax around him, to just be herself without any of the baggage that came along with her past. Everyone within a thirty-mile radius of Sawyer Bay knew about her past. She couldn't walk down the streets of town without someone sending her a pitying look.

She knew what they were saying about her. That she'd never recovered from the tragedy. That she deliberately pushed people away because she blamed herself. It was all true. Tenley was acutely aware of what she'd become. But that didn't make it any easier to forget her part in what had happened. Nor did she feel like changing just to make everyone else more comfortable. It was simply easier to keep people at a distance.

Alex was different. For the first time in her adult life, she wanted to get closer. If Tenley had the power, she'd make the storm go on for another week or two so they could be stranded in this cabin a little longer. There would be quiet afternoons, making love in front of the fire. And then never-ending nights, when sleep could come without dreams.

There was a way to keep him close, Tenley mused. If she accepted his proposal to publish her graphic novel then they'd have an excuse to see each other every so often. Maybe he'd make regular trips up to Door County to see her and they could enjoy these sexual encounters three or four times a year.

Tenley smiled to herself. It was the closest she'd ever come to a committed relationship. But in that very same moment, she realized the risk she'd be taking. Cursing softly, she turned away and walked through the cabin to her room.

"Don't be ridiculous," she muttered to herself as she pulled on her clothes. She and Alex Stamos had absolutely nothing in common, beyond her novel and one night of great sex. What made her think he'd even want a relation-ship?

He probably had his choice of women in Chicago. Why would he choose to carry on with her? It was a prescription for heartbreak, Tenley mused. She'd make the mistake of falling in love with him, living for the times they could be together, and one day, he'd tell her it was over.

She'd learned how to protect herself from that kind of pain and it wouldn't do to forget those lessons now. Alex was a momentary fling, just like all the other men in her life. She could enjoy him for as long as he stayed, but after that, she'd move on.

As for her novel, it would be best to put an end to that right away. Though a little extra money might be nice, she certainly didn't need the pressure to produce another story.

Tenley tiptoed back out into the great room and found her boots and jacket near the back door. The dogs were waiting and, when she was bundled against the cold, she slipped outside, into the low light of dawn. She bent down and gave them both a rough scratch behind the ears. Pup, the larger of the two, gave her a sloppy kiss on the cheek. And Dog pushed his nose beneath her hand, searching for a bit more affection.

"Go," she said, motioning them off the porch. They ran down the steps and into the snow, leaping and chasing and wrestling with each other playfully. The wind was still blowing hard, the snow stinging her face. She tipped her head back and looked into the sky, still gray and ominous.

A memory flashed in her mind and she remembered the sky on the day she and Tommy had set off on their sail. The image was so vivid it was like a photograph. A storm had taken her brother away. And now another storm had brought Alex into her life. The forces of nature were powerful and uncontrollable.

Was that what this was about? Was nature giving her back what she'd lost all those years ago? She drew a deep breath of the cold air. She'd never believed in fate or karma but she couldn't help but wonder why Alex had suddenly appeared in her life. A few minutes one way or the other, a different day or time, and they never would have met at all. Another shiver skittered down her spine and she started off across the yard.

The barn was set fifty yards from the house, a simple wooden structure painted the traditional red. Attached to one corner was a tower that rose nearly three stories off the ground. Her grandfather had built it as a studio, with four walls made of windows to take in the views of the woods and the bay.

Tenley slogged through the snow to the barn door and retrieved a shovel. She cleared off the stairs to the studio, then stepped inside to escape the icy wind. The stairwell was as cold as the weather outside, but when she opened the door to the room at the top of the stairs, it was pleasantly cozy.

Dropping her jacket at the door, she walked to the wall of windows facing the lake. The snow was still coming down so hard, she wasn't able to see more than a hundred yards beyond the barn.

With a soft sigh, she sat down at the huge drawing table in the center of the room. Her grandfather's easels had moved to town with him, but he'd left his drawing table, in hopes she'd find a use for it.

She and her grandfather had always been close. After Tommy's death, he'd been the only one she could stand to be around. And after her grandmother had died, Tenley had taken over the duties of running the business end of the gallery, a job her grandmother had done since their wedding day.

She did most of her business over the phone and, when customers came in the front door, her grandfather usually greeted them. He hated the details of running the gallery and she avoided the customers. It had been a good arrangement. If she weren't working for him, he'd have to hire someone at a much higher salary. All Tenley needed was enough to buy food and clothes and feed for her animals.

She sifted through the sketches scattered over the surface. Her work was a mishmash of genres and media. A pen-and-ink drawing of a hummingbird, a pastel landscape, a watercolor self-portrait. She'd never been to art school, so she'd never really discovered what she was good at.

Grabbing a cup filled with black markers, she sat down at the table. Taking a deep breath, she sketched a scene with her heroine, Cyd. She imagined it as a proper cover for the novel, something that would set the mood for the story inside.

There was a generous portion of Tenley in her character. She was an outsider, a girl who had known tragedy in her life, one who was graced with an incredible power. But with that power came deep moral dilemmas. Tenley often wondered what it would be like to change the past, to alter the course of history.

What would her life be like if she hadn't teased her brother into sailing to the island? Or if the weather hadn't turned on them? What if they'd stayed home or left earlier? Where would she be today?

Tenley closed her eyes and tried to picture it. Would she be married, happily in love with a man, surrounded by their children? Or would she be living in some big city, working as an artist or a writer? She'd always thought about becoming an actress.

Perhaps her parents wouldn't have divorced and maybe her grandmother wouldn't have suffered the stroke that killed her. Maybe the townspeople of Sawyer Bay would admire her, rather than pity her. Snatching up the drawing, Tenley crumpled it into a ball and tossed it to the floor.

She couldn't change the past. And she didn't want to change the future. There was a certain security in knowing what her life was, in the sameness of each passing day. "I'm happy," Tenley said. "So leave well enough alone."

She grabbed her jacket and pulled it on, then headed back down to feed the horses. The dogs joined her in the barn, shaking the snow from their thick coats. As she scooped feed into a bucket, the horses peeked over the tops of their stall doors.

"Sorry, ladies. No riding today. But after breakfast, you can go outside for a bit." The two mares nuzzled her as they searched for a treat—a carrot or an apple. But Tenley had left so quickly she'd forgotten to bring them something. "I'll be out later," she promised.

On her way back to the house, Tenley decided to walk up to the road and see if it had been plowed. The woods kept the snow from drifting too high, but it was clear they'd had at least sixteen or eighteen inches since it began yesterday morning.

By the time she reached the end of the driveway, Tenley

could see they'd be stuck in the cabin for another day. A huge pile of snow had been dumped across the driveway and beyond it, the road was a wide expanse of bare pavement and three-foot drifts.

In truth, she was happy to have another day with Alex. If they spent it in the same way they'd spent the night before, then she wouldn't have reason to grow impatient with the weather. Tenley smiled as the dogs fell into step beside her. "We'll keep him another day," she said.

The cabin was quiet when she let herself back in. She stripped off her jacket and boots, then shimmied out of her snow-covered jeans. The dogs were anxious to eat and they tore through the great room in a noisy tangle of legs and tails.

"Ow! What the hell!" Tenley looked up to find Pup lying across Alex's chest, his nose nudging Alex's chin.

"No!" she shouted. "Come here!"

Pup glanced back and forth between the two of them, then decided to follow orders. Alex sat up and wiped his face with the damp quilt. "Funny, I expected someone of an entirely different species to wake me up."

"Sorry. If you want to get some more sleep, you should probably go to your room. Once the dogs are up, they're up."

"What time is it?" He glanced at his wrist. "I lost my watch."

She opened the refrigerator and pulled it out. "It wouldn't stop beeping."

Alex got to his feet and walked naked to the kitchen, then took the watch from her grasp. He strapped it onto his wrist, silencing the alarm. Then, he looked at the clock on the stove and noticed it was almost noon. "Is that right?" he asked, rechecking his watch.

She shook her head, trying to avoid staring at his body. "No. I don't like clocks. There isn't any need for them here."

Alex frowned, raking his hand through his hair. "What about when you have to be somewhere on time?"

"I never have to be anywhere on time. I get there when I get there."

Alex chuckled. "I wish I could live like that," he murmured.

She glanced over her shoulder at him. He was so beautiful, all muscle and hard flesh. Her fingers twitched as she held out her hand. "You could. Here, give me your watch."

"No. This is an expensive watch."

"I was just going to put it back in the refrigerator."

He thought about the notion for a second, then smiled and slipped it off his wrist. "When in Rome."

She opened the fridge and put it inside the butter compartment. "You've been liberated. Doesn't that feel good?"

"How do you know when to get up in the morning?"

"I usually get up when the sun rises," she explained. "Or when the dogs wake me."

"Don't you have to be to work at a certain time?"

She shrugged. "I keep my own hours." She opened a cabinet and pulled out two cans of dog food. "Here, make yourself useful. The can opener is in that drawer."

"I thought I had made myself pretty useful last night," he murmured.

Tenley felt a warm blush creep up her cheeks. "You want to talk about it?" she asked.

"You…surprised me. I wasn't expecting…"

"Neither was I," she said. "I was curious."

"About me?"

She nodded. "Sure. You seemed like you were interested."

"I was," he said. "Am. Present tense. But I'm even more curious about something else."

"What's that?"

"Whether it might happen again?"

A tiny smile curved the corners of her mouth. "Depends upon how long this storm lasts." So it wouldn't be just a one-night stand. Tenley wasn't sure how she felt about that. She wanted to spend more time with him, even though she knew she shouldn't. But she liked Alex. And he lived in Chicago, so sooner or later, he'd head back home.

A brief, but passionate affair, one that wouldn't be dangerous or complicated. As long as she kept it all in perspective. It wouldn't last long enough to become a relationship. And if it didn't become a relationship, then she couldn't possibly get hurt. Still, she had to wonder what he was thinking about it all. Why not just ask? "What if it does happen again," she asked. "And again. What would that mean?"

He gave her an odd look. "It would probably mean we'd have to go out for condoms?" he teased. Alex paused, then shrugged, realizing that she didn't find much humor in his joke. "It would mean that we enjoy each other's company. And that we want to get to know each other better?"

"Then it wouldn't be a relationship?" she asked.

"It could be," he said slowly.

"But if we didn't want it to be?"

Alex drew a deep breath. "It will be whatever you want it to be," he replied. He glanced over his shoulder, clearly uneasy with the turn in the conversation. "Maybe we should check out a weather report so we can plan our day," Alex suggested. "Where's your television?"

That was it, Tenley thought. She knew exactly where he stood and she was satisfied. Neither one of them were ready to plan a future together. Still, if she did ever want a man in her life, someone who stayed more than a few nights, Alex would be the kind of guy she'd look for. "I don't have a television," she said.

He stared at her in astonishment. "You don't own a television? How is that possible? What about sports and the news?"

"There's never a need. I have a radio. They do the weather every hour on the station from Fish Creek. It's over there in the cabinet with the stereo. But you really don't have to check the weather. The storm is going to last for a while."

"How do you know that?"

"The barometer. Over there, by the door. It hasn't started going up yet. When it does, the storm will start to clear."

"Does that mean you can come back to bed?"

"Maybe we should try a real bed?" she suggested. Tenley tugged her sweater over her head and let it drop on the floor. Then she turned and walked toward her bedroom, leaving a trail of clothes behind her. The storm wouldn't last forever, so they'd best put their time to good use.

chapter three

ALEX wasn't a meteorologist, but from what he could see outside, the storm showed no signs of weakening. Though he had business to attend to, he was content to spend the day with Tenley, sitting in front of a warm fire with a comfortable bed close at hand.

Without his watch, he could only guess at the time, probably early afternoon. But Tenley was right. It didn't matter. He didn't have anywhere important to be. T. J. Marshall could wait.

He rolled onto his side and watched Tenley as she slept. He'd known her for less than a day, yet it seemed as though they'd been together for much longer. In truth, he'd spent more time with her than he had with any single woman over the past ten years. And considering he'd never spent a complete night in a woman's bed, this was another first.

He thought about their earlier discussion. She'd made it very clear she wasn't interested in anything more than a physical relationship. And he'd agreed to her terms. But Alex was already trying to figure out whether there was more between them than just great sex.

He reached out and smoothed a lock of hair from her eyes. She didn't possess the studied perfection of most of the girls he'd dated. Everything about her was much more natural, more subtle. She was…soft and sweet.

Yet she also had an edge to her, an honesty that caught him off guard at times. There wasn't a filter between her thoughts and her mouth, just a direct line. But he was beginning to enjoy that. Though she didn't answer every question he asked, when she did, he could trust that he was getting the truth.

Alex stretched his arms over his head. He needed to call the office or see if he could get an Internet connection. He smiled to himself. She didn't have a television. She probably wouldn't find a home computer particularly useful either.

He slipped out of bed and walked to the bathroom, deciding to grab a shower. He flipped on the water in the shower stall and waited for it to warm up, then looked at his reflection in the mirror. He needed a shave first.

Alex shut off the water, then retrieved his shaving kit from the guest room. After plucking a razor and a can of shaving cream out of the leather case, he rinsed his face off and continued to stare into the mirror. He was exhausted, but it was a pleasant exhaustion, a sated feeling that he hadn't felt in…a long time? Ever. He'd never felt this way after making love with a woman. In truth, intimacy always left him restless.

Alex heard the bathroom door creak behind him and a

few seconds later, he felt her hands smooth over his back. She rested her cheek on his shoulder and watched him in the mirror.

"I thought you were asleep," he said. "I was just going to catch a quick shower and shave." He slowly turned and she smiled. "What do you want?"

"Nothing," she said. "What do you want?"

"I need a shave," Alex replied.

She reached around him for the can of shaving cream he'd set on the edge of the sink. "I can help with that." Tenley sprayed some cream on her palm, then patted it onto his face.

"Are you sure you know what you're doing?"

"No," she said. "But I do shave my legs. It can't be much different. Hand me the razor."

Alex grabbed it and held it over his head. "Be careful. We're a long way from emergency medical care. And this pretty face is all I have."

She took the razor from his hand, then stepped closer. "You are full of yourself, aren't you?" Her hips pressed against his and he slipped his arms around her waist to steady them both. Slowly, she dragged the blade over his skin, her brow furrowed in concentration.

Alex held his breath, waiting for disaster, but Tenley took her time. And as she worked at the task, he found himself growing more and more aroused. There was something about her taking on this mundane part of his life, even if it was as simple as shaving, and making it erotically charged.

With a low moan, he moved his hands down to her hips, his shaft growing harder with every second that passed. Was it possible to want her any more than he already did? Every time he thought his need might be sated, he found himself caught up in yet another sexual encounter, more powerful than the last.

"Quit squirming," she warned. "I'm almost finished."

"Finished?" He chuckled, running his hands up to her breasts. "Look what you started."

"It really doesn't take much, does it?" Tenley teased.

"From you, no." Why was that? Alex wondered. Why did every innocent touch seem to send all the blood to his crotch? What kind of magical power did she hold over him?

"You know," she murmured, "we're lucky we're snowed in."

"What do you mean?"

"Because if we have to take care of your little problem every time it pops up, we'd never get out of the house."

"We could always take a shower together and see how that goes. Maybe it will just disappear."

"I know exactly how to get it to disappear," she said. "Come on." Tenley grabbed his hand and pulled him out of the bathroom, bits of shaving cream still on his face. "You'll love this."

They walked through the house, both of them stark naked. Then she opened the coat closet and rummaged around inside until she pulled out a pair of boots. "Here, put these on."

"Oh, wait a minute. Is this going to get kinky? You want me to be the lumberjack and you're going to be the… I don't know, what are you going to be?"

"Just put them on."

"Why?"

"Do it," Tenley said. She grabbed her own boots from the mat beside the back door and tugged them on, then flipped a switch beside the door. A red light blinked. "Ready?" she asked, her hand on the door.

"For what?"

"Just follow me." Tenley yanked the door open, then stepped outside onto the back porch.

Alex gasped. "What the hell are you doing? You're naked. You'll freeze to death."

"Not if I run fast enough," she cried. With that, she scurried across the porch to the steps, then carefully waded through the drifted snow.

If this was Tenley's idea of fun, then Alex was going to have to expose her to more interesting events—concerts, ball games, nightclubs. Drawing a deep breath, he walked through the open door and pulled it shut behind him. She stood waiting, her hair blowing in the wind, her skin pink from the cold.

"You have to move fast, before you start to feel the cold," she cried.

"I already feel it." He glanced down to notice that the erection she'd caused had subsided and the effects of the cold were beginning to set in. "Tenley, come on. I don't want to play in the snow."

"Follow me," she called. She headed toward a small log building. When she turned and waved to him, her foot caught on something beneath the snow and she disappeared into a snowdrift.

With a sharp curse, Alex took off after her. By the time

he got there, she'd already picked herself up and was laughing hysterically, snow coating her hair and lashes and melting off her warm body.

"What the hell are you laughing about?"

"I picked a bad time to be a klutz," she said. Tenley grabbed his hand and led him to the tiny log hut, then opened the door. She reached inside and pulled out two buckets. "Here, fill these with snow." She grabbed two for herself and scooped them into a nearby drift.

By this time, Alex could barely feel his fingers, much less the other appendages on his body. But when the buckets were filled, she led him inside the hut. To his surprise, it was warm and cozy inside.

Cedar benches lined three walls and a small electric stove was positioned in the center. "Wow. A sauna."

Tenley set the buckets next to the stove and stretched out on one of the benches. "My grandfather built this for my grandmother. She was Finnish and she grew up with one of these. Her family was from northern Michigan. They didn't have indoor plumbing so this is the way they took a bath. Except they'd cut a hole in the ice afterward and jump in."

"We're not going to do that are we?"

"No, we'll just roll around in the snow. It works the same way."

"And this is what your family does for fun?"

"Yes. What does your family do?"

He chuckled. "We don't roll around naked in the snow. We…eat. And argue. Occasionally, we play board games or watch movies. I grew up with typical suburban parents.

My mother would be shocked to hear I was running around without any clothes on."

She smiled. "I was raised a bit differently. My parents were very open-minded. Free thinkers. They taught us that being naked was perfectly natural."

"Hey, I'm all for nudity. In warm weather."

"You'll love it. I promise. It's invigorating. And relaxing." She made a sad face at him. "Don't be such a baby. You city boys don't know what you're missing."

"Believe me, there is no way I'd ever miss this."

Tenley crawled across the bench and stood in front of him. Then she gently pushed him back. "Sit," she said. "Relax. Take a load off."

Alex did as he was told, leaning back against the rough wall of the cabin. Tenley knelt down in front of him, running her hand along the inside of his thighs. "You're very tense," she said.

"It was freakin' cold out there."

"Relax," she said, smoothing her hands over his belly and then back down his legs. Alex watched her as she explored his body, her touch drifting down to his calves. She tugged off the boots and tossed them aside, then massaged his feet.

This was definitely worth the run through the cold, he mused, tipping his head back and closing his eyes. "Those Finns have the right idea," he said.

She pushed his legs apart and knelt between them, pressing her lips to his chest. Alex knew what was coming, but the rush of sensation that washed over him came as a surprise. Her lips and tongue were sweet torture, making him hard and hot in a matter of seconds. He wondered if it might be dangerous to become aroused in such a warm environment, then decided that if he died as a result, he'd go out a happy man.

He'd experienced this same pleasure with other women before, but he'd always focused on his own enjoyment, taking what was offered without thinking much about his partner. But as Alex watched Tenley seduce him with her mouth, he realized that she wasn't just any woman. The pleasure with her was more intense, more meaningful, because she was the one giving it.

He never understood how a guy could be satisfied spending his whole life with just one woman. But he was beginning to see how it was possible. Tenley was like a dangerous drug, alluring and addictive. The more he had of her, the more he needed.

Though he tried to delay, Alex's release came hard and quick. One moment he was in control and the next, he was caught in a vortex of incredibly intense pleasure. When he finally opened his eyes, he found Tenley staring up at him, a satisfied smile on her face.

"I told you saunas could be relaxing," she said.

"I will never doubt anything you say. Ever. Again."

"ARE YOU HUNGRY?" Tenley asked.

Alex distractedly rubbed her stockinged feet as he read, his long legs stretched out in front of him. Tenley sat on the opposite end of the leather sofa, trying to finish *Madame Bovary,* but she found her study of Alex much more intriguing. She'd been focusing on a tiny scar above his lip, wondering how it got there.

"No, I'm fine," he murmured.

They'd returned from the sauna and snow bath, tumbled into bed for another round of lovemaking, then taken a quick shower together. After a long and leisurely breakfast at two in the afternoon, Alex had rebuilt the fire and they'd settled in, listening to the wind rattling the windows and the drifting snow hissing against the glass.

"I should probably go check on the horses," she said. "I was going to let them out for a while."

He glanced up at her. "Don't you ever just sit still? Chill out. Just be with me."

"So, you liked the sauna?" she asked. Though it took every ounce of persuasion to get him out there, Tenley considered the activity a success. Alex, naked, in any environment, was fun.

"It was just about the best thing I've ever experienced," he said, his gaze still fixed on the book he was reading.

"We could play a game," she said. "Do you like Scrabble?"

He snapped the book shut. "Do I have to have sex with you again, to calm you down? Because if that's what it's going to take, I will. Just say the word. I'm willing to make the sacrifice."

Tenley giggled. "I'm just not used to sitting around. I don't read in the middle of the day. I read before bed because it puts me to sleep."

"If I weren't here, what would you be doing?" Alex asked.

"Clearing the driveway. I have a small tractor with a front-end loader. After that, I'd shovel the walk out to the barn. Then I'd probably get the dogs and take a hike out

on the road, to see if it was plowed. Or maybe brave the storm and drive into town for some dinner."

"Is the road clear?" Alex asked.

"No."

"Does it make sense to plow the driveway right now?"

"No."

"Why don't we just talk, then. Have a conversation. I'll ask you a question and you answer it. And then you ask me a question and I'll answer it."

Tenley really didn't like the suggestion. After all, there were a few things she was hiding from him. She wasn't quite ready to tell him she was T. J. Marshall. Though it would certainly make for some interesting conversation, it might change everything between them.

She tried to imagine his reaction. He probably wouldn't be thrilled at her deception. He might wonder what other lies she'd told. But he would have to be happy he'd found her and they'd developed a relationship of sorts. He liked her. How could he be angry for long?

She could always test the waters, Tenley thought. Throw a tiny bit of truth out there and see how it went. "I suppose you're anxious to get into town," she ventured. "I mean, since you have business."

"That can wait," Alex said. "There's not much I can do about it in the middle of this storm."

"The snow should quit in a few hours," she said. "The barometer is starting to rise. Then I can dig us out and you can be on your way." She paused, waiting for his response.

"There's no hurry," he said.

"So you'd like to stay another night?"

He squeezed her foot. "If you'll have me. I'm not too much trouble, am I?"

"No," she said. She drew a long breath, steeling herself for what would come next. "You can meet my grandfather tomorrow morning."

His hand froze on her foot and his brow furrowed. "You want me to meet your family?"

"You came here to see T. J. Marshall, didn't you? That's my grandfather."

Alex gasped, his eyes going wide. "Wait a second. Why didn't you tell me that earlier?"

She shrugged. "I didn't think it made a difference. Does it? Make a difference?"

"You're Tenley Marshall?"

"Yes."

He leaned back into the sofa and raked his hand through his hair, shaking his head. "I just don't understand why you wouldn't have said something."

"Because I thought you might be one of those guys who doesn't like to mix business with pleasure? Because I'm the one who rescued you and I found you attractive? Mostly because I wanted to see what you looked like naked and I figured if you knew who I was, you wouldn't take off your clothes."

Alex thought about her explanation for a moment, then sighed. "I guess I understand. Is there anything else you're keeping from me?"

She shook her head. If she didn't say the word *no*, then it wasn't a full-fledged lie, was it? "My grandfather didn't create that book, though. I run his gallery. I know his work. And that's not his."

"I don't get it. Why would someone send it in under his name? It doesn't make sense."

Tenley jumped off the sofa. "I'm going to take care of the driveway before it starts to get dark. If the weather clears we could drive into town and see about your car."

"Are you that anxious to get rid of me?" he asked.

"No," she said. In truth, Tenley wished she could keep him for the rest of the week. Maybe even for the rest of the month. It was nice to have a man around, if only for the good sex. And the sex was really good. "But we don't have much to eat for dinner. The snow isn't going to plow itself. Besides, it will give you a chance to relax and read."

"I'll come with you," he said. "I can help."

"No, you're the guest. I'll be in soon. You can feed the dogs if you like." She hurried over to the kitchen and retrieved two cans of dog food from beneath the sink.

"You never told me their names, either."

"Dog," Tenley said. "And Pup. The little one is Dog and the big one is Pup," she said.

"Unusual names."

She slipped her bare feet into her boots, then tugged on her jacket. "They just wandered in one day and that's what I called them. Once they decided to stay, I didn't see any reason to give them new names since they seemed quite happy with Dog and Pup."

"Do you always take in strays?" he asked.

"I took you in, didn't I?" She sent him a flirtatious glance, hoping that it might smooth over any ruffled feathers. He chuckled. So she hadn't completely messed things up between them. If this revelation didn't upset him, maybe he'd be fine learning that she was the artist behind the graphic novel he wanted.

She zipped her coat up and pulled the hood tight around her face, then grabbed her gloves from her pockets. Sooner or later, he'd discover the whole truth. And after that, she'd have to try to explain her entire life to him. She could barely make sense of it herself.

Her novel meant money to him. And he'd assume she'd want a share of the financial windfall. But Tenley wasn't sure she wanted to turn a silly little scribble into a job. She wasn't a decent artist. People would criticize and she didn't think she'd be able to take that. Hell, there were a million reasons she could give him to go back to Chicago and leave her alone. But there was only one that made any sense to her.

She was starting to imagine a future with him. Not marriage or children, but a relationship, a connection that went beyond what they shared sexually to something re-sembling affection and trust. She'd already wondered what it might be like to have him present in her life, to speak to him every day on the phone, to see him on weekends…to make plans.

With a soft sigh, she trudged down the hill toward the shed. "I've spent less than twenty-four hours with the man," she muttered to herself. "It's a little early to confuse good sex with a relationship."

But would she even know a relationship if it dropped out of the sky and landed at her feet? She'd never been in love, never wanted to be with anyone for more than a night or two. Maybe after a second night together, she'd want him to go away.

Tenley waded through a huge drift, then grabbed the shed door and slid it open. Her Jeep was inside, still coated with snow from the night before. The small tractor sat beside it. All these thoughts about the future were beginning to drive her a bit crazy.

Maybe it was time to heed the warning signs, to put a little distance between them. If they spent another night together, there was no telling how she'd feel in the morning. She might just fall in love with Alex Stamos. And Tenley knew that was the worst thing she could possibly do to herself.

ALEX PEERED OUT the window, watching as Tenley maneuvered the tractor around the small yard, scooping up snow and dumping it against the trees. He wasn't quite sure how to take her news. Had he known she was T. J. Marshall's granddaughter, he'd have played things a whole lot differently.

Getting the artist under contract was his first priority. Everything else fell to the bottom of his to-do list. Still, even if he'd wanted to, Alex suspected it would have been impossible to resist Tenley's advances. She did crawl into bed with him, so he wasn't completely to blame.

The only way this could go south is if he and Tenley parted on bad terms. Alex cursed beneath his breath. What if she'd already fallen in love with him? If he didn't handle this right, she could sour a deal with her grandfather before it even began.

Alex stepped away from the window and crossed to the fireplace. Holding his hands out to the warmth, he contemplated the possibilities. If he had to choose between Tenley and the book contract, the choice would have to be— His breath caught in his throat.

No, it wasn't that easy. His first instinct wasn't to put business first. He wanted to choose Tenley. The notion startled him. He'd never made a woman the priority in his life. Beyond his sisters and his mother, women were pretty much a temporary distraction. Work always came first.

Alex shook his head. Maybe it was time to start thinking about business. He crossed the room to the phone, then picked it up and dialed the office. When the receptionist answered, he asked for his sister's extension.

"Where have you been?" she asked. "I've been ringing your cell and it kept bouncing through to your voice mail. I've called all the hospitals up there thinking you got into some kind of accident."

"I'm sorry. I lost my cell in a snowbank and I spent the night with the Good Samaritan who rescued me from the ditch. My car got hit by a snowplow and I haven't had a chance to talk to this artist yet. So, I'm going to be here for a while."

"Sounds like you've had a very exciting twenty-four hours," she said.

"You wouldn't believe it," he said. "I need you to over-night another cell phone to me. Send it to the Harbor Inn in Sawyer Bay. Then find a place for me to rent a car. And have them deliver it to the inn. On second thought, rent an SUV. Once I get into town, I'll try to find a wireless network and I'll pick up my mail."

"What's your number at the inn?" Tess asked.

"I'm not there yet. I probably won't be until tomorrow morning."

"Where are you?"

"I'm staying with this…with T. J. Marshall's grand-daughter."

"Oh, that's nice," Tess said. "So things are going well?"

"That's debatable," he said. "And a very long story to tell. But, I should be at the inn sometime tomorrow. I'll call you then."

He set the phone down, then picked up his book from the sofa. *Walden* was one of his favorite books and obviously one of Tenley's as well. She had written notes in the margins and he found drawings at the ends of chapters. Frowning, he walked over to the bookshelves that flanked the fireplace.

He'd noticed the eclectic selection of literature and was quite impressed. But the books hadn't been hers originally. Most of them held copyrights from the 1950s and earlier. The library had probably belonged to her grandfather.

He plucked out a copy of *Jane Eyre* and flipped through it, noticing the notes and drawings. If he looked hard enough, he could see hints of the artist who had drawn Cyd. Alex grabbed another book, *The Catcher in the Rye,* and opened it, only to find a drawing of a young girl on the title page.

The parallels were there to see. In the eyes and in the hands. T. J. Marshall had drawn these sketches and he'd drawn the graphic novel. But according to Tenley, her grandfather only painted landscapes. She'd been adamant that the novel wasn't his work.

Something wasn't right. He wasn't getting the whole story, and Tenley was standing in the way. She worked at her grandfather's gallery. Was she afraid that publishing an edgy graphic novel might hurt his reputation as a serious painter? If that was the case, they could publish under a pseudonym.

Alex needed to meet this man and make his proposal. If the roads were clear, then he'd have Tenley take him into town. If not, he'd go tomorrow morning. But he was definitely not sleeping with Tenley tonight. There was every chance that she was deliberately distracting him.

"Definitely not," Alex repeated. He grabbed the copy of Thoreau and sat down on the sofa. But as he tried to pick up where he'd left off, Alex's thoughts kept returning to Tenley. Sleeping in separate rooms seemed like a good plan, but in reality, he'd have a serious problem staying in his room. And if she crawled into bed with him, then all bets were off.

No, he'd have to get back to town tonight. If Tenley wouldn't take him, then he'd call a cab. Perhaps the inn had a shuttle service.

Over the next half hour, Alex tried to focus on reading, but he found himself walking back and forth to the window, peering out at Tenley as she ran the tractor up and down the driveway. He'd never known a woman who could drive a tractor. But then, he wondered if there was anything Tenley couldn't do for herself. She seemed like the kind of woman who didn't need a man.

When she parked the tractor near the shed and started

back toward the house, Alex returned to the sofa and opened his book. She burst through the door, brushing snow off her jacket and stamping her feet on the rug.

"Get your things together," she said. "The road is plowed. I'll take you into town." She opened the closet door and pulled out a down jacket. "Wear this. You'll need something warm. And find a hat. It's still windy."

With that, she turned and walked back outside, slamming the door behind her. Alex stared after her. "I guess I will be sleeping alone tonight, after all." He wouldn't have to worry about controlling his desires. Somehow, he'd rather that the decision had been his.

Alex went back to the guest room and gathered his things, then found the pair of boots he'd worn out to the sauna. When he was dressed against the cold, Alex walked out onto the porch, expecting to find Tenley waiting there with her SUV. But the woods were eerily silent.

He hiked down to the shed, calling her name, the sound of his voice echoing through the trees. As he passed the barn, he noticed her inside. She was working with one of her horses.

"I'm ready," he said, dropping his duffel on the ground.

"I'll just be a few minutes."

"Tenley, I don't want you to think that I'm angry with you. I can understand why you might want to protect your grandfather's reputation."

She gave him a perplexed look. "All right," she said. "You have business to do and sleeping with me is probably just a distraction. It's better that you go."

"You're not a distraction," he said, contradicting what

he'd been thinking earlier. "I don't regret the time we spent together. Or anything we did. Do you?"

She smiled and shook her head. "No. I liked having sex with you."

He caught her gaze and held it. Was that all it had been to her? Just sex? "Do you want me to stay the night?"

"You don't have to," she said. "The roads are plowed."

"That's not the point," Alex countered. "I'm asking if you want me to stay another night."

"Have you ever taken a sleigh ride?" she asked, striding out of the barn, the horse following her. She handed him the reins. "Hold these."

"What does that have to do with anything?"

Tenley smiled. "Minnie needs exercise and the roads are perfect. They're covered with snow so they're nice and smooth. It'll be fun." She walked to a large sliding door on the side of the barn and pulled it open to reveal a small sleigh. Then she took the reins from his hands and deftly hitched the horse to the sleigh.

"Hop in," she said, leading Minnie toward him. "You can toss your things in the back."

When they were both settled in the sleigh, a thick wool blanket tucked around their legs, Tenley snapped the reins against Minnie's back and the sleigh slid out into the yard. The horse took the hill up to the road without breaking stride and before long, they were skimming over the snowy road at a brisk pace.

The horse's hooves were muffled by the hard-packed snow. Alex drew a deep breath and let it out slowly, listening to the hiss of the runners beneath them. He glanced over at Tenley, the reins twisted in her hands, her gaze fixed intently on the road.

She was amazing. He'd had more new experiences with her in the past twenty-four hours than he had in the past year of his life. How could he ever forget her? And why would he want to? He scanned the features of her face, outlined by the afternoon sun.

It was all so breathtaking—her beauty, the sparkling snow, the blue sky and the crisp silence of the winter evening. She glanced over at him. But this time, she didn't smile. Their gazes locked for a moment and he leaned over and dropped a kiss on her lips. "This is nice."

"My grandfather used to take my brother and me out after snowstorms. We'd bundle up and my mother would make us a thermos of hot cocoa and off we'd go. We'd sing and laugh and my face would get so cold it would hurt. It's one of my favorite childhood memories."

"I can see why. It's fun. Does he live around here?"

"My grandfather lives in town. I told you, he has a gallery—"

"I meant your brother," Alex corrected.

An odd expression crossed her face. Alex wasn't quite sure how to read it. She looked confused and then sad. Tenley shook her head. "No. He died."

Alex was shocked by her reply. He'd come to believe he knew most of the basic facts about Tenley. But what he'd pieced together obviously still had a lot of holes. Very big holes. "I—I'm sorry. I didn't mean to—"

"No, it's all right. Nobody ever mentions him around me. I'm just not used to talking about him." She pasted a bright smile on her face. "People think I'm…fragile. I'm not, you know."

"I can see that," Alex replied. "I don't know a single woman who can drive a sleigh *and* a tractor. Or run naked through the snow."

"People also think I'm crazy," she said. "You'll probably hear a lot of that when you're in town."

He slipped his arm around her and pulled her body against his. "I like crazy." Alex paused. "I'm going to see your grandfather tomorrow. I'm hoping to convince him to let me publish his novel."

"I know," she said.

"And then, after he's signed a contract with me, I'm going to come back out here for another sleigh ride."

They passed the rest of the trip in complete silence. As they drove into town, Alex was struck by the fact that he'd spent an entire day away from what he considered the conveniences of civilization. There were people driving on the streets and lights that seemed a bit too bright and clocks confirming what the sun had already told him—the day was coming to an end. And it was noisy.

He fought the temptation to grab the reins from Tenley and turn the sleigh around. Their time together had been such a nice respite from his real life, much better than a week at his family's beach condo in Mexico.

They wove through the narrow streets of town, snow piled high and nearly obscuring their view of the white clapboard buildings. She pulled the sleigh to a stop. "I don't know where you were planning to stay," she said. "But this is the nicest place in town. Ask Katie for the big room at the top of the stairs. It has a fireplace."

He caught sight of the sign hanging from the porch. "Bayside Bed and Breakfast," he said. "I had a reservation at the Harbor Inn."

"This is better. Katie Vanderhoff makes cinnamon rolls in the morning." She twisted the reins around a ring near her feet, then jumped out of the sleigh.

Alex followed her around to the back, then grabbed his things from the luggage box. "Thanks for everything. For saving me from the storm, for taking me in and feeding me."

"No problem," she said.

This wasn't going to be easy, saying goodbye to her. Alex didn't like the prospect of spending the night alone in bed. Nor did he want this to be the end. "Let's have dinner tomorrow. I'm going to be staying another night and you probably know of a nice place."

She hesitated, then nodded. "Sure. I'll talk to you tomorrow." Tenley turned to walk toward the sleigh, but Alex didn't want her to leave.

He dropped his things onto the snowy sidewalk, then caught up to her and grabbed her hand. He pulled her against him, his mouth coming down on hers, softly at first, then urgently, as if he needed to leave her with something memorable. Alex searched for a clue to her feelings in the softness of her lips and the taste of her tongue.

She surrendered immediately, her arms slipping around his neck. Time stood still and, for a few moments, Alex felt himself relax. She still wanted him, as much as he wanted her. So why the hell were they spending the night apart?

"Stay with me," he said.

"I can't. I have to take Minnie back. And if I stay here, the whole town will know by tomorrow morning. They already spend too much time talking about me." She pushed up on her toes and kissed him again. "I'll see you tomorrow."

With that, she hopped back into the sleigh and grabbed the reins. The horse leaped into a brisk walk when she slapped the reins against the mare's back and Alex watched as she disappeared around the corner. A sense of loneliness settled in around him.

Suddenly exhausted, Alex picked up his things and walked up to the porch. When he got inside, he rang the bell at the front desk. A moment later, an elderly woman stepped through a door and greeted him.

"I need a place to stay," Alex said. "I'm told that I should ask for the big room at the top of the stairs."

"Have you had friends that have spent time with us?" she asked.

"No. Tenley Marshall suggested this place."

The woman blinked in surprise. "You're a friend of Tenley's?"

"Yes. Is the room available?"

She nodded. "How is Tenley? I haven't seen her recently. She used to work for me when she was a teenager. But that was before all that sadness." She drew a sharp breath and shook her head, then forced a smile. "I'm glad to know she has a friend."

Alex frowned. Though he wasn't one to pry into other people's private affairs, he believed he had a right to know a little more about the woman who had seduced him. "Yes," he said. "I heard about all that. You'd think after all this time—how long has it been?"

"Oh, gosh. Ten years? She was fifteen or sixteen. They were a pair, those two. Joined at the hip from the moment they were born. And you've never seen such beautiful children. That black hair and those pale blue eyes. You'd never recognize her now with all that silly makeup."

"I think she's beautiful," Alex said, feeling the need to defend Tenley.

She blinked in surprise. "Well, that's lovely." A smile slowly suffused her entire face. "Let's get you registered and then I'll show you your room."

Though he was tempted to ask more, Alex decided to bide his time. He didn't want to give the town gossips any more to chat about.

chapter four

TENLEY carefully maneuvered the sleigh down the narrow streets to the harbor. Before long, the salt trucks would be out and the snow would melt away, making it impossible to use the sled. They could have brought her truck, but Tenley had wanted time to talk to him, to tell him the entire truth.

Unfortunately, she hadn't been able to figure out a way to adequately explain her reasoning. Forced to come up with an alternate plan, she decided to enlist her grandfather's help. But she needed to talk to him before Alex had a chance to introduce himself. She drew to a stop in front of her grandfather's gallery, then tied the reins to the mailbox.

"What kind of gas mileage do you get with that rig?"

Tenley turned to find the town police chief, Harvey Willis, hanging out the window of his cruiser. He waved and she returned the gesture. "Oats and hay," she said. "And an occasional apple."

"Drive safe," he said. "And get that thing back to your place before dark or I'll be giving you a citation. It doesn't have lights on it." He chuckled, then continued up the road from the harbor.

Her grandfather answered the door after only thirty seconds of constant ringing. He carried a paint-stained rag and wiped his fingers as Tenley greeted him.

"You brought the sleigh out. Give me a few minutes and I'll get my jacket."

"No, we need to talk," Tenley said.

"We can talk and ride," he said.

She nodded, impatient to get to the subject at hand—Alex Stamos. When her grandfather returned, bundled against the cold, Tenley helped him into the sleigh, then handed him the reins.

"Oh, this brings back fine memories," he said, urging the horse into a slow walk. "How long has it been since we've had a ride? Last year, we barely had snow. And the year before that, I spent most of the winter in California with your father. Three years? My, time really does fly."

"Grandpa, I need your help. There's this man—"

"Is someone giving you trouble, Tennie? It's not Randy, is it? Is he making a pest of himself again?"

"No. It's not Randy." Randy Schmitt had been pursuing her since high school and she'd been fending off his affections for just as long.

Tenley fiddled with the fingers of her gloves, searching for a way to enlist her grandfather's help. It wasn't difficult to predict his reaction to her dilemma. But she couldn't think of any way to make Alex's offer sound insignificant.

"I made a little comic book for Josh as a Christmas gift. Just a story with some pictures to go with it. And he loved it so much, he sent it to a publisher in Chicago. Now that publisher has come here, hoping to put the work under contract."

"Tennie, that's fabulous! I didn't realize you were working on your art."

She groaned. "I don't have any art. This was just… doodling. Crude illustrations. The problem is, Josh told the publisher the book was done by T. J. Marshall. And the publisher, his name is Alex Stamos, thinks that's you. So tomorrow, he's going to come by the gallery and try to convince you to sell him the rights to the book. And you're going to tell him you're not interested."

Her grandfather scowled, his eyes still fixed on the road ahead. "Why would you want me to do that? This is your chance to do something on your own. Tennie, you have to grab an opportunity like this. Not many artists can make a living off their talents."

Tenley shook her head. "But I don't have any talent. And I'm just too busy with my work at the gallery."

"You can do both."

"I've never really thought about a career as an artist," she said.

"You've never really thought about a career, period," he said, drawing the horse to a stop at the corner. "Everything went to hell before you had a chance to decide what you wanted to do with your life. You've been afraid to be passionate about anything, Tennie. Afraid if you showed any interest, it would be taken away. But your talent can't be taken away. It's in your genes."

She really had no excuse. Her grandfather was right. But she'd never wanted a career as an artist. She wasn't prepared. "I love my life exactly the way it is."

He shook his head. "No, you don't. Every day, I look at you trying to avoid living, trying to keep things on an even keel. You hide out in that old cabin. You hide behind that makeup and that silly hairdo. You dress yourself in black, as if you're still in mourning. Everything you do is meant to push people away. It's time to take a chance."

He was talking about her art, but what her grandfather said applied to Alex as well—or to men, in general. Reward didn't come without risk. She slipped her arm through his and rested her head on his shoulder. "I don't mean to be such a mess," she said.

Her grandfather laughed. "You've always been a bother. But that's why I love you, Tennie. We're not so different, you and I. I was lucky to find your grandmother. She was a sensible woman and she put me in my place. And I loved her for it. I'd like to think there's someone out there who can do the same for you. Someone who can bring you balance."

Tenley sighed, her breath clouding in front of her face. "Do you ever wonder what he would have been like? He would have changed as he got older. I always try to imagine what kind of man he would have become."

"I know one thing. He would have been mad as hell to see you wasting away in that cabin. He would have told you to get off your butt and make something out of your life."

"He would have," Tenley said with a weak laugh. She

gave his arm a squeeze. "Would it be all right if we cut our ride short? I have some things I need to do."

"Sure, sweetheart." He handed her the reins. "I'm going to walk from here. I need some exercise. And I want you to think about what I've said. Carpe diem. Seize the day, Tenley Marshall."

He jumped down to the ground, then knocked on the side of the sleigh. Tenley clucked her tongue and sent Minnie into motion. Though she could have taken a quick way out of town, she decided to ride past the inn.

She slowed the sleigh as she stared up at the window of Alex's room. What was he doing now? Was he lying on the bed, thinking about the time they'd spent together? Was he reliving all of the most passionate moments between them?

She fought the urge to park her sleigh and climb the trellis to the second-story porch that fronted his room. But someone would see the sleigh and question what she was doing at the inn. There'd be all sorts of speculation. Though small-town life could be nice, there was a lot of bad with the good.

"Get up, Minnie," she called. "Let's go home."

Tomorrow would be soon enough to tend to her future. For now, she wanted a quiet place to think about the past twenty-four hours.

THE WHITE CLAPBOARD inn was as quaint on the inside as it was on the exterior. Two huge parlors flanked the entry hall and a wide, open staircase led to the second floor and Alex's room.

Tenley had been right about the choice. The room, fur-

nished with a mix of real and reproduction antiques, was spacious, but cozy. It overlooked a wide upper porch with two sets of French doors that could be thrown open in the warm weather.

After checking in, he'd walked down to a small coffee shop and had dinner, then spent a half-hour looking for a place to buy a new pair of shoes for his meeting with T. J. Marshall. The only men's shop in town was closed and wouldn't open until ten the next morning, so Alex decided to return to his room.

An attempt to kick back and relax only made him more restless. He felt imprisoned amongst the chintz curtains and the overstuffed furniture, used to the soothing mix of rustic charm and natural comfort in Tenley's cabin.

Alex opened the French doors and let the cold wind blow through his room, breathing deeply as he tried to clear his head. Maybe Tenley had it right all along. Maybe people weren't supposed to live with all those silly conveniences like televisions and clocks and microwave ovens.

Though he'd only spent a day with her, Alex sensed something inside him had changed. He looked at his surroundings with a greater awareness of what was necessary for happiness and what could be discarded. And in his mind, Tenley was standing with the necessities.

He looked over at the bed, to the pages of the novel that he'd spread over the surface, the papers fluttering. Tenley. Something had been nagging at him since he'd left her place, something he couldn't quite put his finger on. He locked the doors against the wind and then crossed the room.

His thoughts focused on the drawings he'd found inside

her grandfather's books, the little sketches that seemed familiar in a way. Gathering up the pages, Alex stretched out on the bed and began to read the novel again, carefully studying each illustration before moving on.

The haze of desire that had clouded his thoughts slowly cleared and Alex realized instantly what had been bothering him. The heroine in the story was Tenley. A girl who'd lost her family in a tragic accident and who had discovered a way to bring them back to life. Cyd was Tenley. But it was more than that.

The story was so personal, so rooted in the heroine's viewpoint that it could never have been written by a man. Nor had it been illustrated by Tenley's grandfather. She'd done the drawings. And she'd written the story.

He rifled through the pages until he found a close-up of Cyd's hand. The rings that Tenley wore were exactly the same as Cyd's. The shape of the hands, the long, tapered fingers and the black nail polish. Hands just like those that had touched his body and made him ache with need.

"Oh, hell," he muttered, flopping back against the pillows. This was all his fault. He'd made some rather big assumptions about T. J. Marshall—pretty sexist assumptions—that had been completely wrong. He was looking for an artist by that name from Sawyer Bay and he'd found one. But he'd never considered that the *T* in T.J. might stand for Tenley.

Alex tried to rationalize his mistake. He'd been blinded by desire, anxious to believe everything she said and even things she didn't say. "The surprises never end," he said.

Tenley had never claimed to be a conventional girl, but

what artist wouldn't want to make a living from their work? There were thousands upon thousands who struggled to make ends meet every day. And he was offering her a chance to do what she loved and get paid to do it.

Alex carefully straightened the pages, then put them back in his briefcase. As he closed it, he noticed the phone and considered calling her and demanding the truth. But if she'd gone to so much trouble to hide herself from him, then he'd have to proceed cautiously. She'd be the one to sign the contract, so his approach would have to change.

Her number was in the phone book under Tenley J. Thomas J. followed immediately after, and below that, the Marshall Gallery. Had he bothered to look in the phone book, he might have figured this out sooner. And maybe he wouldn't have made the mistake of sleeping with her.

Or maybe not, Alex mused. She would have been awfully difficult to resist, all soft and naked, her hands skimming over his body. He punched in the digits of her number, casting aside the images that raced through his head, then waited as her phone rang. He wasn't sure what he intended to say or how he intended to say it. But that became a moot point when she didn't answer. "She's probably outside, chopping wood or rebuilding the engine on her Jeep," he muttered.

Irritated, Alex stripped off his shirt and tossed it onto a nearby chair, then discarded his khakis and his socks. The simplest way to occupy his mind was to lose himself in his work, but he preferred to think about Tenley instead. Perhaps a hot shower would clear his head.

He strode to the bathroom and turned on the water,

waiting for it to heat up. Then he skimmed his boxers off and stepped inside the tiled stall. Bracing his hands on the wall, he let the water sluice over his neck and back, his eyes closed, his mind drifting.

Tantalizing images teased at his brain and he thought about the sauna, about the two of them naked and sweating, of Tenley's mouth on his shaft and the orgasm that followed. Alex groaned. Just the mere thought brought an unwelcome reaction.

If he got hard every time he thought of her, then he needed to find something else to occupy his mind. He reached for the faucet and turned off the hot water, forcing himself to bear the sting of the cold. It wouldn't take much to ease his predicament and Alex considered taking matters into his own hands. But surrendering wasn't an option. He was the one in control of his desires, not her.

He tipped his face up into the spray, waiting for the water to have an effect on his body. But his mind once again drifted to thoughts of Tenley. What would they be doing at this very moment if he'd spent the night in her cabin? Would they be curled up in front of the fire, drinking hot cocoa? Maybe they'd already be sound asleep, naked in each other's arms, after a long afternoon of mind-blowing sex.

Alex slowly began to count backward from one hundred, challenging his body to bear the cold shower. He needed to stop thinking about sex. Even if he wanted to return to her bed, he didn't have a car. There was no way to get back to her cabin. Hell, he didn't even know where her cabin was.

Finally, after his erection had completely subsided, Alex shut off the water and grabbed a towel from the rack above the toilet. His skin was prickled with goose bumps and he shivered uncontrollably. But his erection was gone.

Alex shook his head, then stepped out of the shower and wrapped the towel around his waist. As he walked back into the room, his ran his hands over his wet chest. But when he glanced up, he jerked in surprise. "Jeez, you scared me."

Tenley sat on the edge of the bed, dressed in her parka and fur hat, her big boots dripping water on the hardwood floor.

"How the hell did you get in here?"

She pointed to the French doors. "I climbed up the trellis and came across the porch."

"Those doors are locked."

She shrugged. "They are. But you can jimmy the lock with a library card." Tenley reached in her pocket and pulled out her card. "It's good for more than just books."

Alex stared at her from across the room, afraid to approach for fear that he wouldn't be able to keep his hands off her. Why was she here? Had she missed him as much as he'd missed her?

"I didn't want to sleep alone tonight," she said. "I thought maybe I could sleep here."

"Just sleep?"

Tenley nodded. "I like sleeping with you. When I sleep with you, I don't dream."

Alex knew once they crawled into bed, there'd be a lot more than sleeping on the menu. "Tenley, I think you and I both know that we can't be in the same bed together and just sleep."

"We could try," she said.

Every instinct in Alex's mind and body told him to show her the door. He had an obligation to treat her as a business prospect and the last time he checked, that didn't include losing himself in the warmth of her body. "I'm not even remotely interested in doing that," he said.

Her eyes went wide and he saw the hurt there. "You aren't?"

Alex knew he was risking everything, but suddenly business didn't matter. He could live without her novel, but he couldn't go another minute without her body. "If you spend the night here, I won't hold back." He paused, then decided he might as well be completely honest. Then the ball would be in her court. "I'm going to see your grand-father tomorrow. If he isn't the one who made that story, I'm not going to give up. I'm going to find that person, whoever he—or *she*—is."

She stood, her expression unflinching, and shrugged out of her jacket, letting it drop to the floor at her feet. Then she kicked off her boots and dropped them in front of the door. She still wore the goofy hat with the earflaps. Alex reached out and took it off her head, then set it on the desk.

He hadn't seen her in a few hours, but the effect that her beauty had on his brain was immediate and intense. His gaze drifted from her eyes to her lips. Alex fought the temptation to grab her and pull her down onto the bed, to kiss her until her body went soft beneath his.

Slowly, she removed each piece of clothing, her gaze fixed on his, never faltering. When she was left in just her T-shirt and panties, Alex realized that he hadn't drawn a decent breath since she'd begun. A wave of dizziness caused him to reach out and grab the bedpost.

His fingers twitched with the memory of touching her body as he took in the outline of her breasts beneath the thin cotton shirt. He looked down to see his reaction, becoming more evident through the damp towel. Tenley noticed as well, her gaze lingering on his crotch.

Who were they trying to fool? There was no way they'd crawl into bed together and not enjoy the pleasures of the flesh. Alex untwisted the towel from his waist and it dropped to the floor. Then he pulled her into his arms, tumbling them both back onto the bed.

This was dangerous, he thought to himself as he drew her leg up along his hip. To need a woman so much that it defied all common sense was something he'd never experienced in the past. It wasn't a bad feeling, just a very scary situation. How much was he willing to give up to possess her? And when would it be enough?

TENLEY STARED at the landscape of the harbor at Gill's Rock. "It's lovely," she said, nodding. "The colors are softer than those you used on the painting of Detroit harbor. Are you going to have prints made?"

"Definitely. The prints of Fish Creek harbor sold well. I'm thinking we ought to do some smaller ones and sell the whole series as a package."

"Are there any harbors left to do?"

"After Jackson, I think I'm done with them," her grandfather said. "I'm going to move on to barns. Or log buildings."

"You could start with the cabin."

"I was thinking of doing that. But there's a nice barn on Clark's Lake Road that I've always wanted to paint." He stepped back, studying his painting intently. "Lighthouses, harbors, barns. The tourists love them and I do give them what they love."

Tenley knew the compromises that her grandfather had to make over the course of his life. Though he might have wanted to become a serious painter and have his work hang in museums, he'd come to accept his talent for what it was—good enough to provide for his wife and a family and more than enough to tempt the tourists into buying.

"By the way," her grandfather said, "I like the new look. All that stuff on your eyes…I never understood that. You're a pretty girl, Tennie." He paused. "No, you're a beautiful woman."

Tenley threw her arms around his neck and gave him a fierce hug. "I have to run over to the post office. I think your paints are here. And I'm going to mail these bills, too. Do you have anything you want to put in?"

Her grandfather scowled. "Is there a reason you're so anxious to leave?"

"No. I just have work to do."

"I thought you said that guy from the publishing house was going to stop by."

Tenley wasn't sure what Alex had planned for the day. She'd slipped out of his room at dawn, leaving him sound asleep, his naked body tangled in the sheets, his dark hair mussed. To her relief, she'd managed to crawl back down the trellis and get back her Jeep without anyone seeing her, minimizing the chances for gossip.

"He might. He didn't make an appointment, so I don't know what time he plans to show up. If he comes, tell him I'll be back soon."

"Tenley, I am not going to make excuses for you. The man has come all the way from Chicago. The least you could do is talk to him."

Oh, she'd done a whole lot more than talk to him already, Tenley mused. If her grandfather only knew the naughty things he'd done to her, he'd probably lock the front door of the gallery and call Harvey Willis to escort Alex out of town. "I'll only be a few minutes, so—"

The bell above the gallery door jingled and she heard someone step inside. Tenley forced a smile. "There he is," she said. Clutching the envelopes in front of her, she wandered out of the workroom and into the showroom. Alex stood at the door, dressed in a sport jacket, a crisp blue shirt and dark wool trousers. His hair was combed and he'd shaved and he looked nothing like the man she'd left that morning.

"Hello," she said, unable to hide a smile. There were times when she forgot just how handsome he was. Boys like Alex had always been way out of her league. They dated the popular girls, the girls who worried about clothes and hair and…boobs. They always had boobs. Tenley glanced down at her chest, then crossed her arms over her rather unremarkable breasts.

"Hi. I'm here to see T. J. Marshall."

Tenley swallowed hard. It was now or never. Her grandfather wouldn't take part in the subterfuge, so Tenley was faced with only one choice. She cleared her throat and straightened to her full height. "I'm T. J. Marshall. At least, I'm the one you're looking for."

He didn't seem surprised. "Yeah, I kind of figured that out on my own." He crossed the room and held out his hand. "Alex Stamos. Stamos Publishing."

Hesitantly, she placed her fingers in his palm. The instant they touched, she felt a tremor race through her. He slowly brought her hand to his lips and pressed a kiss to her fingertips. "I missed you this morning," he whispered. "I woke up and you weren't there."

"See, that wasn't so difficult."

Tenley jumped at the sound of her grandfather's voice. She tugged her hand from Alex's and fixed a smile on her face. "Alex Stamos, this is my grandfather, Thomas Marshall. Also known as T.J. Or Tom."

Alex held his hand out. "It's a pleasure to meet you, sir. You have a very talented granddaughter. Did she tell you we're interested in publishing her graphic novel?"

"I've always thought she had talent. She used to draw little sketches in all my books. Drove me crazy. I thought she might be an illustrator someday. She never did like books without pictures." He chuckled softly. "Well, it's a pleasure, Alex. I'll leave you two to your business."

When they were alone, Alex reached out for her hand again, placing it on his chest. "Why did you leave?"

"I figured I'd better get out of there or the whole town would be talking."

Alex gave her fingers a squeeze. "So, what do you think

they'd say if I took you to breakfast? There's a nice little coffee shop down the street from the inn."

"You didn't stay for the cinnamon rolls?"

He shook his head. "Hmm. Cinnamon rolls. Tenley. Cinnamon rolls. Tenley. The choice wasn't tough."

"All right," she said. "But you're buying."

"I wouldn't have it any other way."

Tenley grabbed her jacket and they stepped out into the chilly morning. "How did you figure it out?" she asked as they headed away from the harbor.

"I was flipping through some of those books your grandfather mentioned. There were drawings in the margins. At first I thought they were just crude scribblings, but then I came across one that looked very familiar."

Tenley knew she ought to apologize. But that might prompt a discussion of her motives and even she wasn't sure why she'd kept her real identity a secret from him. "I didn't intend to deceive you. I just didn't want anything to… I wanted to be able to… I wasn't ready…" She shook her head, feeling her cheeks warm with embarrassment. "It's sometimes easier not to get too personal. At least, that's always worked for me in the past."

"So, I'm just one in a long line of uninformed men?" he asked.

Her breath caught in her throat. "No! You're not like anyone I've every known. I thought if you knew, you wouldn't want to sleep with me." She cursed softly. "I wanted you and you wanted me. All that other stuff is just…business."

"I have rules about mixing business with pleasure. Very strict rules."

"You haven't mixed the two. Not yet."

"What are you talking about?"

She straightened. "I haven't agreed to do business with you, Alex, so all we've had is the pleasure part. You haven't broken any rules…yet."

Alex laughed, shaking his head. "Whatever made me think this was going to be easy? God, I thought I'd come up here, do my little presentation, charm you and get you to sign on the dotted line."

"You have charmed me," she said.

"Yeah, I've heard I have a way with women," he muttered. "But do me a favor. Don't say no until I've told you the plan. Consider my offer and if you don't like it, then I'll—I'll make you another offer." He stopped and grabbed her arms, turning her to face him. "But be assured of one thing, Tenley. You are going to sign with me."

"You must have a lot of confidence in that charm of yours," Tenley said.

"It worked on you, didn't it?"

"I think you're forgetting who seduced whom." She started walking again, then turned back to him. "Maybe I should hire an agent. Just to make sure I get the best deal."

"At least an agent would make sure you didn't pass on a great deal. He'd say, don't be stupid. Sign the contract."

In truth, Tenley *was* interested in how much her novel might bring. After talking with her grandfather, she'd begun to see the wisdom in his words. She'd be silly to turn down a chance to make money from her art. But she had no idea what a project like hers was worth. There was the money to discuss—and a few other conditions.

"But an agent will take fifteen percent," he added. "You don't need an agent. I'm going to give you a good offer." He caught up to her as they turned down the main street, toward the inn. "I had a nice time last night. Did you sleep well?"

Tenley nodded. "I did."

"I'm going to stay another night," he said.

"I thought you'd be leaving today."

Alex took her hand and tucked it into the crook of his arm. "Nope. I'm going to stay until I convince you to sign with us. And after that, we're going to go over all the things that need to be done with your story to make it better."

When they reached the coffee shop, Alex opened the door for her and stepped aside for her to enter. The shop was filled with all the usual customers. Morning coffee was a daily ritual for a number of the folks in town, choosing the same seats every day.

Her entrance caused a quite a stir, with everyone turning to watch as the hostess seated them in a booth near the front windows. She handed them menus and asked about coffee. Alex ordered a cup and Tenley asked for orange juice.

"Why is everyone staring?" Alex whispered.

"I don't usually come in here," Tenley said. "It's like Gossip Central. If you want the town to know your business, you just mention it during breakfast at The Coffee Bean. Here, information moves faster than the Internet."

They ordered breakfast, Tenley choosing a huge platter

with three eggs, bacon, hash browns, a biscuit and three small pancakes. Alex settled for toast and coffee.

"Not hungry?" she asked.

"I usually have a bigger lunch," he said. "So, I think we need to talk business."

"Let's not," Tenley said, slathering her biscuit with honey. She took a huge bite and grinned at him. "Sex always makes me hungry. I find that my appetite is in direct proportion to the intensity of my orgasms. This morning I am really, really hungry. You should be, too. We did it three times—no wait, four times, last night. That has to be some kind of record."

Alex glanced around. "Do you really think this is an appropriate topic for breakfast conversation?"

Tenley slipped her foot out of her boot and wriggled her toes beneath his pant leg. "You know what I like the best? I like the way you look, right before you come. Your lip twitches and you get this really intense expression on your face. I love that expression."

She loved the way his body tensed and flexed as he moved inside of her, she loved the feel of his skin beneath her fingers and the warmth of his mouth on hers. Tenley loved that she could make him lose touch with reality for a few brief moments. There weren't many things that she did well, but seducing Alex was one task at which she excelled.

Alex cleared his throat. "Stop."

"Why?"

"Because I don't like being teased, especially in public."

She took another bite of her biscuit and then held it out to him. "You should eat more. You're going to need your energy. We should go skiing. Have you ever been cross-country skiing?"

"Never," Alex said.

"Or skating. There's a nice rink in Sister Bay. And you can rent skates. Do you know how to skate?"

"I used to play hockey when I was a kid. But I'm not much for the cold. I prefer warm-weather activities. I like windsurfing. I go hiking. I like to water-ski."

"We have all that here. Just not now."

"Tenley, I want to talk about this contract."

"Always about business," she muttered. "I find business very dull. And if you're trying to charm me, you're not doing a very good job. If I want to go skating, then you should be happy to take me."

"I don't have anything to wear," he said.

"We have stores here. You'll need some long underwear and a decent pair of boots. And some good gloves. Those leather gloves won't last. We'll go shopping after breakfast."

It was nice to have a playmate, both in and out of bed. Alex made a good companion. He was funny and easy-going and he seemed to find her amusing. And he made her shudder with pleasure whenever he touched her. What more could a girl want?

She grabbed a piece of bacon from her plate and slowly munched on it. With Tommy's death, she'd lost her best friend. Since then, she hadn't tried to find a new one. Alex was the first person she really wanted to spend time with.

"All right," he said. "We'll talk business at dinner."

"At my place," she said. "I'll cook."

"You're not going to distract me again," he said. "I

want you to promise. And I think it would be better if we went out."

Tenley shrugged. "We'll see."

"If you don't promise, I'm going to kiss you, right here and now." He glanced around. "What would the gossips say about that?"

"Go ahead," Tenley said. "I dare you." In truth, she wanted him to accept the challenge. She wanted to shock everyone watching, to make them wonder just what poor, pitiful Tenley Marshall was doing with this sexy stranger.

When he didn't make a move, she leaned across the table, took his face in her hands and gave Alex a long, lingering kiss. She didn't bother to look at the crowd's reaction. Tenley chose to enjoy the look on Alex's face, instead. "I don't make a dare unless I'm willing to back it up."

He licked his lips, then grinned. "Bacon," he murmured. Reaching out, he snatched a piece from her plate. "Maybe I'm hungrier than I thought."

chapter five

ALEX curled into Tenley's naked body, pulling her against him and tucking her backside into his lap. He usually didn't spend a lot of time outdoors during the winter. But since he'd come to Door County, he'd realized just how delicious it felt to spend the day outside in the cold and the evening getting warm in bed.

Though this had begun as a business trip, it was slowly transforming into one of the best vacations he'd ever had. Previous vacations had always been solitary escapes, a time to get away from his social life and focus on himself. But his time with Tenley was making him question why he hadn't enjoyed those holidays in the company of a woman.

Perhaps because he didn't really know any women who shared his interests. The girls he dated weren't really interested in hiking the mountains or rafting river rapids. But Tenley had probably experienced more of those things than he had. "Are you awake?" he whispered.

"Umm. Just barely."

"What do you think of rock climbing?"

"Right now?" she asked.

"No, in general."

"It's difficult to do in the winter," she said. "Cold hands, slippery rocks, big boots. But there are some nice spots around here if you come back in the summer. We could go." She rolled over to face him. Her hands smoothed over his chest and she placed a kiss at the base of his neck. "You should try kayaking. And hiking at Rock Island is fun. But that's all summer stuff. We could snowshoe. Have you ever been snowshoeing? I'll take you tomorrow if you'd like."

"Interesting," he said.

"It is." She sighed, then rolled on top of him, stretching her naked body along the length of his. "And then there's sex. Sex is a year-round thing in Door County." Her lips found his and she gave him a sweet kiss.

Was it possible she was the perfect woman? He'd always imagined his ideal mate to be tall and blonde and eager to please. And though Tenley did excel in the bedroom, she did it on her own terms. There was no question about who was in control. Maybe he'd been looking for the wrong perfect woman.

"Is there anything you wouldn't try?" he asked.

"Scuba diving," she said. "Being underwater scares me. It would be like drowning alive."

Well, there it was. She wasn't perfect. Alex loved scuba diving. "Interesting," he said.

"You know what would be *really* interesting? If you'd get up and make dinner for us."

"Don't you think you're taking this slave-boy thing a bit too far? Just because I want that contract, doesn't mean you can take advantage of me."

She sat up and clapped her hands, her face lighting up with amusement. "Oh, a slave boy. I've always wanted one of those. I think that's a wonderful idea." Tenley crawled over the covers until she was stretched out alongside him, her head at his feet. She wiggled her toes. "Rub my feet, slave boy."

Alex let his gaze drift along her naked body. Would he ever get enough of her? Though he'd only known her for a few days, he'd come to think of her body as his, as if he were the only one smart enough to see what an incredible woman she was.

Grabbing her foot, he rubbed his thumbs against her arch. "How's that?"

"Oh, that feels so nice."

He pressed his lips to a spot beneath her ankle. "How about that?"

"That's nice, too. But don't stop rubbing."

"So, let me tell you about what we can do for your novel."

"Please don't. I just want to relax. Talking about business makes me nervous."

"Do you plan to fight me on this every step of the way? If this is some plan to drive me crazy so I'll leave, it's not going to work."

"Would sex work?" she asked.

"Sex?"

"Yes. If I seduced you right now, would you be satisfied?"

"I'm always satisfied when you seduce me." Alex picked up her other foot. "What are you afraid of, Tenley? Most artists would jump at the chance to sell their work."

"I don't really know what I'm doing," she said. "I didn't go to art school. I haven't studied writing. I have no technique, no style. I'm afraid if I have to produce something, I'll just…freak out."

"You don't seem like the type to freak out. Besides, some of the greatest writers and artists never went to college. So that excuse doesn't fly. What else?"

"That story was personal. What if I only have one story in me? And now that it's out, there's nothing left."

"No problem. We'll cross that bridge when we come to it. For now, we'll focus on the novel you have written. Anything else?"

"Are you going to work on this book with me?"

"Yes. You'll also have an editor to work with once the contract is signed. But if you want me to stay involved, I will. This imprint is my idea, so I am going to have my fingers in it until it gets up and running."

"So, you and I will be…business associates? And we'll pretend that we've never seen each other naked. And that we've never touched each other in intimate ways."

He chuckled. "That's going to be very difficult to forget."

She sat up, crossing her legs in front of her and resting her arms on her knees. "But how will it work, when I see you? Don't you think it will be strange?"

Alex saw the confusion in her eyes. "Because we've been lovers? I don't know. I guess we're just going to have to make it up as we go along."

To be honest with himself, Alex hadn't really thought about the end of their affair. He wasn't sure why it had to end. The passion they'd shared was real and intense, not something that could be tossed aside without a second thought.

Was Tenley worried she was about to become another notch on his bedpost? Like all those other women who'd registered their complaints on that silly Web site? Sure, he didn't have the best reputation, but where was it written that a guy couldn't change?

"Tenley, I want to get to know you better. I don't want to think this will be over when I go back to Chicago."

A tiny smile twitched at her lips. "Me neither."

"Then let's do it. Let's get to know each other. You start. Ask me any question and I'll answer it. Go ahead."

She regarded him shrewdly. "All right. Do you want to have sex with me all the time, or are there times when you're thinking about something else?"

Alex laughed. This was one instance when he wasn't afraid to be honest. "When you're in the room, I'm pretty much thinking about the next time I'll see you naked. And when you're not close by, I'm thinking about the next time I'll be with you—so I can take off your clothes and see you naked."

"Men think about sex a lot, don't they? Women aren't supposed to think about it."

"Do you?"

"Yes," she said, her voice filled with astonishment. "All the time. When I see you dressed, the first thing I want to do is take your clothes off. I like the way you look. I like your skin and your muscles and your eyes and your hair."

"My turn. Tell me about your favorite fantasy."

Her face softened and her expression grew wistful. "That one is easy. I'm at work and I'm sitting at my desk and the bell above the door rings and there he is. All grown up. He still looks the same, but he's bigger. And it's like it never happened, like he was just gone for a few hours, running errands or having lunch."

He'd expected a sexual fantasy, at least that was what he thought they were talking about. But from the look on her face, he could see the emotional toll the confession was taking. He wanted to stop her, to tell her she misunderstood, yet he was curious to know the truth.

"Your brother?"

She nodded. "I used to have that dream all the time. It would be the only thing that kept the nightmares from becoming unbearable. I'd wake up and I'd be so happy. Sometimes, it was different. I'd be somewhere and I'd see him on the street and I'd run after him. Or I'd be hiking and find him sitting in the woods, all alone."

"What happened, Tenley? How did he die?"

She bit her bottom lip. Her voice wavered when she spoke. "Tommy drowned. In a boating accident," she said. "I'm getting hungry. I think you should fetch us some dinner."

He kissed her gently, satisfied that she'd told him enough for now. "I'm not much of a cook."

"There's a bar in town that makes the best pizza. We can order one and you can go pick it up. And while you're gone, I'll feed the horses and make a fire. Then after supper, we'll take a walk down to the bay."

"That sounds good to me," he said, dropping a kiss on her lips. "And then we'll talk about your book."

"What if I just say 'yes' right now? Then do we have to talk about it tonight?"

"Are you saying yes?" Alex asked.

Tenley nodded. "Yes. Yes, you may publish my silly book, Alex. Yes, I'll sign your contract. As long as we don't have to talk about it for the rest of the night."

Alex held out his hand. "Deal." He paused. "Don't shake unless you mean it. A verbal agreement is legal and binding."

She shook his hand. "Deal. Green olives, green peppers, sausage and mushrooms. And get the eighteen-inch. With extra cheese. And hot peppers on the side."

"Can I get dressed first?" he asked.

Tenley rolled over onto her stomach, her legs crossed at the ankles. "As long as I can watch. But do it really slowly."

He got up and began to retrieve his clothes from where they were scattered on the floor. Tenley followed his movements, a brazen grin on her face. "Stop staring at me," he teased, repeating the words she'd said to him their first night together.

"In the summer, I live without clothes."

"Really?"

"I walk down to the bay and climb down the cliffs and take off all my clothes and lie on the rocks in the sun. Sometimes sailboats go by and see me, but I don't care."

Alex could picture her, walking through the forest like a wood nymph, her long, pale limbs moving gracefully through the lush undergrowth. He'd be back in the summer to see that, making a silent promise to himself.

"Why don't you come with me to this bar? We'll eat there. Maybe have a few drinks. Then we'll come back and I'll help you feed the horses."

"Would this be a date?" Tenley asked.

"Yes," Alex said. "This would be a date."

"Then I accept," she said. She jumped up and ran from the bedroom to the bathroom. "I'll have to make myself pretty."

"No," he said. "I like you just the way you are." There was nothing at all he'd want to change about Tenley. And Alex found that fact quite amazing.

TENLEY GRABBED the pitcher of beer from the bar and walked over to the table she and Alex had chosen. He followed behind her with two empty glasses and a basket of popcorn. Before she sat down, he pulled her chair out for her and Tenley sent him a playful smile.

"Your mother taught you well," she said.

"My great-grandmother," he corrected. "She was from the old country. She learned English by reading Emily Post and she somehow got the idea that all Americans had to act that way. Usually Greek families are loud and boisterous. We're loud, but unfailingly polite. You should hear our conversation around the table at Easter."

"My parents didn't believe in social conventions. They let us run wild. We were allowed to say and do anything we wanted. As I look back on it, I'm not sure that was good. It's cute in children, but people think it's weird in adults."

"I think you turned out just fine," Alex said.

Tenley loved the little compliments he paid her. She'd often thought a good boyfriend would work hard to make her happy. And Alex seemed to do that naturally, as if his only thought was to please her. "Do you have a girl-friend?" she asked.

The words just popped out of her mouth and an instant later, she wanted to take the question back. Yet her curiosity overwhelmed her. How could a guy like Alex be single? He was smart and funny and gorgeous. And there were a lot of women in Chicago who would consider him a great catch.

"No," he replied. "I don't really get into long-term re-lationships. I date a lot of different women, but no one seriously."

"I see," Tenley said. Though it was exactly what she wanted to hear—he was unattached—she wasn't sure she liked the fact that he dated "a lot" of women. Was she just the latest of many? "But do you sleep with them?"

"On occasion," he said in a measured tone. "What about you?"

"I don't sleep with women, especially women who've dated you. Although there was a rumor going around town that I preferred girls."

"Do you?" Alex asked.

"I started the rumor. I got tired of every single man in town asking me out. I don't think there's anything wrong with liking girls. You love who you love. I guess if you're lucky enough to find that, it shouldn't make a difference."

"I guess not," Alex said. "I've been thinking that I might be missing out. Maybe I should try the whole relationship thing. See how it goes."

"I wouldn't be any good at that," Tenley said. "I have

too much baggage. Everyone says so. They say my last name should be Samsonite."

Alex laughed, but Tenley had never found the comment particularly funny. She couldn't help how she felt. Putting on a sunny face and pretending she was happy seemed like a waste of energy.

But this was the first time she'd been out in ages, and she was with a man she found endlessly intriguing. And tonight, they'd go home and crawl into her bed and make love. Tenley had to admit, for the first time in a long time, she was genuinely happy.

"Who is that guy over there?" Alex asked, pointing toward the bar. "He's giving me the evil eye."

Tenley glanced over her shoulder, then moaned. "Oh, that's Randy. He's in love with me."

"Really?" Alex's eyebrow shot up. "He doesn't seem like your type."

"He thinks he's in love with me," Tenley corrected. "He's had a crush on me since high school and every year about this time, he asks me out to the Valentine's Day dance at the firehouse. And every year, I say no."

"You'd think he'd get the message," Alex said.

"He's kind of thick-headed," Tenley explained. She looked at Randy again, then quickly turned around. "He's coming over here. Maybe we should leave."

"No!" Alex said. "We have just as much right to be here as he does. Besides, I'm hungry and they haven't brought our pizza yet."

"Hello, Tenley."

She forced a smile as she looked up. He really wasn't such

a bad guy. Except for the fact that he was in love with her. "Hello, Randy."

He shifted nervously, back and forth on his feet. "How have you been doing? I haven't seen you in a while. I heard you had breakfast at the Bean this morning. I thought you didn't like that place."

"News travels fast." Randy had probably heard about the kiss as well, but Tenley wasn't going to get into that. "Randy, this is Alex Stamos. Alex, Randy Schmitt."

Alex got to his feet and held out his hand, but Randy refused to take it, turning his attention back to Tenley. "Can I talk to you for a second?"

"Randy, I'm not sure that—"

"Just for a second. Over there." He pointed to the far end of the bar.

Tenley looked at Alex and he shrugged. "All right." She pushed back in her chair and stood. "Just for a second."

Randy held on to her elbow as they wove through the patrons at the restaurant. Tenley was aware of the gazes that followed them and she knew what they were thinking. It was the opinion of most of the folks in town that Randy was just about the only man who'd be interested in marrying Tenley Marshall. Though Tenley had never given him any encouragement, he persisted with his belief that they were destined to be together.

In truth, Tenley felt a bit sorry for Randy. It must be horrible to love someone who couldn't love you back. She'd made sure to harden her heart against love, but Randy wore his on his sleeve.

"What are you doing with that guy?"

"It's not what you think," she said. "He's just a friend."

"A friend you kiss at the breakfast table. And rumor has it that he spent the night out at your place. Jesse said he pulled the guy's car out of the ditch after you took him home. Now, I can understand that a girl like you might be attracted to a big-city guy like him, but he's all wrong for you, Tenley. He won't make you happy the way I will."

"Randy, you have to give this up. I don't love you. I'm not going to suddenly change my mind one day and marry you. You need to find someone else."

"I know those flatlanders," he said. "They flash around their money and think they can take whatever they want."

His attitude wasn't uncommon. Though the locals appreciated the money that tourists brought in, they didn't like them encroaching on their territory—especially their women.

"Randy, I'm going to go back and sit down. I suggest you finish your beer and go home."

"Hell, no! I've been waiting around for you all these years, thinking that sooner or later, you'd get your act together and see what's standing right in front of you. I'm the one who loves you, not him. He'll go back to Chicago and I'll be here. You'll see."

"But I don't love you," Tenley insisted. "I'm sorry." Frustrated, she turned to walk away. But Randy grabbed her arm and wouldn't let go.

"If you'd just give us a chance, I know I could—"

"Hey, buddy, let her go."

Tenley closed her eyes at the sound of Alex's voice. One moment, he'd been watching them from the table and the next, he was behind her. "I knew we should have had pizza at home," she muttered.

Alex grabbed Randy's wrist. "I mean it. Let her go."

"Get the hell out of here," Randy snarled. "You can't tell me what to do. I'm not your goddamned buddy, buddy."

"I will tell you what to do when you're making an ass out of yourself. She's not interested. Didn't you hear her?"

The next few seconds passed in a blur. Randy slapped at Alex's hand and accidentally hit Tenley in the head. Alex shoved Randy, Randy took a swing at Alex, and Tenley reacted. Without thinking, she drew back her fist and hit Randy squarely in the nose.

Blood erupted from his left nostril as he stumbled back and knocked down a waitress with a tray full of drinks. "I'm sorry, I'm sorry," Tenley cried. "I didn't mean to do that." She held on to Alex to keep him from jumping on top of Randy, yet at the same time tried to help Randy to his feet.

"Tenley Marshall, I'm going to have to take you in." Harvey Willis stepped into the middle of the fight, his considerable girth creating a wall between Alex and Randy. The police chief's napkin was still stuffed in his collar and he was holding his fork in his right hand.

"This was not her fault," Alex protested. "She was just defending herself."

"You pipe down or I'll take you in, too. She wasn't defending herself, she was defending you. Now, I can understand how that might piss Randy off, seeing as how you're not from around here. But punching a guy in the face is assault. And doing it in a restaurant full of people is just bad manners."

"I don't want to press charges," Randy said, holding his flannel shirt up to his nose.

"Well, we'll sort that out down at the station. Tenley, you'll come with me. Your flatlander friend can follow us. Randy, you can walk off the pitcher of beer you drank. The exercise will do you good. Let's go." He nodded to the bartender. "They'll be back later to settle up, Bert. And pack up my pizza for me. I'll send Leroy back to get it."

Tenley struggled into her jacket as she walked out the front door. Harvey's cruiser was parked out front in a No Parking zone. "You can get in front," he said. "I don't think you're going to try any funny business, are you?"

"No," Tenley said. "I don't know why you're blaming me for this. You saw Randy start it. He just won't give up."

When they were both in the car, Harvey turned to her and shook his finger. "Tenley Marshall, you know how that man feels about you. Still, you decide to parade your out-of-state boyfriend in front of him and the whole town. How do you think he's supposed to react?"

"Alex Stamos is not my boyfriend. And I've made it perfectly clear to Randy that I don't have feelings for him. *And,* this is the big one, I didn't realize Randy was there. Had I known, we would have gone somewhere else."

"Well, since this Alex fella has come to town, people have been worried for you. You're not acting the way you usually do."

Tenley's temper flared. "Maybe if everyone would just mind their own business, I could get on with my life."

"Is that what you've been doing? I just think it's a little funny you've been hiding away like a hermit for years and then he rolls into town and you're suddenly a social butterfly. He seems to be the slick sort and you're falling for his tricks."

"Let's go," she muttered. "I'd really like to take care of this before it causes any more gossip."

"Oh, well, I think that horse is out of the barn already," Harvey replied.

They drove the three short blocks to the police station and by the time Tenley got out of the car, Alex was standing at the door, waiting for her, pacing back and forth. "Is she going to need a lawyer?" he asked. "Because if you're going to charge her with anything, then I want to get her a lawyer."

"Oh, just pipe down," Harvey said. "We're going to fill out a report, she's going to pay a fine and then you'll be on your way. We don't tolerate physical violence here, unlike what goes on in the big cities."

"He's the one who grabbed her first. She was trying to get away when I stepped in. And then he took a swing at me."

"I know. I saw the whole thing. So did half the town. But Tenley drew blood, so she's going to have to pay the fine."

As they walked into the lobby, Tenley turned to Alex. "Wait here. I'll be out in a few minutes. And don't start things up again with Randy. He's drunk and he has at least fifty pounds on you. Besides, Harvey treats outsiders a lot more harshly than townies."

True to Harvey's word, the matter was dispatched by filling out a short report and paying a small fine. Since Tenley didn't have fifty dollars in her wallet, Harvey agreed to let her come in the following morning with the money.

By the time they finished, Randy had arrived and was sitting glumly in the reception area across from Alex, staring at him with a sulky expression. Harvey motioned to him and he approached Tenley with a contrite smile. "I don't want to press charges," he insisted.

"Randy, my boy, you need to move on with your life," Harvey said. "Tenley's not interested. There's nothing more pathetic than a guy who won't take no for an answer. You bother her again and I'll toss your ass in jail. By the way, Linda Purnell has been in love with you for going on three years. If I were you, I'd give her a second look." He paused, then directed his gaze at Alex. "As for you, I'm going to be watching you. You keep your nose clean and you and me won't have any problems."

Alex stood and held out his hand to Tenley. "Thank you. We'll just be going now."

When they got outside, Alex dragged her toward his rented SUV. "What the hell was that?"

Tenley laughed. "Next time, when I suggest pizza at home, maybe we should just stay home and forget all this dating stuff."

"No," Alex said stubbornly. "Tomorrow night, we're going on a damn date. And you're going to wear a pretty dress and I'm going to take you to a nice restaurant, and we're going to have a pleasant evening that doesn't involve jealous ex-boyfriends and bloody noses."

"He was not my boyfriend," Tenley insisted.

Alex yanked open the passenger-side door. "Well, I *am* your boyfriend, and if we have to drive to Green Bay to get some privacy, we will."

ALEX STARED OUT the window of the tower studio, taking in the view of the bay beyond the trees. Tenley was seated at the drawing table, a pad of paper in front of her. "All right," she said. "I'm ready. Fire away."

"This isn't supposed to be painful," Alex said. "We're working together on this. To make your novel better."

"Why don't you just give me the list and I'll look it over and we can discuss it later."

"Because I want you to understand what we need before you sign the contract. So there are no misunderstandings."

"Take off your shirt," she said.

Alex cursed beneath his breath. "I'm not going to let you change the subject again, Tenley. Whenever you don't want to do something, you try to seduce me."

"I'm not going to seduce you, I want to try drawing you. So take off your shirt. And the rest of your clothes while you're at it."

"Tenley, this isn't going to get you—"

"Slave boy, you're not listening. I feel the need to draw you and you're supposed to do everything in your power to please me."

This was getting to be a pattern with the two of them, although Alex really couldn't be too upset. What man would grow impatient with a woman who wanted sex as much as he did? They did have the entire day to work on her novel. He could give her an hour or two of forced nudity as long as it was followed by more pleasurable activities.

"First of all, we need to have an understanding," he said. "This can't end up like one of those sex videos that everyone gets to see. This is for your own private viewing pleasure. Agreed? This will not end up on the Internet."

Hell, he'd had enough trouble from scorned girlfriends. Adding naked drawings to the mix would probably send his mother right over the edge.

"I won't even give you a face. Unless people recognize other parts of you, you'll be completely anonymous."

Reluctantly, Alex stripped out of his clothes, then stood and waited while Tenley gathered the things she needed. When she was ready, she took a deep breath. "All right. Turn around and brace your hands against that post. And lean into it."

He did as she ordered. With his back to her, all he could hear was the occasional rustle of paper and a few soft curses from Tenley. His arms were beginning to grow stiff and his shoulders tight when she finally spoke again.

"There. I think I'm done."

He turned around and she held up the sketchpad. Though Alex didn't know a lot about art, he knew the drawing was beautifully rendered, every muscle perfectly shaded. "Wow."

"You're hot," she said. "I'm not sure I got your butt right. But it's a decent first attempt."

"Tenley, it's better than decent. It's very good."

"You really think so?" She stared at the sketch. "You

know, I've been thinking maybe I should take some classes. The university in Green Bay has an art program."

With any other woman, he might have turned on the charm and lavished compliments to soothe her insecurities. But as he grew to care about Tenley, Alex realized that they needed to have honesty between them.

"There are great art schools in Chicago, too," he said. "And you're good enough to get into a top-notch program, Tenley. Sure, you haven't had a lot of experience, but you do have talent."

"I couldn't move," she said distractedly, her attention still focused on her sketch. "My grandfather is here. He needs my help. Besides, I have my cabin and my animals. I couldn't bring them to Chicago."

Though Alex had considered what the future might hold for them, he'd never really appreciated her ties to this place. She was living in a paradise and he couldn't blame her for not wanting to leave. He'd only spent a few days here and he didn't want to leave either. What was Chicago compared to the beauty of this place?

"They have seminars at the Art Institute. You could come for a few days. Meet everyone at the office. Maybe do some publicity shots. You could stay with me."

"I want to try another pose," she said, changing the subject. "Turn to the side and lean back against the post." She stared at him for a long moment. "Put your right leg forward a bit and then hold on to the post with your left hand."

For the next hour, she sketched, posing him in different positions and then quickly completing the drawing. She tossed aside the pencil for charcoal and then switched to pastels.

"All right," she finally said. "You can get dressed."

"You're finished?"

Tenley stared at the drawings scattered across her table. "I think I can do this," she said breathlessly. "I'm not as bad as I thought I was."

"You're sure you want me to get dressed?"

Tenley grinned. "Yes. Well, only if you want to. If you prefer to work like that, then you can stay naked."

"We're going to work now?"

"Yes," she said in a gloomy voice. "You're going to tell me what's wrong with my novel and I'm going to try to fix it." She jumped up. "You do need to get dressed. It's too distracting having you sitting around here naked." She walked over to him and smoothed her hand from his belly to his cock.

Alex groaned as he closed his eyes, waiting for the involuntary reaction that came from her touch. Though he wanted nothing more than to make love to her, he had a choice to make. She was willing to talk business now. So sex would have to wait until later.

Turning away from her touch, Alex pulled on his boxers and jeans and then slipped into his shirt, not bothering to button it. "All right. The first thing, and this is going to be big—we're going to have to redraw everything. Your friend has the original, but even that is a little too rough. We're going to print at a high resolution, so everything has to be very clean."

"That's going to take a long time. I'd have to draw it oversized in order to get it just perfect."

"No, we'll scan it into a computer and have our graphic artist clean it up. But there are some parts that will need additional drawings and changes to the story."

Tenley took a deep breath. "Why don't we start with those changes first?"

Alex pulled up a stool and sat down next to her. He grabbed her hand. He pressed a kiss to the back of her wrist. This was actually going to happen. Tenley was going to sell her book to him and he was going to make her famous. He was also going to make her a lot of money. But it wasn't that thought that thrilled him. It was the fact that he and Tenley would always have a connection.

Over the next two hours, they worked together, going over the editor's notes, discussing the production process, arguing about the plot and drawings needed to flesh out the story.

For the first time since Alex arrived, he saw Tenley excited about the possibility of her novel being published. And he was grateful he was the one to make it happen. It was so easy to make her happy. It didn't require a huge bank account or a fancy apartment or the promise of a comfortable life or social status, things the other women he knew were always searching for.

Tenley responded to kindness and encouragement. Something terrible must have happened to make her so unsure of herself, Alex mused. Though he only knew the barest details of her brother's death, he was determined to learn more.

He wanted to know every tiny detail of her life, everything that made her the woman she was. He wanted to be the man who understood her the best. He wanted to be the man she turned to when she felt frightened or overwhelmed or lonely.

Making himself indispensable to Tenley Marshall was a huge task. But Alex was afraid of the consequences if he didn't. For it was becoming more and more evident that Tenley needed to be a permanent part of his life.

chapter six

TENLEY rubbed her eyes, then pinched them shut. She knew she ought to just set the work aside and get some sleep, but every time she closed her eyes, doubts began to plague her.

It was simple to feel good about herself when Alex was standing behind her, cheering her on. But without him, all her insecurities rushed back. How would she ever do this on her own? Nothing she drew would ever be good enough. She'd always find fault.

Tossing the drawing pad on the floor, she flopped back into the leather sofa. This was entirely his fault. Until she'd taken him home during the storm, she'd been perfectly happy with her life. She found her work at her grandfather's gallery satisfying and her free time was spent in relaxing pursuits, not frantically trying to make something out of nothing.

Grabbing the throw from the back of the sofa, she lay

down and tucked it up around her chin, staring at the dying embers of the fire. She felt caught in a familiar dream. Tommy was on the phone and he was trying to tell her where he was. She'd scribbled down the directions, but they'd be wrong, so she'd start, again and again and again, never getting it quite right.

Her heart would begin to race and her hands would sweat as she became more and more frantic. Finally, faced with her ineptitude, he'd hang up. She felt tears press at the corners of her eyes. Would she ever be able to let go of what had happened? Somehow, Tenley knew her guilt over her brother's death was holding her back. She couldn't change the past, but was she strong enough to change her future?

Alex had put his trust and faith in her abilities as an artist and a writer. He claimed she had a real talent. Tenley had heard those words a million times from her parents and from her grandparents, but she'd never believed them. They were merely trying to make her whole again.

But Alex was a stranger, someone who didn't know about her past. He could be objective. She pushed up on her elbow and stared at the crumpled paper scattered on the floor. She'd just have to try again.

"Tenley?"

She sat up and watched as Alex wandered through the kitchen and into the great room. "I'm here."

"What time is it? What are you doing up?"

"I was just working. Trying to figure out these new scenes for my story."

He stood in front of her, his naked body gleaming in

the soft light from the fire. He ran his hand through his hair, then sighed. "Is everything all right?"

"Sure," she said. Tenley felt emotion well up in her throat, but she swallowed it back. "Everything is fine."

He sat down beside her, slipping his arm around her shoulders. "Sweetheart, don't worry about this. I don't expect you to finish it in one night. Or one month. You can take your time. I'll wait."

A tear slipped from the corner of her eye and she quickly brushed it away before he could see. But from his worried expression, Tenley could tell she hadn't been quick enough. "Sorry," she said, shaking her head. "I'm just exhausted."

"Talk to me."

"It's nothing. I'm just having a little meltdown. I'm tired and cranky and frustrated."

"Go ahead," he said. "You can melt in front of me if you want."

Another tear slipped from her eye, but this time she let it run down her cheek. "Really?"

He nodded, then pulled her closer. Tenley sobbed as the tears suddenly broke through her defenses. Nuzzling her face into his naked chest, she let them fall, the emotion draining out of her with each ragged breath.

For Alex's part, he simply sat beside her, smoothing his hand over her hair and whispering soft words against her temple. She clung to him as tightly as she could, as if his presence would somehow save her from her feelings. Then, slowly, the sadness dissolved, replaced by relief and resignation. She'd allowed her emotions to overwhelm her and she'd survived.

"Better?" he asked.

Tenley nodded. "God, I feel like such a dope. Look at this mess. I couldn't sleep and I just worked myself into a panic." She pressed her hand against his chest and looked up into his eyes. "I don't know why you like me. I'm a mess."

"You're not a mess," he said.

"I've made so many mistakes in my life, Alex. I let so much slip away. I should have listened to my parents. I should have gone to college. I should have studied art. Everything would have been different."

"But maybe not better," Alex said.

"What do you mean?"

"That story you wrote came from your life as it was, from the pain you felt at the time. If you'd done things differently, that story might never have come out."

She sniffled, brushing at her damp cheeks. "I don't know. I tried to be strong, but it was so much easier to just avoid thinking about it. I didn't want to make my parents happy, I didn't want to plan for my future. I just wanted to grieve. And I did, in the only way I knew how."

"That was the right thing for you to do, Tenley. You have to let these things take their natural course. You can't be something you aren't."

"My life should have begun when I graduated from high school or college. But it feels like it's beginning now. And that scares me. I'm twenty-six years old."

"It doesn't scare me. You can hold on to me as long as you need to."

"You're a really nice guy," she murmured, pressing a kiss to his chest. "Did anyone ever tell you that?"

"No. I think you're the first."

Tenley laughed. "Really?"

"You're the only one that matters," he said in a quiet voice. Alex took her hand and pressed a kiss to her palm. "Come on. Leave this for later and come back to bed."

Tenley shook her head. She'd only lie awake and stare at the ceiling until dawn. She needed something to occupy her mind. "I won't be able to sleep."

"I know what will relax you," he said. Alex stood and pulled her to her feet. "A nice, hot bath."

"You're going to give me a bath?"

"Well, I thought we'd give each other a bath. Then we'd go back to bed and sleep until we couldn't sleep anymore."

Intrigued by the suggestion, Tenley followed him to the bathroom and sat on the toilet seat as he filled the old claw-foot tub. She fetched her shampoo and soap from the shower stall and grabbed a washcloth from the rack on the wall.

When the tub was full, Alex undressed her, pulling her T-shirt off over her head and skimming her pajama bottoms to the floor. He held her hand as she stepped over the edge and slowly settled herself.

Then she leaned forward and held out her hand. "There's room for you, too."

Alex stepped in behind her, her body tucked neatly between his thighs. She leaned back against his chest and closed her eyes. "This is perfect."

"Yeah, it is," he said. "I need to get a bathtub at my apartment. A big one, just like this."

"Tell me about your place," she said.

"I live in a two-flat in Wicker Park," he said. "I have the

second and third floor and I have tenants who live down-stairs. It's an old house, built at the turn of the century. But I've renovated it inside. It's comfortable, but it's not as nice as this." He ran his hands through her hair. "This is like a home. It's warm and cozy. I like it here."

"When do you have to go back?" she asked.

"I was supposed to leave for a vacation in Mexico on Wednesday, but I missed my flight. I was planning to be gone through Monday, so I guess I'd have to leave Monday night?"

"That gives us four more days," she said.

"And three more nights," he said. "Doesn't seem like a long time, does it?"

"I'm sorry you had to miss your vacation," Tenley said.

"I'm not. This is the best vacation I've ever had."

She turned over, pressing her palms to his chest as she looked into his eyes. When she'd first met Alex, he'd been so charming, it had been difficult to believe anything he said. But now, as she lay in his arms, Tenley saw the real man beneath the charm, the sweet, considerate, affectionate guy that every girl wanted.

"I could fall asleep in this tub."

"Don't do that. You'd wake up all wrinkled." He scooped water into his hands and poured it over her hair, smoothing the damp strands away from her face. "There. I like you just like this."

"How is that?"

"With your hair out of your face, so I can see your pretty blue eyes and your perfect nose." He bent closer and kissed her, tracing the shape of her mouth with his tongue. "And your lips."

"Do you realize that we've only known each other for just over three days?" Tenley asked.

"No, it's been longer than that," he said.

"Monday night. It's Friday morning."

He seemed stunned by the revelation. "That's…amazing." Alex drew in a sharp breath, then grabbed her hips. "Sit up. I'll wash your hair."

Tenley chuckled. "Slave boy has returned."

"Your wish is my command," he said, grabbing the bottle from the floor next to the tub. He tipped her head back and rubbed a small amount of the shampoo into her hair. "I think I need to get some of this. So when I'm back home, I can smell it and think of you."

It was difficult to imagine what her life would be like once he left. He'd changed everything for her. He'd carved out a place in her world and he fit perfectly. She had four days and three nights to prepare herself—to convince herself she could live without him.

It would be difficult to do when every moment they spent together seemed to be more perfect than the last. But Alex had taught her one thing. She was a lot stronger than she'd thought she was.

ALEX PUSHED OPEN the front door of The Coffee Bean and scanned the crowd inside, looking for Tenley's grandfather. He'd stopped by the gallery, only to find a note on the door indicating that Tom had gone to breakfast. Alex didn't know Sawyer Bay well, but he knew the best place for breakfast was The Coffee Bean.

Tom was sitting at a table with Harvey Willis, the two

of them in deep discussion. Alex hesitated before he approached, knowing that the town police chief didn't have a high opinion of him.

"Morning," Alex said.

Harvey grinned. "Well, there he is. Were your ears burning? You've been the subject of some wild speculation 'round town."

"I'm sure I have," Alex replied.

Harvey got to his feet and indicated his empty chair. "Have a seat. It's all warmed up for you. Tom, nice talking to you. Thanks for the donation. Your pictures always bring a pretty penny in our raffle."

"Thanks, Harvey. I'll talk to you later."

Alex rested his hands on the back of the chair. "Mind if I sit?" he asked.

"Not at all. I've been expecting a visit from you. Would you like some coffee?" He twisted in his chair. "Audrey, bring us another cup of coffee, would you?"

The waitress nodded, then hurried over with a full pot and another menu. "What can I get you?"

Alex scanned the choices, then pointed to the Lumberjack Breakfast. It was what Tenley had ordered the last time they dined at The Coffee Bean. He was beginning to understand her point. After the previous night's activities in her bed, he was ravenous.

"So, I suppose you're here to discuss Tenley," Tom said. "You're worried she might not want to go through with this?"

Alex shook his head. "No. She's agreed to the contract. We're going to publish her novel."

Tom grinned and clapped his hands. "I knew it. I knew something was going on with her."

"Going on?"

"Tenley has had a very hard time of it these past years. Lots of sadness in her life."

"Tell me about that," Alex said. "I know her brother died, that he drowned. And that it made her shut herself off to everyone around her. But that's all I know."

Tenley's grandfather took a slow slip of his coffee. "I'm not going to tell you anything. If Tenley wants you to know, she'll tell you. And if she does talk about it, then I think she's really ready to move on." He sighed. "If you feel a need to know, anyone in town can fill you in. Or you can read about it in the old newspapers at the library. May 15, 1999. That's when it happened." He paused. "But if I were you, I'd want to know her side of the story first. If she trusts you enough to tell you, then I think you might be the kind of man she needs in her life."

"I think I want to be that man," Alex said. "But I'm a little worried. I've gotten to know Tenley—her feelings can shift in the blink of an eye."

"Are you in love with her, Alex?"

He was surprised by the direct question. But then, it was clear where Tenley had gotten her plainspoken curiosity. "I don't know," he admitted. "I've never been in love before. I'm not quite sure how it's supposed to feel."

"I'd appreciate it if you'd be very careful with her heart. It was broken once and I'm not sure she'll be able to survive having it broken again."

"I won't hurt her," Alex said. "I can promise you that. But I can't guarantee she won't break my heart."

"She's a piece of work, isn't she?" Tom chuckled. "Oh, you should have seen the two of them. They were a pair. When they were born, their parents put them in separate cribs and they screamed until they were together again. After that, Tenley and Tommy were inseparable. When they started to talk, their words were gibberish to everybody else. They had their own language. No one understood it except the two of them." He reached into his back pocket and pulled out his wallet. "See. There they are. This was their tenth birthday."

Alex examined the photo. Tenley hadn't changed much. The dark hair and the pale blue eyes, the delicate limbs. "She was cute."

"After Tommy died, my son and his wife couldn't handle the grief. They grew apart, separated, and then decided to divorce. Tenley was uncontrollable, angry, lashing out at anyone who tried to get close. They ended up leaving, but she just flat-out refused. So she lived with her grandmother and me. I thought it was good she wanted to get back to her normal life, but that's not what happened. A few years later, I found out the reason she stayed was because she thought he might come back. That the body they found wasn't really his and that he was alive."

"She's been waiting all this time?"

"She has. But I think she's stopped waiting for Tommy. I think maybe she's been waiting for you. Or someone like you. Someone she could trust. Someone who could give her the same confidence that her brother gave her. I think you've done that for her, Alex. And no matter what happens between the two of you, you need to respect that."

Alex had always shied away from commitment in the past, but this time, he wanted to make all the promises necessary to ensure Tenley's happiness. "I care about her. But if publishing this novel is going to hurt her in some way, I'll turn around and go back to Chicago today."

"No," Tom said. "I think you might be the best thing that's ever happened to her."

Alex smiled. "She's a very talented artist. And an incredible storyteller. I just want readers to see that."

"She and her brother used to draw cartoons all the time. After he died, she just stopped drawing. This is a big step for her. Don't do anything to mess it up, all right?"

"You can trust me," Alex said.

Tom's eyebrow arched up and he fixed Alex with a shrewd stare. "Can I? Will you stick with her, even when she's trying her damnedest to push you away? Because she will, you know. She'll find some excuse to run away and do everything to make you hate her."

"I think I can deal with that," he said, frowning. "I've used that technique myself on occasion." How many women had he charmed then ignored when he grew bored with the relationship? Except for the motivations, what Tenley did wasn't much different.

"You're taking on trouble," Tom warned. "But I'd venture to say the reward will be well worth the battle." He held up his coffee cup in a mock toast. "I wish you luck, young man."

They passed the rest of their time discussing Tenley's

novel and what kind of opportunities publication would offer her. Alex was glad for Tom's insight into Tenley's behavior. Though there were moments when he thought he knew her well, he realized she was like a puzzle. Each individual piece was simple to understand, but it was how the pieces fit together that complicated matters.

When they were finished, Tom paid the bill, then invited Alex back to his studio, anxious to show him photos of Tenley's childhood. But Alex begged off. Tenley had closed herself in the studio at the house, determined to work on her new drawings. And Alex was anxious to see her progress.

But before he went back, he had to pick up his new phone from the Harbor Inn, call the office, then check out of his room at the bed-and-breakfast and move his things to Tenley's cabin. He and Tenley would spend the rest of his vacation together.

He walked back to the inn, where he'd parked the rental, then decided to surrender to his curiosity. He'd seen a sign on Main Street for the local library. It was past ten, so it would probably be open.

As he drove through the snow-covered streets, Alex wondered if it might be best just to let it go. Would it make a difference knowing the whole truth about Tenley's past? It might help him understand her insecurities a little better. And it could explain why it took her all these years to work through her grief.

He parked the SUV in an empty spot on the street and walked the short distance to the library, a small building that looked like it might have once been a bank. A young woman, not much older than Tenley, greeted him from the circulation desk.

"I'm interested in looking at some old newspapers," he said. "From this town, if possible. Back about ten years ago."

"That would be the Sawyer Bay Clarion," she said. "They stopped publishing it two years ago, but back issues can be found in the periodical section. If you want one from any further back than fifteen years, I'll have to go down to the basement and fetch them."

"Thanks," Alex said. He wandered to the back of the building and found the huge books on a shelf near a big library table. May 15th, 1999. He laid the book on the table and flipped through the yellowed pages. The paper was a weekly, so he found the article in the issue dated May 19th.

The headline was huge. LOCAL BOY DROWNS IN BOATING ACCIDENT. The words sent a shiver through him. Tenley had lived through this tragedy. As his gaze skimmed the story, he was stunned to learn that she'd nearly died as well. She'd been clinging to the overturned sailboat for four hours before she'd been found. Her brother hadn't been so lucky.

"It was a tragedy."

Alex glanced over his shoulder to find the librarian standing behind him. "I guess you found what you came for."

"Yes. Did you know them?"

"I went to high school with them both. They were a few grades younger than me, but everyone knows everyone in this town. I think it was the most tragic thing that ever happened in this community. Everyone loved them so much."

"I can't imagine what she went though. But why would they have gone out in bad weather?"

"They were always doing crazy things," she said. "Always getting in trouble. Some folks said it was bound to happen, one of them getting hurt. It's the way they were raised. No one ever said no. There was no discipline. Children need boundaries."

"She blames herself," he said.

"I heard she was the one who talked her brother into going outside the harbor. They were always challenging each other. Dares and double dares and triple dares. Everything was game to them." The librarian shook her head. "She never forgave herself. That's why she's…different."

He slammed the book closed. "I like different," Alex said in a cool tone. He nodded at the librarian and headed back toward the door. "And you can tell everyone in town, if they're wondering."

As he walked back to his SUV, he thought about what it must have been like for Tenley. He was close to his two sisters and couldn't imagine how he'd feel if anything ever happened to one of them. It would be like a part of his soul had been cut away. Not only had Tenley lost her twin brother, she'd probably blamed herself for the breakup of her parents' marriage.

Suddenly, the burden of her happiness seemed like too much to bear. What if he couldn't be the man she needed? What if he failed her in the end? This was all moving so fast. Alex wasn't sure he was ready for it to go any further.

Maybe he shouldn't have pried into the past. It might have been better to remain comfortably oblivious. He got behind the wheel, then turned the key in the ignition. Alex wasn't sure what the future held for the two of them. But if this was love, then he sure as hell was going to give it a chance.

"HAVE YOU SEEN Alex?" Tenley distractedly flipped through the mail, separating the envelopes into bills to be paid and checks to be cashed.

"I did," her grandfather said. "We had breakfast this morning at The Coffee Bean. Had a nice chat. Although I've never seen anyone eat as much for breakfast as he did. Except for you."

Tenley smiled. "I think I'm going to take him snow-shoeing tonight. I love the woods after dark."

"Maybe he's over at the inn."

"He said he had to check in with his office. I hope nothing's wrong." She paused. "You don't think he had to go home, do you?"

"Without telling you? I don't think he'd do that."

"But what if there was an emergency? He could have tried calling me at home and I wasn't there."

"Then he would have called here. Or stopped before he left town. Don't worry, Tennie, he's not going to disap-pear."

The bell above the door rang and she smiled. "That's probably him. I'm just going to drop these at the post office and then I'm going. I promise I'll finish all this up next week."

"We're not exactly going crazy with customers these days," her grandfather said. "Maybe you should think about taking a week or two off. A trip to Chicago might be nice. There's a new impressionist exhibit at the Art Institute."

"I was going to drive into Green Bay. I'm thinking about enrolling in some classes this summer."

"I think that's a fine idea, Tennie. They've been trying to get me to come in and teach a class in acrylics. We could drive in together."

She gave her grandfather a quick kiss, then hurried out into the showroom, anxious to see Alex. But when she walked through the door, it was Randy who was waiting for her. Tenley stopped short. "What are you doing here?"

He gave her a sheepish shrug. "I came to apologize for the other night."

"You don't need to apologize."

"I do," Randy said. "And I'm sorry for being such a pest. But I've loved you for as long as I can remember. I've never said that to you and right now, I'm pretty sure it won't make any difference, but I had to say it."

"I'm sorry," Tenley said, shaking her head. "I don't feel the same way."

"And you may hate me for this, but I don't care." He held out a manila envelope. When she refused to take it, he set it on a nearby table. "I think you should know about this guy from Chicago. I did a little research on the Internet and he's not everything you think he is."

"Take it back," Tenley demanded, a defensive edge in her voice. "I don't need to see it." Cursing softly, she crossed the room and picked up the envelope, then shoved it at Randy. But he refused to touch it. Tenley ripped it in half and then in half again. "Go," she ordered. "Before I punch you in the nose again."

Randy slipped out the door and Tenley glanced down at the scraps in her hands. Her fingers were trembling and she wanted to scream. What right did he have to interfere in her life? People in this town spent too much time worrying about others. They ought to spend more time worrying about their own lives.

"Wasn't that Alex?"

Tenley spun around, her heart skipping a beat. "No."

"A customer."

"It was just Randy Schmitt. He wanted to drop something off for me." She held up the scraps. "It wasn't important." Tenley shoved the papers into her jacket pocket, then picked up the mail that she'd dropped on the floor. "I'll see you later. If Alex stops in, tell him I went home."

Tenley hurried out the door, anxious to leave all thoughts of her encounter with Randy behind. As she strode up the sidewalk to the post office, she passed several people she knew. They smiled and said hello and Tenley returned the greeting.

Usually people avoided her gaze, knowing she wouldn't respond. But things had changed over the past few days. Whatever they thought was going on between her and Alex suddenly made her "normal" again.

The odd thing was, she felt normal. She wanted to smile, even though she was still furious with Randy. In truth, lately, she found herself smiling for no reason at all. She picked up her pace as she walked and the next person she passed, Tenley made it a point to say hello first.

When she got to the post office, she made polite conversation with the postmaster and when she walked out, she held the door open for Mrs. Newton, the English teacher at the high school.

By the time she got back to her Jeep, parked beside the gallery, Tenley felt as if she'd accomplished something important. Though Sawyer Bay could be a difficult place to live, it also had its advantages.

She reached in her jacket pocket for her keys, but found the scraps of Randy's envelope instead. She pulled them out and searched for a trash can that wasn't covered with snow. In the end, she got in her car and set them on the seat beside her.

But her curiosity got the best of her. What had Randy found that warranted a personal visit and a plain manila envelope? All manner of possibilities came to mind. Alex Stamos was a criminal, a happily married man, a porn star.

Well, porn star wouldn't be that difficult to believe considering his prowess in bed. But criminals usually didn't run publishing companies. And she was pretty confident that Alex wasn't married. Maybe he'd been married in the past?

Though that really wouldn't change her feelings for him, she had to wonder why he wouldn't have mentioned it. She picked the papers out of the envelope and spread them out on the seat, piecing them together one by one.

They were pages printed off a Web site called Smooth-Operators.com. From what Tenley could see, the pages were a file on Alex. Beneath each screen name was a para-graph describing Alex—most of them in very unflatter-ing terms. As she read through them, Tenley realized that these were written by women Alex had dated—and dumped.

As she flipped through the pages, she was stunned at the sheer number of women who had something to say about him. He appeared to be a serial dater. He was known as "The Charmer," a nickname that appeared on the top of each page alongside his photo.

"'Modus operandi,'" she read. "'The Charmer finds more excitement in the chase than he does in what comes later. After he gets you into bed, it's bye-bye and onto the next girl. He can't seem to settle on just one mate because he feels compelled to make every woman fall in love with him. He'll love you and leave you, all in the same night.'"

This didn't seem like the Alex she knew. But then, did she really know him at all?

"'Stay away from this man,'" she read.

If this was Alex, and the picture proved it was, then perhaps she ought to be more careful. Maybe there wouldn't be a future for them after all. Tenley scanned the photos of the women next to the screen names. Every single one of them looked as if they'd stepped out of the pages of a fashion magazine. If they couldn't capture Alex's heart, what made her think she could?

She closed her eyes and leaned back into the seat. Who was she kidding? She and Alex had enjoyed a vacation fling, an affair that was meant to have a beginning and an end. When she'd found him, she'd been willing to settle for just one night. Now, she'd have almost an entire week.

It would have to be enough. After he left, she'd move on with her life. And if they saw each other again, they could enjoy a night or two in bed—no strings, no regrets. Tenley quickly picked up the scraps and shoved them into the glove compartment.

At least her relationship with Alex proved one thing. She was ready to fall in love. And someday, maybe she'd find a man like him, a man who made her feel like she could do anything and be anyone she wanted to be.

chapter seven

THE woods were silent around them. Alex held his breath, listening, waiting for some sound to pierce the night air. But there was nothing, just the dark sky and the bare trees and the moonlight glittering off the snow.

"Wow," he murmured. "In all my life, I'm not sure I've ever heard complete silence." He reached out and found her hand in the dark. "There's always some sort of noise in the city, even when it's quiet. It hums."

"Shh! Hear that?"

He listened and heard the flutter of wings behind them. "What is that?"

"Owl," she said. "Probably got a mouse. There are all kinds of things moving in the woods at night. In the summer, it's like a symphony of sound. But in the winter, the snow muffles everything."

He could barely see the features of her face in the moonlight, but he could hear the smile in her voice.

"What if we get lost?" he said. "Will you protect me from the bears and the wolves?"

"We won't get lost. I know every inch of these woods. Every tree. I grew up here." She turned on the flashlight and began walking again, her snowshoes crunching against the snow. Alex followed her until she stopped at a large tree.

"See," she said, pointing to the trunk. Her gloved finger ran over an arrow carved into the tree, the head pointing down.

"Did you do that?"

Tenley nodded. "Underneath all this snow and about a foot or two of dirt is an old cigar tin. My brother and I buried a time capsule on our eighth birthday. We were going to dig it up when we turned eighteen."

"Did you? Dig it up?"

Tenley shook her head. "I didn't have the heart. I can't even remember what we put inside. Maybe this summer, I'll come here and find out."

"What was he like?"

"He was…like me. In every way. It was like we shared a brain. We knew what the other was thinking all the time. I could look at him and know the next words that were going to come out of his mouth. Some people say twins have a psychic connection. When I come out here sometimes, I can feel him. Does that sound crazy?"

"No," Alex said.

"I just wish I could go back and fix the mistakes I made."

"What mistakes?" Alex knew the answer to his question,

but he wanted her to tell him. And to his surprise, she started talking. Maybe it was the fact that she couldn't see him in the dark or that they were out in the cold, alone.

"It was my idea to go out that night," she began. "I dared him to sail out to the island. He said no, but I wouldn't let it go. I kept picking at him and picking at him until he agreed."

"It's not your fault, Tenley. You were just a kid. You didn't know."

"I did. That's the point. I knew it was dangerous. So did he. But I wanted him to admire me. I wanted him to think I was the most important person in the world. I wanted proof that he loved me the best."

"But he did. You were important to him."

"I wasn't. Not anymore."

"I don't understand."

He heard her draw a ragged breath. "Tommy had a girl-friend. He told me all about her, how much he liked her. How he was going to ask her to go sailing with him that weekend. I knew she'd be afraid to go outside the harbor. But I wasn't afraid. I had to prove to him that I was better than she was."

Alex reached out for her, but she pulled away, stepping back into the darkness. "Tenley, what happened was an accident. You didn't cause it. There's a million and one ways that bad things can happen. A million and one reasons why they do. You didn't create the bad weather, the cold water or the wave that turned over the boat."

"We were out there because of me," she said, bitterness suffusing her tone. "Because I was jealous of some silly girl with blond hair and pretty clothes."

He saw the tears streaming down her face, glittering in the moonlight. Alex wanted to take her into his arms and make everything better. But he knew how much it had cost her to tell him. By trying to brush it away, he would only trivialize her feelings. "What if you had been the one to die that night? What if Tommy had lived? And he'd tortured himself the same way you've been doing? How would you have felt about that?"

"Angry," she said. "But I wouldn't blame him. He'd never do anything to deliberately hurt me."

"Don't you think he knew that about you? Don't you think he realized how much you loved him? He wouldn't want you to spend the rest of your life mourning his death. Hell, I don't know Tommy. But if he was anything like you, he'd tell you to stop acting like such a baby and get on with your life."

Tenley sat down in the snow. "I feel like I'm ready to let it go. But I'm afraid if I do, I'll forget him. And then I won't have anyone."

He squatted down in front of her, reaching out to cup her face in his gloved hands. "You'll have me," Alex said.

"No, I won't. You're leaving in a few days."

"I don't live that far away, Tenley."

"Don't," she murmured, brushing his hands away. "Don't make any promises you can't keep. I'm fine with what we've had. I don't need anything more."

This was it, Alex thought. Her grandfather had warned him it was coming, but he hadn't expected her to turn on him for no reason—and so soon. "What if I do? Need more, I mean."

"I'm sure you'll find plenty of girls eager to take care of your needs."

"Do you think that's what this is about? Sex?"

She stumbled to her feet and brushed the snow off her backside. Then she shone the flashlight in his face. "That's all this was *ever* about. We enjoy each other in bed. There's nothing to be ashamed of."

"I don't believe you," Alex said. "I refuse to believe you don't feel something more."

"What I feel doesn't make a difference. Come on, Alex, be reasonable. We can pretend that we'll see each other again, we might even make plans. But once we're apart, the desire is bound to fade. I can deal with that. Don't worry, I'm not going to fall apart on you."

Alex felt a surge of anger inside of him. She sounded so indifferent, but he knew it was a lie. He had seen it in her eyes, had felt it in the way she touched him. They shared a connection that couldn't be broken with just a few words and a wave goodbye.

"We should go back," she muttered. "I'm getting cold."

He knew what would happen when they returned to the cabin. Tenley would find a way to smooth over their discussion and she'd lure him into bed. And once again, he'd be left certain he was falling in love with her, yet completely unsure of her feelings for him.

Alex had to wonder if he'd ever know how she truly felt. Would she ever be brave enough to admit that she needed him? Or that she wanted someone to share her life? Maybe Tenley was right. Maybe they both ought to just move on.

She pointed the flashlight out in front of them and retraced their steps in the snow. Alex had no choice but to follow her. They walked for a long while in silence, but when he saw the lights from the yard, Alex suddenly regretted giving up his room at the inn.

He wasn't angry with her. He knew why Tenley was pushing him away. But Alex wondered if she could ever fully trust him. Or trust any man. He found it odd that her insecurities didn't come from a series of bad relationships, but from never having experienced a relationship at all.

She'd obviously had sex before. She was far too comfortable in bed. But he suspected she treated sex the same way she treated a hike or a ride in her sleigh—a pleasant activity to pass the time and nothing more. Truth be told, that was the way he'd always approached it as well—until he'd met her.

From the moment he'd first touched her, Alex felt something powerful between them. And sex became more than just physical release—it became a way to communicate his feelings for her. For the first time in his life, he was actually making love.

"I think I'm going to work for a while," Tenley said. "I'll be in later. Don't wait up."

"Fine," he said.

They parted ways on the porch, Alex watching as she walked toward the barn. He ought to pack his bags and leave. Let her see how much she liked her life without him in it. Maybe, with some time apart, she'd actually realize what they'd shared was special.

He unbuckled his snowshoes, then stepped inside to find the dogs waiting. "Go ahead," he said, moving aside. They bounded out into the snow in a flurry of flying feet and wagging tails. He watched them play. Dog and Pup.

She hadn't even bothered to name her dogs. Was she afraid they were going to leave her, too, someday? He wasn't sure what the two cats were named, if they even had names. And as far as she was concerned, he was probably just…Guy or Dude.

Alex had cast aside more women than he cared to count. Why couldn't he bring himself to do the same with Tenley? Instead of being apathetic, he found himself angry. He'd made a difference in her life and she refused to acknowledge it. They were better people together than they were apart.

He saw the light go on in the tower studio and stepped into the shadows of the porch. Tenley appeared in the window overlooking the cabin. He watched as she moved about, remembering the previous afternoon and how she'd talked him out of his clothes.

Alex shook his head, wondering how this would all end. Hell, he couldn't believe it had begun in the first place. Had he not ended up in that snowdrift, none of this would have happened. Eventually, he would have tracked down Tenley, made his proposal and been on his way. On any other day, he might have looked right past her, unaware of the incredible woman she was.

But something had brought them together, some great karmic design, some strange twist of fate. And he had to believe that same force would keep them together, even though she was doing her damnedest to drive them apart.

"IT'S BETTER THIS WAY," Tenley murmured to herself. She paced back and forth across the width of the studio, her nerves on edge, her mind spinning endlessly. She wasn't supposed to fall in love. She'd never meant for it to happen. But now that it had, Tenley needed to find a way to stop herself.

Though she'd heard of people who'd fallen in love at first sight, Tenley never believed it was possible. Lust at first sight, maybe. But love took time to grow. How could you possibly love someone you didn't know?

"That's right," she muttered. "You can't love Alex. You don't even know him."

She pressed her hand to her heart. It wasn't love. But it sure felt like something she'd never experienced before. And she'd never been in love in her life.

Tenley stopped in front of the table and picked up the new drawing she'd done for the second chapter. It was as close to perfect as she could make it and it was good. Even she was proud of the effort, and Tenley was her own worst critic.

The fact that she was able to believe in herself as an artist was Alex's doing. She owed him a huge debt of gratitude. But did she owe him her heart? It seemed to be the only thing he wanted from her. Tenley's heart was a mangled mess, shattered in a million pieces and stuck back together again with duct tape and school paste and chewing gum.

Who would want a heart like that, a heart so close to breaking again? A heart that wasn't strong enough to love. Tenley sat down in her chair and cupped her chin in her hand. Slowly, she flipped through her story.

And it was her story. Cyd was everything she'd wanted

to be—strong, determined, blessed with powers that could alter the past. But as she looked at the pictures she'd drawn, Tenley saw that Cyd was just ink on paper. Every move she made was part of an intricate plot planned out ahead of time. She had all the answers.

Real life was a different matter. Tenley had no control over the plot. There was no plan. Nothing was black and white. Instead, she was left to navigate through a world filled with shades of gray.

Did she love Alex or didn't she? The answer wasn't that simple. Perhaps she had the potential to love him. Maybe there was a tiny part of her that loved him already. But if asked for a yes or no answer, Tenley couldn't give one.

She shoved the papers back and stood, the walls of the studio closing in around her. Grabbing her coat, Tenley ran down the stairs and out into the cold night. She wrapped her arms around herself and tipped her head up to the sky, staring at the stars.

What came next in her story? Would she let it unfold in front of her? Or would she try to manipulate the plot? Though it might be nice to possess a superpower or two, Tenley suspected there was no power in the world that could make Alex love her if he didn't want to. She had to be prepared to let him go and to do it without any regrets.

The snow crunched beneath her boots as she walked back to the cabin. The great room was lit only by the fading fire and the light from above the kitchen sink. Pup and Dog came out to greet her and she gave them both a pat on the head. Tenley tiptoed down the hall and peeked into her bedroom. A stab of disappointment pierced her heart when she saw Alex wasn't waiting in her bed.

The door to the guest room was closed and she could only assume he was sending her a signal. She wasn't welcome. Tenley walked back to the kitchen, her wet boots squeaking on the wood plank floor. She kicked them off at the door and shrugged out of her jacket, tossing it over the back of the sofa.

A survey of the refrigerator yielded nothing interesting to eat, but she felt compelled to munch in an effort to take her mind off the man sleeping in her guest room. They'd spent the past four nights in each other's arms. It didn't seem right, sleeping all alone.

Tenley grabbed an apple from the basket on the counter, then walked back to her bedroom. She took a huge bite, then tossed the apple on the bed and began to remove her clothes. But in the end, exhaustion overwhelmed her and she flopped down, face-first on the sheets, still half-dressed. She found the apple and took another bite, then carefully considered her options.

She could do the sensible thing, crawl beneath the covers of her own bed, close her eyes and pray she'd fall asleep before giving in to her impulses. Or she could do the reckless thing and strip off all her clothes, walk into the guest room and get into bed with Alex. Or she could lie here and think of other options.

The cats were curled up on her pillow and she rolled over and pressed her face into Kittie's fur. Kattie opened her eyes and watched Tenley for a moment, then nuzzled her face into her paws and went back to sleep. This was what she'd be reduced to after Alex left—searching for affection from her pets.

She'd survived on their love before he'd walked into her life. So why did the prospect seem so unsatisfying now? "I love you," she murmured to the cats. "I do." But they didn't open their eyes. "I know you love me. You don't have to say the words. I can tell by the way you're lying there that you love me." She paused. "God, am I pathetic."

With that, Tenley sat up and raked her hands through her hair. Then she grabbed a book from the pile on her bedside table. But as she flipped through the pages, one by one, she couldn't find anything that might occupy her mind. She could bake some cookies. Or clean the fireplace. Or scrub the bathroom floor. Tenley drew a deep breath. Or she could walk into Alex's room and do what she really wanted to do—make love to him for the rest of the night.

She crawled out of bed and tiptoed to his door, then slowly opened it, wincing at the squeaky hinges. The room was dark, the only light coming from the hall. Tenley stood next to his bed, then silently knelt down beside it, her gaze searching his face.

There were times when his beauty took her breath away. Men weren't supposed to be beautiful, but she could look at Alex with an artist's eye and see the perfection of his long limbs and muscled torso. This was the kind of man the Greeks sculpted in ancient times, the epitome of the human form, from his well-shaped hands to his lovely feet.

She thought back to the sketches she'd made of Alex. For the first time in her life, she'd felt like an artist. And she'd understood the need for a muse. Drawing Alex brought out her passion for her art. When she looked at his naked body, everything she saw through her eyes came out on the sketchpad.

Her fingers clenched and she longed for a pencil and pad, wanting to capture this scene in front of her. The frustration she felt earlier was gone and now she felt nothing but regret for her sharp words. He didn't deserve them. Alex had been nothing but kind and encouraging. No matter what those other women claimed, he'd been a perfect gentleman.

Tenley didn't know how much longer this would last. She suspected the feelings might fade once he returned to Chicago. But they still had three more days together. The least she could do was put aside her insecurities and make their moments together count for something.

Holding her breath, Tenley crawled into bed beside him, still dressed in her jeans and long-sleeved T-shirt. She felt him move behind her and then his arms circled around her waist and he pulled her against his body. His soft sigh tickled the back of her neck and a moment later, he pressed his lips to the same spot.

Tenley smiled, holding on to his hands and allowing her body to relax. He didn't need to say a word. Just his touch was enough to know that she'd been forgiven. And though Tenley wanted to strip off her clothes and make love to him, there was something wonderful about just being in his arms, lying next to him in his bed.

They had three more days and two more nights. There would be plenty of time to reignite the passion between them. She closed her eyes and waited for sleep to take the last of her tensions from her body.

But the noise in her head refused to quiet. Tenley drew a deep breath and then let it out slowly, before turning in Alex's embrace. Facing him, she smoothed her hands over his features, memorizing the feel of them in the dark.

When he brushed his mouth against hers, Tenley realized he was awake. She touched her lips to his and slowly the kiss grew deeper and more passionate. But there was an edge of desperation to each caress they shared, as if they both knew that the clock was ticking down on their time together.

With each soft sigh and each whispered word, Tenley grew more frantic to feel him inside her. When he began to undress her, she impatiently tore off her shirt and kicked out of her jeans. Once she was naked, Alex pulled her beneath the sheets, into the warmth of his body.

He was already hard and as he moved against her, his shaft pressed into the soft flesh of her abdomen. This was all she needed in life, this wonderful warm feeling of anticipation. Alex could smooth his hands over her skin and she'd lose herself in a wave of sensation.

There was more at work here than just physical attraction. She ached for that moment when she felt most vulnerable, when their souls seemed exposed. At that instant, the past melted away and Tenley felt alive and aware. Though she'd had men in her bed, not one of them had ever made her feel a fraction of what Alex did.

She reached for the box of condoms on the bedside table, surprised to find just one left inside. He smiled as she smoothed it over the length of his shaft, his breath coming in soft, short gasps.

He rolled her beneath him, then pulled her leg up alongside his hip. Probing gently, he found her entrance and in one sure motion, he slipped inside of her. Tenley groaned at the thrill that raced through her body.

There was nothing in the world that had ever felt this good. And Tenley knew this was what it was like to want a man so much her body ached for his touch and her soul cried out for his love. If this was all she had in the world, she could be happy forever.

But happiness didn't always last. It could be snatched away in the blink of an eye. At least she knew when the end would come. And she'd be prepared.

THE RINGING WOKE Alex up from a deep sleep. He opened one eye, searching for the source. It wasn't his watch. That was still in the refrigerator.

"What is that?" Tenley murmured, turning her face into the pillow. "Turn it off."

"I can't find it. Where's the clock?"

"It's not an alarm clock. I don't have an alarm clock."

Alex sat up and searched the room, then noticed the sound was coming from his pants, which were tossed over a nearby chair. He stumbled out of bed and picked them up, then found the new BlackBerry in his pocket. He pushed the button and put it to his ear.

"What?"

"It's Tess. I'm sorry to call you so early but we have a huge problem. The new press just went down and we're in the middle of the Marberry project. It's Saturday and none of the techs are answering their phones. We're supposed to deliver this job on Monday and we've still got to run it through bindery. I need you to come home."

"Aw, hell." Alex rubbed his face with his hand, trying to clear the sleep from his brain. "It's going to take me a while. I can probably make some calls from the road. I'm going to call Marberry first and see if we can't push back delivery. How much of a hit can we take on our price?"

"Five percent at the most. But don't offer him a discount on this job. Tell him we'll discount the next one. At least we know we'll get him back as a customer, then."

"Do you have to talk so loud?" Tenley groaned. Alex sat down on the edge of the bed and put his pillow over her head.

"Who is that?" Tess asked. "Oh, my God. Are you with a woman? Good grief, Alex, send her home, get in your car and point it toward Chicago. I'll see you in...five hours."

"I've got to pick up my car from the garage and they won't open until eight or nine. It'll take me at least six hours to get back, so schedule a meeting with the production team at three. We'll get this sorted out."

Tess hung up and Alex flopped back down on the bed, the phone still clutched in his hand "I have to go," he said.

Tenley pushed up on her elbows, her hair sticking up in unruly spikes. "Go where?"

"Back to Chicago. We've got an emergency with one of our presses at the Elgin plant."

"No," Tenley moaned. "You're supposed to stay until Monday."

Alex rolled over and drew her into his embrace. "I know. Maybe I can come back. I'll take care of business and if everything's all right, I can drive back late tonight. I could be back here by midnight."

She closed her eyes and for a long time didn't speak. Alex thought she'd fallen asleep again. But then, she opened her eyes. "You have to go," she said. "We only had a few days left anyway. It's all right."

"No, I'll come back," Alex insisted.

Tenley shook her head, then pressed her finger to his lips. "No. It's better this way. You need to get back to work. And I need to work on the novel. I can't do that with you here."

"How about next weekend? I could drive up on Friday night." All Alex needed was a promise that there would be a next time. He didn't want to leave without knowing exactly where they stood.

Tenley reached out and smoothed her hand over his cheek. "Alex, we both knew, going in, how difficult this would be. You're down there and I'm here. Throw in the whole business thing and it gets too complicated. I'd like to believe we're both smart enough to see that and save ourselves the pain of trying to make a relationship work."

Alex couldn't believe what he was hearing. He'd never been dumped in his life and this sounded suspiciously like the big heave-ho. He brushed the hair out of her eyes and turned her face up to his. But all he saw in her eyes was complete honesty. Had he misread the depth of her feelings for him?

"So this is it?" he asked.

"I know you've done this before," Tenley said with a small smile. "A guy like you doesn't stay single for as long as you have without breaking a few hearts. It's easy."

"This doesn't seem easy to me," he said.

"It will get better." She leaned forward and brushed a kiss across his lips. "At least I didn't break your heart and you didn't break mine. I think we both got out of this feeling pretty good."

She was right. Still, he wanted her to want him to stay, so much that she would grasp at any chance to see him again. That was what women did. They got all crazy and clingy and demanding. But then, Tenley hadn't ever acted like the women he'd dated. So it would make sense she'd just cut him loose without a second thought.

"You're sure about this?"

"Absolutely sure," she said.

He frowned. "So, I guess we'll be talking to each other about the novel. You'll work on the changes. And when they're done, we'll discuss them."

"Yes. If I have any questions, I'll call you."

Alex sat up and swung his legs off the bed. Then he ran his hands through his hair. This just didn't seem right—hell, it didn't *feel* right. Every instinct in his body told him not to leave her like this, to make it clear he wanted more than what they'd already shared.

She slipped her arms around him from behind and rested her chin on his shoulder. "I am going to miss you. I like having you here when I wake up."

"That's a good reason to see each other again, isn't it?"

She crawled out of bed and pulled him to his feet. "Come on. Get dressed. I'll make you something to eat while you pack. And I'll call the garage and tell them you're coming for your car."

Tenley grabbed her T-shirt from the floor and tugged it over her head. "Wait a second," Alex said. "Not so fast." He pulled her against his body and kissed her, smoothing his hands up beneath her shirt until he found the soft flesh of her breasts.

Tenley giggled. "Wanted to cop one last feel?"

"Hey, I'm a guy. I have to have something to think about on the ride home."

Tenley dragged her T-shirt back over her head and threw it on the bed. "All right. I'll cook breakfast in the nude. That should give you plenty to think about for the next two or three days." She gave him a devilish smile, then walked out of the bedroom, a tantalizing sway to her hips.

Alex poked his head out the door and watched her as she moved down the hallway. Tenley had the most incredible body. And she didn't even work at it.

He gathered the clothes he'd left in Tenley's room and took them back into the guest room, then dug through his duffel for something comfortable to wear. He found a clean T-shirt, pulled it over his head, then stepped into his last pair of clean boxers. His missing jeans were mixed in with Tenley's laundry and he tugged them on, then searched for his socks.

"Scrambled or fried?" she called from the kitchen.

"Just toast," Alex called. "And coffee. Really black." He might as well get back to his regular routine as soon as possible. Besides, he wouldn't be spending the day and night with Tenley, so there wasn't much need for extra energy.

When he got out to the kitchen, he found Tenley standing at the counter, sipping a cup of coffee, still completely naked. She handed him a mug and then retrieved his toast from the toaster.

"I like this," he said, letting his gaze drift down the length of her body. "If a guy had this every day, he'd never get to work in the morning."

"It's a lot better in the summer," Tenley said. "I'm freezing."

Alex gathered her up in his arms and pressed a kiss to the top of her head. "You are, by far, the most interesting woman I've ever met, Tenley Marshall. I'm not going to forget you, even if you do make breakfast with your clothes on. Go get dressed."

She ran back to her bedroom and reappeared a minute later in flannel pajamas and slippers. She sat down next to him at the end of the island, sipping her coffee and waiting for him to finish his toast.

"I did have a wonderful time," she said with a warm smile. "I'm glad I stopped and rescued you."

"I'm glad you did, too." He reached out and slipped his hand through the hair at her nape. Gently, Alex pulled her forward until their lips met. He knew it might be the last time he kissed her, so he tried to make it as sweet and perfect as possible. When he finally drew back, Alex looked down, taking in all the small details of her face, committing them to memory.

There was a time when he thought her odd, but now, Alex was certain she was someone so special, so unique that he might never meet another woman like her again. He drew a steadying breath, then stood. The longer he waited, the more difficult this was going to be.

"I have to go. Now. Or I'm never going to leave."

Tenley nodded. "All right." She hugged him hard, then pushed up on her toes and gave him a quick kiss. "I'll see you, Alex."

He wanted to gather her in his arms and show her what a real goodbye kiss should be. But in the end, Alex took one last look, smiled and turned for the door. "I'll see you, Tenley."

The trek out to his rental car was the longest walk of his life. Every step required enormous willpower. When he looked back, she was standing on the porch in her pajamas, the cold morning wind blowing at her dark hair. He waved as he drove past the house to the driveway. And all the way to town, Alex tried to come up with an excuse to send him back to the cabin.

Tenley was right. They'd been caught up in a wildly enjoyable affair, but that was all it had been. Passion had turned to infatuation and he'd mistaken it for love. Love didn't happen in four days or even four weeks. And though his interest in other women had always faded quickly, Alex knew that his feelings for Tenley would be with him for a very long time. He would never, ever forget Tenley Marshall.

"YOUR PERSPECTIVE is off here."

Tenley studied the drawing, then nodded. "You're right. I always make that mistake." She cursed softly. "This is why I should have gone to art school. People will see things like that and know I'm an amateur."

"No, they won't. This is highly stylized, Tenley. You can break a lot of rules. In fact, in this kind of work, you can make up your own rules. It's your universe. I'm just pointing out some areas you might want to consider," her grandfather said.

"Right," she murmured.

It had been three days since Alex had walked out of her life. He'd called twice, but she'd ignored his calls, knowing it would be easier if they didn't speak for a while. Still, she'd listened to the sound of his voice on her voice mail over and over again.

She'd been working on the novel nonstop, but her progress had been cursed with fits and starts. With only her own resources to depend upon, Tenley found herself second-guessing the decisions she made. Her first impulse was to call Alex and discuss her concerns with him. But she realized that if she wanted to be an artist, she'd have to stand on her own. Or fail.

Though failing had once been a viable option, the more time she spent on the novel, the more Tenley wanted to make it work. This was a great story, a story that was so tightly woven into her own that she had trouble separating herself from Cyd. She'd grown to like the girl. She was strong and resourceful and determined. She was a survivor.

Yet even with a new story swirling around in her head, Tenley still couldn't keep her thoughts from wandering to Alex. She hadn't thought it would be this difficult. Once he was gone, she assumed her life would get back to normal. Sure, she'd think about him occasionally, but thoughts of him would soon fade.

In reality, she'd become obsessed with remembering. Each night, before she fell asleep, she'd go through each image in her head, lingering over them like a photo album. Yesterday, she'd actually made a drawing of Alex in the perfect state of arousal and she was quite taken with it, until she realized it was bordering on pornography.

On the floor in front of the fire, in the sauna, in the studio, in his room—everywhere she turned there were reminders of him.

"Tenley!"

"What?" She stood up, spinning around to find her grandfather standing behind her, his arms crossed over his chest.

"How long are you going to be like this?"

"Like what?"

"Your young man has been gone for, what, three days?"

"Yes, three days."

"And when is he coming back?"

"He's not. And he's not my young man. He's just a guy I knew for a while."

"I see. And how long do you plan to mope around?"

"I'm not moping. I'm just distracted. I have a lot of things on my mind and not enough time to think about them all. Speaking of which, if you don't go through those bills of sale and mark the inventory numbers on them, I'm going to have a lot more to be crabby about than Alex Stamos."

"This arrived for you today." Her grandfather held up a large envelope. The logo for the university in Green Bay was emblazoned on the corner.

Tenley took it from his hand. "Thanks."

"So you're going to start school?"

"Yes," she said firmly. "This summer. I'm going to take a writing class, too."

"Why not spread your wings a little further, Tennie? Check out some other schools. The Art Institute in Chicago has a great school. You could go down there and stay for the summer, really immerse yourself in something new."

Though the Art Institute might have a fabulous school, Tenley knew why her grandfather was pushing that choice. It would give her the opportunity to rekindle her relationship with Alex. The thought had crossed her mind more than once. But she wanted to simplify her life, not make it more complicated. "I can't do that. I have responsibilities here. I have my dogs and cats and horses to care for. And I don't have the money to stay in Chicago for the summer. If I go to Green Bay, I can drive back and forth."

"I'll give you the money," her grandfather said.

"No, you won't. You don't have the money to give me."

"No?" He laughed. "I have a lot of money. Money you don't even know I have. I've put it all in a trust for you. I don't think you should have to wait for me to kick the bucket before you can use it. So I'm going to give it to you now."

"I can't take your money," Tenley said. "You should spend it on yourself."

"I intend to. In fact, now that you're planning on attending school, I might just go somewhere warm for the winter."

"You hate California," she said.

"I was thinking about Greece."

Tenley gasped. "Greece? Since when?"

He picked up a paintbrush and examined it closely. "I've always wanted to go to Greece. Your grandmother hated to fly, so we couldn't go. And after she died, I had you to watch out for. But now that you're moving on, I think I should do the same."

Emotion welled up inside of her. She'd never meant to be a burden on her grandfather. She was supposed to care for him, not the other way around. "I'm sorry. I didn't realize that you— You should go. Oh, it would be wonderful. Think of all the things you could paint." With a sob, she threw her arms around her grandfather's neck. "Thank you for being so patient with me. I'm sorry it took me so long to figure things out."

He patted her back. "Not to worry. It all worked out in the end. You found a man and that's the only thing that matters."

"I didn't find a man," Tenley said stubbornly. "Alex went back to Chicago. He's gone."

"What difference does that make? If he's the one you want, then a few hundred miles won't matter. When I met your grandmother, she was living in the Upper Peninsula. and I was living in Minot, North Dakota. We managed to find a way to make it work."

"I don't want to make it work," Tenley said. "I'm not ready to be in love."

Her grandfather shook his head and chuckled. "It's not like you can prepare for it. It just happens and when it does, you have to grab it and hang on for dear life. It doesn't come along that often."

Tenley took her drawings and put them back inside her

portfolio, then zipped it up. "Well, I don't want to be in love. Not right now. I have too many other things I have to do. It would just get in the way."

He reached out and placed his hand over hers. "Tennie, I really don't think you have a whole lot of control over that. Don't get me wrong, I've always admired your resolve. But on this one you're wrong." He tapped her portfolio. "Good work. When you're done, I think a trip to Chicago might be in order. It'll give you a chance to check out the school at the Art Institute."

"What would you do without me during the summer?"

"I was thinking I'd hire one of those college students who are always wanting to intern at the gallery. Someone who's not so much trouble."

Tenley giggled. "You're not going to get rid of me with insults." She picked up her portfolio and walked to the door. "If I go to Chicago for the summer, you'd have to take care of my dogs and cats. They'd have to move in with you. And we'd have to board the horses."

He held out his hands. "A small price to pay for your happiness."

She zipped up her coat and walked out the door into the chilly afternoon sun. Once, her days had been spent in a holding pattern, just waiting for something to push her forward again. Alex had done that for her. He'd given her a reason to move on and for that, she'd be forever grateful.

Someday, she'd tell him that. Someday in the distant future—when she'd be able to look at him and not wonder if she'd given up too soon.

chapter eight

TENLEY had been to the Art Institute several times when she was younger. As she walked down the front steps, looking back at the classic facade, she let the memories wash over her. Her parents had been together and Tommy was still alive. They'd rushed up the front steps, racing each other to the door, hoping to see everything in just one day. And while her mother and father lingered over the paintings, she and Tommy found their favorite spots.

Tenley had been fascinated by the miniatures, like little dollhouses with each tiny piece of furniture perfectly reproduced. Tommy was drawn to the Greek and Roman coins, comparing them to his collection of Indian head pennies at home.

It had been one of the last times they'd traveled together as a family. But to her surprise, the memory didn't cause the usual ache in her heart. Instead, she felt only a tiny bit of melancholy as she recalled the affection they'd all had for each other. Tommy had lived a short life, but he had been well loved.

Maybe that was what life was all about—searching for a place to feel accepted. Since Alex had left, Tenley had made the decision to walk away from the past and begin again. Though she was excited at the prospect, she was also a bit frightened.

She'd spent the afternoon strolling through galleries, studying the artists and wondering if they'd ever had the same doubts she was having. To pacify her grandfather, Tenley had met with an admissions specialist for the Art Institute school and, in the end, decided to apply for a three-week session in June and another in August. Six weeks away from home during her grandfather's busiest season would be difficult, but he'd assured her he could get along with temporary help.

Housing was offered by the school, but it didn't allow for pets. So Dog and Pup and her two cats were going to have to live at her grandfather's place while she was gone. Josh could take care of the horses, moving them over to his family's farm to make it more convenient, and she'd drive home on the weekends to make sure everything was running smoothly.

Yet, even though she tried to focus on the business at hand, her thoughts constantly shifted to the real reason she'd come to Chicago—Alex. They'd spoken several times since he'd left, mostly about the novel. But sometimes they drifted into conversation about their time together.

Though neither one of them wanted to make the first move to rekindle their romantic relationship, there always seemed to be a tension simmering right below the surface—as if the thoughts were there, waiting to be expressed.

Tenley stepped to the curb and held up her hand to hail a cab. A few seconds later, a taxi pulled up and she got inside. She reached into the pocket of her portfolio for Alex's business card and gave the cabbie the address.

Though she'd come to Chicago to see Alex, her excuse for the trip was a meeting she'd scheduled with her editor. She'd finished the requested revisions and had completed the new artwork for the changes. Rather than sending them via courier, Tenley had decided to deliver them personally.

Marianne Johnson, her editor, felt it important they meet, but Tenley was really hoping to take a few moments to say hello to Alex. It had been nearly three weeks since he'd left and even though she thought of him every hour of every day, she was beginning to forget the tiny details that had fascinated her so. The closest thing she had to a photograph was the picture from the Smooth Operators Web site. And then she had her drawings, but none of those had a face with the body.

All she needed was a few seconds to recharge her memory. As the cab wove through the late-afternoon traffic, Tenley tried to imagine how it would be. She'd stand at his door and say a quick hello. He'd ask her to come in and sit down, but she'd beg off, explaining that she had a meeting scheduled with her editor. He'd ask her to dinner and she'd tell him she was driving back that night. He'd say the traffic was bad until later and she ought to wait.

All she really wanted to know was that she and Alex could deal with each other as business associates. The past was the past. It might not have been so important before, but in the past few weeks, Tenley had begun to imagine building a career as a graphic novelist. She'd already come up with four or five new ideas for stories.

The headquarters for Stamos Publishing was located in the South Loop in a huge brick building that had been modernized with new windows and a gleaming entrance. One corner was constructed entirely of glass, revealing a printing press in full operation.

Tenley paid the cabbie, then hopped out of the car, clutching her portfolio to her chest. She'd left her Jeep parked in the lot at the hotel, her bags in the trunk, preferring to let someone else do the driving while she was in town. Later tonight, she'd pick it up and head home.

She checked in at the front desk and was given a badge to clip onto her pocket. A few seconds later, Marianne Johnson burst through the door, a wide smile on her face. "Tenley! Gosh, it's a pleasure to finally meet you." She held out her hand. "How was your drive down? The weather looked good."

"I actually came down yesterday afternoon. I went to the Art Institute this morning and spent most of the day there."

"Wonderful! First, I want to take you by Alex's office. I know he's in and I'm sure he wants to say hello."

"Oh, I don't want to bother him," Tenley said, suddenly succumbing to an attack of nerves. What if he wasn't thrilled to see her? What if they had nothing to say to each other? She'd built this meeting up in her mind for three weeks, ever since Alex had left Door County. And now that it was here, she wanted to run back home.

"It's no bother. When I told him you were coming, he insisted we stop by. Come on."

They wove through a warren of hallways, past small offices and large conference areas, all occupied by production personnel. Marianne took her back to the pressroom and explained to her that her novel would be printed at their new plant in Elgin and that she would be invited to do a press check once the process had begun.

By the time they stepped inside the elevator, Tenley's heart was slamming in her chest and she could barely breathe. What if she couldn't speak? What if everything she said sounded stilted and contrived?

"Our sales and marketing offices are up here," Marianne said, after they arrived at the second floor. "We're so excited about publishing your novel. I think this new imprint is going to be the best thing that's ever happened to this company."

Unlike the production offices, the second floor was quiet, the hum of the printing presses barely audible. Marianne took her through a set of glass doors, then smiled at the receptionist. "Alex wanted us to stop in," she explained.

Tenley took a deep breath. She'd brought a new outfit for the occasion. She wore a hand-woven jacket with a bright chartreuse turtleneck, a short black skirt and leggings underneath. Lace-up ankle boots and a studded belt finished off the ensemble. In her opinion, it was edgy and cool and it made her look like a real artist.

"Alex? I've got Tenley here."

Marianne stepped aside and directed her through a wide doorway. Tenley pasted a smile on her face and walked in. The moment their eyes met, she felt as if she'd been hit in the chest with a brick. Her heart fluttered and her breathing grew shallow and she felt a bit light-headed. "Hello." It was all she could manage.

"Hello, Tenley. Come on in. Sit down."

His voice was warm and deep and caused a shiver to race through her body. "Oh, I can't stay. Marianne and I have a meeting. And then I have to get back on the road. I've got a long drive home tonight. I just wanted to say hi." She gave him a little wave and a weak laugh. The words had just tumbled out of her mouth so fast she wasn't sure what she'd said. "Hi."

"Don't be silly. Your meeting with Marianne can wait." He glanced over at the editor. "Right?"

Marianne nodded. "Sure. Just give me a call when you're through." The editor disappeared down the long hallway, leaving Tenley standing alone in the door. Wasn't this how she'd imagined it? What was next?

"Come on in. Sit," he said, pointing to the chair on the other side of his desk. "God, you look…incredible."

"It's the new clothes," Tenley said. "Now that I'm an artist, I have to start dressing like one."

"They suit you," he said. "But then, everything looks good on you. I seem to remember a funny hat with earflaps. I liked that hat."

"I didn't bring it along. I didn't want to look like a complete bumpkin."

"So, are you really going back tonight? Because you can't. We have to have dinner. I'll take you out and show you the town." He reached for his phone and punched a button. "Carol, can you make a reservation for Tenley Marshall at the Drake? Confirm it for late arrival on our account."

Tenley shook her head. "I can't. I have to get back. I promised my grandfather."

"One of the suites would be good," he said to his secretary. When he hung up the phone, he nodded. "Just in case you don't want to go. You'll stay for dinner, right?"

"Sure. The traffic will probably be crazy until later on, anyway. So, yes, I'll stay for dinner."

"Good. We have a lot to catch up on. I can't believe you're here."

"I am," she said, slowly lowering herself into the chair. She set her portfolio on the floor, fumbling with the handles. Why had conversation suddenly become so difficult? She couldn't think of a single thing to say to him. He looked the same, maybe a bit more polished. He wore a finely tailored suit and a white dress shirt that showed off his dark features. If he'd picked out his clothes to please her, they were certainly doing the trick. He was as handsome as ever. "How have you been?"

"Good," he said. "You know, this is crazy. Good, fine, you look great." He circled around the desk, then stood in front of her, pulling her to her feet. Without hesitation, Alex cupped her face in his hands and gave her a gentle kiss. "That's better."

"I remember that," Tenley murmured, her gaze dropping to his lips.

"So do I." For a long time, they stood silently, staring at each other. And then, he blinked and glanced at his watch. "It's almost four. Let's go now and we'll have a few drinks before dinner and—"

"I have to see Marianne," she said, grabbing her portfolio.

"Right."

"But I won't be long. I'll come back at five and we'll go then."

"Sure," Alex said, following her to the door. "Her office is down there on the right. Name's on the door."

Tenley nodded and started down the hall. At the last minute, she glanced over her shoulder to find him watching her. "Stop staring at me," she said.

Alex laughed out loud and Tenley hurried down the hall, enjoying the sound. It hadn't gone badly. It could have been worse. They were able to be in the same room without jumping into each other's arms and tearing clothes off. And though the kiss was a bit more than what friends might share, they'd been a lot more than friends.

If this was all it was, Tenley could be happy. There was no anger or regret between them. Only good memories and a warm friendship. She could move on from there.

When she got to Marianne's office, she walked in, only to find another woman sitting in her guest chair. The woman jumped up and held out her hand. "Hello," she said. "I'm Tess Stamos. And you have got to be Tenley Marshall."

"Yes," she said.

"I'm Alex's sister. I work here, too. I loved your novel,

by the way. It's about time women start kicking butt in those books, don't you think?"

"I do," Tenley said.

Tess was tall and slender, with dark hair and eyes. She appeared to be a few years older than Tenley, but she had a confidence that made her seem just a bit intimidating.

"So, you saw Alex? He's been going crazy all day waiting for you to come. He usually doesn't let a woman get him so rattled. You must be special."

"We're friends," Tenley said.

Tess observed her with a shrewd look. "I think you're more than that. Alex has even mentioned you to my mother, which means he's willing to put up with her nagging just so he can talk about you around the dinner table. But please, don't break my brother's heart or I will have to chop you into tiny pieces and run you through the printing press. I can do that, you know. I'm head of production."

With that, Tess Stamos waltzed out of the room, leaving Tenley with nothing to say except, "She was…nice."

Marianne circled her desk and took Tenley by the arm, guiding her toward a chair. "Don't let Tess bother you. She deals with loud printing presses and stubborn press opera-tors all day long. She's used to speaking her mind."

As they went over the new drawings and story changes, Tenley's thoughts were occupied elsewhere. She'd expected a warm welcome, but there was something more going on. This wasn't just a casual visit, at least not for Alex. He'd been anticipating her arrival and had even told his sister about her. But then, as a new author, she would naturally be the subject of conversation around the office.

There was no need to read anything into Tess's words. Nothing had changed. Everybody was simply being kind and solicitous, just good business practice.

And at dinner tonight, she'd restrain herself, putting aside all the memories of their passionate encounters at her cabin. She was determined to make this relationship comfortable, to redraw the lines and follow the rules this time.

And though her heart ached a little bit for what they'd lost, Tenley could bear it. She was stronger now and able to look at the attraction between them with a practical eye. Though it would always be tempting, in the end, it just wasn't meant to be.

ALEX GUIDED THE SEDAN down Lakeshore Drive, impatient to get to the restaurant so that he could turn his full attention to the woman sitting beside him. It felt so good to have her back in his orbit again. Though they hadn't touched since he'd kissed her, just knowing he could reach out and make contact made him happy.

"How's your grandfather?" he asked.

"He's good. He says hello. He's working on a new series of paintings. Barns."

"And how are things in town? Is Randy giving you any problems?"

Tenley shook her head. "Actually, we're dating now. He just wore me down and I had to say yes. We're planning the wedding for June."

Alex frowned, then noticed the teasing smile twitching at the corners of her lips. "I'm very happy for you."

"What about you?" Tenley asked. "Have you been dating anyone?"

Alex was surprised by the question, but even more surprised by his answer. "Tenley, it's only been three weeks. I'm not interested in dating anyone."

"I just thought a charming guy like—"

He suddenly realized what she was getting at. "Oh, wait. I know where this is going. You looked me up on the Internet, didn't you? And you came up with that silly Web site."

"SmoothOperators.com. I didn't, Randy did. He gave me the full report."

"When?"

"Before you left. He dropped by the gallery when I was working."

"Damn, he doesn't give up, does he?"

"He's dating Linda Purnell now. So, yes, he has given up. Unless he's carrying a secret torch for me." She glanced over at him. "Why haven't you started dating again?"

"Because I haven't met anyone half as interesting as you." In fact, Alex hadn't even bothered to go out since he got back to Chicago. He spent most of his evenings at the office, getting back to his apartment in time to catch the end of a basketball game or a hockey match. The rest of the night, he spent staring at his BlackBerry, trying to convince himself that not phoning Tenley was a good thing.

"I know what you mean. There aren't that many interesting single guys living in Sawyer Bay. Though prospects improve in the summer."

Alex reached out and grabbed her hand, lacing his fingers through hers. It felt so good to touch her. "We could skip the restaurant," he said. "We're just a couple blocks from the Drake. We could order room service and spend some time alone."

She smiled weakly and Alex immediately regretted his suggestion. He was moving too fast. And it was obvious her feelings for him had changed.

"I don't think that's a good idea," she said.

"You're probably right. Best to maintain a professional relationship. But it worked out pretty well for us when we did it the first time."

"Yes, but that was just for fun."

Alex watched the traffic as it slowed in front of him for the light. What did she mean by that? Was that all he'd been to her, just a few nights of fun? Maybe all this distance was simply her way of letting him down easy.

As they drove along the lakeshore, Alex pointed out the major landmarks. Acting as tour guide kept the conversation light and interesting. But in his head, he was cataloguing all the questions that needed answers. Why couldn't she love him? She didn't really believe that ridiculous Web site, did she?

They were so obviously compatible, both in and out of bed. He loved talking to her. She didn't babble like most of the women he'd dated. And she wasn't obsessed with her looks or her clothes. Over time, Alex had realized that it was the little things that he found so attractive.

Tenley didn't wear makeup, at least, not anymore. From the moment she got up in the morning until the time she went to bed, she never once looked in the mirror. She combed her hair with her fingers. She wore clothes that were comfortable and shoes that didn't kill her feet.

And she read books. She didn't watch silly television shows or buy fashion magazines. She had a stack of classics on her bedside table. She was smart and talented and witty.

"And when you have a free moment, you go out and do something useful with your time," he muttered, "rather than going to get your nails done."

"What?"

Alex glanced over to find Tenley watching him with an inquisitive expression. Had he said that out loud? "Nothing," he said. "Here we are." Thankfully, the parking valet provided a distraction. He opened Tenley's door for her and helped her from the car, then circled around to grab the keys from Alex.

When they got inside, Tenley excused herself and headed toward the ladies' room. Alex waited outside and watched as two women went in and came out before Tenley. What was she doing in there? He reached for the door and pulled it open. "Tenley?"

"What?"

"Is everything all right?"

He heard a sniffle. "Yes?"

Alex stepped inside, then locked the door behind him. He heard the tears in her voice. She was locked in the center stall and he rapped on the door. "Come on, Tenley, open up. I don't want to have to crawl under."

He heard the latch flip and he pushed the door open. She sat on the toilet, her eyes red, a wad of toilet paper in her hand.

"Go away," she said.

"No." Alex reached down and took her hand, then pulled her out of the stall. "Why are you crying?"

"I don't know." This brought a fresh round of tears and she turned away from him and sat down on a small chair in the corner. "God, I hate crying. I feel so stupid."

"Are you upset with me?"

"No." She paused and wiped her nose. "Yes. Maybe. You just make it so difficult."

"What?" He pulled her into his arms and smoothed his hands along her waist. "I don't mean to."

Alex's fingers found her face and he tipped her gaze up to his. Her eyes were red and watery and he brushed a tear away with his thumb. He didn't have the words to make her feel better because he didn't know what was wrong. So Alex did the only thing he knew would take her mind off her troubles. He kissed her.

But what began as a sweet, soothing kiss, slowly turned into something more. Her mouth opened beneath his and he took what she offered. How many nights had he lain in bed, thinking about this, about the next time he'd touch her and kiss her and make love to her? This wasn't exactly the setting he'd imagined, but at this point, it didn't matter. Tenley was back in his arms again.

He grabbed the lapels of her jacket and pushed them aside, desperate to find a spot of bare skin to touch. They stumbled back against the sinks and Alex picked her up and set her on the edge of the counter, stepping between her legs.

She had too many clothes on and there wasn't enough

time. He glanced over his shoulder and considered the stall for privacy, but decided against it. The door was locked. If someone knocked, they'd have to stop. But until then, he—

"No," she said, pressing her hands against his chest. "Don't do this."

Alex was stunned and he immediately stepped away. "What is it?"

She pulled her jacket back up and slid off the counter. "I can't do this. I—I have to go." Tenley hurried to the door and pulled on it, but it wouldn't open. "I need to go."

"Tenley, wait. I'm sorry. I didn't— It's just been such a long time and I—"

She finally realized the door was locked and when she turned the knob, it opened. He followed her out into the lobby, but she headed back out to the street.

"Tenley." He took her hand. "Where are you going?"

"I have to go home. I can't stay here."

"Don't. I promise, I won't kiss you again."

She raised her hand for a cab, but he pulled it down. A cab screeched to a halt in front of the restaurant. Christ, he could wait all day for a taxi and now, when he didn't want one, there were ten available. She pulled the door open.

"Wait," Alex said to the driver. "We're not through."

"Go," Tenley said.

"No! Wait." He reached into his pocket for his wallet, ready to pay the driver to do as ordered.

But Tenley pulled the door shut. "Go, now!" she shouted at the driver.

Alex could do nothing but curse as the taxi roared off down the street. The valet stood at his desk, observing the entire scene with a dubious expression.

"Bad date?" he asked.

"Yeah, you could say that."

"Well, at least you didn't buy her dinner." He grinned. "Do you want your car?"

Alex nodded. He sat down on a bench, his breath coming in gasps, clouding in front of his face in the cold air. What the hell had happened? Where was the woman who'd crawled into his bed and seduced him on the night they met? Or the woman who ran into the snow stark naked?

Something had happened to the free-spirited Tenley he knew three weeks ago. How could someone have changed so fast? He reached for his cell phone. She'd spent the previous night in a hotel and left her car parked there. Maybe if he tracked her down, he might catch her before she left.

Alex stared at his phone, then shook his head as he realized the impossibility of that task. The bottom line was Tenley didn't want to be with him. Whatever they'd shared had faded. And he'd just killed what was left of it with his behavior in the bathroom.

When the valet returned with his car, Alex gave him a fifty-dollar bill and slipped behind the wheel. He'd made only one mistake in his life and Alex suspected he'd never stop regretting it. He'd left Tenley that morning after his sister had called.

He should have stayed. He should have lived up there

with her until he was absolutely certain she was in love with him. He knew her heart was fragile and yet he thought they'd just be able to pick up where they'd left off in a week or two. Only in the meantime, Tenley had erected a wall around herself, too high and too thick for him to broach.

He'd missed his chance with her and there was absolutely nothing he could do about it.

TENLEY LOOKED at her reflection in the mirror, trying to see herself as others might. Gone was the streak of purple in her hair. Gone was the dark eye makeup and the deep red lipstick, the black nail polish.

She smoothed her hands over the bodice of the red vintage dress. She'd found the garment in a trunk in her grandfather's attic and had thought the shawl collar and wide skirt made it a classic design. When she'd brought it down, her grandfather had grown all misty, remembering the night her grandmother had first worn it.

In her ongoing effort to get out more, Tenley had invited her grandfather to the Valentine's Dance, held at the fire hall in town. The dance was one of the biggest events of the winter season. Everyone attended. Jimmy Richter's Big Band came in from Green Bay to play and the Ladies Auxiliary made cake and pink punch. Anyone who was single was invited to attend, from teenagers to retirees.

Tenley suspected her grandfather had ulterior motives for accepting the date. Rumor had it he and Katie Vanderhoff had been seen together at Wednesday-night bingo for the past four weeks in a row. Though he might have wanted to ask Katie to the dance, Tenley knew the potential gossip would have scared him away. Considering the suitability of the match, the gossips would have had them married off before they stepped on the dance floor.

Tenley heard a knock on her door and she took one last look in the mirror. "You can do this," she murmured. "It's just a silly dance."

But it was more than that. Since her trip to Chicago, almost two weeks had passed. She'd begun to see her life in a different light. She wanted to find someone to love her, a man who might make her feel the way Alex did. But Tenley knew it would take time. She wouldn't fall in love in a week or even a year. There were too many things in her past that kept her from surrendering so easily.

But she had felt something with Alex and she was certain she could find that again if she only got out there and started looking. She had made one vow to herself. No more one-night stands. Sex for fun was a part of her past. From now on, she intended to act a bit more circumspect.

She grabbed her coat from the bed, then hurried to the door. The dogs tried to follow her outside, but she slipped out without them. "Sorry," she said.

Her grandfather stood on the porch, dressed in his best suit, his hands behind his back. He slowly brought out a plastic box and Tenley was delighted to find a corsage there. "It's an orchid," he said. "I used to buy your grandmother white orchids all the time. She loved them because they lasted so long."

Tenley took the box from his hand. "I'll put it on in the

car. It'll freeze out here." She hurried down the steps and hopped inside her grandfather's Volvo. Shivering, she rubbed her hands together and then held them close to the heat. "Are you really sure you want to do this?" she asked.

"Your grandmother died four years ago. I think it's time I got out there and met some ladies. Not that I want to get married again, but I would like to have some company if I decide to see a movie or dine out."

He'd combed his bushy hair and shaved off the usual stubble that covered his cheeks. "You look very handsome," Tenley commented. "All the ladies will want to dance with you. I heard you've been spending time with Katie Vanderhoff."

He grinned. "Maybe. It's those damn cinnamon rolls. I stop by for coffee in the morning and she feeds me one of those and I think I'm in love. That's how your grandmother won my heart. With her apple pie."

"Well, you'll have to be sure to ask her to dance. Just make sure I get the first and the last one."

Tenley flipped the visor down and looked at her reflection in the mirror. Her hair looked silly, all curled and poufed up. As soon as she got to the dance, she'd take it down.

"You look very pretty," her grandfather said, steering the car onto the road. "No more blue hair. Or was it purple? I can't remember."

"I've decided to be perfectly normal for one night. I'm even wearing underwear."

"I don't need to hear about that," her grandfather said, wagging his finger, "although, I am glad to hear it. I wouldn't want to have you twirling around on the dance floor wearing nothing beneath your skirt. And I do love to twirl a girl."

By the time they got to town, Tenley was nervous. She'd been off the social radar for so long she knew her appearance would cause a lot of speculation. Everyone in town knew about Alex and her romance with him. But as far as they understood, that was still going on, long distance.

If they asked, she would have to tell them the truth—she and Alex had parted as friends. Friends who didn't speak to each other. Friends who couldn't possibly be in the same room without wanting to tear each other's clothes off.

The dance was already well under way when they arrived. Her grandfather grabbed her coat and hung it up, then held out his arm gallantly, a broad smile on his face. "You look lovely. Absolutely lovely. I wish your grandmother could see you. You look just as pretty as she did on the night we met."

"Thank you," Tenley said. "Are you ready?"

"I am. Are you?"

She nodded. They walked toward the entrance to the hall and stopped at the ticket table. Harvey Willis's sister, Ellen, was selling tickets and complimented them both on their snazzy attire.

The interior of the firehouse had been transformed. The trucks had been moved outside for the night and lights had been strung from the overhead beams. A small stage was set up on one end and the band was already in the midst of their rendition of "Moon River."

To Tenley's relief, there were plenty of familiar faces in attendance. If no one asked her to dance, she'd at least be able to chat. But as she scanned the room, her gaze came to rest on a face she hadn't expected to see.

Her fingers dug into her grandfather's arm as she gasped. "He's here," she whispered.

"Who's here?"

"Alex. He's standing right over there."

"Oh, look at that," her grandfather said. "Now, doesn't he look handsome. And what's that he has in his arms? Looks like roses."

"Did you know about this?" Tenley asked.

"Well, he did call a few days ago. Wanted to know if the dance was on Saturday or Sunday night. I just told him what he wanted to know. I also mentioned you'd be attending." He unhooked Tenley's hand from his arm and gave her a little push. "Go on. Talk to him before some other girl snaps him up."

Tenley slowly crossed the hall. Everyone was watching, even some of the guys in the band. Her knees felt weak and her head was spinning, but she held her emotions in check. She was not going to break down and cry. Nor was she going to throw herself into his arms.

She stopped in front of him, swallowing hard before speaking. "What are you doing here?"

"I heard you were planning on attending and I didn't want to give any of these single guys a chance to charm you."

"How did you know about the dance?"

"You mentioned it. You said Randy asked you every year."

"You remember that?"

He nodded. "I remember everything you said to me."

She glanced over her shoulder at her grandfather and found him grinning from ear to ear.

"I brought you something," Alex said. He handed her the roses. "I'm sorry there's so many of them, but I asked for the nicest bouquet and this is what they gave me." He took them from her arms. "Here, we'll just put them down."

"Thank you," she said.

"And there's candy and a card, but I thought I'd save that until later. They're out in the car."

"Gee, all you forgot was the jewelry," she teased.

"Ah, no. I didn't forget that." Alex reached into his pants pocket, but when he didn't find what he was looking for, he patted down his jacket pockets. "Where did I put that?"

"I don't need any more gifts, Alex. The flowers are fine."

"No, you'll like this one," he said. "At least, I hope you will. Here it is." He held out his fist, then opened it.

Lying in his palm was a ring…a diamond ring…a very large diamond ring. Tenley gasped, her gaze fixed on it. It was the most beautiful thing she'd ever seen, a pale yellow heart-shaped diamond, surrounded by tiny white diamonds.

"What does that mean?" she asked. Was this a proposal? And if it was, did he really expect her to accept with all these people watching her? Or maybe that was why he'd done it here, so she couldn't refuse. "Alex, I don't think this is a good idea. You know how I—"

"Tenley, don't talk, just listen. Yes, I know how you feel. And I understand your hesitation. Your experiences in life haven't made it easy for you to open yourself up to loving someone. But what we shared that week in your cabin was something special and I don't want to let that go."

"Is this a proposal?"

"It's whatever you want it to be," Alex said. "You decide. All I know is I don't want to lose you. I want you to be mine, for now and for as long as you'll have me. I want you to be my valentine, Tenley."

"But I—"

"Don't say no. You can't say no. Because I'm going to keep coming back every weekend and every holiday until you say yes. I'll buy a place up here and I'll come over every morning and take you to breakfast. And I'll sit on your sofa every night and rub your feet. We'll go for walks in the woods in the winter and we'll take our clothes off and lie in the summer sun."

He took her hand and slipped the ring on her finger. "I'm giving this to you so that you understand I won't change my mind. For as long as you wear that ring, I'm completely yours."

"But how are we going to do this? You live in Chicago and I live here."

"I'm not sure. At first, I'll come up on the weekends. And maybe you can come down and visit. We'll figure out all the details later, Tenley. We don't have to decide everything right now. All we have to do is make a commitment to try."

He was making it so easy for her to say yes. And she wanted to say the word, to throw herself into his arms and tell him it was quite possible that she did love him. Not just possible, very probable.

"I was thinking about spending some time in Chicago. There are some classes I want to take at the Art Institute this summer."

He smiled. "Really? Because that's just a quick train ride from where I live. You could stay with me. I could take you out and show you the city. You could even bring the dogs and cats. I've got plenty of room for all of you." He dropped down on one knee and held her hand. "Say yes, Tenley. Tell me you're willing to try."

"Yes." The word came out of her mouth without a second thought. "Yes. I am willing to try. And I will be your valentine."

Alex stood up and pulled her into his arms, lifting her off her feet and twirling her around on the dance floor. The crowd around them erupted in wild applause and Tenley looked up to find everyone in the hall watching them. A warm blush flooded her cheeks and she buried her face in the curve of Alex's neck.

"We're causing a scene," he said.

"I know. Don't worry. It will give them something to gossip about tomorrow morning."

"Are you all right with that?"

She nodded. "I think I can handle it."

Alex set her back on her feet, then took her face in his hands and kissed her. That brought even more applause and a few moments later, the band broke into their rendition of "My Funny Valentine." Alex swept her out onto the dance floor.

She'd never really danced before, but Alex seemed to know exactly what he was doing. She followed his lead and before long, they looked like experts. Everything always seemed so much easier when he was around.

Life, love—and dancing.

epilogue

ANGELA tacked an index card on her bulletin board. "The Charmer," she said. "I've discovered ten archetypes of the typical male seducer. Once women learn to identify each type, then they'll be prepared to judge their relationships more objectively."

"So, who are you planning to interview for this chapter?" Ceci asked.

"I wanted to interview Alex Stamos. He seemed to fit the type perfectly. But when I called him last week, his sister told me that he's been involved with a woman for nearly two months. That doesn't fit the pattern."

"Do you think he could be in love?" Ceci asked.

"No," Angela said. She paused. "Well, maybe. But that would be an aberration. The majority of these men never change."

"Yeah, but we'd like to believe they could," Ceci said.

"Well, I'll just have to find another man to interview.

The Charmer is the most common of the archetypes. It shouldn't be too difficult."

Angie sat down at her desk and picked up the description she'd been working on. "The Charmer is all talk. He knows exactly what to say to get what he wants and he enjoys wielding this power over women. He will often delay a physical relationship, waiting until it's your idea to hop into bed together. While you're certain that sex will take the relationship to a more intimate level, he knows it signals the end. He quickly moves on after blaming you for getting too serious, too fast."

"Sounds good," Ceci said. "But it would be nice to believe that, given the right woman, any guy could change his bad behavior." She sighed. "Kind of makes me wonder what happened to all those guys I dumped because I thought they were hopeless causes."

In truth, Angela had been wondering the same thing. Was she wrong about these men? Could you teach an old dog new tricks? Or were some of these men just lost causes? "I suppose we have to be optimistic," she murmured. "If not, we might as well just give up now, because the bad ones far outnumber the good ones."

"I guess I'd really like to know how much time you should give a guy before you cut your losses and move on," Ceci said. "I've been with Lance for three months and he still refuses to call me his girlfriend."

Angela gave her friend a weak smile. "There are always exceptions to every rule. We've just got to figure out a way to find those exceptions."

Angela stared at the index card. Alex's change of heart

certainly didn't bode well for the theories she planned to present in her book. But for every one guy who left the single life behind and fell in love, there were a hundred more serial daters out there breaking women's hearts.

She was on a mission to make a point. And if Alex Stamos wasn't the man she thought he was, then she'd find another Charmer to take his place. After all, she could spot a smooth operator a mile away.

★ ★ ★ ★ ★

The Harlequin® Blaze™ series brings you
six new fun, flirtatious and steamy stories a month
available wherever books are sold, including most bookstores,
supermarkets, drugstores and discount stores.

If you enjoyed these 3 stories from
the Harlequin® Blaze™ series
by bestselling authors

Stephanie Bond

Leslie Kelly

Kate Hoffmann

you will love other books
from the Harlequin®
Blaze™ series!

*The Harlequin® Blaze™ series brings
you 6 new fun, flirtatious and steamy
stories a month available wherever
books are sold, including most
bookstores, supermarkets, drugstores
and discount stores.*

HARLEQUIN®

Blaze™

is proud to introduce...

New York Times bestselling author

Brenda Jackson

SPONTANEOUS

Kim Cannon and Duan Jeffries have a great thing going.
Whenever they meet up, the passion between them
is hot, intense…spontaneous. And things really heat
up when Duan agrees to accompany her to her
mother's wedding. Too bad there's something
he's not telling her.…

Don't miss the fireworks!

*Available in May 2010
wherever Harlequin Blaze books are sold.*

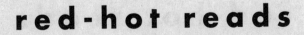

red-hot reads

www.eHarlequin.com

HB79542TR